RACHEl
A HARP IN L(

M000113590

RACHEL ETHELREDA FERGUSON (1892-1957) was born in Hampton Wick, the youngest of three children. She was educated at home and then sent to a finishing school in Florence, Italy. By the age of 16 she was a fierce campaigner for women's rights and considered herself a suffragette. She went on to become a leading member of the Women's Social and Political Union.

In 1911 she became a student at the Royal Academy of Dramatic Art. She began a career on the stage, which was cut short by the advent of World War 1, whereupon Ferguson joined the Women's Volunteer Reserve. She wrote for *Punch*, and was the drama critic for the *Sunday Chronicle,* writing under the name 'Columbine'. In 1923 she published her first novel, *False Goddesses,* which was followed by eleven further novels including *A Harp in Lowndes Square* (1936), *A Footman for the Peacock* (1940) and *Evenfield* (1942), all three of which are now available as Furrowed Middlebrow books.

Rachel Ferguson died in Kensington, where she had lived most of her life.

BY RACHEL FERGUSON

NOVELS

False Goddesses (1923)

The Brontës Went to Woolworth's (1931)

The Stag at Bay (1932)

Popularity's Wife (1932)

A Child in the Theatre (1933)

A Harp in Lowndes Square (1936)

Alas Poor Lady (1937)

A Footman for the Peacock (1940)

Evenfield (1942)

The Late Widow Twankey (1943)

A Stroll Before Sunset (1946)

Sea Front (1954)

HUMOUR/SATIRE

Sara Skelton: The Autobiography of a Famous Actress (1929)

Victorian Bouquet: Lady X Looks On (1931)

Nymphs and Satires (1932)

Celebrated Sequels (1934)

DRAMA

Charlotte Brontë (1933)

MEMOIR

Passionate Kensington (1939)

Royal Borough (1950)

We Were Amused (1958)

BIOGRAPHY

Memoirs of a Fir-Tree: The Life of Elsa Tannenbaum (1946)

And Then He Danced: The Life of Espinosa by Himself (1948)

RACHEL FERGUSON

A HARP IN LOWNDES SQUARE

With an introduction by
Elizabeth Crawford

DEAN STREET PRESS
A Furrowed Middlebrow Book

A Furrowed Middlebrow Book

FM3

Published by Dean Street Press 2016

Cover by DSP
Cover painting an adapted detail from *Children in an
Interior* by Carl Vilhelm Holsoe (1863-1935)

First published in 1936 by Jonathan Cape

ISBN 978 1 911413 73 8

www.deanstreetpress.co.uk

It is too late! oh, nothing is too late
Till the tired heart shall cease to palpitate.
Cato learned Greek at eighty; Sophocles
Wrote his grand Oedipus, and Simonides
Bore off the prize of verse from his compeers
When each had numbered more than fourscore years

LONGFELLOW

INTRODUCTION

A FAMILY – a House – and – Time. These are the ingredients whipped by Rachel Ferguson (1892-1957) into three confections – *A Harp in Lowndes Square* (1936), *A Footman for the Peacock* (1940), and *Evenfield* (1942) – now all republished as Furrowed Middlebrow books. Her casts of individuals, many outrageous, and families, some wildly dysfunctional, dance the reader through the pages, revealing worlds now vanished and ones that even in their own time were the product of a very particular imagination. Equally important in each novel is the character of the House – the oppressive family home of Lady Vallant in *A Harp in Lowndes Square*, comfortable, suburban Evenfield, and Delaye, the seat of the Roundelays, a stately home but 'not officially a show place' (*A Footman for the Peacock*). Rachel Ferguson then mixes in Time – past, present, and future – to deliver three socially observant, nostalgic, mordant, yet deliciously amusing novels.

In an aside, the *Punch* reviewer (1 April 1936) of *A Harp in Lowndes Square* remarked that 'Miss Ferguson has evidently read her Dunne', an assumption confirmed by the author in a throwaway line in *We Were Amused* (1958), her posthumously-published autobiography. J.W. Dunne's *Experiment with Time* (1927) helped shape the imaginative climate in the inter-war years, influencing Rachel Ferguson no less than J.B. Priestley (*An Inspector Calls*), John Buchan (*The Gap in the Curtain*), C.S. Lewis, and J.R.R. Tolkien. In *A Harp in Lowndes Square* the heroine's mother ('half-educated herself by quarter-educated and impoverished gentlewomen') explains the theory to her children: '… all time is one, past, present and future. It's simultaneous … There's a star I've heard of whose light takes so many thousands of years to reach our earth that it's still only got as far along history as shining over the Legions of Julius Caesar. Yet that star which is seeing chariot races is outside our window now. You say Caesar is dead. The star says No, because the star's seen him. It's your word against his! Which of you is right? Both of you. It's only a question of how long you take to see things.' The concept of 'simultaneous time' explains why the young first-person narrator, Vere Buchan, and her twin brother James, possessing as they do 'the sight', are able to feel the evil that haunts their grandmother's Lowndes Square house and uncover the full enormity of her wickedness. In *A Footman for the Peacock* a reincarnation, one of Time's tricks, permits a story of past cruelty to be told (and expiated), while *Evenfield*'s heroine, Barbara Morant, grieving for her mother, takes matters into her own hands and moves back to the home of her childhood, the only place, she feels, 'where she [her mother] was likely to be recovered.'

For 21st-century readers another layer of Time is superimposed on the text of the novels, now that nearly 80 years separates us from the words as they flowed from the author's pen. However, thanks to *We Were Amused*, we know far more about Rachel Ferguson, her family, and her preoccupations than did her readers in the 1930s and early 1940s and can recognise that what seem whimsical drolleries in the novels are in fact real-life characters, places, and incidents transformed by the author's eye for the comic or satirical.

Like Barbara Morant, Rachel Ferguson was the youngest of three children. Her mother, Rose Cumberbatch (probably a distant relation to 'Benedict', the name 'Carlton' appearing in both families as a middle name) was 20 years old when she married Robert Ferguson, considerably older and a civil servant. She was warm, rather theatrical, and frivolous; he was not. They had a son, Ronald Torquil [Tor] and a daughter, Roma, and then, in 1892, after a gap of seven years, were surprised by Rachel's arrival. When she was born the family was living in Hampton Wick but soon moved to 10 Cromwell Road, Teddington, a house renamed by Mrs Ferguson 'Westover'. There they remained until Rose Ferguson was released from the suburban life she disliked by the sudden death of her husband, who was felled by a stroke or heart attack on Strawberry Hill golf course. Fathers in Rachel Ferguson's novels are dispensable; it is mothers who are the centres of the universe. Rose Ferguson and her daughters escaped first to Italy and on their return settled in Kensington where Rachel spent the rest of her life.

Of this trio of books, *Evenfield*, although the last published, is the novel that recreates Rachel Ferguson's earliest years. Written as the Blitz rained down on London (although set in the inter-war years) the novel plays with the idea of an escape back into the security of childhood, For, after the death of her parents, Barbara, the first-person narrator, hopes that by returning to the Thameside suburb of 'Addison' and the house of her childhood, long since given up, she can regain this land of lost content. The main section of the novel describes the Victorian childhood she had enjoyed while living in 'Evenfield', the idiosyncrasies of family and neighbours lovingly recalled. Incidentally, Barbara is able to finance this rather self-indulgent move because she has made a small fortune from writing lyrics for successful musical comedies, a very Rachel Ferguson touch. What might not have been clear to the novelist's contemporaries but is to us, is that 'Addison' is Rachel Ferguson's Teddington and that 'Evenfield', the Morant family home, is the Fergusons' 'Westover'. In *We Were Amused* Rachel Ferguson commented that since leaving Teddington 'homesickness has nagged me with nostalgia ever since. I've even had wild thoughts of leasing or buying Westover until time showed me what a hideous mistake it would prove'. In writing *Evenfield* Rachel Ferguson laid that ghost to rest.

But what of the ghost in *A Harp in Lowndes Square*? Vere senses the chill on the stairs. What is the family mystery? Once again Rachel Ferguson takes a fragment of her family story and spins from it what the reviewer in *Punch* referred to as 'an intellectual ghost story'. The opening scene, in which a young girl up in the nursery hears happy voices downstairs, is rendered pathetically vivid by the description of her frock, cut down from one of her mother's. 'On her small chest, the overtrimming of jetted beads clashed …' This humiliation, endured not because the family lacked funds, but because the child's mother cared nothing for her, was, Rachel Ferguson casually mentions in *We Were Amused*, the very one that her own grandmother, Annie Cumberbatch, inflicted on her daughter Rose. 'The picture which my Mother drew for me over my most impressionable years of her wretched youth is indelible and will smoulder in me till I die.' Rachel Ferguson raised the bar by allotting Sarah Vallant a wickedness far greater than anything for which her grandmother was responsible, but it is clear that she drew her inspiration from stories heard at her own mother's knee and that many of the fictional old lady's petty nastinesses – and her peculiarly disturbing plangent tones – were ones that Rachel Ferguson had herself experienced when visiting 53 Cadogan Square.

The *Punch* reviewer noted that in *A Harp in Lowndes Square* Rachel Ferguson demonstrated her 'exceptional ability to interpret the humour of families and to make vivid the little intimate reactions of near relations. Children, old people, the personalities of houses, and the past glories of London, particularly of theatrical London, fascinate her.' Rachel Ferguson's delight in theatrical London is very much a feature of *A Harp in Lowndes Square*, in the course of which Vere Buchan finds solace in a chaste love for an elderly actor (and his wife) which proves an antidote to the wickedness lurking in Lowndes Square. As the reviewer mentioned, old people, too, were among Rachel Ferguson's specialities, especially such impecunious gentlewomen as the Roundelay great-aunts in *A Footman for the Peacock*, who, as marriage, their only hope of escape, has passed them by have become marooned in the family home. Each wrapped in her own treasured foible, they live at Delaye, the house inherited by their nephew, Sir Edmund Roundelay. The family has standing, but little money. Now, in the early days of the Second World War, the old order is under attack. Housemaids are thinking of leaving to work in the factories and the Evacuation Officer is making demands. 'You are down for fifteen children accompanied by two teachers, or ten mothers with babies, or twenty boys or girls.' This is not a world for which the Roundelays are prepared. Moreover other forces are at work. Angela, the sensitive daughter of the family, watches as, on the night of a full moon, Delaye's solitary peacock puts on a full display, tail feathers aglow, and has an overpowering feeling he is signalling to the German planes. What is the reason for the peacock's malevolence? What is the meaning of the inscription written on the window of one of the rooms at the top of the house: 'Heryn I dye, Thomas Picocke?' In *We Were Amused* Rachel Ferguson revealed that while staying with friends at Bell Hall outside York 'on the adjoining estate there really was a peacock that came over constantly and spent the day. He wasn't an endearing creature and … sometimes had to be taken home under the arm of a footman, and to me the combination was irresistible.' That was enough: out of this she conjured the Roundelays, a family whom the *Punch* reviewer (28 August 1940) assures us 'are people to live with and laugh at and love' and whom Margery Allingham, in a rather po-faced review (24 August 1940) in *Time and Tide* (an altogether more serious journal than *Punch*), describes as 'singularly unattractive'. Well, of course, they are; that is the point.

Incidentally Margery Allingham identified Delaye 'in my mind with the Victoria and Albert', whereas the 21st-century reader can look on the internet and see that Bell Hall is a neat 18th-century doll's house, perhaps little changed since Rachel Ferguson stayed there. Teddington, however, is a different matter. The changes in Cromwell Road have been dramatic. But Time, while altering the landscape, has its benefits; thanks to Street View, we can follow Rachel Ferguson as, like Barbara Morant, she pays one of her nostalgic visits to 'Evenfield'/'Westover'. It takes only a click of a mouse and a little imagination to see her coming down the steps of the bridge over the railway line and walking along Cromwell Road, wondering if changes will have been made since her previous visit and remembering when, as a child returning from the London pantomime, she followed this path. As Rachel Ferguson wrote in *We Are Amused*, 'I often wonder what houses think of the chances and changes inflicted on them, since there is life, in some degree, in everything. Does the country-quiet road from the station, with its one lamp-post, still contain [my mother's] hurrying figure as she returned in the dark from London? … Oh yes, we're all there. I'm certain of it. Nothing is lost.'

Elizabeth Crawford

PRELUDE

IN THE SCHOOLROOM in Lowndes Square, a child, in her ugly, unsuitable frock of plum-coloured satin, cut down when discarded from one of her mother's, bent over the cutting out of a doll and its cardboard wardrobe, and shivered as she worked.

Windows and doors in the upper regions of the five-storied house fitted ill: nobody ever attended to them. The nursemaid had 'forgotten' to bring another scuttle of coal up all those flights of stairs; nobody except Sir Frederick and Lady Vallant rang bells.

It was past bedtime, a landmark easy to forget, for the Vallant children were given no supper, but the nurse was flights below at hers, the nursemaid out for the evening. Underneath the lilac sky the lamplighter had gone his rounds and the lights pricked the harness of passing, clopping hansoms into sparks.

Anne was stiff with cold and concentration, and slid off her chair, a little, odd old-womanish figure in the ridiculous frock, that martyrdom which made heads turn when one went out with Mamma. On her small chest, the overtrimming of jetted beads clashed as she raised the doll's profile dresses to the light. Myra would love it. If one could make her *laugh* for pleasure … meanwhile, doll and wardrobe must be hidden, and if suspected, denied, and if found, lied about, especially if one were fool enough to falter that it was for Myra.

Matter of factly Anne hid the toy before putting herself to bed.

As she lay in the darkness, voices sounded, two flights below – the drawing-room flight, that would be.

But Mamma wasn't giving a party?

Young voices. …

'Now for it, Jamesey.'

She warmed to that voice.

'Yes. This is the dam' drawing-room.' A young man's voice.

'Got the thermos?'

What was a thermos?

'Here. I wonder how long we shall have to wait for them to-night?'

But Mamma and Papa weren't out? The brougham hadn't been ordered round? If Hutchins had made a muddle … even servants, menservants, weren't safe from Mamma.

Cautiously Anne Vallant got up and pattered in her shrunk flannel nightgown to the stair-head and the young voices.

But you couldn't see down all those stairs.

Simultaneous time ... the past co-existing with the present and the future.

'*All time is one.*' It was Anne who, years later, said that to her own children, James and Vere, but it was they who were to prove it.

It is often a shock to have one's inner beliefs, delicate, improbable and personal, put to actual test. It leaves us speculating upon what Anne, the woman, would have made of that evening in Lowndes Square, when – still the younger Miss Vallant – she peered over those banisters and heard a young, unknown man and woman many flights below, and warmed to the voices of her son and daughter who were to be.

CHAPTER I

I

IT IS ON record that when mother found that she was going to have a baby she said to father, 'Oh Austen, look what you've done now!'

I can see them, strolling along that quiet suburban road, as they discussed the coming upset to their life. Years later, I *did* see them, and found that, as was to be expected, the remark of mother's was in that vein of humorous, tolerant resignation I was to know so well when it was my own turn to be born. No bad feeling and outcries and no false sentiment from her, mental attitudes which have always seemed to me to be the great blots upon the post-war and Victorian mothers respectively. I don't know which is worse.

What Austen, my father, had 'done now' was Lalage, my elder sister. What, two years later, he did next was to be the last of his family, James and myself.

When mother knew that twins were upon her she cried that it was pig-like to have litters and refused point-blank, with all the Vallant obstinacy, to take exercise in the day-time. 'I am a billowing scene, Austen,' said the poor little thing, 'and it's all sufficiently vile and disgustin', and I won't inflict the spectacle on the village.' And she didn't. James and I were born in September, and all through those scorching days and sultry nights she lay low, coming out only after dinner to walk in the moonlight with Austen. 'That blaring old brute,' she called the moon.

And three days before we were born she took her last silvered walk. Father stood still in a field and said, 'You know, they ought to be rather dotty. They've had three solid months of nothing but moonlight. It'll be too much to expect them to be like other people.' The thorough-paced tactlessness of the remark luckily amused mother, who hung on to a stile and laughed and laughed.

II

A few days later she was shown James and me and said to the nurse with faintish interest, 'They don't look a bit like lunatics, but like those little cheap celluloid dolls one bought in the Lowther Arcade,' at which the nurse decided to be offended, and, I rather gather, left 'before her month'. Mother says she can't remember a thing about her except that her shoes ('great boats') squeaked, and that she had an infuriating habit of saying 'b'pardon?' when she didn't hear you. But having twins wasn't all laughing at father and celluloid dolls, and for months mother, slight and frail, was very ill indeed. And it was then that father said, 'Anne, we'd better send for Lady Vallant – ah – your mother. She could keep an eye on things'; and mother (she has often admitted it in our lifetime) with a little twisted smile and in that tone of voice which commonly goes with a shrug, refused, weak as she was, her grey eyes anxious, but her tongue valiant and obstinate. Besides, the Mater would probably refuse to come.

The Mater. It was the name of mother and the aunts, her sisters, for their mother. Even as a small child I sensed before I knew the meaning of the word or even guessed that it was Latin, a lack, a wanting, and James has since told me that he felt the same. One said nothing, then. Children take most things for granted. Mother, then, was desperately ill and recovered: it was suggested that her mother be sent for and the idea was downed without explanation. Anything that touched or worried mother affected

James and me, and that small incident we have since elected never to re-see, as boy and girl, even as ageing man and woman. It was to be a straining at a gnat and swallowing a camel, but oh! the comfort of one's gnats!

III

We lived in that large suburban village for thirteen years, and mother, London born, hated it steadily.

Often to this day, James and I make pilgrimage by bus to revisit old stamping-grounds and we realize all she must have gone through. To this day, fusty cabs (no taxis) droop for custom outside the station, and the pollarded trees in those still avenues are unstirred by anything more noisy than a tradesman's trap. In the spring, lilac hangs heavy in the air, red-purple and with a scent that only your bush with Victorian roots seems to possess, and in the winter the ice still forms on the Jubilee fountain outside 'the Baxters' house'. Guiltily we love it all, our grown-up sight registering only superficial contempt. You can't kill a first love easily, and our sometimes incredulous realization of ugliness and ignominiously-planned homes is largely enhanced by seeing them through our mother's eyes.

And so over the bridge along the asphalt passage which to this day echoes one's footsteps with a sound of 'balc, balc', and into our road, and we lean on the gate, and the almond tree has been cut down and a new pane of glass put into old Sims's glory hole where he used to clean the knives and buzz a tune that later emerged into 'Soldiers of the Queen' (we broke the pane out of unforgivable, meaningless devilry in 1900), and really, those are all the innovations. And we hoist ourselves (no time for manners) on to our fence, and lo! the row of artichokes is still there, and the fowl-run that mother herself had had erected, and if one dug in that border, an earthy penny would come to light, dropped by me when I was seven.

There is a motor bus now to take us back to London; it starts from the Station Hotel. We ignore the hotel. As children it had had nothing to do with us whatever, and so can have nothing now … My outer eye apologetically sees that it is probably the oldest house in the village, with a large ramshackle garden full of character, and of trees that were veterans when Pope roved the tow-path to his villa, and Pepys passed through on his way to Hampton Court. But in youth we were hustled past it by relays of nursemaids, because on Bank Holidays drink *was* drunk, and the red-coated soldiers in their pill-box hats were considered 'ignorant' by Bessie and 'jumped-up dogs' by Ethel.

Our house we liked well, slightly haunted though it was, in that stupid knockabout way that usually means only the more harmless poltergeist with no interesting history at his back. Certainly the noises in the kitchen when 'the servies' had filed up to bed were something to remember, and occasional domestic ankles were clutched and windows tapped, and once James was jolted right out of his cot.

Our point was the fusty, awkward roomy attics, and, above all, the garden. The temptation to enlarge upon every path and currant bush I am going to resist. I, too, have been bored to whimpering stage by others with reminiscent fish to fry, and oh! how they fry it! and with what exclamations and sizzling!

But I have often, since those days, lamented that better gardens than ours, larger, and much more worth looking at and being in, should offer so much less absorbed occupation to you when you are grown up. It wasn't that we attempted, as children, to 'garden', it was that, to a child, there is that fulfilment, that sense of endless interest, of 'something going on' and all-sufficing that I, for one, have lost for ever. When, now, I am invited by friends in the country to 'spend' the day or week-end, their gardens give me a sense of unrest. It is as if one occasionally visits a person with whom one used to live; all the features are there, but the sense of context is gone. The historic garden or house, of course, is another matter. That, in time, was to give James and me a different problem altogether. But this I swear: that lend enchantment to distance as you may, those summers *were* hotter, the afternoons longer, the winters more sparkling and the sun more red (a very toffee-ball) than ever they have been since, and all the flowers more sweet. I have since been supported in this belief by the elderly, who tap barometers and give one dreary weather statistics, and even by letters to the press from authorities, who know the Latin name for every plant and so miss all the fun, poor souls!

IV

There was very little illness in our childhood, except when I caught influenza and my cot was taken from the night-nursery and put in the spare room away from James. They tell me that on the night I nearly died, he, a passage removed, turned as cold as ice, and moaned in his crib. The doctor (he whose garden wall gave on to the Jubilee fountain) was quite apologetic about it. We know now that the whole affair was only a trivial manifestation of that odd psychic bond that unites twins and some humans not even related, and about which, certainly in those days, the world was not interesting itself.

At about nine years old, onwards, we intermittently had the same dreams, tallying to the smallest detail. Nobody took any notice, and it couldn't be helped, and who wants dreams described? The relation in detail of one's dresses and dreams, together with plots of novels and plays one has read and seen should be made a penal offence, except perhaps to Mr. Henry James, to whom I would give the floor for a nightmare. Nobody else I can think of is qualified to touch that. It is a half-world, slipped between earth and heaven, and peopled with evil knowledge of all furtive, secret thought, and set to thin high winds from hell; winds that don't blow, but *undulate* in layers. ...

No. Henry James, emphatically!

Being ill was immensely worth while, as it involved lots of presents, and I shall always associate chicken-pox with a cylindrical kaleidoscope at the end of which were clashing fragments of coloured glass. 'And how it is done,' said James, aged seven. 'I for one wash my hands of the whole business.'

We were never given to pulling toys to pieces; we sensed that a mystery must ever remain one. Didn't the very bread of our dear Maskelyne and Cook depend upon the preservation of secrets? We called the firm 'Masculine and Cook' in all good faith. It was probably this fascinated acquiescence in marvel that made us unable to be impressed by the miracles in the Bible, to the shocked disappointment of the governess. But on thinking it over I still believe that we had a case. Are the loaves and fishes more wonderful than wireless, and hasn't Mr. Masculine's successor, Mr. David Devant, with his magic kettle, at least equalled the water into wine?

Illness, too, meant visits from Penny, the kitchen tabby, who rather ignored us, in health, but out of whom affliction, as it does with so many people, brought 'the best'. As James once said to the nurse, 'Penny may be difficult, but he's always been very good to me'. So with the first hint of trays below, Penny lumbered upstairs and put his great striped fiddledum head round the door. He learnt to hide right down the bed and only once gave himself away when I was peppering my lunch, and Penny said 'Pig … WHIFF' very loudly and put his bonnet-strings back flat to his head. If mother were there she would say 'Oh *let* him stay, Ethel, they're all enjoying themselves'. Mother was always the pleader for happiness. 'He *likes* a party, bless him,' and the nursemaid, content in absolute non-comprehension, had to give way.

When we weren't reading or dozing we played games of our own invention. One was 'Shakespeare', and it was calculated, if you weren't very much on the spot, to raise temperatures. Quotation was forbidden, but the point was that you must speak to each other in an extempore Shakespearean scene; if you failed to respond in under ten quick seconds you lost a point. James, arms round knees, would say in that falsely hearty way that so many characters seem to keep for each other on the stage.

> My good lord Cardinal, the King is wholly grieved
> That … that in this matter of the Prince's marriage
> The tide and the occasion do succumb

and he would point a hortatory finger at me, adding, 'ONE two three …' Upon the third count I managed to shout:

> Oh what a martyr'd pestilence am I
> That these young lovers should become
> A cause of bawdiness and sneers in France

'ONE two …'

Poor Lalage was always late for the fair and would falter

'Lord Abergavenny, God knows I never liked you much
But if ... oh lor ... but if the nameless tide
And ... something ... sea and bellying sail ...'

Here, mother's voice came from the landing where she was putting away the linen. *'Abergenny! Abergenny!* You'll be saying "Pytchley" and "Cholmondeley" next, and shaming me before the quality.'

But father was our real family stickler and never could resist a grammatic tilt with anybody. When the cook quarrelled with the housemaid in the hall and said 'Whatever made you do that, Ella?' father, wholly uninterested in the cause of dispute, opened the billiard room door and shouted, 'Don't say "whatever!" "Ever" is quite superfluous in that sentence!' which stopped the row in a twinkling.

We compiled part of a Handbook Of Etiquette For All Occasions. Father had once harangued Lalage for 'ejecting' some gristle on to her plate and had said, 'As soon should I expect to see a lady spit into the butter-dish' so our first entry began with that.

'If anything on her plate is not plesent after eating it she should ashore her host that it was very good but too jenerously rich and turn lightly to the wether.' (Mother's comment was, 'perfectly Oriental politeness. I can't rise to it!')

Another hint ran: 'At a party where a lady may meet a gentleman nobody should say stomach or flea', for a nurse had once said that to Lalage. But not all the entries were derivative, and one of James's contributions was *For The Wedding*: 'A bride should not bounce to the alter, but carry one glove in the hand.'

v

Every morning father went off to the City in a silk hat and carrying a rolled umbrella and a neat packet of sandwiches cut in the kitchen. We thought it a very grown up thing to do, but he was always more of a parent than mother. Mother really wasn't a parent at all, and I think she knew it and was glad, and that that may have accounted for the way she threw herself into whatever we were doing. That was how we saw it, then. All the other mothers in the neighbourhood played games as a concession, and I can't imagine that any of them would, as mother once did, look out of the larder window where she was consulting with cook about lunch, and say 'Mince ...' then, under her breath, 'Oh dammit, they've begun', and rush out of the house to secure a good place.

Curious how some people *fill* a room. Others can be there without being anything except dwarfed and possessed by their surroundings. Mother furnished any place she appeared in. I can't, I think.

There is one room in the house we live in now which, quite frankly, I couldn't get on to terms with for five or six years. It had nothing for me, and began by disliking me, and James as well, in an aloof way. I felt that I was taking an unfair advantage by being in a position to make it serve me by using it. And then one day I began to write of her and of Cosmo Furnival in it, and it gave way. I can't describe the process except that I felt it was flattered. It warmed at once.

Everyone has these rooms if they'd only realize it. And the most important thing is to find out what a room's trouble is. Usually, it is simply neglect, physical or social.

And so mother furnished that suburban garden she detested, and so we played.

CHAPTER II

I

THERE CAME a time when one of us asked her if she and her brothers and sisters played 'our sort of games', though I have forgotten the details of enquiry. But I remember he answer: 'Oh, we had our games, of a kind.' And I remember every detail of the scene of the question; a warm autumn evening with one blackbird fluting; James sitting on the garden roller, massaging Penny's furry stomach to see him start bicycling and pedalling as cats do; I on the edge of the wheelbarrow, pressing open poppy pods to discover what coloured 'ballet skirts' came spreading out. Mother was watering the garden with Lalage following and being allowed to pinch off dead heads. James said: 'How many of you were there, darling?'

Mother showered the last of the water over a bit of rockery and said in that tone which, under cover of humour, was meant to put one off, 'Oh, six or seven or eight or nine'.

'No, but *really?*'

Obtuseness (like Monmouth's 'melancholy') was never James's greatest fault, and I shot a look of surprise at him. Well – it was a fine evening, we'd had a successful circus, with Mother as Scintilletta, The Barest Back'd Rider in The World, skipping and drawing kisses from her mouth; we were already half an hour beyond our bedtime and were to have eggs for supper instead of bread and milk. I made allowances for him.

Mother said, 'There were Auntie Sophia and Emmeline and Uncle Stuart, Julian, James and me. Seven of us'. And her face was white.

That night, James in bed said to me, 'Did you hear? Mother said there were seven of them'.

I was alert in an instant. I knew that tone in his voice; it always meant some stress. I said 'Well?' as briskly as might be.

'There was Auntie Sophia and Emmeline and mother and three Uncles. *That's only six.*'

My heart began to thump, then Lalage remembered something.

'She can't do sums,' she hissed hopefully. 'You know what it is when she does the housebooks every Monday.'

We didn't even go through the form of suggesting that we tackle mother upon the subject. We knew that that would be one of the impossible things of the world, and Lalage caught the general atmosphere and followed our lead, senior though she was. What she contributed to us was that tendency to a comfortable common sense of her own which we subconsciously found healing. I see it more clearly now. Neither James nor I could have remembered and used the tradesmen's books at that moment.

11

It would be misleading to say that from that evening we spied upon mother. It was, rather, as though James and I, fearfully and unwilling, were impelled to some discovery the nature of which we were ignorant, beyond the fact that instinct told us that it was unlovely and best left alone. The spying – childish attempts to trip mother into further discrepancies and statements which refused to tally – was of course intermittent. Healthy children (and we were that) can't sustain these things for long at a time, or the imaginative would go out of their mind. It was that James and I, quite plainly, were never able for an instant to believe in that particular inaccuracy of mother's, in spite of her notorious arithmetic. On looking back, this seems to me rather odd. Tentatively, with much screwing up of courage, one or the other of us would add to our hoard of information.

Grandmother – Lady Vallant – the Mater – lived at Vallant House in one of those large and pillar'd London squares. Vallant in Hampshire was her country place ('Oh, it was a beautiful house enough. Queen Anne.')

That was anyone's information. It is still the Vallant seat. The Vallant children, our aunts and uncles, were much there in their youth. That too. One had to wait for months, sometimes, for fresh items. Often they arose out of our own concerns, as when Lalage's godmother sent her a doll for Christmas and mother told us, quite deliberately (no trapping) that she once had one herself 'a horrid beast. A rag doll. Ugly'. We never asked her who sent it. It was, for us, a doll that came and went from the unknown, its only purpose as an item to be hoarded by us.

'A horrid beast'.

'But a toy,' urged James. I knew what he meant. He was imploring comfort from me for that child who was our mother, in her London schoolroom. After all, as I told him, we knew from our own nursery reading that Victorian children didn't have many books or pleasures.

'And once,' cut in Lalage valiantly, 'Granny gave them a queen-cake for a "pretend" tea-party.'

I often wonder what pastrycook made that fabulous queen-cake which was to be the future mental solace of a nursery of three children.

Lady Vallant was 'a beauty in her day'. We instantly collected to consider this and to find a photograph of her, a yellowed cabinet with Lady Vallant set in an oval. 'I think she's got a face like an egg', said Lalage.

We didn't. It wasn't, of course, a face calculated to appeal to a child's elementary standards; it had too much drive and purpose; aquiline nose, strong dark brows, thin lips and dark eyes, too small and set too close together – points which naturally escaped us. This was the person who had given the queen-cake, who must have known about that doll, but who also had the power to bring that suppressed look to mother's face and a strained, hesitant tone to her voice when she mentioned 'the Mater'.

Poring over the photograph, we tried to wrest more knowledge from it, to read into it understanding of what we already possessed. Every time something fresh came to hand, more grist to our mill, we dug out the photograph again.

Susan Vallant.

'Oh, the Mater didn't understand children' … 'I remember seeing the hall stacked with game that people sent them. Of course *we* never got any' … 'No ice was ever sent up to the schoolroom and the butter always went rancid' … 'Raging at the servants. It was awful'. And once (it smote us) 'We never had any Christmas or birthday presents'. All this tossed to us intermittently in mother's guarded way with that twisted smile the Mater seemed to evoke. And yet, on the other hand:

'They gave wonderful parties, we all got invited … oh, they lived just across the square' … 'Our coming out dresses …' Cheerful, normal, *presentable* items like that, that we clung to before dispersing to piece things together. I think we took the line 'no home can be *completely* – wrong (we shied off any other definition) that has cakes for dolls' tea-parties, and coming out dresses and good parties across the square'.

It was entirely characteristic of us to assume disaster and then mitigate it with consolations rather than to take happiness for granted and be appalled by hints that all was not well. You can think any person or thing into a bogey if you concentrate enough, and give it strength and power by your tribute of apprehension into the bargain and that 'perfect love casteth out fear' is half a lie I have always known, for the greater the love the more the dread.

III

It was, to me, an actual relief to meet Lady Vallant face to face in our own garden. My passion of protectiveness towards mother knew that it might be literally a coming out into the open. Mother broke the news of her visit to us quite matter of factly ('she's never seen the house, you know'). We accepted the grandmotherly whim as we did the fact that she never sent us presents or tips or letters, or came to be with mother when we were born, but dwelt aloof and cussèd in Lowndes Square. 'The Vallants *are* rather rum that way', mother had often said, 'Aunt Emmeline and the uncles are a bit Vallantish too'.

It came to be a cheerful term of reproach amongst us.

'Don't be a Vallant.'

James and I chose Lalage to watch for Lady Vallant's arrival along the road, because Lalage is plucky and stolid and wouldn't muff things, and is, of course, the eldest, and poor Lalage turned crimson but trotted to her post all the same.

Our grandmother had hired a station fly, had even made the journey to the village in that casual train from Waterloo which we knew so well from the yearly visits to Drury Lane pantomime. Lalage says that she told the cabby 'Wait here', with no softenings of 'please', or explanation. It upset her, she said, as mother was always as considerately polite to those who served her as she was to her friends. Lalage went forward, held out her hand and said, 'How do you do? I'm Lalage', and led her through the kitchen garden door to the lawn.

What happened next was that as Lady Vallant glided forward on tiny feet James looked up and suddenly screamed, mother came running and saw the little group.

Have I imagined it through prejudice, or did mother, on reaching us, make to spread out her arms and pen us in behind her? There is certainly no doubt but that we, too, had the same idea simultaneously. And we won. We stood, all three, in a row in front of her and held our ground.

Mother with 'the old lady' (our grandmother couldn't have been then more than fifty-odd, but was of an age when young women wore caps at thirty) was quiet, attentive, and all her sparkle and fun was in abeyance. Of course, Lady Vallant was a visitor

... She spoke in a plangent, penetrating voice for all she never seemed to raise it.

Oh, she was handsome, though. Devilishly so.

She was perfectly civil to us children – I don't know why this baffled us except that it, as it were, left us weaponless without being disarmed, and all her attention, if you could call it that, was for mother. They discussed the family like a pair of strangers. Only once did Lady Vallant seem to turn into a real person when James, unprompted, stolidly offered her cake.

'He is well grown.'

And it was after this that James and I began, vaguely at first, and intermittently, to develop what the Scots call 'the sight'. It was, I imagine, always latent as it is in most people, and emotional disturbance had woken it from sleep.

IV

The first intimation happened in the middle of a winter walk with Bessie, a stupid stop-gap nursemaid. The whole episode was rather tripperish and obvious and I shouldn't dwell on it at all but for what mother said about it when James told her, for it was upon James that the mixed blessing fell first, at Hampton Court.

I was in another apartment at the time, for what that is worth, and Bessie and Lalage comfortably bundling up and down the Haunted Gallery.

James, it seems, had gone through my apartment furnished only with its tester bed of encrusted embroideries, had found a door and opened it. The room was handsomely furnished with tapestry and chairs (he had since told me that toys were littered about the floor). He took this fact 'quite sitting' and wasn't in the leas surprised, 'because, at seven, one doesn't know enough to be surprised *with*'. In a high chair was 'a small, pasty looking kid in velvet'; the man staring out of the window he recognized at once. That flat feathered cap on the table ... that golden beard ... that girth. What seems to have struck James most was that he was eating an apple. I suppose a child seldom associates historic people with homely acts; he isn't encouraged to, where all are Bills of Attainder, executions and the puttings away of what for nursery use, is called 'favourites'.

Henry said, 'No more tennis for me. This cursed leg of mine,' and little Edward VI, according to James, 'just hunched his shoulders and looked cross'.

As far as we can make out, James hung about the door, watching and quite accepting everything, until Henry spoke and began eating the apple. If Henry had caught sight of him and bluffly guffawed and shouted 'by my halidom, a likely knave!' or any similar costume-novel toshery: if even he had downed a flagon of sack, I think James would have held his ground and seen and heard more. The loss to the world! As it was, King Henry ate an apple and talked like a person, and this seems to have unnerved James, who fled to find me. He was upset and excited enough to tell Bessie, who said, 'Why what an impudence! Telling me a big story!' (oh, Board schools!) and James turned very red and hesitated a moment and kicked her.

And when that had been smoothed over by mother, when, quite inevitably, the next history lesson touched upon Henry VIII, James looked up and said to Miss Johnson, 'He wasn't like that *really*, you know. I've seen him.'

This ended in a disorder mark for impertinence. (Oh, gentility and colleges!) So once more the matter was referred to mother.

It couldn't have been an easy interview, with James to soothe as well as an agitated and indignant woman. Mother, eventually, plumped for James, knowing the misery of a small boy at being in any way set apart from his fellows, and the end of that was the resignation of Miss Johnson.

And then mother tackled James, passionately interested in the thing for its own sake, but shelving that, for his.

'I see ... yes. Not being booksy. Yes, I think I should have felt the same. But after all you know, Jamesey, they were *people* just like you and me.'

He looked at her, worried. 'But ... they're dead.'

And then mother, half-educated herself by quarter-educated and impoverished gentlewomen, began to speak, humble before her own deficiencies, gappy, probably inaccurate, virgin of any science, talking to us both like a shy schoolgirl, backed by heaven knows what of secret conviction and therefore succeeding entirely (I reproduce it in the light of wider knowledge on our part, and short of her explanations of difficult words).

'Look here ... all time is one, past, present and future. It's simultaneous.' Then (she could never resist analogy however wide of the mark), 'Think of your phonograph record of Dan Leno's monologue on Eggs. You don't know Dan, but somebody has discovered how to capture his voice for just you in the nursery. You've a little bit of him upstairs, just as you got a little bit of Henry at Hampton Court. ...

'There's a star I've heard of whose light takes so many thousands of years to reach our earth that it's still only got as far along history as shining over the Legions of Julius Caesar. Yet that star which is seeing chariot races is outside our window now. *You* say Caesar is dead. The star says No, because the star's seen him. It's your word against his! Which of you is right? Both of you. It's only a question of how long you take to see things. That's what I mean by time being simultaneous. Look here,' and she took a sheet of paper and a pencil and drew a big circle. Inside the top she sketched two manikins ('That's you and Vere, just born.') She drew a dotted line clockwise round the circle. 'This is both of you growing up and getting older and older the further you move away from the manikins; but the more you get away from them, the nearer you come to them, and when you touch again, that's so-called death, but it's birth as well.'

James liked the tangibility of that circle. So did I. It stuck in the memory. He said, 'Would that Edward kid like a toy?' Mother considered. 'There you have me! You see, that toy's *not in history*, and one must stick to the rules of the game. Probably if you gave him one now it would go right through him and fall on to the floor. But we might *try*.'

So we put on our hats and walked along the roads and lanes to Kingston to buy a fairing for Edward VI.

V

We chose, after an argument (in which mother, who adored silliments, took her full share) one of those little chubby two-inch books of photographs which, when whirled back by the thumb, gave a most enthralling Illusion of motion. I've never found one since. Those booklets were the forerunners of the cinema, and ah! how much more glamorous! The thing came (of course) from

'Pilborough's, that two-steps-down, bow-window'd moss-roof'd shop of all joys, cheap, imaginative, and glittering.

In the Palace, James, after a little misguidance, found his door and we took deep breaths all round and opened it.

From the result, I now deduce that all psychic sight is not of equal strength. Mother, for instance, saw the room as it is, bare and polished, but sensed a recent domestic occupation. I saw defectively, in patches; that is to say that whereas the one wall was bare, the other was hung with tapestry, very indistinctly seen, and of the nursery chair I could see no higher than the arms. It was my first experience of 'simultaneous time'.

James (confound him) saw the complete scene as he had before, and pointed, and shouted 'There they are!', and the noise rang all down the corridor and brought up an official in no time, so that we had no chance to do anything but throw in Edward's toy in a hurry, and it fell prosaically on to the floor.

In time, James and I were to focus with exactly equal distinctness, and my theory about the way we all saw that morning is that, except for the sight of James, which seems, for some quirk, to have matured earlier than my own, we had with that Tudor glimpse no family tie or blood relationship backed by urgent personal emotion. I throw the suggestion out tentatively in view of what occurred years later.

The morning ended, because nobody had been particularly good and it was nobody's birthday, in ices and lemonade at 'the Miss Burtons' in Market Square.

CHAPTER III

I

WHEN POOR Miss Johnson, pinkly resentful, had gone ('Johnson, passenger to Harrogate'), Mother filled in the hiatus and taught us herself. We rummaged for all we could find about Edward VI, and he seems to have been a nasty, precocious little swot who wouldn't have improved on acquaintance. Mother sensibly threw in her hand about arithmetic and it ended by Lalage teaching *her*. ('Mother! When *will* you remember to pay back twelve for the shilling column? You must pay back, you know. It isn't *like* you not to.') And Mother, bent over her sum, looked up and said it had never struck her in that light, and what fools mistresses were, and that she'd never learnt so much before. I can quite believe it. The governesses chosen (if she did choose them) by the Mater seem to have been a woeful lot of incompetents. 'But then, no one cared.'

I shot a look at James and he shook his head; he was quite simply enjoying lessons and didn't want to be upset by Vallantry. Lalage cocked her head at us both for a cue and we signalled negatives across the red cloth.

We learned to read out of books we liked, and my first light of words as distinct from isolated letters was that Edward Lear limerick on the subject of the old man of Spithead who opened his window and *said*, and mother suddenly laughed aloud and said it was exactly like Mary of Scots' Latin prayer. We used to chant the two interchangeably:

> There was once an old man of Spithead
> Who opened his window and said
>   'Languendo, gemendo
>   Et genu flectendo',
> That doubtful old man of Spithead.

I suppose we all failed completely over grammar because it appealed to no literary or dramatic instinct, or to anything at all. Even mother could do nothing to englamour it for us. We tried everything; we even got down to being Grand Inquisitors with heretics who would get put into the Iron Maiden if they couldn't answer satisfactorily about extensions of predicate, or whatever it is, but as James said, 'It's no good, darling. The Maiden's full up again'. Even music was rather a penance. Mother taught us our notes by making them into sentences. 'God Bad, David Fell Ananias' ('It was *Goliath*, my dear,' from Lalage), and 'Egg Good, Breakfast Delightfully Fresh.' Practising could only be endured by making it a concert at Queen's Hall, and we had to go into Kingston to buy James a false moustache at the hairdresser's before he would seriously settle down to scales and became Holstein – no Signor or Heinrich nonsense, he was too big a name for that. Just Holstein. If he was tiresome about getting started

And having got her, it was, somehow, her party from the moment she came in at the door. There was no trick about it; it was all the more effective in that she made no attempt at assertion.

For years we strove to break down her odd initial apathies, her gentle unwillingness to appear. It was Lalage who said to James and me, 'I know! *She's seen better days.*' We promptly filed into the house to find out if they had been and mother laughed and said, 'Of *course* they were, ducklingtons!' until she caught James's eye and stopped chaffing us. And then she said one of her things that silenced without convincing. 'Don't we have good times together?' and, hitting below the belt because it was an appeal to our chivalry and to abandonment of the subject, 'You're all I want, my ancients'.

I was in the billiard-room with mother and father (no James to support me) when the invitation to the County ball arrived. I had never been present, formerly, at mother's opening of the envelope though we all accepted it that she never went, except father, who (I suppose he did it every year) began to urge her to go, and she began to hedge and be flippant ('I can't flatter m'self the ball will be abandoned because I'm not there'). By the time she had got as far as that I was almost impatient with her myself.

'But Anne, love, you are so fond of dancing.'

So she was, if her performances at our parties in the back drawing-room and conservatory, or with ourselves on sudden, private occasions, were anything to go by. Tiny flattered boys, carefully pattering round her in stubby buckskin shoes: curates flushed and admiring: old Doctor Baxter: father, very correctly achieving his share of the steps, all were fish to her net when the music began.

'I know. But I don't think I'll go.' A finality I recognized though he failed to immediately. And she turned white and began to roll red balls along the cloth, and after a while I ran to the nursery to find the others.

James was making out a list of people who might expected to send wreaths to his funeral, and called out Lalage, 'Well, *I* make it twenty-nine, if you count the servants', and Lalage, pasting scraps into a book, said 'You can't count four more in; they might club together and I don't really count Sims because he'll probably get them out of the garden and that isn't the same as a shop wreath'.

'The onlookers won't know that,' argued James, but they stopped at once, because James saw my face, and Lalage took her cue from him.

'What else did they say?' Lalage asked practically.

'Father said, "It isn't as if it were going to be like the ordinary local affairs, but everyone will be there",' I answered, carefully quoting like a constable in the police court, 'and then he said "I hear that the Lawrence girl's coming out at it. She'd be eighteen, now, I suppose".'

'And mother still wouldn't go?'

'It was then that she wouldn't more than ever,' I said, unaware I had registered that impression at the time.

'Perhaps she hasn't got a frock fit to go in?'

The suggestion was so puerile that we merely looked Lalage. Mother was never what was called a 'dress woman', her conversation never full of clothes, but she always looked charming and unlike every other woman in the place. More or less heedless of fashion, her evening gowns were usually one-piece Liberty velvets, square-necked, laced with cord from shoulder to hem, and the other mothers sensibly never attempted imitation.

'Well, it's just *like* her, you know,' said James, his hands in his pockets, and except that we were all upset over the look on her face and the way she rolled billiard balls, there we had to leave it. The Lawrence girl could obviously have nothing to do with mother – the Lawrence girl was short and plump with round brown eyes and a 'bright' manner with men and was thought to be extremely pretty and 'fetching', and the seal of success was set upon her when people began to say that she would marry early. Mother called her 'the Boarding-house Belle' and said her social manner was Marble Arch.

And then we stopped arguing because Bessie put her head round the door to tell us that the baker had told cook there was skating on the Long Water, and we set off with a great clashing for Bushey Park.

'Suppose we all got drowned,' remarked Lalage, 'how *awful* it would be for mother.' She was probably following out a train of thought beginning with the wreath game and ending with mother and the County ball.

'Puff!' said James. 'People don't get drowned three at a time except at sea.' But all the same we tossed up for one of us to remain on the path while the others were on the ice and I lost, and watched James and Lalage being precariously fitted to their wooden skates (it involved a nail being hammered through the heel and there was a tremendous to-do with straps) by one of that small crowd of shabby loafers who sprang up from nowhere when the ice held, and the moment James and Lalage had sailed away they became extremely witty and polite to each other, so I knew that they were being Charles II and Nell Gwyn, and had to console myself with being Rochester guying the scene on paper. Just as I had begun the first line ('Oh damn these empty pleasures') which I thought very strong, a kindly woman came up and asked me my name, and I said 'Rochester' – I didn't mean to be impertinent, but I was getting interested – and what I was writing, and I said 'A scurrilous lampoon upon the foibles of the age', which was a line I had memorized from a large Stuart biography, and just then Charles II came a heavy purler on his behind and I hurried up to get a better view, while the woman, moving off, said to her companion, 'That little Rochester girl's nurse ought to be spoken to'.

And always in those winters there were parties to get ready for.

The nursery, too, was a good place to which to come back. It was haphazard, comfortable in no taste or style at all, and therefore a room to be used to the full. And on the walls were framed Christmas supplements, sentimental and largely Bavarian: warming, friendly, bad art that I have liked ever since!

CHAPTER IV

I

MY FIRST GLIMPSE of personal tragedy happened at a party, and was over James becoming, out of the blue, enamoured of a smaller child in golden curls and pink satin.

We had come in late, as usual, Lalage and I in leaf-green Liberty silk bound with gold cord and golden sandals on our feet. We were always beautifully clad, I remember, and the mothers were always trying to copy. James was in black velvet with a jacketless silk shirt, and looked like a small *maître de ballet*. Queer, how one remembers all one's life details of place or dress or food if they were passed by, worn or eaten when something vital to oneself was happening. I can remember the sweets I was sucking when told of my father's death: that we were walking under a scaffolding in Sloane Square when mother first told us how babies were born; that on Mafeking night there were sponge cakes and 'liquid chocolate' for supper, and that it was just outside the Piccadilly tube that mother said to Lalage, 'You really *must* try to like going to parties, lovie'.

The game (Oranges and Lemons) was held up while we were passed round, and quite soon we were having partners brought up for us to choose from. And James chose the pink satin and sat out a dance with her and was by her side for tea, and avoided my eye. And my heart stopped.

Nine sees trouble as a whole picture; it can't be expected to warm to the knowledge of the perishable nature of pink satin, nor does it at nineteen; even at twenty-nine, I think, the bone and the hank of hair bulk larger than that final blow, the mental affinity.

I dramatized the future (which was, of course, to prevail unremittently). James leaving me … James no longer even liking me … James despising me. I left him no leg to stand on! One must face things. …

I sat about and snubbed the boys. I retreated to the hall and was ignominiously rescued by a daughter of the house and 'taken upstairs'; she, at twenty, of no occupation, already taking refuge, poor wretch! in 'having a way with children', especially before the trickle of male guests, City friends of her father, a fact perfectly sensed by me, as children, all unsuspected, do. And after supper (orange and red jelly in real hollowed orange skins), the hostess and the daughter hunting us, and cries of 'James, sing!' and 'Vere, dance!' And we had to perform long duets from *San Toy* that, in an unguarded moment at home, we, with our retentive memories, had come out with after only having seen the play once, and listened twice to the score. And James, quite good in a

Huntley Wright song ('Scotchee man a great success, wears his legs in evening dress'), and myself in 'La Belle Parisienne' and the ladies' maid song from *The Country Girl* ('You must let her read a little or she'll want to read a lot'), and the usual storm of applause and squeals of excitement, all of which had no significance for us whatsoever, except that we rather shrank from it than otherwise – we were so used to it, and did our turns with the accuracy of professionals.

And driving home in the cab, Lalage was buffer between James and me. We huddled back in our wraps as sulkily as opera stars. And after all, he had forgotten pink satin in a week, which enraged me for the waste of good emotion!

Lalage had no parlour tricks, and I don't know when this fact first penetrated our understanding. We took it for granted that she was never called on to 'do' anything, and rather envied her for years. But I do remember (again!) every detail of the occasion when James and I first knew that she was unhappy about it.

The party was at the Kanes in their shrubbery'd house in an avenue and was a birthday affair to celebrate the appearance upon earth of Estelle, one of the spindling little girls, whose mother was determined that at least we should have no limelight that afternoon, and removed a sticky scarf crusted with discs of glass and six photograph frames and a lamp from the piano that Estelle might have music for her step dance. (What, by the way, is a step dance? Or what, rather, is a dance without steps?) In Estelle's case it was a tying of a length of silk round her hips and a rushing into every corner in the room, there to bend and posture to the accompaniment of a vast deal of rattling and banging of a tambourine with a hand-painted picture of Vesuvius in eruption upon its face. By the time she had been at it for three minutes James was nearly hysterical, and I was pretty far gone. The audience of children passed via apathy and restlessness to spasmodic conversation, and a small boy in a green linen smock said loudly, 'I mean to be a plumber', and quite suddenly some tactless Miss piped 'James! Vere!' and they were all in an uproar at once, while our hostess, biting her lips, said how nice that would be.

It was while we were starting the 'Alphabet Duet' ('Oh my lover you are clever, but you've never taught me yet') that I missed Lalage from the massed circle of children on the floor, and managed to give James a special look. He broke off at once, said 'Excuse me,' and we ran into the hall.

She was crying, quite quietly, and wiping her eyes with her raspberry chiffon frock. We sat on either side of her, and I said, 'Is it tummy or lavatory, or didn't you get what you wanted at tea?' And as she shook her head and hid her face deeper, I said, because I guessed in a flash, 'Jamesey, she *minds* ... about our performing, you know', and James turned very red and almost shouted because he was so sorry, 'Then we mustn't do it any more'.

That was not to be always possible. Also, I think I knew that the declaration was no good to Lalage. She wasn't out for sacrifice from us, but for a share of life for herself.

It was an uneasy cabful that turned in at our drive. This James and I agreed, was a case for mother, and when we had disposed of Lalage, we went to look for her.

She was dressing in pale amethyst velvet for the Shakespeare Reading at which she was to figure as Ophelia. The Readings were held once a month at the members' houses in turn, and when the station cabs and Harkness's flys gave out, the members often had to wait for their cab to 'drop' someone else before returning for themselves, and mother has sometimes picked up hair ornaments and pins and handkerchiefs (and once a bottle of heartburn tablets) off the fly's musty floor, items that she would redistribute to their owners on arrival. Luckily, this evening it was the turn of our house to receive, and James and I started about Lalage at once, and had a long talk. Mother hugged us tight, and said, 'She's shy, like *me*'. And as we were leaving to go to supper, 'I'm glad you realize about Lalage, and it's sweet of you. She's not a bit like you two, and ... well, help her out all you can'.

She was making much of the business. The significance of that escaped us as we were making much of it ourselves. Proudly – we felt like positive parents – we strutted to the nursery.

After supper and bath we hung over the banisters and listened. The curates were awful as Horatio and Marcellus, and once some man lost his place, and we prompted him loudly. Mother was very sweet and appealing and true in the songs, though her voice was a mere thread. She, too, had no parlour tricks.

In November – it must have been early in the first week, as we had been busy all the morning in the garden after lessons supervising Sims making our guy – mother, hatless, in a fur jacket, came out, and there was something in the way in which she walked round the guy that prepared me for news slightly unwelcome. Half-heartedness and inattention wasn't like her. Our parties on the Fifth were always events, 'and what we spend on fireworks, worms wouldn't believe', mother used to say.

'Mother! Come and sniff! He smells delicious, of potting-sheds and Sims's trousers,' shouted Lalage.

And then Penny rushed out sideways and was up the guy in a flash and crouched, glaring with pleasure and wearing his teeth outside, like a walrus.

'Oh pick him off!' Lalage shrieked, 'if he learns to do that he'll do it on the night and get his dear stripings singed.'

'Well, he'll flog up to town and order another pair,' answered mother, 'he's a dressy beast, aren't you, my stout?' She picked him down, adding, 'and to-morrow we're all going to London to see grannyma.'

It was probably owing to the guy and Sims and Penny and mother being out with us there in the patchy frost in the garden, and that to-morrow was always a long way off, for James called out cheerfully, 'Is *that* all?' and Lalage asked what we should have for lunch. Mother answered, with apparent irrelevance, 'We'll have sandwigs before we start', and, 'afterwards we'll go to Hamley's and buy ourselves fairings'.

It was a wrench to leave the garden, next day, and we were all predisposed to resentment, a state of mind which mother made no attempt to soften. She just assumed we wouldn't let her down and let it go at that.

We had had Vallant House described for us so often that our only sensation upon seeing it was one of surprise that it should be so familiar. Mother's talent for mimicry held good also over description and her pungent phrases one sentence would sometimes account for a whole room had engrained the house far more upon our imagination than would the most accurate inventory.

The hall: *Raked by the Pater's study … flights of beastly china cockatoos up the stairs.*

The drawing-room: *Oh, it could have been a beautiful room only the Mater ran to knick-knacks and china-cupboards and things one was always falling over or skidding on or knocking against.*

The Mater's bedroom: *Dead. Just a bedroom. A hotel room.*

The schoolroom: *A draughty cupboard at the top of the house.*

Or the unfinished phrase: *I never saw the servants' quarters at all in all the years I lived there … drainage bad … nobody seemed to mind. …*

The butler admitted us, and mother's face softened as she shook hands with him.

'How are you, Hutchins?' And the old man flushed and murmured and called her Miss Anne and then corrected himself, and his eye fell on us. It was a searching glance for all its brevity – it concentrated most upon Lalage – but we, or something else, seemed to have passed a test. Mother said, 'Here they all are', named us and told us 'Hutchins is a very old friend of mine', and James and Lalage and I put our hands into his – it held them all. And then began the ascent to the first floor past all those china cockatoos.

Mother asked, 'How is her ladyship?' and Hutchins suddenly and momentarily became another person and grimmed his lips and said that she 'kept excellent health', and we were shown into the drawing-room.

Lady Vallant certainly looked extremely well as she sat, erect, in her rich silks, the lace veil on her head falling to her shoulders, diamonds gleaming at neck and fingers. Perhaps the silk of her gown was a shade too bright – a deep rose colour, which her contained and tormented expression lightened sometimes by the curiously satyr-like look of faintly malicious amusement, didn't seem to match. I can see her still so clearly as she was that afternoon, and I still think the key to her outward appearance lay in the word 'sardonic'. As for the room she sat in, it was exactly to mother's description except for an easel that she had forgotten to mention upon which was propped a woolly watercolour suggesting some talent-at-bay resorted to by a still unmarried great-aunt, and which to the nervous or maladroit constituted the greatest pitfall in the room. And Lady Vallant had a knack of inspiring nerves. ...

Several incidents marked that, our initial visit to the old woman, the first domestic enough.

We filed down to the dining-room and to a wonderful luncheon – it began with Palestine soup and ended with hothouse fruit. As we had all, at mother's instigation, fortified ourselves heavily in advance, with sandwiches, this was a set-back that made James shoot a glance of reproach at her as he reluctantly refused salmi of pheasant. She accepted his look with a tiny shrug and smile behind which lurked irony. Lady Vallant, sunk in her carved armchair, said, 'I hope they are enjoying their food, Anne', and mother answered, 'It would be impossible not to, Mater', and looked at her plate.

Quite soon after that, the footman, sidestepping to avoid Hutchins who was pouring wine for mother, nearly dropped a fork, but retrieved it deftly. Lady Vallant said, 'You've spilt some gravy on the cloth'.

'No, my lady.'

'Don't contradict me.'

My heart was beginning to thump and I shot a glance along our ranks. Mother's lips were compressed but she mustered a warming smile for me. Lalage's eyes were beginning to fill, and James's face had flushed scarlet.

'My lady, there is no gravy on the cloth.'

'Leave the room.'

And then James (the man of party) slid off his chair and pattered up to the old woman, knuckles drumming on her chair-arm. There was luckily no time to consider what mother's feelings must have been. It might have stopped him. It might ...

'Lady Vallant, it wasn't his fault. And it was a clean fork, anyway,' and James took the thing from the man's hand and held it up. The old woman just looked at him and said plangently, 'Go to your seat'. There was a faint flush on her cheek which we put down to temper. Then she swerved to mother. 'Why do they call me Lady Vallant? Tell them I don't like it.'

Mother met it, said adequate things about Lady Vallant being seen by us so seldom ... didn't quite realize ... and that passed, except that when conversation was resumed, Lady Vallant steered it to servants and said 'I keep them on board wages or else they eat their heads off' – this, with Hutchins in the room, immobile at the sideboard.

It was our first experience of heartlessness.

As we were filing out of the dining-room, James said urgently, 'Can we see the kitchen?' Luckily Lady Vallant didn't hear; as leader she was already halfway up the staircase. It was then, I suppose, that mother let us know that she had never seen the basement, either.

After this, it seemed to be a more or less understood thing that Vallant House was to be included in our London visits, slipped between shopping, calls at other large houses, on cousins, old friends of mother's and Lalage's godmother who lived in Sloane Street. We all cheerfully hated the Vallant House visits. It was about the liveliest and most wholesome emotion we were ever to feel for the old lady. It wasn't only the behaving well, for that applied on any call, although at Vallant House we three deliberately threw in more of behaviour, unrelaxed and purposeful, than we attempted elsewhere; it was a watching of our grandmother's face, a listening and preparation for her to say something hurtful to mother; it was, above all, the realization that in this house, of which one hour discomfited and oppressed our spirit, mother had lived for eighteen years.

As time went on it seemed that, of us three, I was to be odd man out. I didn't register with Lady Vallant; it was upon James and Lalage that she concentrated, if you could call it that, for even we could sense that she didn't understand children or value them.

We argued it out in the nursery: James, of course, as the only boy of the family, and Lalage, because she wasn't in the least like either of us. It seemed a very neat and obvious arrangement.

And all those years she was clever with us, as clever as a woman can be who isn't aware that she is pitted against antagonism and hasty, immature prejudice.

She began to give us money. At Christmas and after the visits we got into the habit of accepting five-shilling pieces and sovereigns. Apart from the fact that most children are mercenary little brutes we saw no way of refusing that wouldn't recoil on mother. Also, the action seemed to humanize Lady Vallant. And mother would stand aside watching the delicately bony fingers doling out coins with a faintly sarcastic smile.

CHAPTER V

I

FATHER DIED two years later; he was run over by a train and killed instantly. Ironically enough he, who rather hated cats, lost his life trying to save a kitten which had bounded out of the waiting-room and jumped over the platform as the train drew in.

Father lay in his coffin in our billiard-room: we could see its shape from the hall as we went up and downstairs. Mother suggested, 'Don't you want to go in and see him?' and we all said no. She thought it over. 'Better try, learn to face everything', then, with arms round us all, 'he looks just the same'.

We filed in, James first, and stood in a row trying not to tremble and feel sick, but we made ourselves take a look, and a long one. The room was banked with wreaths and I have dreaded the smell of Madonna lilies ever since.

Even Lady Vallant had sent a wreath.

We came out and tried to avoid mother but she was waiting, indomitable, in her grotesque crapes and lawn (black-streamered bonnet for out of doors, stiff white cap for the house) that convention decreed, and James found his voice and of sheer embarrassment asked quite at random after the kitten. 'He saved the little thing, Jamesey.' It was, I am pretty sure, a loving lie; she excelled at them.

Mother, always reasonable where public opinion was concerned, still refused to take us to the funeral, defending her point of view to intimates with all the Vallant obstinacy and her own spirit. Colloquial, flippant, paining plenty of those good, real dears whom the curates called 'sweet women' (and who remained loyal and lovable in spite of it!).

'Funerals are so dam' bleak … no. Let 'em remember him as he was … Oh, one sends for the clergyman at these times as one would for any other tradesman … One's body's a great problem; one ought to disintegrate into the ether. I do think they've managed these things so badly.

Nor were we put into mourning. We all saw that if you have really been fond of anybody and if black clothes mean grief, then to come out of black at the end of a year is a betrayal. Mother bore the ugly brunt herself, and standing in front of the glass, exclaimed to us all, 'I look *exactly* like Mrs. Nickleby!' And so, we chaffed her and laughed together against closed blinds and in the sultry smell of lilies. Fathers have had worse passings.

Some woman friend, low-voiced, murmured to her, 'If you could only *cry*', and mother said, 'That sort of thing gets one nowhere. I've been all through *that*'. She didn't know I'd overheard. It haunted me for weeks. What she did know was that any tears from her would have knocked down our defences. And on the day of the funeral she sent us off to Kingston to a matinée, to see Miss Valli in *Alice in Wonderland*. 'If the servants or Bessie ask where you've been, tell them for a walk; they wouldn't understand. And you'll have to go into the pit or you may meet a lot of the kids from the village *and* their mothers Take care of 'em, Jamesey,' and mother, very whitefaced and crape from head to foot, took up her Prayer Book in a black-gloved hand.

It was our first outing alone. In the road at the side entrance we were entertained by a man with a disc of black felt who said that he was Queen Victoria, a nun and Napoleon, and later on a quavering woman sang a song from *The Country Girl* and we joined in the chorus – it was one of my usual solos at parties, and the poor thing got the words wrong and muffed the time and took the final A an octave lower, and we thought it so awful that Lalage gave her her lucky threepenny bit. James bought the metal tokens and ran and found us good places, brandished us to them and said to a stout mother, 'Will you move up just a little? I have my ladies with me.'

In the interval Lalage said quite suddenly, 'Are we orphans, now?' Altogether impossible not to swell with assorted importances.

Father's death left us very badly off, a fact mother circled round with us for a considerable time – she had her own bearings to get. It was the stoppage of the order for Liberty patterns of velvets for her gowns which first put me, personally, on the track of the situation. I kept it to myself for days, it seemed so unbelievable. From this to telling James and Lalage, and from that to assuming we were penniless was, for us, the work of a moment. It ended by James and me sneaking up to London to earn money. We left Lalage at home; we both felt that seamy sides weren't for her, and it was essential not to frighten mother by a wholesale departure. Also, it was to be Lalage's job to tell mother we were out for the afternoon planning a surprise for her.

There were four shillings in my money-box and one and six in James's tin post-office that we were saving up for (me) a box of 'chocolate bricks' that I wanted because I liked the grouping of the words, and (James) for a lady's hat covered with sequins which he'd seen in a second-hand shop we had passed on the afternoon walk. He would probably never have been allowed to keep it, but he craved for it with the unreasoning and mysterious urge of childhood.

We rehearsed at the end of the garden behind the apple trees, where in autumn we pulled delicious dowdy russets and found, half buried in dead leaves at the roots of the one nut bush, great acid-green 'cookers' which had thudded down during the night. Lalage and I had cut up an old hat we'd found in the boxroom, and tried for an hour to be nuns and Napoleon, but the results were awful – we couldn't do it quickly enough and didn't know the twists, and it has given us a respect for pavement performers that we have never lost. Lalage hung over a branch with her hair starred with apple blossom and was too envious and interested to laugh. Only once did we sight success and that was when I folded the felt into a shape that distinctly recalled the Princess of Wales's bonnet, but when I tried to repeat it I found the bonnet was an accident, and I couldn't. So we just fell back upon selections from our usual party programmes.

We managed to get to the station without any set-back. Sometimes when at a loose-end in the afternoons we would saunter down there to watch trains come in and put pennies in the slot machines and re-examine the coloured picture of hell that hung in the first class waiting-room – apparently second and third class passengers were considered to be saved, so that our casual appearance on the platform attracted no notice, and we even got a carriage to ourselves, and were so wrought-up by this and by nervousness that we forgot to look out of the window for such landmarks as 'the Gregory's garden' and 'Miss Puce's cottage', and for that moment when the line took such a curve that we could see the engine and half the train as well, and which we, for some still unfathomed reason, called 'the race'.

At Waterloo we had enormous difficulty in finding our way to the theatre district; father and mother had seen to all that part for us at pantomime time, and we had to take a growler to the nearest pit queue, spending on it our return fare and trying not to think what would happen if we didn't make it. There were of course 'the relations'; there was as a last resort, Hutchins, about whom we both felt that he was capable of collusion ... 'Unless, of course,' worried James, 'it wouldn't be fair to borrow it out of his board wages'. Board wages certainly sounded bleak, and for some time we all believed it meant sleeping on a plank.

At the first theatre we stopped at, the play began at two o'clock and the queue was already heaving and shuffling out of sight up the gallery stairs, but eventually we landed in the Hay-market, and we got out and paid the cabby and faced the line of theatregoers. We had long ago decided that, if nervous, we were to remember they were only people and not a race apart; that probably they, too, had emptied money-boxes to get there at all; that they couldn't get at us because they were in line, whereas we could cut away at any minute, so James just hummed our key in my ear and we began, and nothing happened at all for what seemed like half an hour and was probably half a minute. The queue seemed shock-proof. Things came and sang and contorted and twisted at them and they just looked about and read the *Pall Mall Gazette* and the *Girls' Own Paper*. And then, quite suddenly, individuals began to take us in and listen to a line, and speak to their companions, and stare and murmur, and so it spread. We had applause, which I have since had reason to believe unusual; on the other hand, we didn't get half the money we could have collect-ed, because of our clothes. There was a shyness, an uncertainty when we passed along the line with one of cook's smaller pud-ding-basins. There were apologetic grins, and young men turning red, and one man gave me half a crown and took his hat off to me to be on the safe side.

We took eighteen shillings, and coming home we were both sick with excitement and fatigue out of different windows. I had glanced up at the theatre hoardings and saw the name of Cosmo Furnival and thought it had brought us luck. Mother and father had once gone to town to see him act, and it seemed to make the theatre and side street comforting. Mother must have stepped on the very pavement we had ourselves; in that building there were people father had spoken to for tickets and programmes. ...

We poured our takings on to the table in front of mother and told her everything; we had agreed that, as this was to be the means by which we kept the family, it was useless to hedge. And then, of course, mother, hugging us both, explained how impossible it was, and having done that repaid us by going into the whole question of our future.

We were, it seemed, able to 'scrub along', which was unsatisfactory – we preferred sensational contrasts and could willingly have adopted Little Nellish rags where the coming reduction of pocket-money and other things was merely humdrum and exasperating. We left the dining room and sat round the drawing-room fire which a capricious spring wind was causing to smoke a little, and the incandescent burner to curtsy and whistle. Mother was forcing herself to tell us everything at one blow, shelving her natural reserve and that superimposed code by which Victorian parents concealed facts however vital or trivial from their children. Therefore she blurted:

'I'm afraid that it'll mean no Rugby or University for you, Jamesey. Will you mind ... awfully?'

I don't think she realized that it is useless to ask anyone whether the deprivation of an untested experience will disappoint them; again, in the Victorian manner, she was talking to the only male of her family from the point of view that 'all the Vallants went to Rugby'. James understood at once that he was unable to do something that the world considered essential, and looked solemn for the sake of appearances, and to match mother's tone of voice and then, answering the expression on her face, 'Of course not. I don't care'.

She said, 'But of course you'll have to go to school'.

'Away?'

'I'm 'fraid so. You see,' and here mother came out with one of her indiscretions, 'if one doesn't go to a decent school, one's apt to turn into a Bunthorne.'

He cocked an appreciative ear. 'Howell and James?' Lalage and I were concentrating solely on velvet coat and cap and floppy ties. Until quite twenty years old we failed to assimilate the implications of Bunthornism, just as it took Lalage twenty-five years to realize that the Mock-turtle wasn't a rather dear beast created by Carroll, but an elaborate and mundane joke about soup. But mother pulled herself up. 'I mean that it isn't good for you, Jamesey, to live with three lorn females.'

'But I *like* lorn females!'

'Duckie, I know you do, bless you! but you'll like to meet chaps of your own age.'

It was to be, we saw. And as we sat toasting our shins and accepting it, mother after a longish pause, said, 'Would you three mind awfully if we left this place?'

That was brass tacks with a vengeance. We could find nothing to say. Mother hurriedly started upon reasons: house too large now – cutting down servants – garden too large – Sims's wages – later, if James went to St. Paul's School, saving of fares as he would be a day boy – It was all devilishly plausible. Protest, even argument, was silenced because we all knew that she hated the house and the village – it was typical that she called house, garden and environs 'this place'. I forget which one of us, struggling with catastrophe and embarrassment, faltered a query as to the future of Penny, to be instantly overwhelmed with reassurance. And later when we settled in London there were the cousins to make friends with. That meant 'the Seagrave kids', children of Sophia, mother's elder sister, and 'the Verdunes', offspring of Aunt Emmeline, and why mother lined them up as an inducement I don't know. I think she was too disoriented to be clever about everything, that night. We three assumed tragically and instantly that we were to leave home at the end of the week. Actually, we lived in our house for another year.

II

That summer holiday was memorable as being the last one we should pack for from home. Next summer, it seemed, we should not be able to afford a holiday owing to the expense of the move and James's school fees. To us it meant that we were watching cook cutting sandwiches for the last time ever on that table in that kitchen. Future cooks and sandwich-cutting, we all felt, wouldn't be the same to the table in a strange kitchen. And indeed I have often thought that the susceptibilities of furniture and china have never been sufficiently allowed for by families. Even a much-used saucepan must have its dreary little memories when put into the dustbin at last, and as for chairs! Is it inconceivable that, apart from their feeling for their room and their owners, the tree-life persists in them? Have not seeds buried with mummies for two thousand years sprouted under the very eye of the excavator? You cannot live with a thing and use it without humanizing it to a certain extent, and those men who bluffly announce that their pipe is their 'friend' have hit upon a truth more subtle than they know; and perhaps those women who (always contemptuously) get called 'slaves to their household goods and chattels' are only, in their turn, more unconsciously susceptible to the dormant life in oak, mahogany and walnut?

For the last seaside time we left Penny's money for fish and milk, chose dolls and books and went all round the garden, knowing that when we returned at the end of September it would be entirely different because for two months it had lost touch with us, and had been pushing on its own private affairs unwatched. The garden always took two or three days to 'come round', and show us the alterations.

We went to picturesque, hideous, dear old Ramsgate and found it as usual smelling of hot asphalt, tar and fish, and I fell in love with a beach singer – one of six in sullied white, and one morning he gave me a kiss and James smacked his face, and 'Uncle Tony' said 'Now then, sonny, who're *you* pushing?' which disgusted me, and we fled. We scuffed along in silence halfway towards Broadstairs and James once muttered 'It's abominable!', and I, even then unable to jettison the adored, said 'I *liked* it', which was rather a lie, as nobody could possibly enjoy being kissed on a crowded beach littered with paper bags and lumps of gnawed nougat, and I knew that to save our Uncle Tony's kiss I should first have to switch it over to surroundings of my own contrivance – say, the Marina Gardens at night. But James was desperately upset at the remark; he was, in that second, amply paid back for the pink satin episode which had so undermined *me*! And I think that it was at that exact moment in our green jerseys and sandshoes, within sight of Dumpton Gap and with a heat haze buzzing, that we realized that, when all was said, he bore a label called 'boy' and I another marked 'girl', and all it might be going to mean if we allowed it to. The impending school life contributed, for about things like that there is no free will, and the older you grow the more adhesively does the world expect you to fix your label to you, until a man and a woman can't see each other for sex, and until, as a result, premiums are put upon those men and women who can produce the greatest amount of it. And the danger of all boys' schools is that they can cause the young male thing to lose sight of the kind of person he was originally meant to be. He must scoff at all forms of beauty which are not of muscular origin: conceal any love of music (except for facetious instruments like the bassoon) together with any love of verse other than limericks, and above all hide any natural appreciation for colour and scent, and learn that one is soppy and the other a stink. He must read no book which has a woman in it because it is orientally assumed that his thoughts about her will be unclean, and his very great reward for conformity is the stunning yarn which grips and rattles and is chiefly occupied with revolvers and violence. He must remember never to allude to mother or sisters other than slightingly, and be prepared, if he should commit the sin of love for another boy, to be expelled.

I wonder if any school will ever have the courage to grant the small change of affection to the bewildered cravers of ten, eleven, twelve and thirteen, and to allow for the real necessity of superficial sentiment in the very young? But no! A kiss is beyond the pale. Better the other thing. Let it come to a head and then expel the lad.

Later, tension is relaxed at the University, and he makes a belated effort to scramble back into his personality, which perhaps accounts for the number of available sets; the brawn set, the swot set, the religious, Swinburne or womanist set. But I suppose that (like British justice) the system is for the greatest good of the greatest number, and there is no getting over the fact that the present-day scoffers at the Old School Tie are, on the whole, detrimentals of one kind or another, sitting on a very vat of sour grapes; people you could not count on in a national crisis, or wholly smile upon your daughter marrying. ...

James had always disliked cricket but played it with assiduity and I am glad to remember that, if any point of herd-etiquette arose which found him unprepared, he had the sense to write home at once for hints (mother had not had brothers of her own for nothing) and that Lalage and I backed her up and could nearly always be counted on to be brusque and caustic and common sense with him.

CHAPTER VI

I

I CAN remember to this day our last hours in our old home, and the almost unendurable unhappiness we went through. In the case of James and myself, we were not only coping with obvious grief at leaving the house and garden, but with that oversensitized notion of our betrayal of inanimate things that we had always shared. It is the same emotion in reverse that, all our lives, we have experienced when visiting any historic castle or old country house; the feeling that the past is so close to us and is holding its scenes and secrets from us. It's maddening! It also gives one a feeling of mental suffocation for which, I suppose, the reason is that the past of the rooms and grounds is so photographed on the ether that one's own personality is blurred, like the operator's hand when some awkward gesture sends it across the magic-lantern picture.

I only know that James and I have had to crawl back, defeated, over the grass of many a ducal park to the waiting motor coach leaving the rest of party giggling and exclaiming in the halls and galleries of the house, and once, James caught sight of a famous seat over the low, flint park wall and said 'That's no good. I can't go in'. The mansion, quite kindly, had conveyed that he and it had no point of contact. So he sat and smoked in the coach and told the party he had hurt his foot.

On the last morning in our home we all scattered to have a final private view of every room and every landmark in the garden. The idea was unfortunately common to all three, and when we encountered each other we were cross and made ludicrous excuses. I met Lalage suddenly round the lilac bush on the drive and she said 'I thought I'd dropped a pencil', and when James knocked against me in the box-room he announced angrily that he 'came up for something he'd forgotten, and to avoid tripping over the trunks'.

Sims, instead of bending over radishes, had come in his best clothes to say good-bye, and stood in the hall 'like a person', which was intolerable, and in the kitchen a row of graduated ovals across the wall under the house-bells marked the place where hung the great plated dish-covers. In the bare drawing-room which had held so many lamplit Shakespeare readings I went, and declaimed:

> 'Though yet of Hamlet our dear brother's death
> The memory be green …'

because I wanted to leave the room something to be going on with.

We were all astonished at the send-off we were given at the station. Everyone we knew seemed to be there: the contemporaries of a dozen nurseries, 'the little Fishers' (who always had a monster cracker at their Christmas parties), the spindling Kanes from the house in the avenue down which they would presently stroll back to lunch (that was a pang), and numerous others who, to us, represented their surroundings far more than themselves, and whose names I can't repeat even now without visions of hoops in Bushey Park, skates on the gravel pits, Morris curtains and hand-painted door-panels, dancing class and Easter-egg hunts with their glitter of silver foil among the daffodils. And among the mothers stood all those women with whom our mother, appreciative and affectionate always, had never quite succeeded in establishing that intimacy – of 'running in' and domestic confidence, that they wistfully desired. Most of the husbands, bar the City men, were there as well, except those who had gone off earlier to golf at Sudbrook Park. Even a curate appeared (Marcellus), and when he caught sight of mother, he wheeled in a perverse agony of shyness and began to examine the tin advertisements of the Owl and Waverley pen, Owbridge's Lung Tonic and a monster pod of Carter's peas, and when mother took his hand, he began to cry, and his nose, Lalage said, 'turned the most *lovely* shade of mauve'.

Poor Marcellus! He'd loved her and we never guessed. Had mother? It would be like her to know, to pity, and to continue to imitate his sermons, which indeed were pretty fatuous.

And then the vicar came on the platform, looking, as usual, like Savonarola in a top-hat a size too large, and put his hand on her shoulder, and said, 'I should like us to say a little prayer,' and mother said, 'Oh Mr. Royce, *please* don't let's!' and he laughed with grim affection and said she was always an undisciplined person, and blessed us all. And then Lalage and I seemed to be being kissed by the most unlikely people, who apparently felt that a final and imminent departure would shield them from reprisals, as a mob loots the ruins after a fire. Little Freddie Hayter burst into tears as he tiptoed to reach Lalage's face and asked her to marry him, and Lalage, suddenly affected, began to cry as well and sniffed that she 'hadn't time to'. Another worm i'th' bud! Poor freckled Freddie, who, all those years, was to us but a covert coat, gaiters, picking up chestnuts, feeding the deer and a nurse with a cleft palate; and here he was, 'a person' for a matter of minutes.

Everyone gave us presents; you would have thought we were going on a voyage instead of forty minutes down the line to London. To crowd to the train window and see them all left on the platform, to hear the jingle of harness from one of Harkness's flys, to glide past the book-stall from where so many numbers of *Little Folks* had been put aside for us was so painful on the grand scale that we had no sensation left, and were able to behave like ordinary passengers.

James had put a penny in the slot of the revolving gipsy, and she leered and whirled and stopped at a section marked 'Riches and wealth', which galled him, but he had spent the penny because, so he told us, he meant to come back in a year, and if her finger was still at Riches and Wealth he would know that nobody had used the machine since himself. The idea was comforting; we felt we still had a stake in the station.

And the next thing we knew was that James went off to school at Eastbourne, and that Mother, Lalage and I were settled in a little house just off Campden Hill.

Before he left, one thing happened which none of us had foreseen. Lady Vallant sent for James. We had forgotten all about her for months, and now the Vallant feeling washed over us again like a wave. On the face of it, it was a reasonable request, and a proper one, but our grandmother had a knack of selecting only those moments of social fitness which happened to suit her private book, and of skipping any sort of continuity of family feeling or obligation. She had not advised, commented upon or helped with the move: she had sent no line of welcome to await us in our new little hall, and now she was coolly commandeering James, whose very hours with us were numbered.

He refused to go, truculently and with indignation. Mother, wasting no time, asked him to as a favour to herself, which of course settled it. I offered to accompany him, and was dissuaded. Lady Vallant, it seemed, detested uninvited guests, and had even been known (here was a new item) to refuse to ring for more hot water if bidden guest arrived at five instead of four-thirty when the hostess had had her own cup of tea; had often refused her own daughters, 'parched with shopping' as Mother put it, the dregs of the teapot as it stood.

'But, Mater, I don't mind if it is off the boil.'

'No, no, dear. Leave the pot alone. It is stewed.'

'I don't mind that, either.'

'Leave it alone.'

Mother, sub-acidly imitating the scene.

'Well, *I* think she's mad,' said James daringly, for which Lalage and I were grateful to him.

'Oh no, she's not.' (After all, mother was, incredibly, her daughter.) Then, side-tracking James, 'She'll be quite nice to *you*'. And, with a little, bitter smile, 'Granny likes men'.

And so the man, in his first bowler hat and new over coat, went to call at Vallant House.

I was uneasy. I hung about to waylay him, and where he came home at six o'clock, I saw how right I had been. His eyes were too bright and his face was anxious. He threw his bowler on to the settle and shovelled me into the dining-room, shutting the door.

'That's a *beastly* house,' he began.

'How ... specially, I mean?' I seemed to know that he hated it quite apart from the fact that it was the home of Lady Vallant. He was at a loss: plunging about for reasons.

'I can't stand the stairs. They're beastly cold. I said so to Hutchins. He said he hadn't noticed it, but he looked pretty pasty himself.'

It was no use to expect any sort of coherent story; James was too busy sorting impressions, and when he'd come out with them, discovering that putting them into words rendered them capable of other interpretations, so about the staircase, he added, 'I suppose *he* was cold, too'. He brooded morosely, and then dived a hand into his pocket and threw a wad of bank notes on to the table.

'Ten pounds. *She* gave it me. I didn't know how to refuse.'

'No.' After all, we'd all taken money from her in our time and under mother's eye, at that. But – ten pounds!

He wove his neck in his collar. 'She kissed me', and looked out of the window and turned scarlet. 'She asked if I liked her dress, and of course I had to say yes, and then she showed me photographs of herself and said I should have seen her twenty years ago ... and then she began about all of us. She seems to take rather a special interest in Lalage, for some reason, and wanted to know if she was what she called "robust", and began to talk about her being so unlike us. And then she started on mother.' Here James broke off, listening. I said, 'It's all right, she's upstairs, reading. Go on and be *quick*.'

'She said she supposed that we were all terrified of her, and that mother had made us hate her. ...'

'What?' I almost shrieked.

'*Shut up!* She'll hear. And I said we weren't, and she hadn't and that mother very seldom spoke of her ... she seemed a bit flummoxed at that.'

'Jamesey, that was clever of you!'

He shook his head. 'Wasn't. I mean, I didn't *mean*, to score off her. I was just doing the polite and it came out that way.'

'And then what?'

He frowned. 'She began to talk pi-jaw.'

'Pi-jaw? Lady Vallant!'

'It was a bit thick, from her. You see, she doesn't know we know a bit about her already.' That was a point, and we sat savouring it. 'She showed me a book of hymns she'd written in eighteen-seventy-something.'

'Hymns!' Somehow it didn't fit in, to us, even then I added at random, 'What were they like?'

'Awful. One didn't go right when you said it, and the rhymes were "save" and "love" … *you* know. There was one about

> "The evil that we do, O Lord,
> Shall be washed white as snow."'

He thought again. 'And she asked me if I didn't think so too, and of course I said I didn't know, and she said she knew I should be 'very good' and talked about "Gawd".

'I know that,' I chipped in. 'Mother always told us, she did. She called fivepence "fippence", too.'

'And then Hutchins and the footman came in to clear tea and draw the curtains, *and she was nice to them.*'

This human gleam had evidently made an impression on James. Not a pleasant one.

'How?' I asked.

'Oh, she asked for her handscreen and grinned at Hutchins and said she was a trouble, and she was sure I'd show myself out to save him coming up the basement stairs.'

'Was Hutchins pleased?'

James looked at me, his ruddy little poll shorn like an orange against the impending school. 'I think he hated it.' His eyes widened. 'You see, he knew she was showing off. She'd forgotten about lunch … that day.'

'And did you show yourself out?'

'No fear! I would have, but Hutchins was waiting in the hall. He "hoped I'd had a pleasant time" and sent messages to mother.'

There was nothing else to tell or to hear. We should chew on James's visit at our leisure. And then we remembered the money. James said 'We'll tear it up'. I said, 'You can't do that. You'd better keep back one pound in case mother asks you if she gave you a tip,' and, resentful of being robbed of even a portion of his gesture, he had to agree. It was early September but there was a fire in the grate, more because mother, on no evidence, mistrusted the former tenants and wanted to 'air' the rooms, and we tossed the whole wad of notes on to the flames. It was impossible not to be thrilled. ...

At dinner, mother didn't even allude to money in connection with James's visit. He told her what he chose, shooting glances at me for guidance. He selected what I myself would have: Lady Vallant's photographs, her dress, Hutchins's messages, and the hymns. It was passing off very successfully, I was thinking, until I happened to look at mother when James had got to the hymn book. She took a sip or two of water and the glass was shaking in her hand. It was too late even to kick James's shin under the table; and then I saw he hadn't noticed. He sat eating his roast mutton and elaborating the awfulness of our grandmother's verse.

III

Lalage and I went to a small private school on Campden Hill. We were happy there and never overworked, and my memory of it will always be bound up with lilac, may trees, laburnum, syringa and the plays of Euripides in an eternal warmth and impossible summer. The headmistress, a gentle, uncertificated woman with a flexible nose and a bun, had a passion for school plays, and selected the Greek drama as being the most respectable, whereby we spent a large portion of nearly every term declaiming about curious and bloody vengeances, morbid elopements with a wordy fellow called Death, and singularly uncivil passages between sons and aged fathers.

We inevitably made a lot of friends in Kensington, discovered that Church Passage had a real village shop which sold masks, peg-tops and net bags of beads, together with sugarsticks and newspapers, and at night, by hanging out of our little bedroom windows, we could carry on conversations over the network of

back-garden walls, continue arguments, or complete plans and
quarrels begun that morning in the cloakroom with two or three
of our school friends. When the picture postcard craze came on,
the night rang with declarations.

'Well, *I* love Lewis Waller.' Or (more often)

'Are you over Martin Harvey?'

'I *hate* his wife, don't you?' (This, from a nightgowned woman
of fourteen).

'Is Hayden Coffin married?'

I only wish I could have a tourist's view of that dump reserved
for wasted emotion. It must go twice round the earth! And not
one parent in a hundred realizes the premature pangs endured
by thirteen, fourteen and fifteen. It gets called Outgrowing Their
Strength and anaemia and The Awkward Age, but is usually an
actor or a schoolmistress, and the fact that these untested devo-
tions are laughable and essentially insatiable doesn't detract from
their pathos, or from the tolls they take.

To-day, girls mob but do not hero-worship; they will wait
for hours to see the hat of Douglas Fairbanks emerging from the
boat train, but they neither dream of nor idealize him. Mass production breeds its mass-emotions that one film failure will stam-
pede, and there is no faith in them, and more's the pity. I wouldn't
give a toot for any daughter of mine who couldn't make a love-
fool of herself as an adolescent.

Having no garden to speak of – the Campden Hill house
possessed a greasy square of meaningless ground bordered with
catty laurels – we made do with Kensington Gardens, and the
keepers little know that once we planted, hurriedly and crooked-
ly, a patch of mustard-and-cress in the Flower Walk. We disputed
as to the design, and decided that as it was Royal earth it would
be polite to compliment the princess Louise, so we sowed an L
and what we hoped would be recognizable as a crown. (The L,
for some reason, never came up at all, and only half the crown.)
But it was enough. We had our stake in the Gardens!

But if our garden didn't please us, it seemed to satisfy Penny,
and he would sit for half-hours at a time chittering at the pigeons
and scintillating his whiskers when the birds alderman'd about
the garden and gobbled crumbs. And he married a lot. Mother
said, with reference to Penny's latest spouse, a ginger who lived

three gardens away, 'These everlasting receptions are a great strain. Shall Searcey do the ices?' And when we complained of the pigeons' greed and of the fact that they scared away the thrushes and blackbirds she said that they were very like humans, that their interests were so few that crumbgrabbing was their substitute for shady company-promoting.

The garden was not the only thing which restricted us. We were very badly off, and for the first time in our lives had to struggle with hooks and buttons, hair-doing and even darning. Mother's Liberty gowns were cut down for us, as she saw that the artistic racket was not only fashionable but effective as well for those who could carry it off. It was hit or miss, and it succeeded. Our birthday, Christmas and Easter presents, in those years, were new dresses, and she sold many a piece of silver and jewellery to the little antique shops in Notting Hill Gate that our frocks might be the prettiest at the party. She was insistent on this point, overriding our assurances that 'the old green' or 'our oyster-whites' would do; gently obstinate, curiously, secretly determined, she bought the new material.

She once said, 'It's agony to wear ugly clothes …' and stopped, very suddenly, and changed the subject.

CHAPTER VII

I

IT TOOK US a long time to 'get the relations sorted'. Most of our cousins were older than ourselves and were headed by 'the Seagrave kids', who, in point of fact, were, at the time of our move, four endlessly lanky young women of up to nineteen years old, with the face that goes with brogue shoes and tweed hats, and about as much bosom as imported rabbits. Our family ran to girls.

Of our Aunt Sophia Seagrave the most one can say is that she would be the last woman in London to abandon an At Home day and silver photograph frames on the grand piano.

Many years ago, apparently, Aunt Sophia had decided in what lights to present her daughters to the world.

Helen was 'just like a boy' and was made to have riding lessons in the Row, in a voluminous habit and a truncated top-hat, accompanied by a housemaid whose implicit task it was to scotch any flirtation between Helen and the riding master, for which Aunt Sophia was perpetually prepared.

Beryl was 'our outdoor one', and was frequently sent packing into the home counties with the sewing-maid and a tin box of sandwiches.

Flora was 'Oh, she's never in the house! We hardly *see* her, my dear! Country house visits ...', the planning and dovetailing of which, according to the Verdunes, gave Aunt Sophia a lot of thought and penmanship, as she sat at her creaking and inconvenient (but period) escritoire in the immense drawing-room in Emperor's Gate.

Theodora, the eldest, she had selected as family beauty who was immensely admired by men. 'Always a new face in the drawing-room,' Aunt Sophia would proclaim in a loud drone, and the phrase became a catchword between James and mother for years. And when Seagrave invention flagged, they gave book teas to which you came with a gardenia in your furs as *La Dame Aux Camellias*, or holding a tattered sock cobbled with red cotton for *As A Man Sows*, while the butler handed tepid China tea and looked horrified, and Uncle Maxwell hid in the morning-room (he was 'Always a nose in the papers').

I asked mother what she thought our Seagrave label might be, and she smiled, derisive and a little bitterly, and said, '*We* are "Poor little Anne". We don't entertain and our turning doesn't reassure coachmen.'

Which was true, for there was a distinct tendency on the part of the aunts with daughters of their own to exclude us from their parties lest our dresses would not pass muster, and an even more distinct one when they gradually found out that our garments were the most original in the room.

Of the other relations we preferred 'Aunt Emmeline's lot'; the Verdunes were more of an age with ourselves and had the Vallant looks – aquiline and rather saturnine – and the Vallant tongue. Also, their minds and bodies were not so violently protected from life as were the Seagraves', although they, too, were well off. One felt that it would be possible to go to the devil with the Verdunes, which in those days meant sallying out alone to Earl's Court Exhibition.

We liked their schoolroom, with its Hassall poster of *The Only Way*, and making caramels on the landing was possible, with Aunt Emmeline entrenched two or three flights below. It was with 'the Palace Greeners', as we called the Verdunes, naming them after their address, that we were able to swop Seagrave stories, and from Barbara that we learned their own Seagrave labels.

'I'm "That Naughty Puss",' Barbara explained, her elbows on the schoolroom table, 'and Evelyn is "going to be good-looking but such a stoop, mah—ee dear", and Dolly is "it's such a pity that Emmeline doesn't take a firmer hand".'

Dolly grinned, and roasted chestnuts. 'That's because I was seen kissing a Sandhurst cadet behind one of Sophia's hired palms,' she said. 'You see, she wanted him for Theodora, and he wasn't having any … well, I mean … who would?', and she screwed her eyes and laughed, open-mouthed.

'But I will say that Aunt S. does one well at dances … a jolly sight better than mamma.' To this, Lalage and I had nothing to say. It jarred us; but we were there to learn. We raised politely questioning eyebrows. It was enough. The Verdunes meant to go on, in any case.

'Mother's very Vallantish in some ways. She freezes our men, so we have to make our own arrangements … but I prefer it to Sophia's method, in the long run.'

'But … she was a Vallant, too,' fumbled Lalage.

'Yes, curious, isn't it? So's your mother, if it comes to that, and she simply isn't like the same family. I should think Aunt Anne is rather a dear, isn't she?'

Evelyn interrupted (we were grateful), 'If it comes to that … we're all Vallants,' and didn't seem to like the realization.

So it came about that, of all the related possibles, it was with the children of mother's eldest sister, Emmeline, that we were able to discuss the family. From them we even learnt of in-laws and cousins (all grown-up) who were destined to remain for ever little but names to us; of others which some exaggerated piece of schoolroomism later helped us to 'place'.

'There was great-uncle Ivor Stonor ... grannyma'sbrother. He lived in the country and had a *regiment* of daughters all called Hester and he dogwhipped their young men.'

'But ... did they go on having any?' Lalage, already pitiful, put in.

'No. They're *all* unmarried, except one that isn't alluded to, who popped off with a farmer. They've got faces like lavatory seats, oval and utterly blank.'

'Uncle Ivor got religion before he took to dogwhips.'

We sat there, learning and listening, a little shy before these glib London seniors, with their shining armour on imperviousness. And then Barbara, poking a nut off the brass bars, said, 'He's not grandmother's brother for nothing'.

II

So it was with the Verdunes that we were able to speak of Lady Vallant.

We learnt that, to the Seagraves, she was just a grandmother, impersonal, and neither to be feared nor sought. Placidity and sanity reigned here, it seemed.

To the Verdune girls, she was a joke, pure and simple; here was criticism, spirited, slapdash and thick-skinned, a rowdy, reassuring attitude that had never so much as occurred to us.

'I loathe grannyma's lunches. One never gets enough to eat. It's all huge silver dish covers and underneath four pennies on four sticks of firewood that she calls cutlets. But we stoke up beforehand, at home. It makes mother furious, but I'm not going to stand any of Vallybags nonsense.'

'Of course the poor old brute's rather pathetic. It must be pretty beastly to know that nobody likes you.'

'And the way she hangs on to her youth. Mother say she never throws away any dress she was admired in. She's got cupboards bung-full. Palmer hates it because she never gets any perks. Trust Susan for that.'

Palmer sounded like a maid. I was determined at any rate, to keep *this* conversation alive. 'She was a beauty,' I remarked, half in question, half in assertion.

'Oh lor yes, I believe so. "Always a new face in the draw-ing-room, mah–ee dear." Mother's often said so.'

'All *I* can say is, there must have been more men in those days, or they were easier to please.'

'Wonder how grandpa liked it?'

'Oh, she ran him entirely, I gather.'

'*I* only wonder she was willing to have all those children.'

'They did, in those days.'

'But – seven, Dolly!'

I started because I couldn't help it, glanced at Lalage and knew this was going to be left for me to cope with. I managed to say 'Seven?' and sound passably facetious. Dolly was ticking off on her fingers.

'There were mother and Sophia and your mother' (to me) 'and Uncle Stuart, Uncle Julian, Uncle James (he was killed in the Boer War) and Myra.'

My hands had begun to tremble and I had to put them under the red serge table-cloth. I ran my eyes along the mantelpiece to steady my mind, noting the procession of glass pigs, the invitation cards, the little trumpery silver clock pointing to five minutes past six, and the vases which supported glossy postcards of Martin Harvey, N. de Silva, Evelyn Millard, Edmund Payne in a Gaiety theatre group and Cosmo Furnival in some costume play. Then I heard myself saying 'Let me see ... Myra ... it's so difficult to get them all sorted.'

Barbara said, 'She died. Uncle Julian and Uncle Stuart live in the country, at Vallant, most of the year. You wouldn't know them, they're very shy birds. ...'

'... and Uncle Julian's nearly blind. ...'

'Is he so old?' Lalage asked that.

'No. I gather it was a piece of Vallantism. Susan's doing. She wouldn't consult an occulist when he was at school and jeered at him for being a milksop when his eyes hurt him and he cried.'

'Oh *no*!' – it was Lalage again, her eyes nearly black in a white face. The Verdunes nodded. 'Mother let that out only a year or two ago. Quite casually. Imagine it!'

I hadn't time for that, though the pang would hit me later. To fifteen, poker-faces do not come easily, and I hoped mine was being adequate as I said, 'But Aunt Myra' (somehow, I was very careful about the prefix) 'what did she die of? I've forgotten.'

'Oh, I think there was something the matter with her spine, or she went into one of those declines people did ...'

Evelyn said, 'Aunt Anne would tell you. Wasn't she your mother's favourite sister?'

I answered, 'Yes,' and nudged Lalage (after all, she is the elder), and she capped me nobly with an off-hand 'Of course'.

That night, I wrote off to James:

'There *was* a seventh. Her name was Myra, and she died. She was mother's favourite sister ... the Verdunes say so. Why do they know? Can one ask mother? Write the Myra part on a separate sheet so that I can show your usual letter to her.'

I dodged out into Campden Grove to post the letter at the corner grocer's. At breakfast, a day later, a letter from James was on my plate:

'Is anything the matter? Last night, at prep, I suddenly came over all rum ... it felt like pins and needles in one's head, and being afraid of everything. Can't describe it. The chap next me hacked me on the calf because old Brewster was on duty, and I pretended I wanted to know the time, and Ash said, "Five past six," and got fifty lines.'

The letter was dated; it was the night we had had tea in Palace Green.

Part of his answer said:

'Funny our letters crossed. About M. Can't think how the Verdunes come to know anything we don't. I suppose mother doesn't want it talked of, or she would have. But why has Aunt Emmeline told them? They aren't on terms with her, are they? I mean, not as we are. One's a right to know, but I shouldn't care to take on the job myself, with mother. It's like her age; she must *be* one, but one doesn't ask. And after all, as the V.s say, people did go off in declines. Dickens and Thackeray say so, and the Egerton Castles are full of "vapours". ....'

In short, James, like myself, didn't believe for an instant in the plausibility of the Verdune story; he was trying to bolster me up generally.

III

In what seemed to be an incredibly short time, James was a St. Paul's boy, almost as tall, as tall, and taller than, mother. (I wonder why it is that it always seems an impertinence when children overtop parents?) He was horribly embarrassed when his voice broke and refused, like an expectant mother, to go to any parties, and in the year it happened, he and I seem to have lived in a perpetual state of dodging out of the drawing-room because visitors were there or imminent, and prowling the streets, or sitting in each other's bedrooms.

'It's such a stinking advertisement of sex,' James would hoarsely hoot.

'It's beastly,' I agreed, 'but now we *are* on the subject pretty foul things happen to us too, Jamesey.'

He nodded. 'Yes, I know about that.'

'Then I hope you know it right. I couldn't stand it if *you* had got hold of the wrong end of the stick about us females, or if you'd only got hold of bits of the stick from some sickening boy. So if there's anything you want to know – ever – always ask me.'

There was, and he did, and I told him and I'm glad. After all, aren't sisters the best training for their mistresses and wives, just as brothers are, or might be, for our lover and husbands?

Incidentally, I swept away, with a little embarrassment and incoherence and plenty of slang, some fairly grotesque and messy misconceptions under which he'd been labouring, and he suddenly looked less harassed. 'And, drink fair, Betsy,' I ended, 'I may want to know no end of oddments from you.'

'Come on.'

'Not now. But don't grow up and be a Young Man and forget, or welch on me.'

'No. Promise.'

CHAPTER VIII

I

JAMES WAS WHAT, in a girl, would have been known as 'an immediate success' with the relations. Mother, viewing the cards which suddenly became embedded in the scrollwork of the mantelpiece, looked at this tall thing that was hers, and said, her hands on his shoulders:

'Men are always in demand, my dear; there are so dashed few of 'em! Go and have the best time you can, but don't forget that it's partly the state of the market.'

It was a risk, and she took it. Possibly she had memories of the fatuous stage in her brothers, and of the ultimate crashes that awaited masculine youth which had mistaken its comparative rarity for its own fascinations. Or it may have been that she guessed James to be an idealist, easily shattered. What she didn't dare allow for was the fact that James and I, in the last resort, made our own discoveries, and always would.

We soon found that the London ballroom wasn't the same thing as our parties where every face was familiar, and dances had been, or could be, fixed days ahead, during the morning walks. We came to the business from what would pass as the country, and young at that, so I suppose our impressions were sharp.

We made what I must grandiloquently describe as our London debut at the coming out dance of Beryl, the third Seagrave cousin. It was a betwixt and between affair owing to our conflicting ages, and even Uncle Maxwell was forced out into the open, and leant against the outside of doorways, and even took three alarmed steps on to the parquet floor until the music, striking up a waltz ('Gold and Silver') caused him to remember the occasion, and retreat.

The Seagrave girls received under the eye of Aunt Sophia. They wore pale, bright satin and gold tissue roses in the corsage, and Beryl had an unexpected wreath the size of a crumpet pinned above her frizzed fringe, and their matching satin shoes were very long and pointed and later in the evening turned up and grey, and when a new name was announced, they shouldered forward giving an unsupported impression of struggling through a hedgerow, and shook hands grippingly and with hoots of laughter. And there was a tray of programmes from which pink and blue pencils dangled, clashing, and the inevitable moment when they became hopelessly snarled and had to be rent asunder by the butler. And halfway through the evening the leads wore down to stubs and all future assignations were totally unreadable, which led to a great deal of disappointment, and occasionally to sighs of deliverance.

And then the Verdunes arrived and stood there surveying a, to them, familiar scene with sardonic grins before beginning to set about the organization of their evening, which they did with efficiency and humour and entire lack of scruple. There was no absence of finish about the Verdunes; they could 'put on their clothes', which had what the French describe as *chien* without laying themselves open to the tuttings of chaperons, and it is an undoubted fact that some people have what call 'smart faces'. The Seagraves never succeeded in suggesting other than over-grown schoolgirls, and were Barbara said, guaranteed to make a four-guinea hat look like twelve-and-eleven.

11

We stood together, James and Lalage and I, and took it all in. James was in his first dinner jacket; I was in mauve chiffon, Greekishly cut, with golden sandals (from Burnett's, in Chandos Street – our one extravagance), and Lalage in sheer white silk embroidered with silver leaves to her silver feet. Because we were, as usual, in no fashion at all, I suppose it succeeded. Also, we were a novelty to that room. Certainly I, personally, had a good time that night which was not, I found, to be counted upon at future family balls. James as an attractive young male of course made his way, and Lalage gravely didn't care. Whether dancing or listening she contrived, I thought, to look like a soul in a roomful of bodies. ...

Aunt Emmeline appeared and James said, 'Who's the De-stroyer?' and had to be reminded, and indeed she suggested one; handsome, business-like, in iron grey with graceful lines, and po-tentially lethal. She took, I saw, not the faintest notice of her daughters: she was just there. And then it occurred to me that mother was not; struck me, in spite of the fact that for days I had known she had not meant to come ... we accepted it, as usual, took it on its face value as being yet another of her quiet inten-tions towards our independence and social sturdiness. Maids and chaperonage were financially ruled out, for us. So be it. It must be right or she couldn't have acquiesced ... we were poor relations.

There could be, I suddenly realized, no 'coming out' or 'season' for Lalage and me. If we should achieve a coming out or coming of age ball it would be because the dates dovetailed with a Seagrave or Verdune début. I didn't mind for myself, but for Lalage, who apparently didn't care at all.

Luckily one can get through a lot of thinking in a very few seconds, for the habit of unsuitable reflection is, in me, ineradicable. I have never been able to lose myself entirely in the purely social scene, and am, moreover, liable to sudden desires to leave it if only for ten minutes. At that point I was, for some reason, mentally reviewing the Verdune's schoolroom, and wondering if they had sat there discussing the dance that afternoon, and whether their shoes fitted, and if – a favourite speculation that has unaccountably pursued me through life – the fact of eating the same food at supper, at the identical minute, with complete strangers, created any bond, physical, psychic or psychologic – even chemical! – between them, and if so, whether, quite unaware, they took on ever so faintly any of each other's characteristics? The thought of being united, mystically or materially to, say, Sir Henry Irving through a caviare sandwich or a cup of artichoke soup is not without its points!

And at this stage in my musings, Aunt Sophia swept by and droned, 'Oh, you picturesque mite! Quite a Constable.' She probably meant Reynolds or Greuze, but all Old Masters were the same Old Master to her; she had a knack of getting the shape of compliments, combined with complete inaccuracy of detail.

'She means you look like three poplars and a puddle,' hissed James, suffocating with laughter.

One thing at least I learnt at the dance, and it was that in any ballroom, the alliances of the schoolroom are blown into air, and even friendship between girls is in abeyance. It was not even smiled upon to talk to them about immediate topics, and as for resuming any interesting discussion …! The discovery daunted and depressed me it was, I knew, a social attitude that neither James, Lalage nor I was built for. We were eternally interested in people irrespective of social considerations or personal advantages. A fatal characteristic, it appeared. Later, we learnt to recognize, accept, and slough it.

I remember that at some dance where James early discovered ennui, he rambled down to the kitchen and helped the maids wipe glasses for half an hour, and talked, wrapt, with the cook about a play they had both admired, while many a time have Lalage and I sneaked upstairs to gossip with any old nurse the family retained. And it wasn't empty programmes, either. The old women soothed us, and the reality of their overcrowded bed-sitting rooms was a very tangible thing. And we sat, huddled in our satins and silks, and had long, comfortable snobbish talks about the Royal family (and were pulled up uncommonly short if we made slips and muddled Tecks and Fifes, or confused, say, Chatsworth with Haddon Hall). And a brew of tea or cocoa followed, with toddlings to the cupboard and a setting out of a bright canister. Any fool can offer you champagne. But if you can win a lonely, diffident old woman, living in her memories, to give you of her tea, then and not till then have you triumphed.

Or James and I would edge away and get in a few turns at a music-hall and then return to the ballroom forty-five minutes later, humming 'Wot cheer me ole brown son, 'OW ARE YER?' and lose it in 'The Passing of Salome', and find the dance still wonderfully 'as before' and nobody one penny the wiser. Sometimes we would even mark off spaces in our programmes to remind each other of the time.

I still have a ball card inscribed:

    10 Harry Champion

    11 Marie Lloyd

    12 Cinquevalli

But wonderfully soon Lalage and I ceased to be novelties to dance hostesses, and even James couldn't always help us out.

The shynesses of the later teens are forgotten by most women and Lalage's agony of embarrassment on being asked which dance she could spare and finding herself saying 'Let's have "A Hundred Thousand Kisses",' would now be merely comic. My shyness at first took the form of positive aphasia at the subjects men expected one to talk about. In those days it was draughts, the heat, the band and the dances of other hostesses. In these days it is perversion, cocktails, negro actors and adultery, and I'm open to conviction as to the relative monotony of either. But at least, to-day, if men and women go to dances, they go to dance and not to get themselves married.

Sometimes one got kissed behind screens or under palms. This usually meant that the fiery lover had temporarily exhausted the floor, the heat and the Eton and Harrow, and was obeying nature in her curious 'abhorrence' of a vacuum. When this happened, one of three courses was open to you. You either moved off, conscientiously wiping the kiss off your cheek (the Edwardian usually aimed badly) with your kid glove and wondering if you were a fallen woman who might be described as 'who did'; or you were quite preposterously thrilled, and lived over the episode all night, until the morning revealed the fact that you not only did not remember the young man's name but had never caught it at all; or you said 'Shall we tell The Parents to-night?' which was, according to the Verdunes, how the second Seagrave girl secured her husband. Good manners were his downfall. Polite to the last, he stood at the altar, unfailingly courteous he accompanied her for a month to Switzerland, chivalrous to the end became the father of three daughters.

I wonder how many dead melodies drift round those dusty chandeliers, setting them remotely tinkling in a thousand dismantled homes from which the daughters are married and gone, the last guest sped, and a To Let board lashed to the balcony ... they have served their turn, and our gratitude cuts them up into ungainly maisonettes, by which, haply, a civil servant falls heir to the sewing-maid's room and a resting actress sprawls and smokes in the sacrosanct study of one's very uncle. And what the house must suffer one doesn't like to think.

III

It was mother and James who were indignant when invitations to Lalage and myself began to taper off. For ourselves we didn't care; I because I early saw the business for what it was, and was (and still am) liable to be overcome with laughter at that exact moment in sentiment, pseudo or actual, when the only permitted expression is seriousness, and Lalage because over-many outside contacts confused and distressed her. The triviality of social exchanges would never be of the stuff of life to her. It was said by exasperated matrons, in implied relation to the bouncing, vigorous but unmarried charms of their own daughters, that she lacked something, 'I don't know what'.

I did. It was not that Lalage lacked, but that she possessed some quality of the spirit which the thunder of dance bands drives out of the room. A Verdune dared to say to me, with the freemasonry of age, sex and what she took for granted to be a common aim, 'Looking like a very beautiful lost soul at dances doesn't go *down* very well, does it?'

Some man a little more perceptive, said to James, 'Your elder sister is very difficult to stop looking at'.

James was interested and saw to it that the theme was elaborated. His friend added, 'There's something about her eyes. It's as though she were remembering an injustice.' And that man became my brother-in-law. And I can think of no one to whom I could more easily have entrusted Lalage. I started with a predisposition to liking ever since their conversation about her as reported by James; and Hugh had the sense to bide his time, to make no claims, and the courage to risk losing her altogether by self-doubt and dispassionate reviews as to his ability to make and keep her happy. I can even picture him doing it, long sensitive hands clasped, eyes which missed nothing, weighing a future with all the painstaking thoroughness with which he pleaded in Court, and face which would remain impassive to the world if the case of Hugh *v.* Lalage went against him.

We had met Hugh Lyne at the Verdunes. I happen, capriciously, to remember the very words that were used although my own perception was asleep, letting the social side have its turn. So many of the best things in life ultimately come to one through preliminaries utterly insignificant. The rule of the game seems to be that you must be unaware. If you enter it in a state of expectancy, with hope or dream or plan, it will not come to pass. What happiness if it were otherwise! Carroll knew, when he sent forth Alice to the rose-garden.

Dolly Verdune was being lively and daring with Hugh, which is to say that she lit a cigarette at him and said damn. I always dislike watching anybody bungling his work. Dolly's dash and looks were authentic and appreciated by me to the full, we all make fools of ourselves at some time or another; but our foolishness should be original, and not fake. She was challenging him to invite her to the Law Courts and he consented – how refuse? – with the rider, 'But of course, Dolly, it means no smoking, no talking, above all no snapshots, and don't forget to rise when the judge enters', and he turned and saw Lalage standing there. I think he imagined her to be a great deal younger than she was; also, she had an unfashionable way of listening, wrapt, like a child, for he smiled at her and she said, 'Please, I've always wondered, but whose business is it to collect the farthings for damages, and where are they kept?'

He savoured the question, and suddenly laughed, and said he hadn't the faintest idea, now she mentioned it. Years afterwards, he told me that it was probably the farthings that had made him really see her. 'It was', he said with a faint grin, 'such a fairy-tale question.'

But Hugh had come too early. Life is ungenerous about dates, environments and circumstances; there is too often the loose screw somewhere in the machinery which keeps matters at a standstill, and as far as Lalage was concerned we all were to have some bad moments.

The mothers of beauty bear a double burden: that of impending and almost inevitable loss plus the knowledge that the enemy may appear from any and every quarter. One man kept right off drink for six weeks while he believed he had a chance with Lalage, and when amazedly, pitifully refused, naively drew her attention to the fact. He has made good that six weeks, since …

There were the men who coaxed interminably and pled; the men who tried to rush her against her better – or indeed any – judgment, into consent, and there were the men who threatened.

It taught me a lot. It demonstrated to me that at a pinch even the best of men when in love scrap as a matter of course that code of honour which they observe in business office or at the card table and to each other, and about which they are so entertainingly strong and silent, but that where women are concerned they are capable of conduct, cowardices and dishonesties that would get them kicked out of any decent club or service.

James and I must have been a great trial to them. I was suave and, cued by James, galled their kibes in a hundred ways, and sometimes got kissed myself, as the third party intervening in a dog fight is kicked by the owners by accident. James, as a man, had a freer hand, and saw a side of the game denied to me. When any of Lalage's admirers seemed about to become serious, James would take them out to dinner. The minor resultant casualties were an undergraduate who, warmed by some bad claret, began to boast of barmaids; another, a man of thirty, took in James on most counts until he suddenly began to talk about being a gentleman. Major eliminations included a man whose collection of dirty stories turned out to be typical of his attitude to matrimony, and another who was up to the ears in debt and preened himself *à la* Rawdon Crawley on his agility with small tradesmen's bills.

And the thought of Lalage as the official property of any of these men nearly made me ill.

I V

The strain on James was infinitely greater. He was only nineteen when all this began and the irony of it was that his guest-detrimentals thought they were showing him what that type calls Life.

James and the man of the moment would sit together at club and restaurant tables, looking like nephew and uncle and do his conscientious best by the boy, while James listened and egged him on and suppressed revulsions and rages and sometimes nauseas as well. James was so bent on missing nothing that might tell against the other and confirm home-made suspicions that his concentrated avidity passed for normal adolescence as understood by his companion of the evening, and James got all he bargained for and a bit over, I gather. He would come home drained, would dash his hat down upon the hall settle and creep up to me to avoid being heard by mother or Lalage. I would listen in bed as he slumped in my creaking little armchair by the gas fire I had lit.

'*He's* no go. Bullies waiters to show off. Oh lor, I've eaten so much too much!'

He looked worried. 'Any girl may marry one of that kind without knowing. Some of these chaps are obvious, of course, but I've found out much more by accident. It can't be much fun to be a woman.'

Or there was the night he came home, defeated.

The man was undesirable for Lalage in some way I have forgotten, but – he'd seen through James. It was forty against nineteen, and experience won. He chaffed James, and cleverly, and James could only follow suit to the extent of seeing himself caught out. The man sheered off Lalage, I'll say that for him, but it shook James's nerve. The climax had somehow been reached when the man paid for the dinner, tipped, and fairly took charge. The bill, it seemed, hadn't even been proffered to James. And the wine list. 'We must have a bottle of something light for you, young man.'

The perfect, apparent, uncle – except about the eyes. And at that time one couldn't even take refuge in the thought 'there are men like Hugh'. He was still 'a man one met at the Palace Greeners'.

'… and the deuce of it is that I'm always liable to be sent right out of London for the firm.'

'I shall be here, Jamesey.'

'But,' he looked at me, dazed with fatigue. I guessed what he was going to say, knew I was right when he tailed off into, 'It isn't the same, with you'.

It wasn't. I suspected that my own effect upon men, while attracting situations more immediately difficult to cope with, was of a safer type, while the aloofness and rather dreamlike quality of Lalage involuntarily challenged the worst specimens, those who could never rest until all reserves and secrets were torn out, and because her very existence was a taunt and a reproach; so that their resentful puzzled gropings towards any unity with her inevitably took the form of an attempt to drag her down to their level. It is not unpathetic. If she ever loved, she would probably be a one-man woman to the end, or be smashed and wasted. That was her danger, and that our job of work.

But James had too much on his mind with office routine and Lalage's affairs to be burdened with my own. I hadn't pictured matters as working out quite that way but if it had to be, well, so be it. I could look after myself had had to on many an occasion which I kept to myself. Laughter could cut both ways, and I was no woodland nymph with blue-black hair. I doubt if James even thought of me as female at all. We were James and Vere, so much the same person that I sometimes chaffed him while he was struggling with his evening shirt, and would say, 'Don't make me drink too much at dinner, Jamesey' or, if I was off to a theatre with some man friend James would hold up a monitory finger and caution, 'Remember woman, I will not kiss that fellow in the taxi!'

I am fairly sure that neither of us believed in the possibility of ultimate separation. We just made Roman holiday together about life and people.

CHAPTER IX

I

AND BECAUSE we were to each other as we were, and it was evidently a part of living and being an adult person, I was not too badly shaken on the night that James parted with what is inaccurately called innocence and came home drunk into the bargain.

I had gone to bed early, mother and Lalage earlier still, for I often stayed up or kept awake to talk with him and pull the evening to pieces, generally speaking. That night I had fallen asleep over *Dodo*, my last waking thought concerned with pessimistic speculation as to whether there existed such universal providers of feminine charm, and I woke very suddenly.

It was nearly three o'clock and there was something wrong – with *me*. It was frightening because not definitely physical. I don't know if a vague recital of symptoms will be particularly helpful, especially if I say that the leading one was a sensation that part of my own personality was dimmed while my actual body remained normal. I felt that were any decision called for, that part of me which made it would fail me. There was a feeling of what can best be described as a suspension of character – I ceased to be able to count on myself and became merely potential. A development, an eccentric sideline, of this I inadvertently tested when trying to throw off whatever had come upon me.

I began to force myself to think of books, and my mind could fasten upon nothing but two greasy novelettes I had once incredulously dipped into when the servants had gone to bed. Here, I found complete failure to recapture contempt. When I belaboured my brain to Dickens and Thackeray, there was a blank wall. I couldn't even recall the titles, let alone places and people, or any admiration, love or kinship – I had to *remember* that Dickens was my oldest love. And there followed a brainfag and a despair that almost drove me to mother's room. I fought that down with what was left of me, and some time later James came in, and I missed the rhythm of his routine movements and dragged myself out of bed and down to the hall.

He was trying to make the stairs, handing himself about as a parrot does in its cage.

For all one's clever reading and glib printed fact, one isn't very adroit, at nineteen.

I got him up to my room and I was shaking with fright. I made no attempt to undress him, because those slick disrobements are, I discovered, easier described in books than accomplished single-handed in real life by the inexperienced and distraught; but I got his shoes off and his socks and managed to rid him of overcoat and scarf, and by giving him an open-hander with my fist, get half his body on to the bed, and the rest of him by lifting his feet. I re-lit the fire and sat by him, and presently – books aren't always wrong and I'd used my eyes in the side streets on Saturday nights – the expected occurred and he was sick. Later, he opened his eyes while I clutched his poor little basin, and saw me, and I suddenly remembered the Dickens titles and love – and even Miss Pinkerton's Select Academy, The Mall, Chiswick; remembered with joyful loathing cook's novelette, and almost giggled at one sentence which ran, 'She gurgled with happy laughter and melted into those strong arms'.

I said, 'Glad to see you, Jamesey. Been on the tiles?'

'Tiles …' he lay back very white and chilly, considering this. 'I've been … everywhere.'

I made myself let it go at that; James shouldn't tell me anything through a mere inability to stop talking. I wasn't out for confidences that would be regretted later, and prepared myself to lose those hours in his life for ever.

But by ten-thirty next night he was in my armchair, in that mood in which all three of us had hurried to our mother, as children. To us, admission was synonymous with an absolution it would never have occurred to us to look for in the church, or, having received, would have so entirely believed.

I said the first part of it for him, sitting propped against his knees on the rug.

'Well, that needn't be done again, Jamesey, unless, of course, you feel any hankerings that way.'

'It was that chap who wouldn't let me pay the bill.'

'Oh. Ah … I thought perhaps it might be.'

'I meant to meet him on his own ground … and after all, I *am* nearly twenty.'

'So am I, Jamesey!'

His hand tightened on my shoulder. 'You mean, you're just sick with me?'

'Fool! My dear, the only thing that keeps most of us from it is the fear of consequences. It gets called chastity.'

He stirred. 'But … we *are* different. Mrs. Gummidge, y'know, feeling it most.'

'How d'you know? How can men be honestly sure what we feel? D'you know what a girl told me once?'

'What?'

'It was, of all places, at that New Year party at the Palace Greeners. This girl … can't remember her name, but I'll call her Harriett because she was so senselessly plain, not ugly, which is always a chance, and exciting, but plain. When I saw her sitting there and trying to look happy while the Verdunes sported all round her among the men, it struck me for the first time in my life that we should never know what plain people suffered. It must be like going about without a sense … like being born blind or deaf. To go to parties knowing that a man's eyes will never look at you for one instant … it's unimaginable. …

'These girls don't commit suicide; they go to parties. The pluck of it! Hundreds and thousands of 'em all over. England all taking it for granted … and don't talk to *me* about "inner beauty" or "the soul shining through the eyes". To begin with, it doesn't most of the time, and in the second place there's only about one man in a hundred who's up to that, if it did. And he won't be at the party. …

'This Harriett I noticed at once, and I went and cultivated her … which, incidentally, damned most of *my* chances that evening. And ... well, I imagine she unloaded something on me that would have made Aunt Emmeline cut her off her list. She said, "Every time I read in the papers of some servant girl who has had a baby through being assaulted, I am consumed with envy".'

'My good Lord!'

'Mine, too. And that's a woman who's never been even offered any temptations, Jamesey.'

'I see where you're heading.'

'The fact is, we shall never get straight on this sex business, Jamesey, because you men are brought up to acquire escapades as you do your first shave and dinner jacket; escapades become a test of virility instead of a natural impulse, so that I don't suppose even you know where your original fastidiousness ends and rockbottom desire begins. That's what I resent.'

'Well ... I've found out where fastidiousness begins, all right.'

'Do I hear?'

He stirred in the creaking chair and took his hands from my shoulders. None of us three seems able to endure small personal contacts when anything of importance has to be said or done. I'd noticed it so often in myself, from the days when as a tearful penitent I'd evaded laps until the business was cleared up.

'What put me off was that she expected me to kiss her.'

I sprang to that. Sisters must snatch understanding where they can, and this was a thing which instantly jarred me too, on principle. I said, 'I suppose the idea is that you aren't getting your money's worth without'.

'I couldn't kiss her, and didn't. And she was offended.'

'Well ... yes, I can just grasp that. I suppose when all's said a woman never quite loses her idea of charming, you know. If you do her out of that, you're showing her up for the only thing she stands for. Most people need some sort of illusion to help 'em along ... but that knocks one pretty hard, doesn't it?' I settled again and put my arm on his knees. 'You were a trump not to, Jamesey.'

'And ... the rest of it?'

'Oh, that! Blow that!' I faced him. 'You know, I'm not sorry it's happened at last. If it's the correct thing to do' – here we laughed together – 'far be it from me to prevent you from joining the procession. I should writhe if I saw you turning into a pale young curate because of me, or Lalage or mother'.

He had a handful of my long plait in his hands, and his face was at peace, and because the thought of sentiment would have flayed us both, I Roman-holiday'd with that useful, dreadful facility of mine which, all my life, has prompted me for better for worse, to concealment.

'What would Aunt Sophia say! "Oh-h, you promiscuous puss!"'

And we were ourselves again, ready to toothcomb the universe.

I I

Sometimes I was able to be of use to him. Any good looking man who is unattached, attractive and a dancer becomes a target, where to be unattached was enough heaven knows, without those makeweights nature had thrown in for James.

Of course he lost his head occasionally, and, more often his judgment, and it was here that I intervened, sometimes as Judas to my sex, sometimes as Chiffinch to his Charles when the girl was vulnerable and unhappy. The difficulty was that his absence of personal vanity together with his one-time inability to understand the importance which most women attach to trifles was apt to let him in for situations that an older, more complacent hand could have foreseen and countered. Once or twice in those days he would come home entertainingly at a loss to know if he might be considered to be engaged or not. He'd certainly never proposed, and yet ...

'Wait for the breakfast post,' mother would say, kindly patting him on the head, 'perhaps that will throw some light.'

She chaffed him but she was anxious, more anxious still to give him his head. His affairs at least I could share with her, and she refused to take a hand. 'Mothers are only once removed from mothers-in-law in the scale of ridiculousness, darling.' But sisters are not commonly guarded against or allowed for, and, armed at times with some stray and infinitely illuminating hint from her, I took up my position. 'The chucker-out,' mother called me.

James's girls could be tiresome and sometimes very gadflies, but it was the older women who were the real menaces. They could be as unscrupulous, as unmaternal as men could be to me … The parental streak, grossly exaggerated as a desideratum for women, is somehow never expected of the male. Personally I wouldn't give a snap of the fingers for a man who was without it, for me, and the adorable quality of fatherliness I began to take for granted was a non-existent and impossible thing.

But James's older cliéntele – the Houris, as we called them – were minus the larger bowel of compassion, and the fact that James was too young to marry, too poor and didn't even want to, merely seemed to amuse them. Also, they were cads and obtuse in failing to recognize that his kindness and warm, basic sound-ness of heart and nature were to be respected. They merely trad-ed on it. Body-snatchers. If he had a mind they left it assumed, unvalued, unexplored, and they were clever in ways that I can never rise to. The man's woman who offers an effusive jawbone to women friends and keeps an eye swivelling round for attractive males commonly is. How many a time have I found myself willed out of the room by these harpies, there impotently to fume in speculative rage and confusion as to how it was done!

Some of them were worthless without being in any way pa-thetic. They had homes, looks, money and sometimes husbands as well. The prospect of James being kicked downstairs by their life partners was only flattering. It was these I cultivated, to these I was Judas. I would sit in their over-ornamented, under-venti-lated, evasively-lit bedrooms while they harried their maids, and followed every move of their toilette – that type, I discovered, has few reticences, and would lounge in a pair of silk stockings, feathered slippers and nothing else while she chatted to me, pa-tronized me, unloosed on me her affairs financial or amorous and asked amused and impertinent questions about my own.

I would deliberately accentuate young girlery whenever it could be safely assumed, would arrive with my hair in a plait and a large black bow; I would look shy and wide eyed and admiring as I sat there letting off lie after lie and hating her, I who like, admire and love my own sex. But some hates are blessed and cleanly things.

To some of them I said that James was secretly engaged and I once was reduced to throwing mother to the lion and hinting that if my brother ever married she should share his home. And, trailing wearily downstairs, I was sometimes waylaid myself by husbands, and – if I could lay tongue to a vulgarer word I would use it – spooned with and pawed on the landing.

'Has anyone ever told you you've got rather nice eyes?

'How do you do? Yes, plenty of people. Good-bye.'

And (*sotto voce* because of the maid), 'What a pity we can't see each other oftener.'

'Oh, I hardly think so (*forte*), good night.'

At home, I would throw the spoils to mother, keeping them from James against emergency.

Some of the women took presents from him; to that type he was a man, made to be mulcted, not a hard-up boy earning his keep. When it suited them they forgot the lovable youngness that had begun the whole business originally, and for the evening he was the eternal prosperous payee. It gave me a mistrust of the prerogatives of battening, wiles and coaxing that I was to find painfully hard to abandon, even temporarily, and even with the right man.

III

It gave me an understanding of young male things might have missed entirely, and because of James, I don't think they were ever the losers by knowing me. Like Scarpia, 'half Confessor and half devil', I listened to their addled views on life as seen from a window in Balliol; I let them sharpen their little claws on me and kept a lynx eye on their disbursements. Because I had met them chiefly through James, either from his office or club, they paraded before me their new-found code of ethics on the subject of the sacred immunity of 'the sister of My Friend'. It had its humorous side, and it broke down at least once.

The poor child, tipsy with freedom, his own profile, his quarterly allowance and a bottle of moulin a vent – all of which he was eager to mistake for me – had marshalled me upstairs and quaked at the waiter, who flourished napkin and wine-list, and finally left us. My host, folding his arms, said, with an equal mixture of tentativeness, defiance, apology, and pride:

'This is a private room.'

I looked round. The Italian restaurant with a French cook in a London street had staged the orgy with a bamboo chiffonier, a grocer's calendar, an oil painting of the kind that the Lupino family would not hesitate to dive through in a pantomime, and two vases filled with paper apple-blossom. I looked respectful. Inwardly I was doing worried mental arithmetic and wondering how much less time his money would last out, and if his family was finding it rather a struggle, and whether he'd told his mother where he was going, and if his father would be unintelligent and make him a scene, or whether he was of that infinitely more repellent and hopeless type, the Ha-ha-my-boy parent who can still enjoy a borrowed feed of wild oats, and says 'Cherchez La femme' in the accents of Dover-at-Calais.

To laugh at Peter would be brutality; to feign alarmed distress and so give him a run for his father's money was probably beyond my powers as an actress. I was pretty sure I was his first night on the tiles. It is not an unresponsible post if you choose to make it so. He was my age, which is to say ten years younger; he betrayed it; reviling the menu to me and hastily acquiescent to the waiter; plucking his tie askew until my hands itched to adjust it (how often I'd done it for James!), and knew I must keep them to myself because all the boy's social values were still topsy-turvy, while I offhandedly refused liqueurs because I was determined to send him home sober. And I wondered what sort of a man this was going to turn into, and who he'd marry, and why, and when and where, and drifted off into one of my speculations about the oddness of the fact that, somewhere in England, the church was waiting in which he would be married, and that somewhere in the country (or the Channel Islands or Holland) were growing the grandparents of those bulbs whose descendants would provide cut flowers for the ceremony. And suddenly I thought that somewhere in the world, possibly quite near me in London, the man that Lalage would marry must be inevitably having his dinner too (and hoped he was behaving himself!). And James ... his future wife might have been christened that morning, if he married late in life ... or sleeping off a birthday party in her little crib, her face flushed with recent excitement, tears and cake. ...

Through the mists, Peter's voice came back to me.

'You do look stunning this evening.'

Goodness only knew what had gone before, but I was glad he was pleased with me; my small black velvet hat I had made myself and adapted from that worn by one of the Houris. They have their uses. Her hat had probably cost twelve and a half guineas, my own cost as many shillings and made me look quite twenty-eight.

I looked about and saw that dinner was over. Peter was already very pink with wine and embarrassment, and it came to me that the poor boy didn't even know the by-ways of verbal invitation (and indeed they have to be well done), and quite maddeningly, because to laugh was unthinkable, a phrase heard by me and subconsciously recorded at some afternoon of 'progressive whist' when the final competitor appeared, returned punctually, like a facetious pat on the head.

'Shall we make a start?' Even the hostess's face came back to me, and her hair, pompadour'd under an invisible net, and the table on which were the silver match-box and photograph frame prizes.

I should have liked to have said, 'What's the good of this nonsense, Peter? We don't care for each other and, that being the case, you don't know it, but you're being merely impertinent.' As it was I pulled on my gloves, smiled at him and said, 'Let's go to the Hippodrome, I want to see that *Under The Sea* thing'.

It took him unprepared, and he looked at once pilloried and immensely relieved, and he took me home at eleven-forty-five and went back to his own with illusions, I hope, intact, because untested, or with disillusions postponed, and with half his little posturing accomplished, or sufficiently so to give scope for the experienced shake of the head or the patronizing smile and an elaborately-honourable withholding of 'names' for his contemporaries who were ripe for trouble as well.

I went upstairs to find James, and couldn't, and in the hall saw the family slate which got inscribed with messages strange and many.

'Gone to Mudie's.'

'Barbara rang up.'

'Sandwiches in dining-room,' or

'Penny in garden, try get him in.'

This evening the writing was James's.

'Collared by Vallant. Back about midnightish.'

CHAPTER X

I

I HAD FOUND enough work on the salary of which to dress my-self and pay fares and sundries. You had, I saw, to have money and a background to be a successful female loafer; if you could keep open house, every time you descended the staircase from your sitting-room and opened the drawing-room door it was 'a party', while the unfilled hours between luncheon and tea, so infinite-ly dreaded by the unmarried daughters of the house, could be converted into an engagement by ordering round the carriage. But in a home life like ours, the drawing-room door opened on to nothing more social than Lalage darning stockings, and our carriage was the rather extravagant taxi or the bus. Evening dress was the heaviest item, for it was then that one pursued the affairs of James or Lalage – sometimes even of one's own.

Occasionally we all four went out together for a cheap jaunt, and really enjoyed ourselves, with no fish to fry or wet blanketing to be done. James and I would choose the restaurant, for the set-tings that we could weather weren't always right for mother and Lalage, except for the feeling I always had that their very presence in any room, of associations however sordid, cleansed it.

My odd-jobs were part time; I wouldn't allow myself to be spared too long from the family. My employment was not distin-guished, and in the space I allowed myself between selection and decision, I sized up the current situation. It misliked me strangely.

Unless you could attack a profession with long preparation and study and the academic brain which can cram facts and pass examinations, you were, I saw, even now between the devil of Miss Matty's tea and sweetshop and the deep sea of hobbies and idleness. Education involved capital, and I knew the intellectual life was not for me. I can only use my brain for people.

Or you could hang about the house and wait to be married, as the Seagraves did quite guilelessly, and the Verdunes, behind a barrage of chaff and rather bowdlerized rakishness. You were domestically assisted, if you were a Seagrave, by a mother who trumpeted girlhood's points in the very hall and fairly stunned men into becoming husbands, like a genial butcher crying beef-skirt on Saturday night.

If you were a Verdune, you took the aloof, rather splendid and half-true line that 'girls marry themselves'. You did not forbid banns, but you certainly didn't forward matters.

If you were a Stonor, you apparently lurked with walking-sticks, and turned the suitor out of the house, if family history was to be believed, or married out of the school-room, as mother had, to escape the older-generation Vallant atmosphere for ever.

What line mother took about our futures we neither knew nor dreamed of asking. The Verdunes passed to us the story of Aunt Emmeline at table pronouncing that 'Your aunt Anne isn't giving Vere and Lalage a chance'. The Seagraves on the other hand were instructed by Aunt Sophia that we went out far too much.

Theodora Seagrave had, it seems, eagerly explained away our suspectedly dashing successes to her family.

'It's always easier if you've got a brother.'

What nobody knew was that 'your Aunt Anne', looking like a Florentine madonna, had once said to me:

'Have a good time. Try not to acquire a baby because we can't run to its keep, but if you *should* get swept off your feet, see he's sound in wind and limb … and really I think that's about all.'

From old Lady Vallant we expected nothing, at a time when even an extra hundred would have made all the difference. To her we were a sort of family shop to which she sent for what she wanted (it was usually James), and on sale or return at that, as he complained.

II

And so I took my first post, and valeted an old lady in Church Street, Kensington, and read *The Times* to her and the lives of Generals, and it was then that Aunt Emmeline decided that I was being scamped by mother, a criticism that made Lalage's eyes darken with anger. I was merely amused. Also, I love age in man or woman; it can be so kind, so restful. And then I have an incurable avidity for trifles. I'm told (and how often I've read it!) that the existence of a hired companion is monotonous. I never found it so. How can it be while there are three meals a day to order (and shop), the arrivals of friends with their different clothes and faces and all *their* lives to guess at, and above all, the coming of the postman with more news, bringing quarrels, misunderstandings, invitations and suggestions together with stray births, deaths and marriages, items any one of which shifted the pattern of our kaleidoscope for the entire morning (and sometimes for the day), and gave rise to a whole new set of discussions and activities, from setting out 'the fringed napkins' from the linen cupboard to ordering a wreath from the florist in Notting Hill Gate, and subsequently sharing indignation when 'the tribute' was tardily acknowledged by the bereaved ('and those daffodils with the mauve tulips ... quite the prettiest in the cemetery, my dear. It's inexcusable of poor Caroline').

And then, the day I was really taken into the old lady's life, as distinct from just serving her, and confided in about My Son In Bombay, whom I pictured as a Jos Sedley, all shirtfrill, liver and curry, and was disappointed to find, from a faded photograph, was hatchet-faced, mild and moustached. We sometimes served him up at my own family board, and mother would say, 'My son in Bombay would hate this rice', of James, surveying the underdone mutton: 'They do these things better in Boggley-Wallah. My God! I wish my son in Bombay would bring home a pine for tiffin.'

And it was somehow fun to pass our house when out on my old lady's errands, and to know I couldn't run in because that would be 'defrauding my employer of my time'. It made me feel two persons in one; and sometimes mother or Lalage was actually at one of the windows and would see me and wave, or call out, and then I would look oppressed and give them a bitten-off nod.

Above all it was fun to dress the part in frocks almost theatrically severe, and muslin collars and cuffs and a sham gold chain with a rolled gold locket on the end that I had found in a pawnbroker's, and which had the name 'Lottie' engraved on the reverse.

Poor Lottie, who couldn't redeem her pledge! She must be very dead by now.

Sometimes the old lady and I had a treat, and toddled off together to the cinematograph at the Polytechnic, or to Maskelyne and Cook, and lo! it was now Maskelyne and Devant, and one felt that half a dynasty had fallen, and most unfairly resented the adroit and chatty newcomer, in spite of his Magic Kettle, which object gave me and my old lady grist for discussion for the whole of next morning.

And once we walked (starting in good time because her pace was slow) to the Coronet Theatre and saw a very bad play called *The Tulip Tree* with an indifferent cast headed by Cosmo Furnival, who gave the only real performance. My old lady adored it all and whispered, 'I've heard he's a very good-living man', to which I, answering in character, replied, 'I'm afraid all actors are sad dogs'; and when our tea-tray was clinkingly placed upon my lap, she asked the attendant how many spoonfuls had 'gone to the pot' and shook her head at the first sip. And then home, after leaving her comfortably settled (for the *Evening Standard* had come in while we were out).

Sometimes I would take a hatless after-dinner stroll, often with mother or Lalage, and we would go slowly past her house, and if the drawing-room was still lit up I knew all about *that* – whist with the old Misses Venner who lived round the corner in Brunswick Gardens – and at ten-thirty they would break off and nibble the cakes I had bought at Barker's that morning.

And so my mornings were cuffed and cosy and my nights were deceptively smart hats and fencing with ineligibles – a cloud by day and a pillar of fire by night!

III

I came in one morning with a knife-like headache and my old lady was all aspirins and cologne and concern and offered me hot milk, which I managed to refuse as I contrived, somehow, to get through *The Times* and the china-washing (she wouldn't let me go out), and suddenly she stopped the reading and turned her skirt over her petticoat and said, 'My dear, you should be so happy. I often think looking after an old woman is no life for you', then shyly, because she had been drilled from her cradle that 'personal remarks were in the worst of taste', and bravely because she was fond of me, 'I wish you could marry some good man'.

Part of me was grimly amused as I thought of the night behind me. One of my miscalculations. I had had supper with him after a play and found out too late it was *me* he had his eye on, and not Lalage; that he was the type which has no mercy at all upon any woman-thing if he finds her amusing, and who everlastingly confuses even the smallest amount of worldly wisdom she betrays with a willingness to go to any lengths. It is as though he were saying 'Oh, so you do know that veuve cliquot isn't burgundy, and can take up an allusion. Then you deserve all you get'.

With this type only the Miss blatantly fresh from a convent school is immune, and that only because to injure genuine ignorance is bad form. And – he'd done his best to make me tipsy (and very nearly succeeded). As he stood giving directions to the taxi-man I opened the further door and got out.

I said to my old lady, 'Let's get this straight. I came to you in the beginning because I needed the money … I still do, but I'd stay on on half what you pay me, because I'm happy and you're so sweet'.

She flushed (the prettiest pink!) and shook her head from the colossal depths of her experience that was one nice old gentleman with sidewhiskers, dead these forty years, whose portrait hung in the dining-room, and because I was so dreadfully afraid she would soon be arch with me, or put me on that crystal pedestal upon which so many old people delight to enshrine the young in years, I changed the subject in a hurry.

And just as we had settled down together, just as I knew all her ways, and she allowed for those of mine that were fit for her to see, she died. And I began to realize, dimly and for the first time, why it is unsafe for one generation to become attached to another.

It should have warned me.

CHAPTER XI

I

I WAS OUT of work but had little leisure to worry over that; I had enough on my hands at the moment.

This time it was old Lady Vallant.

Our move to London had not improved our relations with her, it had during the years only heightened and elaborated our original impressions and sustained the tradition.

The popular, or discussable, grounds for complaint among Lalage, James and myself included her high-handedness and parsimony. 'Not a funeral note', as once said with a wry grin to the other two. And we resented being sent for. That, too, could be talked over, also the fact that the Seagrave and Verdune girls didn't seem, as by hints infinitely cautious we had found out, to be subjected to similar levies upon their liberty. They just paid regular calls with the aunts in Lowndes Square.

Lalage came out with the suggestion, at first hearing brilliant, that our grandmother was flaunting us in the family face as an example of her own indifference to money, but this on consideration was abandoned, for if Lady Vallant had really been sufficiently aware of our poverty to take such a line, why did she never help us? And she did know, and if not, there were her own daughters, Sophia and Emmeline, to carry the matter.

That alone hardly made for love; but for her James could have gone to Rugby and university, Lalage could have had her fill of concerts and theatres and a coming-out ball of her very own, and mother – but why go on? We saw in time that it couldn't be easy to be the poorest three of sisters all living wellnigh within bowshot.

One of the Vallant-things which we couldn't discuss freely was the pressure of the old woman on our mother; the fact that we had always sensed it made it none the less painful. Once or twice James had hurried back from the City, impelled by some urgency, to find her returned, tired out, from Vallant House; at least twice I had done the same, cutting off my dear old employer almost in midsentence, to find, beyond the fact that mother had been with Lady Vallant and was but recently returned, there was nothing to do for her and very little to hear. For I am pretty certain now that at that time Lady Vallant was giving nothing away, or even had any particular devilfish to fry, and that the visits were 'calls' and nothing more. That the sessions devitalized our mother we, even then, could attribute to the influence of the house itself, in the light of what we'd pieced together for nearly all our years.

It was when James left school and went into father's business that Vallant, as he called her to us, emerged. He was the victim, at nineteen. We made quite a joke of it. He would come back at night and describe her dresses to us – she even rented a box at the opera for the Italian season, one year, the amenities of which were never offered to us. And that amused us too; a distinctly Vallantish touch. We actually had our moments of believing that the old creature was in freakish process of merging into a normal person; the grande dame (she could be that) with her handsome grandson ... showing him the world of fashion ... a miniature version of The Grand Tour. ...

And then, when these outings went on and on I became uneasy. This wasn't in the Vallant vein. Wasn't James being made a fool of? Were people – those whose money herded them into the same public places every season – beginning to notice the old woman and the young man? Would enough of them know the relationship to be appeased? And even if they did, does it ever do a boy any good to be in such constant attendance on a veteran?

If Lady Vallant had dressed the part it might have passed along; there is something peculiarly reassuring about lavender silks. But according to James, 'Vallant goes all the bundle on her kit on our jaunts, tiara on Melba nights and all. And I *think* she rouges'.

Well – she'd been a beauty, we'd all had that bit of information doled out to us; it was sometimes the only tale upon which mother seemed able to fall back.

I for one definitely didn't like it. I remembered the £10 tip before he went to his boarding-school, and in another flash James's hot flush and his little-boy revolt against his grandmother's kiss. The little-boy disgust I'd taken in my stride – who wouldn't? – at the time; now I began to wonder.

And mother's remark tossed off one night was not reassuring.

'I've never known the Mater darken the doors of the opera. She's practically tone-deaf.'

Lalage said with a trace of resentment – she'd temporarily lost her way about the situation and was just genuinely disappointed.

'She might ask us, sometimes.'

Mother's answer – she, too, had lost grip of things – was prompted impulsively by the unhappiness, however trivial, of any of us.

'It's just like her. I'm afraid imagination isn't Grannyma's strong point.'

II

And then Lady Vallant asked James to make his home with her and was of course refused, and this led to a family row which was, to me, a positive relief. Here at last was a tangible thing, a normal family fracas, endlessly discussable with anybody and from any point of view you cared to take. Also, it was our first actual collision, and a contemporary one, every incident of which we could check and verify. It upset mother, as did all scenes, and I took good care during the weeks of bad feeling never to let her be alone with the old woman at Vallant House. It wasn't easy, and I lost a post through it.

In time, our grandmother saw my game, thought nothing of requesting me out of our own drawing-room, and I went for the sake of peace. And once, at Vallant House, when I entered behind mother, she looked at me – just that – out of her black, close-set eyes and said, 'Oh, it's *you*'. And the next time, 'You will prefer to have your tea in the dining-room'. And the dining-room it was, but I would have fed in the coal-cellar sooner than leave.

The footman served me, never Hutchins. In time, I gave up even being announced and would turn automatically into my dining-room, and then Hutchins would come padding in, 'Hoping I had everything I wanted, Miss Vere', I was cold and said so, and he hesitated and lit the fire, and there was a row about that, I heard. The fire, it seemed, was never lit except when her ladyship was giving a dinner party, or, on off days, between definite hours.

'Very high-handed.' That came back to me, too. And I had been gossiping with the servants.

I was enraged, and wrote the old woman what James called a civil stinker; I showed the draft to mother and she begged me, for her sake, not to send it. I had to give in, but the injustice of the vulgar accusation would rush over me at night, doing me out of hours of sleep. And mother's attitude to the injustice aspect was hardly calculated to soothe.

'Justice ... she never had much idea of that for any of *us.*'

It was small episodes like these which made the old woman inscrutable. While she confused the issues with general eccentricity you could, I saw, never absolutely distinguish between that which in her conduct was just innate perversity and that which might be a clue of ultimate significance. All the Vallants were *farouche*; was could tally that up through the enforced reunions of family weddings. The uncles, Lady Vallant's sons, elderly, grizzled, speechless with shyness and taking it out in brusquerie which in a family less socially authentic would have been classed as the bad manners that it was.

'Move up' (this to Lalage, in church).

'Well, Anne ...' and the top-hat of elderly block unlifted. This, in the church porch.

Or there was the story of Uncle Stuart, entrenched at Vallant in the country, upon whom a couple of neighbours incautiously called – an unpopular move in itself – all the Vallants fear the extempore. And of how at eleven o'clock the servant came in with one whisky ready mixed in the glass, and Uncle Stuart drank it and then growled.

'Did you want something to drink? The cellar's locked now for the night.'

Mother flushed, fluttering to these handsome old boors she saw so seldom and who – I honestly believe they never realized it – shunned their own sister like the plague of very social terror.

It was at the wedding of the Seagrave who was kissed at her own dance ('shall we tell The Parents?') that on the steps outside the church I was collided with by a man. As he apologized I ruled him automatically out of the Vallant clan. He peered at me.

'You're Theodora, aren't you?'

'No. I'm not,' I snapped, 'and I'm not Beryl or Barbara or La-lage either.' I was tired and rude and glad of it; if I'm half a Vallant why not take advantage of it. 'I'm Vere Buchan.'

'Oh ... Anne's girl?'

'Yes, I'm Anne's.'

He put on spectacles, thick-lensed and disfiguring. And then I could have lashed myself. It was Uncle Julian, mother's youngest brother. It was, suddenly, the Palace Green schoolroom, the post-cards of Martin Harvey and Cosmo Furnival, the family of glass pigs and Barbara's voice: *'And Uncle Julian's nearly blind. ... Is he so old? No, I gather it was a piece of Vallantism ... she wouldn't consult an occulist ... jeered at him for being a milksop when his eyes hurt him and he cried.'*

I put out my arm to him. 'Will you help me down the steps?' – a stupid piece of Quixotry. Of course he took me up on it – the Vallant brains at least are normal.

'Eh? Nothing the matter with *your* sight, I hope?'

I lied promptly. 'No. My shoes hurt me.'

He helped me – I steering him, and I nearly turned my ankle after all on a cracked flagstone I hadn't seen because my eyes were brimming. Luckily he couldn't see that. I urged him to come and call on us – gave him his own sister's address – and he said he would. And the suggestion crystallized by mother in a letter, and he actually did come and visit us, and seemed pleased, and confused a little, and rather astonished at himself. By the time he had half emerged as a person he struggled up from his chair and left. I took the handsome old man to the gate and he gave me an uninterested hand in an absent sort of way, and partly because he was my new-found uncle, partly to 'larn' him, and mainly because my heart was sore for him, I kissed him.

He started as though stung. Somehow that was more pathetic than his eyes.

I would have done so much for him. Together we might have gone on those inexpensive, silly jaunts I love. I was immensely proud of my aquiline hawknosed old beau. I would have made him laugh, and he would have taken care of me, by wish and by kinship. We would have loved and liked each other, a mutual adoption of inclination, sinking the uncle-and-niece business. He would perhaps have advised me, taught me about men from the man's point of view, directly and decisively, lent me his judgment and experience. Together, as man to man, I might have got the whole family story out of him. This ever-recurrent treading on eggshells was getting on my nerves. And yet, would he have told me anything, even supposing I had achieved our alliance? I had had, over the years, a fairly comprehensive insight into the Vallant powers of cast-iron reserve. And to get even half-way to that stage I know now would have taken the rest of his life; but who was I to complain, when he had jettisoned his own sister for over a quarter of a century?

My disappointment was ridiculously great. 'It's no use. He won't play,' I said to mother.

'They don't, you know. They were never taught to. In our youth it was each man for himself and devil take the hindmost.'

So, it was Lady Vallant, as usual. Because of her, one more individual had been warped and thrown away: because of her, no doubt, that Uncle Julian had never married, or Uncle Stuart either. Too grounded in diffidence, and enraging, even contempt-ible, in grown men. But – what a grounding it must have been!

Mother had run from it, and Sophia and Emmeline had con-trived, somehow, to keep on the right side of the old woman, if their manner, commonplace and indifferent when they spoke of her, was anything to go by. In any case women are tougher, more adaptable, than men.

Yet, even in the aunts there were Vallant traces; in Mrs. Verdune a chilly reserve which had early caused her daughters to 'make their own arrangements'. That did not sound like love. And even comfortable, absurd Aunt Sophia took it out in over-advertise-ment of her family, a shrill challenge to the world that may well have had its origins in self-doubt.

The lady doth protest too much, methinks.

Vallant traces which were to result in one bad Verdune *mesalli-ance*, impulsive and reckless, one loveless Seagrave match, and in Flora Seagrave, tardily exhibiting a little character and sickened with Aunt Sophia's tactics, never marrying at all, the bride and spinster being solely blamed for the *mesalliance* and the single state by both our aunts. The Victorians – or was it only the Vallants? – seem unable to see straight or honestly about themselves, and have, in regard to others, a real genius for being blind to what it doesn't suit them to see.

CHAPTER XII

I

IT GAVE THE family food for discussion for months, during which, very typically in that it had its roots in ruction, we all saw more of each other than commonly we did in years. During the time that I could spare from the tedium of typewriting lessons that I picked up cheap in Earl's Court Road, for I saw that this knowledge would raise my market value, I took my share in family council.

Indeed, it was Dolly herself who rang me up – I can't think why. I had always believed that the Verdunes and Seagraves were the allies and that our humbler circumstances and juniority would rule us out of confidence, as it did out of nearly everything else.

Dolly was in the old school-room now termed 'Boodles' in recognition of its present half-club half-boudoir status.

The same Edwardian paper was on the walls but the postcards of Martin Harvey and Cosmo Furnival were gone from the mantelpiece, and two of the glass pigs were missing. Modern fiction had nudged the geographies and histories from the shelves, and Barbara's athletic phase left over from her gymnasium period as represented by the comfortable litter of indian clubs and petersham chest-expander had been cleared up for good.

'Well of course it's about my disgrace,' began Dolly. 'It was most decent of you to come. The other two are fearfully bored with me about Arthur because they're so fed up with mother for craping all over the house. And one can't talk to the Seagrave

gurls because they're such *dam* fools. And somehow one can't tell
Lalage much. She's so frightfully good, isn't she? Now you aren't
a bit the same ... I say! I didn't mean that, quite.'

'It's all right, I know what you mean.'

'Lalage always strikes me as being ... not exactly not all there
but sort of arrested ... childlike; it's deuced effective, but it always
makes one feel rather ... what? blatant. She isn't a bit like any of
us, is she? Mother says she's awfully like the aunt who died. Myra,
you know.'

I sat up at that. Aunt Emmeline, again, alluding matter of factly to her daughters with whom she had never been friends, to
that shadow of whose very existence our own mother had never told us. And mother must have foreseen that sooner or later
somebody would mention her dead sister to us.

It may have been disloyal, but in that moment I was exasperated. Also, complete silence was a distinct risk which mother all
these years had run. It might all have come out in public before
any of the Seagraves and Verdunes – surely mother had had better
luck than she deserved!

I was losing the thread of what Dolly was saying.

'... well, I mean ... mother is too trying. *Is* it reasonable? I
know Arthur isn't a gentleman, but we are fond of each other.'

'What kind of not a gentleman?' I asked. 'Half-sir or plumber's mate?'

'Three-quarters-sir. *Perfectly* presentable.'

'Where did you meet him?'

Dolly gave a shout of semi-guilty laughter. 'We picked each
other up at the Shepherd's Bush Empire, the return bus was ages
coming and he lent me his umbrella and we jawed about the
programme. Why not?'

'You mean that in any drawing-room a formal introduction
isn't a real guarantee of character either?'

'Of course.'

I thought. 'Honestly you know, I've never been able to go as
far as that. If you marry a man through a respectable introduction, then if he's a complete fiasco, you *can* blame your hostess
for harbouring stunners, but with pickups you've only yourself
to blame.'

'Well, I'm going on with it, and Vere, you don't know how boring the house is; one can't go to matinées more than twice a week and mother won't give me a *thing* to do in the way of even arranging the flowers. She simple doesn't realize we're grown-up and talks to us as if we were still in the school-room. She's getting awfully Susanish ... Dammit! I'm twenty-eight ... D'you remember old great-aunt Jane? No, of course you wouldn't, she was before your time. We only saw her once or twice ourselves. She once said, "The Stonors make *bad* mothers.' My hat! she was right!'

'But Uncle Bertram ... don't you and he hit it?'

'Oh yes, but father's completely under mother's thumb. There it is again. It was just the same with grandpa and Susan. Meanwhile, I'm simply loafing. Could you stand it?'

'I don't know. I've never tried.' I didn't mean to be ironic.

'I said to mother when it all started, "Well, what have you got against Arthur?" and mother (it's *so* like her) said, "Oh, you'll go your own way, you always have", which of course is true. Mother's got a perfect genius for putting one in the wrong without being really right herself; she can always silence one and never convince.' Dolly Verdune took a chocolate and hitched her ankle over an armchair. 'What line does Aunt Anne take?'

'Well ... she doesn't like it,' I admitted, 'but she's come down to thinking that if it's going to make you happy, even happier, you must have your own way.'

'She is a dear, isn't she? I always said she's the only Vallant who isn't cracked. What a crew! ... I wish one of us could marry your nice James. I don't mind telling you we've all had a smack at him, first cousin or no!'

What a lot of things can go on in families unsuspected! But I did remember one telephone call I'd answered, and a Verdune voice ingenuously asking, 'Could one have James to dinner tonight without any of you?'

The passage bell rustled its wires and tinkled. The parlour maid on the drawing-room flight was summoning the youngest Miss Verdune to the tea table.

CHAPTER XIII

I

I WENT HOME, found James and said, 'I've been to the Verdunes'.
Dolly says that Lalage always strikes her as being "arrested", and
it seems that she's exactly like Myra. What about it?'

The best of James is that he always gives one his instant attention without any abstracted just-one-minutes, forgetfulness
or postponements by enquiry about preliminary details. He was
packing for the midlands where he was due for two days on business, but switched off to me as a lever is pulled over.

'Arrested ... she means not up to sample? Too guileless for
her age sort of thing?'

'N-no ... I believe Dolly's hit on something I've always
thought without knowing it. Jamesey, do you remember in the
old days how we used to rather depend on Lalage and relied on
her common sense and stolidity? We even made her be the one
to welcome Lady Vallant at the gate!'

'But, she was always the first to jack up ... the delicate one.'

'I know, but that needn't count. Eldest children often are.' I
fell silent. Even for James I had something pretty far-fetched to
express, and difficult in itself. We were too close to see Lalage
clearly; it was the old story of the outsider, if not exactly seeing
most of the game, at least by unrehearsed, slipshod comment setting one on the right track. I said,

'Here was Lalage, just like us up to about ten years old ... until, that is, she first saw Lady Vallant. Doesn't it seem possible that
Vallant's arrival may have started up something latent in Lalage,
something that if she were with mother and you and me might
have kept in abeyance?'

'What kind of thing?'

I shrugged helplessly. 'Something ... arresting, I suppose.'

'Physical or mental?'

'Personally, mental, I believe, but don't let that put *you* off.'

He was leaning against the mantelpiece and shook his head.
'No, I know what you're after, but if Vallant has such an influence
as that, it must be hereditary, and Lalage would be in for it sooner
or later in any case.'

'Not necessarily. Shock starts things, physical *and* mental.' I paused. 'You screamed when you saw Vallant.'

'Lor! What a young sawny! I'd forgotten that. Looks as if I'd minded the old woman more than Lalage did.'

'I don't agree. Your screaming could have been the healthy reaction of a healthy child to something – beastly. Lalage did nothing.' – I stared at James – 'because it hit her harder.'

'Aren't we being a bit wise after the event?'

'Right-o. Let's get back to Lalage. Well now, we've always known she wasn't like us ... openly, I mean. Can't face things ... fish out of water at dances, and so on (and Lord knows it isn't from want of men!). It's awfully difficult to see straight about Lalage because we shall never know what sort of person she'd have become if she'd never seen Vallant and never come to London ... she was all right at school because it was an influence in itself, and a pretty strong one. But ever since she left school at eighteen and was open to any outside force that came along, her personality *faded.*'

'But my dear, look at the Seagraves! They never *had* any!'

'No, but they were always *in the world*; they're gawky and eager and eager and elbow'd, but they're real people. Enormously tangible.'

'Well?'

'Jamesey, would it be possible to stop living, at eighteen, and yet not be dead?'

He was staring right through me. I went on, 'People often say after some grief or shock, "my life is over". That's what I mean. That Lalage is alive, but her "continuity" is ended.'

'What do we do?'

'Ask me another.' I made a wryish face. 'I may have to cultivate Lady Vallant.' It would be possible; we were once more on visiting terms in Lowndes Square.

'Vere, once and for all, can't we ask mother?'

'I can't. I'm as much scared that she'd tell us as that she wouldn't ... and, James, I can't cope with things indefinitely.' I turned my head away. His arm was round my shoulder.

'My poor old dear, you aren't having a very good time, are you?'

'Oh I can manage, Jamesey.'

II

Indeed, I could have done with a little joy. It is when this realization comes that one flies to the concrete for reassurance: that one was missing the long annual holiday once taken as a matter of course and that two weeks at the sea was only enough to upset routine and liver: that I was working in an office (tiring for the back) and (if it happened to be the spring) that the spring was always very enervating.

In such moods women fly to palmists, planchette or prayer. I refused, this time, to succumb – except to those stray, colloquial petitions which for some reason I have let off, anywhere and everywhere, since childhood. Why not? If God is in church He is equally in the grocer's and the restaurant. Personally, I am invariably more conscious of Him in such non-professional places, and if I have often felt that He hasn't 'answered' me, isn't it fair to give Him the credit for that tongue of mine which has averted the impossible situation, for that long-sight which, enabling me to see beyond the minute, has saved me on more than one occasion from stupidity, rashness and scandal?

And as for palmists: I have the greatest belief in the best of them in spite of their tendency to seize both my hand and James's and tell us both that 'two children mark your hand'. Three times we have been told this, and as we get older, the polite incredulity of the seer, together with a tendency to actual indignation when refuted, becomes more marked.

On the last occasion I had been to have my hand read I had resorted to the business through a need of some pointer, something which might give me a line on Lady Vallant, on Lalage; something which, meaningless to the palmist, might have much of significance for myself. And she made absent pronouncement that I had a singular capacity for loving and hate, and was 'far too independent'. But what appeared to interest her the most was even more exasperating. It ranked in my mind with the large fortune, the long voyage and the dark woman. She asked:

'You have lost your father?' and I agreed.

'And I think I am right in saying that your mother has recently married again, or is about to?'

'Ye Gods!' This was being about the limit, and, as palmists so invariably are before flippancy, mine seemed annoyed.

'My mother isn't dreaming of marrying again, or ever did,' I answered; as usual going down before atmospherics. She bent her head.

'That's very extraordinary, it's here quite unmistakably. It's a man … not young, I think … who certainly stands close to you. And it isn't a fiancé, he seems to be married already.'

Damn the women! And for this I had parted with five precious shillings.

'He is rather tall, dark hair going white, and I get the impression of a crowd round him, or near him. …'

I left feeling like a scullerymaid with a Dream book.

III

The next morning I went half an hour late (for the first time) to my office, where by now I was rather a star turn among the students and fifteen-year-old beginners.

James and I had sat up late in my bedroom talking; we were guying the palmist and I overslept.

My teacher, Miss Royal, put a pile of manuscript by my place.

'Miss Buchan, I am so sorry, but you've just missed some work, a rush order came through at nine-thirty and I didn't dare wait for you. It would have been good for you and – er – paying, you know.' Even now she couldn't quite treat me as she did the rest and would often offer me tea from her pot in the private room. A pity, I thought. Heaven knew I was no money'd amateur filling in for an amusing whim between luncheon party and dance. It is better to know life's worst, stripped of all misconception. …

'Yes, there was a play wanting typing. Parts. It was Cosmo Furnival.'

'Good Lord!' I said cheerfully, 'he must be a thousand years old.'

I was inwardly riled to pieces at losing the money. …

IV

In the little room where we hung our hats and coats I stumbled over the small, dejected figure of our pupil-teacher, whose duties included the reading aloud of newspaper extracts to the Intermediate and Advanced shorthand students. For quite a minute I struggled against the conviction that she was crying, then succumbed.

'Anything I can do, Gladys?' (unless, of course, it was money).

'Nothing, thank you ever so, Miss Buchan.'

'Ah, but perhaps there is. Well, I'm here if you feel like it,' and I deliberately turned my back on her. A longish pause.

'It's only ... ooh, you'll think me so silly ...'

As I probably should, I said nothing, foreseeing a young man with a pompadour or a tiff with My Gurl Friend.

'It ... it's Mr. Cosmo Furnival.'

'*What?*'

'Oh Miss Buchan, I *did* so want to be the one t'be sent to his house!'

Well, whatever my faults, I never find confession ridiculous, however fantastic or foredoomed. Here, I could remember so well the old Martin Harvey-Hayden Coffin days; indeed, I was rather pleased to find still burning a spark of the Edwardian flame!

'I see,' I answered, 'but Gladys, you know he must be quite sixty-five by now.'

'Oh ... not sixty-five, Miss Buchan!'

Already the idol was tottering.

'Fact, I remember ...'

'Oh, do tell, Miss Buchan!'

I racked my brains for the little I knew. Since my schooldays I had taken scant stock of the theatre world – too busy in other directions.

'Well, when I was a small child, my mother and father once went up to London to see him act, and my cousins had a postcard of him on their mantelpiece ...'

The sudden, incredulously-recollected memory of James and myself singing for money outside Furnival's stage door I had (unwillingly!) to suppress.

'Cheer up, my dear. There's sure to be another chance soon.'

'D'you reely think so?'

'Why not? It's happened once, it can happen again, if he's pleased with us; careful, prompt and accurate; dramatic work a speciality,' I quoted from our prospectus.

She was off on another tack. 'But, can he reely be that old?'

I leant upon the wash basin. 'Gladys, somebody (forget who) once wrote "love is not love that alters where it alteration finds". I hope I've got it right. It simply means that if your Cosmo Furnival had a disfiguring illness to-morrow, or lost his sight or his legs or his income and his theatre, you'd round on him … throw him over. I think there's more to it than collecting pleasing picture-postcards … if your Mr. Furnival is worth your affection, you've got to return the compliment by qualifying for him, as you do for your shorthand.'

'But … he's *married*, Miss Buchan!'

'My dear, if you love anybody or anything, must it always be with an eye to grabbing it for yourself? Can't you go to the National Portrait gallery without fretting because you can't own the Kneller Monmouth? … I don't mean that you've got to take a pious, noble pleasure in the thought that the picture is giving pleasure to others, but that you should appreciate it for its own sake.'

She patently couldn't. Her tests were eligibility and a good profile. Goods, undamaged. In fresh condition and right side up with care. It's a good concrete viewpoint with which to face life, I suppose; almost enviable in its vulgar, direct simplicity.

And so Satan rebuked sin and was fifteen minutes late for luncheon. *Not* one of my lucky days.

CHAPTER XIV

I

AND THAT AFTERNOON I was due at Vallant House with James – one of our duty calls, slightly increased in number since his refusal to make his home there.

I had a suspicion that the old woman disliked our arrival in pairs or groups. Always ungenial to me, her dissatisfaction seemed to be invariably more marked when the couple was James and myself than it was over any other combination. … This, at least, isn't being wise after the event; I sensed it often, in those days.

The visit followed the customary routine of ministrations by Hutchins and footman, caustic order and reprimand from their mistress, sharp comment from those small thin lips and the close-set eyes which sardonically summed and appraised, and on our side, strained politeness and absolute unreality. One hour with our hostess, even in a good mood, was an ordeal. What a week, a year, many years must be, and have been!

She said, 'I wish you would telephone in advance when you mean to come here'.

I was a little surprised, not of course at the crudeness of the remark so much as that we had always been urged by mother to make these calls, and she ought to know the rights of the old woman's mental processes. And then I understood, for the parchment-coloured claw decked with diamonds was fluttering down the silken dress. Lady Vallant had been taken by surprise, and not in her favourite gown. And James was the visitor.

I apologized for us both aloofly, and just as we had bogged down into a review of Dolly Verdune and Arthur – the old lady knew very little and I held my tongue – James rose and stood with that expression of polite expectancy, that slight stooping of the shoulders, with which men prepare to meet an introduction.

At first I didn't understand: looked at the clock whose hands still indicated that at least another twenty minutes must be filled before our release, and remembered that in any case it was my business to give the signal and not his.

He seemed to be standing there interminably waiting, a faint astonishment in his eyes; even the old lady noticed it and said sharply, 'Sit down, sit down!'

He obeyed.

'What's the matter with you?'

'I ... thought that lady was staying for tea.'

'Which lady?'

'I think she said "Chilcot".'

We both froze at the look in Lady Vallant's eyes. If she had raved at him one could have borne it better; it was the combination of those eyes with the collected, almost conversational, tone, that was somehow so awful.

'You are drunk. Ring the bell and leave me.'

Outside the door I murmured to James, 'I'm going to collar Hutchins'.

'What for?'

I smiled wryly. 'I "gossip with the servants", you know. Well, now I'm going to.'

'Right.'

In the hall I said, 'Hutchins, can the shutting of the front door be heard in the drawing-room when you let visitors out?'

'No, Miss.'

'Very well. Then we needn't go through the business of shutting it. Will you come and speak to us in the dining-room for a minute?'

He followed us in, closing the door.

'Hutchins, who was Miss Chilcot?'

I was keyed up for practically anything, as far as anyone can know whose breaking-point has never been tested, and his answer, banal and sane, almost made me sigh with relief.

'Governess to the young ladies, Miss.'

'Oh yes …'

'And she left?' this from James.

'Yes, Mr. James.'

'Did you like her?'

'Very much. She, if I may say so, was quite the most,' he hesitated for a split second and found a word that I felt pretty sure was a substitute, – 'satisfactory of any of the ladies.'

'How long did she stay?'

The old man was looking a little harassed. 'About six months.'

'Was that a shorter or longer time than the others?'

'Shorter, sir,' he hesitated again, 'very much shorter.'

He plunged. 'Forgive me, Mr. James, but why do you ask?'

'Oh, that's all right, Hutchins. Miss Chilcot's name happened to come up in conversation this afternoon.'

I said, 'Would there be a photograph of her?'

'I should hardly think so, Miss Vere. There might be in the boxes upstairs; the top floor has never really been cleared up since all the young ladies married. Her ladyship never goes up there, and she was never one to go in for photos.'

'Except her own,' snapped James. He shouldn't have said it, of course, but I sympathized.

'Hutchins, could you go up and have a look, and if you find one, send it to my brother's office, not to Campden Hill?'

'Yes, certainly Miss.'

'Thank you. By the way, what age was Miss Chilcot?'

'Not a very young lady; must have been thirty or over when she came here.'

'That'd make her over seventy now. H'm ... I suppose you haven't her address?'

'The address she engaged from I remember, being accustomed to collect the outgoing letters for the evening post. It was (he gave the number) Rosary Gardens, South Kensington.'

'But ... if she was a Londoner, why didn't she go home every evening?'

'Her ladyship always engaged resident governesses, Miss. She ... was out such a lot herself ... and the entertaining here, and all ...'

I compressed my lips. James said abruptly:

'Do you know why this Miss Chilcot left so soon?'

It took both his hearers aback. I hadn't had time to decide the putting of that question, and as for Hutchins, there was clearly some internal conflict or confusion in process.

'I really couldn't tell you, Sir.'

At that, the fat being in the fire, hoping as well that the old man meant nothing more or less than his reply, we could afford to look expectant and slightly incredulous. He gave up (or did he?).

'There was, I understand, some disagreement with her ladyship, the nature of which naturally never became public in the servants' hall.'

We had to leave it at that.

Where we walked to on leaving Vallant House I don't really know to this day. We found, I remember, a bus of unfamiliar number that eventually put us down in Sloane Square after a vague journeying along streets hot, dusty and depressing.

James, half voluble, half silent, and overstrung (we were both the latter) relived the afternoon for me.

'... well then, the door opened and this woman came in, in out-door clothes, so of course I thought she'd come to tea ...

and she stood there behind Vallant and Vallant went on talking *all through* what the woman said, and yet I heard both voices separately ... like in an orchestra, you know. ...'

'What did she say?'

'"It's Miss Chilcot. I've come to say good-bye."'

'Anything else?'

'Yes. "I wish to God I could have stayed".' He broke off, thinking, 'and yet, Vere, she was dying to leave'.

'Then?'

'Well, I thought in a muddled way, it was rather rum for anyone to come in and then go at once ... until I saw her clothes, and then I noticed they were utterly out of date, like those old bound volumes of *The Quiver* that we used to hoot over when we were kids. So then I knew she was a goner.'

'Ah ... but perhaps she isn't.'

I V

The photograph – very yellow and faded – arrived four days later. James brought it to me, late at night, for safety.

'It's Chilcot, all right. *And* with the aunts. Plain woman ... good eyes ... fighting chin ... That's Sophia looking like a bantam's egg. That might be mother ... no, it's aunt Emmeline. She's got the family nose already.' We turned over the oblong of cardboard:

> Ryman
> High Street
> Vallant
> Hampshire.

'The village Bassano evidently. I bet it was the Chilcot who took the kids to be done. Vallant'd never have troubled, damn her.'

'Give me the Rosary Gardens address.'

I bent once more over the photograph.

'Mother isn't there.' I pored over the ungainly group.

'No, my dear. And neither is Myra.'

And three days later the War broke out.

CHAPTER XV

I

JAMES JOINED UP at once although the office tried to get him earmarked as indispensable. He hated the whole business and was too old to be able to regard it as a cross between a house-match and Arthurian quest. He believed that the War, together with all panic, was more or less brought about by newspapers, that if war wasn't assumed months in advance in the public press, it would probably never happen; and that the catastrophic idea gets into the air, like a poison gas.

'If you believe in the power of thought, you've got to take the rough with the smooth. "When two or three are gathered together in Thy name Thou wilt grant their requests" we all believe. But what price two or three million people gathered together and concentrating on the wrong things? It's mass thought that does it, not which side's running the show.'

He paid a round of farewell family visits, including one to Vallant House. I went with him, I was beyond counting the possible future cost. He was *my* brother, it was *his* war and he was the only available Vallant on active service.

Our grandmother, practically ignoring me, rang the bell, assembled the entire staff of nine and conducted a long, emotionalized prayer-meeting, partly extempore – she dwelt, I observed, upon the more destructive aspects of warfare and there was a lot about 'the wicked man' and 'proud stomachs'. It ought to have been dreadfully funny, judged by almost any standard of humour including that of the cartoonist, who would, I think, have appreciated the row of decorous, print-clad female backs, the polite resignation of the young footman, the pop-eye'd incredulity of the knife-boy and the contours of butler and cook.

It failed to amuse me; for in spite of the fact that the old lady kissed James's forehead and even blessed him, I received two impressions, as fantastic as disagreeable.

One was that Lady Vallant enjoyed the thought of war.

And the other was that she was glad that James was in for it. What she didn't know was that as she blessed him, he had quickly crossed himself over his heart.

And when the blasphemous farce was over, Hutchins took us downstairs.

'I wish you every possible good luck, Mr. James, and my affectionate respects to Mrs. Buchan.'

'Thanks awfully, Hutchins. Will you write to me? I'd value that a lot. And as for this business, I'm going to France on the principle that one takes quinine to fend off a fever, but that isn't to say that quinine is exactly my favourite tipple.' He threw an arm round the old man. 'So long, dear old chap.'

II

All the way home I was debating this latest piece of Vallantism. Rightly or wrongly I came to the unshakable conclusion that she had annexed James in the first instance to fan the embers of her vanity, had wished him to live with her to gratify an undying acquisitiveness or to hurt us, and that, refused, she had merely turned savage.

She was relieved to be getting him out of the way. In plain English, we were now three women with no man in the house. And one of those women was her own daughter, drilled into diffidence and still nervous, for all her acquired sophistication.

III

Six months' training at Tidworth and James was off. His hands were on my shoulders.

'I feel a swine for leaving you to it, Vere. Keep me posted about Vallant, and look after *them*. ...'

And not once, I think, did I ever have to support, among others, the burden of fear for James. I knew he would come back.

IV

It was for Hugh Lyne that I had the only qualms; with him I had no inner bond and for him therefore no secret wisdom. He missed much of the War through his age, and went out in that intermediate period between the calling up of the elder men and the final desperate drive of conscription; and he went fortified by what is called 'an understanding' with Lalage. Marry her before the War was over he would not, and although I theoretically applauded the point of view, I couldn't help thinking that this exaggerated highmindedness about the possible loss of limb or sense was about on a par with the chorus-girl conviction, held by a certain type of woman, that a first grey hair and a crowsfoot will lose her for ever the allegiance of her husband or her lover. Apart from that, I had hoped they would marry soon. I was uneasy at the effect of the War upon Lalage. She was paler than ever and seemed to be losing weight. For months I was sidetracked, believing that James and Hugh were the cause, until something she said to me made me aware that no such sad normality was there. She was possessed by a sickness of the soul.

It was at the time when jokes were in circulation about The Hymn of Hate. For some reason this seemed to strike at her more directly than air-raid or reported atrocity.

We were standing by her window and watching the searchlights, and she suddenly began shaking, and said, '*Anything but the hate. I remember hate*'.

I asked, as casually as might be, 'What hate?'

'I can't say. I would if I could. It's something I just know that I know.'

I could get nothing more.

v

What I hadn't allowed for in the rush of getting James off, of earning my living, worrying over Lalage and Hugh and trying to be at home as much as possible, was Lady Vallant. I had literally overlooked her.

She was – this from family hearsay – in a very difficult mood. Even the aunts noticed it: 'difficult' was the easy Seagrave contribution. Aunt Emmeline, ever more pessimistic and therefore more definite, put it to mother that 'the Mater is going to pieces'. I guessed that no sort of solution would be arrived at until our own visits were renewed. They had to be, in common decency, at such a time.

We were not kept waiting long, and it was upon mother that the storm broke. I couldn't get at what was going on. Once more, mother received our grandmother at our house, went steadfastly to hers, to return white and spent. And I, tired out myself, discounted the whole thing. We'd been through all this before, for years!

Mother's and Lalage's resistance wasn't being strengthened by War work. Every day they went off to Kensington Square to roll bandages and make 'two by two' and 'four by four' swabs, and would return about the time that I did from office or outside commissions, their lungs full of fluff, with aching backs and ears still full of war and rumour. It was work, light and unheroic, but with such types it was grand stuff for the sustenance of mental bogeys. I, more hardened, found myself, too often, doing the same myself. Also, I was nagged by reproach at not doing the spectacular thing myself – in any direction. I couldn't drive a car, I was squeamish about blood to useless-point, I knew that the control of numbers of women was beyond my character, which is of that *petit point* variety that is lost in the mass, or tends, fatally, to over-emphasis of the individual by too great interest, enervating sympathies or unconsidered dislikes which reproached my sense of justice. We needed what I could earn; how much my mother and Lalage needed me no government office would allow for – but it didn't increase one's self-esteem.

One day was the counterpart of the other for Lalage and mother; I at least had variety in my tedium. And at night, James to be written to, and, for the first time, reticences to be observed with him lest some quite unconsidered line of mine be the one that should prey on him and lower his efficiency – until he wrote and told me what I was doing and ordered me to tell him everything. And then arose the problem of his answers which would be devoured in turn by mother and Lalage. I solved that by telling him to send what we called his 'Vallant despatches' on separate sheets inside the demonstrable letter.

Always the last one up, I got into the habit of going round the house at night and listening at the doors of mother and Lalage – for what I hardly knew, save that it satisfied some protective urge of mine, or that if one could catch one of them in grief, one could surprise them into sane explanation. …

CHAPTER XVI

I

I BEGAN TO spend my evenings with Raymond Owen. I would see that mother and Lalage were comfortably settled, would leave my destination and its telephone number at their elbow, would often ring them up in the middle of dinner or during the interval at theatre or music-hall.

Owen didn't like it; he began by chaff and ended by sulks. It was tiresome and I recognized it, and went on doing it. Owen was in love with me. He was what, in discussing the Seagraves with James, I had described as a tremendously real person. He was concrete, and I badly needed tangibility at that time; he made me laugh, by jokes broad and narrow, and my sense of proportion being undermined, I thought that they might restore me by shock tactics, as I told him. He was elderly and I wanted to be looked after myself, for a change. I didn't even want to know what sort of a character he really was. I was dogsick of probing and introspection and psychology and manœuvring. If I was making mistakes – let 'em all come! I even scrapped my conscience and let him pay for my meals and my theatres. It was being done all round me by my own sex. It seemed to be part of the business of being a woman, in war or peace, and the fact that this sort of gold-digging dependence had always gone against the grain with me and clashed with what principles I've got and with all my common sense probably only meant that I was a fool.

Also, he said he loved me, and that was a warmth in itself I was over-eager to believe. He wasn't even in the army – 'too ancient and indispensable' he told me – and I was glad of even that, being wearied of war and trench stories and the whole collection of khaki jokes and catchwords.

And so the band played 'Dixie' and I sat there and thought I was as happy as one was ever likely to be.

II

My search for news of Miss Chilcot took me nearly three months. It was done in my free time, and that again had to be occasionally given to mother and Lalage. I hoped that no necessity for downright lies would arise, but for years now the family was more or less broken to my work which was apt to take me, within limits, to the most unlikely places at unconventional hours, what with rush orders and general keeping of faith with our clients.

The office had been enlarged, more trained staff and paying pupils admitted, and I had drifted into a semi-official position and was considered reliable, which I valued.

I began the hunt in Rosary Gardens to find, as I had expected, that the house had changed hands three times since Captain Chilcot's day.

So, she was a soldier's daughter? 'A fighting chin', James had said. ...

The house-agents were as helpful as was possible. When had the Chilcots left? And the books for 1883 were brought down from upper shelves.

We traced him to a villa in Chiswick; the Chiswick agents believed he had moved to a certain address in Barnes. I found it; small and pretentious, in the Tube station style of architecture. The captain had died there in 1890 (that would be about the time that Lalage, James and I were toddling about the garden of our old home, when every pulled radish was an adventure and the apple trees seemed two hundred feet high). In this house-agent's office there was a chill, and a tendency to shrugged shoulders which I took to be an indication that the memory of the captain was not revered. I thought rapidly that his descending scale of accommodation could only mean money trouble, and hinted it. The captain had, in point of fact, died owing money.

And the family? Scattered, it was supposed. Wasn't there one who was governess to a Lady Vallant? Which one would that be, Miss Buchan?

That meant a letter to Hutchins. The Christian name was Alma; and a letter to the agents. Miss Alma Chilcot.

At this point I drew blank. In the end it was my own work which put me indirectly on the track. I had offered to take a parcel of typescript to Holland Park Avenue and (as usual) the number I wanted was the only one that seemed to be non-existent. I turned back and secured a description of its locality from a baker's shop, and it was while I was climbing the steps that it oc-

curred to me that shops selling necessities were my possible link
with the Chilcots. The captain may have got into arrears with his
rent, but the need for loaves went on for ever. I promised myself
that baker's shop on the first opportunity.

When I went to the shop a week later I learned that it had
changed hands only two years ago (and heaven only knew how
many times before that). I was tired and dispirited and went into
the little back room – a badly converted tea-lounge, all paper
fans and advertisements of tea and fancy bread, and no cloths on
the unsteady tables, and had a cup of tea and a cake that tasted of
old hatboxes. I began to take it for granted, always my way, that
these obstacles were a hint from fate that the Chilcot episode
was closed to myself as an individual; also I was saddened a little
because that morning I had read Peter's name among the list
of officers killed. Peter, whose country wedding I had planned,
whose very flowers I had raised! Had he, I wondered, had time
for any love in his life since that disarming and impertinent effort
towards me?

And then, again in my way, it occurred to me that bakers' were
not the only shops which dealt in necessities, and I paid and left
and found the grocer nearest the Chilcot house. Actually, there
were two shops, and I stood near them and waited for a sign, and
requested God to do something about it under my breath – I
never thought that by going to both shops in turn I should find
out something or nothing in any case. I chose the nearest shop
because in the window a large tabby so like dear dead Penny,
was asleep on a sack of dog-biscuits, its striped arm bound like a
ribbon round its face, a fat, smug smile on its patent-leather lips.
Also, the proprietor, glimpsed over a wall of tinned fruit, was old
and pleasant, and one always turns in preference to age.

I bought a pound of barley (the Chilcots were beginning to
become rather an item in my budget) and then got started. The
old man remembered the Chilcots well. A great loss, the captain.
A real gentleman, not one of these jumped-up dogs. The Miss
Chilcots often came in for this and that. Your ma's governess?
There now! He had heard that one of 'em was dead and the others gone to live in the country with relatives. Scattered, like. Two
of 'em had set up together in rooms in Barnes, but that was – it
must be – fifteen years past, and he hadn't heard nothing since.

The address of the rooms? Oh yes, when they was here they still dealt with us for bits of things, but the orders got very small. ...

I left with my warm and grateful thanks and went to the address he had given me. The house, in a cul-de-sac, was two-storied; children, immune, chalked up cricket stumps on the end wall, and the visiting tradesmen were carts peddling firewood and flabby greens.

But the orders got very small. ...

The landlady was uninterested and naturally suspicious on general grounds. She was impervious to any appeal to sentiment and gave me her facts with a businesslike acceptance of indigence one could not break down. The elder Miss Chilcot had had some 'help', she knew, from 'a charity'; that evidently lowered her in the woman's eyes although it paid her claims against the sisters. 'The other one' – yes, Alma – had refused public assistance (which also roused the staid contempt of the landlady) and had 'gone out' every morning 'at addressing envelopes' and such until she broke down, like. She was now in The House.

Which workhouse, and when?

Two-three years now, it must be. 'The old one' had gone away, she didn't know where.

III

Another week went by before I could visit the workhouse. I had written to the authorities and described myself to the porter at the gates as an old friend.

I supposed it was because I was a bit run down that my legs trembled, that, or the endless stairs. Nobody barred my entrance into the infirmary, indeed the door of her ward was ajar and I walked in. My work had made me used to every description of strange door, of enquiry, answer and mistake, and just as I was walking slowly – trying not to stare at the faces in the iron beds spread with their scarlet blankets, yet not to miss the face I had memorized from the photograph – the Sister advanced and stopped me.

'Yes, you may see her, but don't stay long.'

I had already my permission from a higher authority, but I controlled my anger. This woman was queen of her dunghill, after all.

'Is she ... ill?'

'Excuse me, but who are you?'

Explanation again: one *must* be patient.

'Oh yes, very well. You must expect to find a great change.'

I V

Miss Chilcot's bed was in the farthest corner; it gave her a fractionally greater share of privacy for which I was thankful for both our sakes. Looking down at her as she lay there, unpropped by pillows as were most of the other inmates, one's thoughts were in too great a flurry to allow of decision as to whether she was wonderfully like her photograph, or a total stranger unfamiliarized in one's mind by overlong pondering and speculation. And the social side and manner of approach was clamouring for immediate attention.

She spoke to me with a quiet acceptance of my visit, her own environment, and a backwash of authority which delighted me. She contrived, in that public ward, to surround one with the four walls of social security. It was only when I told her who I was that her manner became vulnerable and she answered me as though, if possessed of the physical strength, she would have forced herself upright on her pillow.

From then on it was she who was the questioner. It was her right. And her thanks, hurried in absently in parenthesis, for my thought for her, was evidently only tribute to ingrained courtesy. She was subtly my hostess, and, whether by politeness or impassioned interest, the family news must be heard by her; outlines of Vallants, Seagraves and Verdunes, while my eyes flicked to my wrist-watch and I cursed the ramifications of the clan.

I saw fairly soon that it was going to be wellnigh impossible to get from her that for which I had come. This was a woman, once more and for fifteen minutes transported to her own world and class, speaking its language. Also, she wished to talk and talk about mother, our home, James and Lalage and even me. And that too was her right.

Only once did I deliberately abandon manners and interrupt her.

'You remember my grandmother well, of course? She is still alive.'

No comment, only a pause. 'Does your dear mother see her often?'

I said yes, grimly enough, and then, quite desperately, for there were but a few minutes more, 'My elder sister is said to be very like aunt Myra.'

The pause was longer and her breathing heavier. And even then she put me at the disadvantage with another question:

'Does Mrs. Buchan speak much of your aunt?'

Well – I might as well let her have it and lay the foundations for our next meeting, leaving Miss Chilcot a week in which to assemble, remember and inform.

'No ... no, she doesn't. Never did. That's what I came to you about, Miss Chilcot. Grandmother is *harrying* mother, always has, I believe. I dislike her, and so does James ... oh, there's no *time* to tell you! ... she seems to leave the aunts alone. ...'

Miss Chilcot's small veined hands were clenched on the counterpane.

'She needs standing up to ... Lady Vallant.'

'Please! What? I can't hear you,' I implored.

'... I failed. I blame myself very bitterly for cowardice.'

'You! I know better!' I looked at her. 'Whatever you did was right.'

She flushed a very little. 'Thank you, my dear, but you're wrong ... you must tell me what it is you want of me.'

'Everything. I don't understand the situation. What really happened to Myra? Why is she never spoken about? The Verdunes ... aunt Emmeline has spoken of her to them ... *naturally*, you know ... but we're always treading on eggs. It's – getting on my nerves... if we were on the usual bad terms with mother it wouldn't matter. But we aren't. ...'

She was thinking. 'I'm so *sorry*. It's not right that you should be touched, as well, by it.' She followed another line of thought.

'Does your mother know you are seeing me?'

'No.'

'Ah! I don't like that.'

'You can't like it less than I do,' I flared, 'but if it's something about that cursed old Vallant woman that a little trouble and
horse-sense will –'

'S'sh!'

'I'm sorry, but we owe her *nothing*, except grudges.'

There was evidently a look on my face that got through to
her.

'I'm not at all surprised, only – pained. And – are you quite
sure you aren't making a mountain out of a molehill? ... Are
you not perhaps, expecting something sensational that mayn't be
there?'

'I've got to the stage when I'd almost rather it *were*. I'm standing the war and James at the war –'

'Would you believe me if I told you that I don't know about
your aunt Myra?' (even then she retained her ceremonial prefix-
es) 'that I was never altogether *sure*... I'm sorry, Miss Buchan, this
I'm afraid has upset me ... a little. Come and see me if you will
next week. I have much to decide. It's so difficult. Disloyalty ...
she *was* my employer... but it's your dear mother one must think
for. One isn't prepared to make mischief.'

The ghost of a hint has always brought me to my feet. In face
of this I left at once.

V

I walked slowly down the tiled passage, oppressed by self-re-
proach in that I had ignored Miss Chilcot all these years and
then only come into the remains of her life to add my trouble
to all hers. I had, as usual, forgotten to allow for the impinge-
ment of personality on my own, was already weakened by it in
my purpose, while the truth that I had only heard of her a few
months ago somehow made no difference at all. The fact, to me,
remained that she was always there, and that I had neglected her.
That I had made my entrance again at the wrong time in another's life and couldn't accept it hardily, or even help. And there
was the business of whether to give mother a chance to see her.
Miss Chilcot had never even hinted at that, which was possibly
characteristic. It would give immense, immediate, and probably
mutual pleasure; on the other hand, my sudden production of her

old governess would require full explanation, and my instinct was against it. Luckily, Miss Chilcot hadn't asked how I came to hear of her, had obviously taken for granted some stray Verdune gossip as having been my clue to herself. And I wished that the orange-and-black tiles of the floor wouldn't run together so, while the very air seemed to buzz like an electric bell. I knew I mustn't have any sort of collapse inside this building at any rate, or someone would send me home in a taxi and I might be betrayed into saying things.

I found a chair outside one of the wards and sat on it and was prudent about hanging my head down. Through the door I saw the doctor going his rounds, and later would enjoy the way he did it; even the Sister had to drop attendance on him in sheer panic for her dignity and deferential perquisites. He gave the impression of knowing the red-tapery and etiquettes of hospitals, of having served and scrapped them. He strolled but his eye assimilated: he hissed between his teeth or sang semi-sotto voce the hits from revues. One liked it because the old women did not patently adore him or turn wistfully to him or smile at him with pale, dim eyes of trust. They simply 'took him sitting' except for sundry bold crones who called out intimate details of their innards, upon which he merely said:

'Now then Mrs. Tuke, don't be gutsy.

> "*You're* here and *I'm* here,
>   So what do we care?
>   Li ta ta *tar* dee-dee dee. ..."

and then a sudden thump on to a chair and a stethoscope produced, and (without punctuation), 'You've had a quick one Sally you old fool I can smell it I don't mind if you don't but you'll have that pain till you stop no you can have half a pint with your dinner and bottled if you can run to it Oh I'll make it all right with Sister. What? It's absolute rotgut makes you see two of everything this wood alcohol.'

I would talk to him myself about Miss Chilcot. Also, this would give me an excuse for occupying my refuge, the chair, for a little longer.

He came out grasping leather gauntlets and newspaper and I hauled myself to my feet. 'May I speak to you a moment?'

'Certainly. In here,' and he crowded me into a small room opposite. 'Now then?'

'It's about Miss Chilcot.'

'Friend of yours?'

'My mother's old governess.'

He leant against a table, fluttering his eyelids in assent, a little personal trick that, somehow, reassured as to his attentiveness.

'I only discovered her existence by accident.'

'Yes, I know how it is. I may as well tell you she may go off any day now. It's a tragic story, these distressed gentlewomen are a great problem. Won't ask for help until it's too late to do anything.'

A wave of nausea swept over me. 'She was – starving?'

Again his eyelids fluttered assent. 'We've done all that's possible. These debility cases at her age are practically hopeless, and her people are no good. In the same boat themselves, I gather. I have an address to write to when she goes.'

'I wish to God we could have her with *us*, but I can't have my mother upset.'

'She's all right here, my wife often comes to see her, the old lady enjoys that. Trouble with this place is that there's hardly anyone of her class. The women aren't half bad sorts, most of 'em, but of course their language is a bit thick sometimes.'

'Is there anything at all I can do, or bring?'

'Just keep her petted. She might be glad of some books. Well ...' The interview was evidently at an end. His eye fell on me.

'You look as though a little attention wouldn't do you any harm. Like me to give you a look?'

'It's awfully good of you, but you see if there wasn't anything the matter, it would waste your time, and if there was I haven't time to cope with it.'

'Hah! What a refreshing point of view ... doing War work?'

'Nothing to speak of, I'm a sort of typist-cum-secretary thing.'

'Oh yes.' He was scribbling in a note-book. 'Might get that made up, take it three times a day after meals. It won't do you any good of course, but it'll buck you up.'

'I will indeed, and ...?' Why is it that this utterly artificial diffidence about fees is ever present, even when the man deals in them for his livelihood, and the woman lives by very shillings?

'Oh that's my treat,' he smiled at me, 'it ought to be a sort of greenish-yellow colour and taste foul; I always hate remembering prescriptions.'

I was entertained. 'Then perhaps you can tell me why doctors flip the backs of their knuckles on one's Collarbone?'

'There's a capital reason for that that'll come back to me one day. Meanwhile it looks well and does no harm at all. Oh well, I must be off. By the way my name's Filson.'

'Mine's Buchan, and thank you so very much.'

'Not 'tall. Good-bye.'

He was gone and I was sorry; I wanted him to stay and fool and perhaps tell me about his wife of whom I liked the sound, who must in point of fact be a jolly woman to have had the sense to marry him, and who was visionary enough to befriend Miss Chilcot. And who was I to expect it or anything?

I wondered suddenly what his version of Lady Vallant would be. Probably obtusely breezy, or treating her as a Freudian subject, only G.P.s probably didn't accept Freud, and indeed he must be an unprofitable line, compared with pills.

Meanwhile there was home to be got to and a long letter to James to be written, part of which asked, 'Can one throw Chilcot in Vallant's teeth?'

His answer: 'It wouldn't do much good and Vallant wouldn't care a damn. She wasn't compelled in any way to look after a gov's future, though I bet C. was sent packing for nothing in the first instance. ...'

CHAPTER XVII

I

ON THE MORNING after my visit to the workhouse Lady Vallant sent for mother, and for the moment I was shaken. It looked too like coincidence to please me. I even canvassed the possibility of Miss Chilcot having written to her, isolate, out of touch with the situation and full of misplaced Christian forbearance and Victorian sentiment; yet I remembered her face when I flung our grandmother into our talk, her voice, her silences. The Chilcot texture was of all time, and not to be pinned down to an epoch.

I said, 'I'll go, it's about my turn and a bit over,' and mother's expression was what I had foreseen, relieved, grateful and apprehensive.

As I turned into the square I planned, if necessary, to use Miss Chilcot, and then saw how impossible it was, in that Lady Vallant would take it out in oppressing mother, and so both of us. Miss Chilcot was evidently an unpopular subject in Lowndes Square. Never had the old woman more nearly given herself away before us than on that afternoon the governess had returned to say good-bye. Somehow, it must be a tussle between the three of us: James, the old woman and myself, a fight so obviously concentrated that no eccentric flight of even Vallant injustice could divert the blame to Lady Vallant's daughter.

II

And after all the old creature was only afraid of air-raids. She became positively human in her apprehensions. The effect on me would normally have been acquiescent, were I not fortified by mistrust. Also, I was antagonized and honestly surprised by her cowardice until a later sentence gave me the key to her uncharacteristic fears.

'One has read of these raids nearer the coast and of the deaths they have caused. But they do not always kill, but disfigure.' And even then I couldn't be sorry for her, for her vanity and loneliness and unloved existence. I tried to see her objectively, as a strikingly handsome old lady, a 'character', as all those things which (including age) I so admire. And it was no good at all.

She said, 'There is always prayer. Never forget that', which did not help matters along, with me. She added, with that arrogant oblivion of generations common to so many old people, 'Anne was always neglectful of religion'.

'Of set prayers, perhaps,' I answered sharply.

'Don't take me up like that. With your aunt Emmeline and with Sophia I had no trouble at all. ...'

She asked after James, and I said he was down for leave, which did not seem to gratify her.

'And your sister, Lalage?'

'She isn't very strong; the war seems to upset her more than most people.'

'A weak nature, probably over-indulged. Your mother was always too indulgent ... Lalage ought to marry and have half a dozen children, that would knock the nonsense out of her.'

'She is going to marry,' I said, trying to keep my temper and not show in my face what I felt about the briskly sadistic attitude to marriage. Our grandmother had had all her own children without anaesthetics, that was family history. But – was chloroform established in her own youth? And even if it were, wasn't her denial of it from social convention which was stronger than her vanity, or just from pointless, ignoble Vallant obstinacy? The woman who suffers unnecessary pain I have always thought abnormal. It might account for much, in my grandmother. ...

'Ah yes, the barrister ... And you? I hope you're not fast?'

I could have laughed aloud.

'I aim to please,' I answered. She was attacking me and so no riposte mattered.

'To please, of course; you should learn to manage men. I hope Anne is seeing that you meet suitable people.'

I did crack at that. 'Would you say that on our income and in our house much entertaining was possible?'

'Not so loud! It worries me. You should be married, too. You are getting on, looking worn, and I dislike your hat, dear ... Our class needs children.'

I was getting tired of the old woman. This was just unprofitable babble; it would take a Doctor Filson to cope with her in this commonplace, betwixt-and-between mood ('Now then, Susan old dear, we've had about enough of you, what?'). I said, almost without glancing at it, 'What a beautiful satin that is', and struck a chord at once.

'It is one of Grainger's, of South Molton Street. They are reliable, they have always made for me. Your grandfather admired their cut,' she rose slowly. 'Come to my room and we shall see if you have taste in dress. I am giving a dinner-party to-night.'

I smiled as I followed the little toiling figure upstairs. Very Vallantish, that item of news, softened by no half-apology for our own exclusion from the feast, decorated with no further explanation.

Her bedroom – the only room apart from dining- and drawing-room into which I had ever been shown, brought back memories of old luncheons and of us three children removing coats, hats and gaiters.

It was the same as ever: as mother had once said, like a hotel room. Dead. One wondered which of the aunts had been born in that large brass bed, and spared a passing pang for the little thing that was our mother first seeing the light in the meaningless square of space. The furniture, good, even fine, could achieve no effect, being placed with no regard for its period whatsoever, a mental attitude that brought a splendid mahogany cupboard, ripe and beaded, as neighbour to a Victorian table of Tonbridge ware, like a mosaic brooch a thousand times enlarged; the walnut tallboy was scarred all down one side. Upon it the maid (I had seen it) struck matches. Coals were shovelled from a Cromwellian cellarette. 'No taste, and no feeling for beautiful things. She never had,' mother had once told us. 'She used to twist up Baxter prints to light the gas with; they were stacked anyhow in an old portfolio and we used to paste them on to the nursery screen.'

But the press containing Lady Vallant's dresses occupied an entire wall space; it was polished and properly kept. The shrine. Its doors, opened by the maid, revealed serried lines of velvet, lace and silk, cloaks and furs. Many of the gowns seemed to me to be hung in strata of various periods. My grandmother was evidently a hoarder. I even caught sight of a tiny fringed and jointed parasol at the back.

My eye turned to the dressing-table. Modern stuff, very modern, and new since my own childhood, with triple mirror. The pots and jars dotted all over it would have done credit to an actress, and all rendered futile by the raucous cross-lights from the never-superceded incandescents which cast a greenish tinge upon our faces as in an aquarium, and probably accounted for the maid's heavy hand in *maquillage*. The one electric bulb in my own bedroom had, heaven knew, given me similar difficulties!

Meanwhile, the maid was looking at me with respectful, tentative curiosity and Lady Vallant threw her a 'Stand aside', and to me, 'Now!'

It was part of the hit-or-miss of life that our *rapprochement* should take place over clothes, a factor with which it had never occurred to me to reckon. There was nothing seriously the matter with my own taste except perhaps for a rather engrained tendency to dwell upon the softnesses of Liberty, and I had no objection to a temporary armistice with Lady Vallant over anything which kept her off the family's bones. My opportunities had been scanty, as the odd man out of us three Buchan grandchildren I had until now remained outside her interest, which James commanded as an eye-taking male, and that curiosity, furtive and baffling, which fell to Lalage's share, and which as the years passed appeared to be degenerating into an assured sort of contempt, easy to confuse with that mild insolence that prevails among close relations, but upon which I had ever kept watch. ...

I would tell Lady Vallant exactly what I thought, whatever the upshot. On the whole it is safer to be yourself in all circumstances; one loses by it often but the gains are incalculable. I have so often noticed when tempted to shout with the immediate crowd that if you can refrain, your character – the sum of your outlook – as it were 'comes round' again, like fashions, and then you are entirely right with yourself and the world as well.

As for the clothes, I couldn't help being interested in them for their colour and texture and their atmosphere.

I touched, rejected and criticized, giving reasons for and against, seeing them always in relation to Lady Vallant, foreseeing her effect in them upon her guests. I carefully handled frills of lace any one of which would have paid three times over for everything I myself would wear that night. I was dining with Raymond Owen and must assemble my best. And my grandmother watched me, almost human, yet ever on the alert to reprove an imagined carelessness. She offered me nothing from the loot of cupboard or jewel-boxes and I didn't expect it. Between whiles I was intensely conscious of her, of the misleadingly intimate nature of our surroundings; thinking intermittently how easy it would be to say something personal to her, some near-friendly appreciation of her features, and how for ever impossible! Impossible because she was set in her ways, I in my mind towards her, and the room in its past. Also, the visit was passing off well, unusually so, and no unconsidered remark must be let fall.

And so I gowned her with tongue and eye and received in exchange considerably more than I had mentally bargained for. She suggested – it was, rather, in the nature of a statement – that I should come and stay with her 'if these air-raids are worse'. And under all the arrogance and self, I seemed to sense for the first time a trace of human dismay, a touch of family feeling however belated and against which I should probably harden my heart.

Going home I reconsidered this. It might be to the good that I got into Vallant House as an inmate, unless, of course, the house was too far gone to appreciate it, in which case the conflict between us would be a to-the-finish affair, inimical and mutually pitiless.

III

That night I was wearing a dress which had at least given us a lot of fun in the making. I had had the idea for it on emerging from a prolonged wallowing in the Elizabethan period, when the notabilities seemed to specialize (particularly for State processions) in costumes 'pounced' and 'powdered' with fleurs-de-lis. No dress-making journal had anything at all to say about powdering, and there was a conspiracy of silence upon the subject of the pounce. Mother, Lalage and I put on designs whenever we felt like it (and I once found that Lalage had included in a fold a tiny cat's head with 'Penny' on the collar).

I had long ago given up trying to be smart and current in my dress, and modern hats have a way of making me look conspicuously absurd.

But Owen would like my appearance. I was at that stage in his regard when nearly everything I did was right. It would be restful, after Lady Vallant, to be approved.

I suppose it was that I was satisfied with my dress, self-satisfied with my management of the afternoon with the old lady and with my Chilcot prospects that, quite suddenly, I told Owen about the affair. I expected a comment of method and downrightness, with its edges rounded off because the speaker cared for me personally. I wondered that this source of help hadn't occurred to me before, but the business of becoming attracted had taken time, and the healing of being liked I had enjoyed as long as possible – one is only human. But I judged that by now we had arrived at that comfortable middle stage, after glamour and before ennui, which would permit confidence.

With an automatic remnant of caution I shot a glance at myself in the nearest mirror. Hair all right so far, face – in spite of Lady Vallant – not looking its age to-night, and I had just arrived at the problem of Lalage when Owen said quite kindly, 'Can't you forget your blessed family for *one* evening?'

I V

I answered 'Of course' very cheerfully, and I believe I laughed. I certainly remembered that his money would pay for the dinner, wine and tips, and knew that it should be for the last time. If I had consistently paid for myself, I might have also bought the right to a little plain English as well. ...

He said, 'Hullo, there's old Cosmo Furnival over there. How he does go on and on'.

I followed his look with a backwash of schoolgirl curiosity. Raking the large room, my eye again caught my reflection in the mirror and I saw that between my attempt at confidence and its reception effects had been produced which would have justified my grandmother's criticism. I was quite pleased about it; enjoyed with perverse jauntiness the fact that my light and careful make-up now looked patchy and haggard and that my dress suddenly resembled something left over from the greenery-yallery epoch of peacock's feather and Passionate Brompton.

I recognized Furnival at once, after all the years. I have a knack of penetrating disguises, and this time his was the more tricky one of everyday life and evening dress. He was in a corner with a party of unidentifiable people; tall, I could see his iron head above the rest as he listened and took his coffee and detached his monocle to polish it on his handkerchief. I wondered where poor little Gladys was, and wished most heartily she could be in my place – Cosmo Furnival looked up then and over towards our table and I was sourly amused that if indeed he saw me, he was seeing me at my worst.

I murmured 'Posing old fathead' quite meaninglessly, because I was hurt with Owen.

'He often comes here. Like to meet him?' Owen was already raising an eyebrow at our waiter for the bill.

'No thanks. Why should I?'

It pleased him, and I was in the mood which takes a confused and slavish pleasure in giving satisfaction, anyhow and anywhy.

That should have been the end of Owen, for me, but it wasn't. Apparently, everything in one can't be killed at once, and if the imaginary best goes, the second best remains.

On another night we went on to a club that Owen assured me was the last thing in this and that. It seemed to me to be singularly like the restaurant we had left, minus the good food, wine and service, but being over-suggestible, I began to see it through his eyes at once, and actually got a certain horrified elation out of dancing with a stranger, though I had a Victorian-Edwardian voice in my ear which dowdily informed me that this was not nice. I could almost see the face of the voice, and annoyingly enough – for was I not enjoying myself and being modern and seeing life? – I could grin at it without feeling in my real self that the voice was being ridiculous at all. I bowed to it and succumbed to the present and was a failure with both. It was evidently my fault that I had to go on telling myself that in this L-shaped room we were all being very daring and having the time of our lives; nor on the other hand could I rid myself of the fixed notion that the place was a den of iniquity, and yet all round me were dazzling children, ten years my junior, who danced and murmured and drank and generally carried on, if not with obvious pleasure, at least with an air of knowing all the ropes in the rigging. Theirs were lives as slick, easy and effortless – and as soulless – as a service flat. One envied, yet one deplored.

I discovered that I knew very little even about myself. A man's voice behind me asked his partner if she was coming back to his digs for the night, and my only sensations were an interested listening for her answer, which was drowned in the crashing of 'When We've Wound Up The Watch on the Rhine', plus a slight surprise at the essentially inconsiderate nature of the invitation given to a girl without toothbrush, pyjamas or suit-case with day clothes inside – an aspect of illicit dalliance which is eternally evaded by the novelists, who at this point always shelter behind a smokescreen of asterisks.

Yet when a baby-faced creature of seventeen squealed that her sandwich was bloody nasty, I was shocked.

The Vallants don't know how to play. That side of them was probably my share of the family kink. I put my elbows on the little table, three inches from a bottle of champagne which had its ration of gold foil round the neck and a traditionally-shaped cork but no label, and which had cost thirty-seven and six, and reflected that if aunt Emmeline were in the room her reactions would be terribly similar to my own, except that she had the courage of her convictions, and would leave. Hearty obtuseness and innocence would rescue the Seagraves who would enjoy it all enormously, while aunt Sophia would be amply capable of going round the room collecting introductions and towing the hypnotized males up to her daughters.

Mother …

She would see through the whole thing at a glance, sit there tolerating, and contrive to make the room a temporary home out of two chairs, one table and a bottle.

The small band, with a preliminary tap on the trapdrum, began to play:

> Jus' see those tip-collectors,
> Those upper-berth inspectors,
> Those Pullman Porters on parade!

Owen was revelling in it all, delightedly trotting in the arms of a very pretty coloured girl who had snaffled him with an easy directness worthy of the Verdunes! I watched them benevolently, thought 'That's "living in the moment", and I can't do it'.

I took out my little engagement diary and furtively did sums. The night's work seemed to be going to make ten pounds look uncommonly foolish for my poor Owen, but I did contrive to fend off a waiter who tried to whip away our quarter-finished bottle and palm a fresh one on to the table. That was nearly two pounds to the good. All this was amazingly tiring. There seemed to be no ventilation at all, and I hoped I wasn't going to be a wet blanket by looking ill, and began to paint a fresh face on, a thing I'd never done in public before because the cynicism of the act always offends me, but here it was merely conspicuous not to.

Not that Owen would notice if one were ill, or if he did it would only annoy him. It is important not to be tiresome.

V

A woman of quite seventy-five jogged past me in a picked little two-step, neat as a thrush's, and if the very young man supporting her were her grandson, the family resemblance was even less marked than usual. She had a heavy make-up – it looked more like greasepaint than the uniform of powder, rouge and lipstick; her wrinkled eyelids were smudged with grey-blue above and below so that the result suggested ill-treatment rather than allure, and her withered lips were too indeterminate to derive advantage from red outlines.

A lieutenant, swinging by, was knocked into by her shoulder and cried, 'Hah beldam! Methinks thou art astray!' and she becked at him, pleased.

I was furious, and putting out my foot, managed to send him sprawling.

I have heard so many people brutally mocking these old dancing women; but why should they not take pleasure where they find it? The worst that any of their denouncers have ever been able to say is that it is undignified, but isn't loss of dignity deplorable at any age? And at least they dance for pleasure and not for home and husbands – like the Seagraves! If it comes to that, I have never been able wholeheartedly to despise the gigolo, who, apart from sundry repellent but strictly personal characteristics, seems to me to be supplying a businesslike demand as useful and definite of its kind as one of Cook's couriers. The woman without a background has a thin time, at any age, and if she can afford to pay for partner, escort and attention, roundly and sensibly, why not? 'Then she can pay a woman companion', seems to be the answer to this, and the fact that the elderly, salaried *âme damnée* is not only not the same thing at all, but positively labels and shelves her employer as an unwanted left-over in the keen eyes of commissionaires, waiters, staff and guests with their terrible power of giving or withholding comfort, good time and dignity is alluded to by nobody. And if I have made up my mind never to be an enamelled harridan, but to relapse, rather, into lace and lavender or epigrams and gout, it is not because I believe that all gigolos are perverts – poor tired wretches! – or that all their old women expect to sleep with them at least once, but because London night life for women opened its doors just in time for me to be young in it myself, and to see and feel the dreadful intolerance of youth to age, its thoughtlessness and easy failures in penetration.

Dance, little old ladies! And indeed you're enjoying it more than we are!

You've worked for it by ordeal of basement mansion, tyrannical mate, over-large family and atrophy of your unsuspected brain; by male contempt for you at thirty, by hansom that was Fast and bicycle that was Unwomanly and vote that was Unsexing, and pretty legs that were never seen. And if ever James has a son, we'll bring him up to appreciate old women and, at worst, to see them for the sad forlornities they really are under the paint – and belike to scrape some of it off before taking them a jaunt. And I thought that if ever I own a large house, I will have routs galore for nice, mellow, crusted old couples, and encourage them to flirt, delicately, and revive old flameships, and manœuvre those who should have married each other and married somebody else into adjacent gilt chairs, and watch them gently savouring mulled burgundy. And there shall be partners aplenty for all those whose dancing days were very numbered in youth, and who never tasted life or kiss or look because their noses were snub or their ankles thick – the eternal Harriets and Miss Chilcots of life. And if it takes half a glass too much to make them burgeon, burgeon they shall, and the snub nose shall be discovered to have a talent for brilliant mimicry, and the ankles a gift of repartee, and Miss Chilcot, urged to the piano, silences us, happily, with her voice which nobody guessed at because her complexion was 'poor', and anyway there were six sisters to educate.

And there will be no marriage or giving in marriage, but plenty of flirtation and giving in flirtation, and no jazz bands at all.

Perhaps a quadrille or two, and a waltz, and the Lancers after supper. And at twelve-thirty, my private fleet of hansoms, jingling, shall arrive for the hard-up guests, and clop from my door full of dears called Adrian and Julian and Cosmo and Lydia and Carlyon, and similarly pleasantly preposterous names.

'Mr. Carlyon's carriage stops the way!'

'The maid for Miss Virtue, Miss.'

'A little foggy to-night, Sir Cosmo.'

'May I have the pleasure of seeing you home, Miss Chilcot?'

Ah me! What good times there are in the world for every-body, and they're being missed right and left for the stupidest reasons.

VI

It was about the time when I was thinking that we ought to go, I to the home, hot-water bottle and book I was longing for, that a woman came and sat at our table and said, 'I've been watching you for ten minutes', a compliment I could not return as the room had long been too packed for the study of types.

She was one of those small-boned, ultra-fair women with tonged-looking hair, who always contrive, without having it, to suggest tuberculosis, and upon whose fragile chests even the min-imum of jewellery appears excessive. The passée chorus girl who was never on the stage: the consumptive who never coughed.

I did polite things with my eyebrows, and she said, 'You're here with Raymond, so you needn't lie about it. Well, I'm Mrs. Owen.'

I said, 'Oh yes?' civilly. My heart was thumping, not, as I knew she assumed, out of panic, but because I dreaded a public scene. I sat, weighing the chances in the light of my experience of James's houris.

'Never occurred to you that he was married, eh?'

'I never gave it a thought.'

I hadn't. Such a likelihood had, of course, presented itself to my mind, but Owen had made no allusion from the start to his home affairs, and one just doesn't say 'Are you married or single?' any more than one asks 'What is your income?' More young women of my class get into this type of mess through misplaced courtesy than is commonly realized. Added to which, I had had no designs upon Owen of any description, except for under-standing, soothing, and the bolstering up of my never too robust self-confidence.

'"It's the war" of course,' she added with a brisk spite which somehow daunted one. 'How long has this been going on?'

I suppose if I had been older or cleverer, or anything not my-self, I should have riposted 'How long has what been going on?' I didn't, and doubt if I should even now, because I knew exactly what she meant.

I answered, 'I've known Mr. Owen for about seven months. We first met through my work; he wanted a substitute typist and my office sent me.'

'Oh … of course.'

And even that I understood. The typist and the wealthy em-ployer and the chase-me-Charlie preliminaries ending in the night-club. The case was so complete, the picture so perfect, that I could have laughed aloud, except when I remembered the nu-merous small presents that Owen had tried to give me and that I had always refused from the first, and of which one must say nothing at all, and when I thought of the procession of chain-tea-shops we had sat in during those first weeks, places chosen because they were near the office and over whose marble-topped tables letters could be signed as we ate our tepid muffins. Indeed, it was probably those qualities in myself least likely to appeal to his wife which had first made Owen focus me as a person; the facts that I was punctual, fairly accurate, didn't suck sweets while he was dictating or comb my hair all over his desk, and that I set my face against books, scent and chocolates, never said 'Pardon me' and 'Go on!' and hadn't a breach of promise look in my eye.

I had liked him well, after working a fortnight for him; en-joyed vicariously all that massive authority: bluff though some of it probably was, it was what I needed after the delicate family atmosphere. And having reached a certain stage of mutual liking, I imagine that the rest had followed with him through goodness knows what of domestic dissatisfaction about which, again, one made no enquiries.

'And you're in love with him, of course?'

'No.' I couldn't tell her that if there had ever been a chance of that, Owen had killed it stone dead in his attitude to Lalage. It baffled her to silence, and I wasn't experienced enough to take any advantage of the lull although I would answer any questions. The story, as Americans say 'listened badly', and I knew it. In this sort of situation neither prosecution nor defence can usually prove anything, and there is nothing left but words, and the nature of those, again, depends upon character and temperament. But I put up a flurried petition that whatever was going to occur might end at myself and not overflow into my home.

Mrs. Owen found her husband with her eye and saw the coloured girl.

'Seems he's left you, now.'

'Yes.'

She was fishing about in a sea of assorted angers, hesitating which to hook first, and then the music stopped with an affected, dissonant wail, Owen smoothly stranded his partner, hurried up to me and saw his wife with a slight start into which anyone might be betrayed if confronted with an unexpected and familiar face.

I got up and said I would go 'unless anybody wants me to stay'. It seemed that nobody did, and we all stood there trying not to catch each other's eye while I struggled, unaided, into my cloak and collected what seemed to be endless personal trifles from the table: handkerchief, cigarette case, matches, diary – I felt like an under-rehearsed parlourmaid on the first night of a cocktail comedy. Mrs. Owen's voice came to me through the confusion of the minute.

'Yes, I think you'd better, you dirty little thing.'

It was, I suppose, rather similar to a blow in the face from a fist. For a blessed second or two I couldn't take in the words, then, realizing, was unable to believe that this had actually been said to me.

At the outer door I found Owen by my side. He had 'seen me off', I'll say that for him, and was obviously furious in a red, suppressed kind of way.

'Vere, I can't say how sorry I am I've let you in for this.'

'It would have been fairer, I suppose, to have warned me,' I said, mechanically. I was stupid with shock and fatigue. The commissionaire watched us tentatively and hopefully.

'I'll see Madam O. apologizes.'

'No. No, Raymond, let it alone for heaven's sake, you'll only make it worse. Let it all rip. Good-night.'

CHAPTER XVIII

I

FIVE DAYS LATER I was walking down the Infirmary passage. Every now and again I sank my nose into the huge bunch of flowers I had bought for Miss Chilcot; their scent drowned the smell of chill efficiency and carbolic. They had been paid for with Owen's money, the balance due to me when I cleared out of his office for good. He had given my agency an excellent testimonial in which he 'greatly regretted being unable to offer Miss Buchan a permanent place on his staff', and I kept a poker face while Miss Royal purred over it.

'That's so nice, Miss Buchan. I always say that there's nothing, if you know what I mean, like sending out ladies. They never make difficulties. Always able to cope… and really, you'd be surprised what can go on in offices … I don't mean in a really *nasty* way, but *awkward*.'

'Rather a good epitaph to an employer,' I suggested, '"He was lovely and pleasant in his life and in death he was not Nasty but Awkward".' But, internally, I was not amused. I was worried about my apparent continued capacity for being hurt. It is disabling when there is work to be done, and although my feeling for Owen had hardly earned the right to grief, he had done his best to put me in the way of grief by encouraging waste emotion in his own snatch at happiness. I ought to be used to that, by now. But it shook one's faith in general kindliness.

The Sister was barring the ward door in a rather extra manner, it dawned on me; she must have recognized me, or this was just another slick weaving of red tape.

'I'm sorry to tell you that Miss Chilcot passed away yesterday afternoon.'

There was my Doctor Filson, and I heard myself repeating his name.

'Doctor Filson is not here.'

'But he'll be round soon! I can wait.'

One would wait endlessly. I felt that nobody but this whistling, crosstalking man with the fluttering eyelids – half healer, half comedian — would do. For me, this time. All he was and knew, for myself alone, if I only possessed it for five minutes. And this woman was looking prim and offended.

'You can see Doctor Cavanagh if you like.'

I threw chicanery to the dogs. 'Sister, where is Doctor Filson? I ... I promise you nobody but him will do.'

Perhaps it is that one is urgent and uncontrolled so seldom that when one does let go, one's demands have a special significance; anyway, I won, if you could call it winning.

'Doctor Filson has joined up.'

'Oh, my God!'

For a second I even thought of running for comfort to his wife. They say that husbands and wives often grow to resemble each other and was it too much to expect that Mrs. Filson, through life with the doctor, should have acquired some of his strengths?

But I remembered that she was Mrs. Filson, and that wives don't help one.

The Sister, more than ever the official because I had sworn in her passage, said 'Miss Chilcot had some things for you, and a letter. You may use one of the nurse's sitting-rooms to go through them in. Come this way please'. She handed me over to a young ward maid who brought in the 'things' and my letter and asked me to ring for her before leaving and left me.

11

Before reading the letter I had to go round the room, getting a line on it. I can never settle to anything until I am on some terms or other with the four walls which enclose me.

This little place had nothing much to say; it was neat and civil and a little chilly, like the nurses who used it. I chose one of the three chairs — a padded rocker — and opened the envelope. The letter was a long one, and Miss Chilcot must have written it over several days. Indeed, the opening date was that on which we had first seen each other.

It was a letter enormously characteristic of the writer, confirming, to me, the impression I had received at once: that in no circumstances could Alma Chilcot ever be ridiculous. So, in the

closely-written sheets, I could derive no amusement from her little archaic turns of sentence, her points of view about trifles, her
Victorian underlinings of the unexpected word or the sprinkling
of unnecessary capital letters which caught the eye everywhere.
'My dear Miss Buchan,

'I suspect it is Possible that I may not be here when you
kindly visit me again, but the doctor is so kind that I cannot read
his *real thought*.

'I have been thinking of you so much, and of That Matter
you spoke of, and it is Difficult to write about as I feel that I may
convey Wrongful impressions in a letter which a word would set
right when I am no longer there to speak it. In any case, Dear
Girl, I have tried to be Kind and I am sure you will remember
that.

'I told you that I failed with your Grandmother. Miss Buchan
the reason was that I could not endure my *situation*, tho' indeed I
tried to stay on for the sake of your dear Mother and your Aunt
Myra. I fear that Lady Vallant made it Hard for me to remain
on that *account*. She is a bad woman, a bad mother and a wicked
Christian. I could not pray with her, in Vallant House, and pre-
sumed to tell her why. Her anger was very terrible, but God gave
me strength and I said my Prayers for those unhappy children in
my own room.

'This escape was not possible to Them, and it was a habit of
Lady Vallant to make Anne and Myra leave their beds and come
to a sort of Confession. She once made Myra stand for an hour
in the cold with only her nightgown on, for some childish fault.
It was half an hour before, by chafing her feet, I was able to warm
the child. It was the sound of her tears that brought me to her side.

'Tuesday.

'Your Grandmother thought much of worldly Things and of
her *person* and dress, and your aunts and uncles suffered from this
in *many* ways. I have often seen your aunts and your mother sent
out in clothes utterly unbecoming their Station, and in this respect, Myra and Anne were the worst treated. Even your Grandfather commented upon it, but to no avail. Sir Frederick could
do nothing – about anything, and I feel sure that this Soured him.
He and the children might have loved each other, else. As it was,

I think he could not but be reminded of his failure in authority as head of the house whenever he met them at Prayers or on the staircase. I never heard him address an affectionate word to any, tho' he once gave Emmeline a shilling on her birthday.

'The strain upon sensitive children was Very Great. I myself was one of a large family which had to practise drastic Economy through our straitened means, but should have been *ashamed* to let any child of mine be so improperly clad.

'I did what I could for them with my needle in my spare time, and was sometimes enabled to effect improvements. I did not dare attempt too much lest Lady Vallant notice.

'Miss Buchan, that was not all. They were not properly *nourished*, especially in sickness. The dishes, at best, came to the schoolroom from the dining-room and were thus never hot or punctual (the schoolroom was at the top of the house), but far more often the diet was different from that of Sir Frederick and your Grandmother. Even the butler (Hutchins) was *indignant*, but it was impossible to complain to the servants. They did *what they liked* unless it was a dining-room matter

'*Wednesday.*

'when nothing was suffered amiss by Lady Vallant, and in the time I was in her service I never saw a luxury upon the children's trays. Many a time I have slipped out to buy them little tempting morsels and strong Soups, which the butler would most kindly heat for me in his own pantry if our schoolroom fire was low. Thus it came that Hutchins and I were led into an association which, tho' not Right, I cannot regret, and would do again. He saw that just complaints could not be made to the kitchen, for the fact is that your Grandmother led her servants such a life of it that they seemed to retaliate on the children, where they knew they were safe.

'For the least thing which *displeased* her, Lady Vallant would deprive the children of a Meal. My dear, they were growing girls and not robust – especially Myra. I often wrote to my Mother for advice as to their welfare and care.

'Hutchins told me much. If he is still at Vallant House, you *can trust him*, believe me. He is a good man.

'He said that when your aunt Sophia had the Pneumonia (the draughts in the schoolroom were very bad) your Grandmother came to enquire for her but once. But S. was very hardy, so, I think, was Emmeline. I could tell it in their attitude to that house. Sophia even under my charge talked quite openly of an early Marriage for herself, which, tho' I discouraged as being immodest, I could not but see was for her happiness. Emmeline resembled your Grandmother closely, would seem to obey and go her own way. Lady Vallant had respect for this, that is why it is Important that if ever *you* should be in unhappiness from Lady V., you should understand this. Be *brave*. I was not. I should think you were, from my sight of you. You have, I am sure, had a happy home life, my dear child, and that gives courage.

'Later.

'From the first I found myself devoted to your mother and Myra. Pity, it is very true, is akin to love. I showed it – unwisely, as I see now – not knowing your Grandmother as I was to later. She made things terribly difficult for me, and on at least one occasion I spoke my mind. I would have done so to the end but that it made life worse for those Two Dear Children.

'My dear, Myra was lame from birth – did you know? Her hip, I think. She walked always with a slight limp and felt it most keenly. Your Grandmother made many a joke about her gait, when angry. Anne protected her whenever *possible*, and Lady Vallant (if one dare say so of a mother about her child) disliked Anne. It was as tho' any love in that house was cause for suspicion. It Brought them into *deceit* for which I could not blame or chide them. They never lied to *me*. Their every motive was misunderstood, and once when Myra timidly embraced Lady Vallant, she repulsed her, saying, "what are you trying to get out of me?"

'Since, I have often thought that your Grandmother provoked the children in order to punish them. I suspect that her treatment of Anne was due to Anne's loving care of Myra.

'As for Myra, it is unbelievable that anyone could have disliked the child, but I am sure your Grandmother hated her. I have thought and thought, and I can only suppose that she was either *Envious* of the girl's looks or contemptuous of her *infirmity*. Pride or vanity, I do not know. I should ask God's forgiveness for these wicked thoughts, but shall not. He knows, and will strike in His good time. I have heard that Mother mock her child before the servants.

'Thursday.

'While I was there, your Aunt Emmeline came out into Society. A Ball was given for her by friends across the Square. Sophia, tho' only seventeen, was allowed to go as well, and the girls wore the only stylish gowns I had ever seen upon their backs. Even your Grandmother realized that they must be suitably clad. They looked most handsome, and quite *irradiated* the old schoolroom, tho' I ever preferred the faces of *my* two charges.

'For days before the Event Myra talked to Anne and myself of the *gaiety* in store for her sisters. She attached an altogether disproportionate importance to the Ball and I enquired the reason.

'It seemed that the poor little thing believed that it was a kind of Freedom and Happiness which befell young ladies at eighteen, and she would reckon the months – even the hours – that she herself had yet to wait. I think she even believed that on that Day her Mother would *change*, and love her. She was just over fifteen years of age.

'My dear Child, it is about this matter that I really feel I am not entitled to write. As I told you, I was never quite sure.

'Emmeline and Sophia had gone downstairs, your Grandmother was receiving gentlemen in the drawing-room– she did not, so far as I know, see the Girls off. She displayed no interest even in her own daughter's coming out Ball. I was writing to my Mother in the schoolroom, describing the unusual gaiety for her benefit. Anne and Myra in their nightgowns ran to the stair head and Anne, ever the more daring, crept to the drawing-room flight with her sister. I blame myself for not stopping them but was always rejoiced for them to have a pleasure however small and they wished to secure a last glimpse of your Aunts in their finery. Anne laughed with pleasure and made some admiring Comment and Lady Vallant heard and quitted the d. room. I could distinguish no *words*, only that she was in one of her rages, and my heart sank. Then came a cracking sound and a cry – two cries, I think. I hurried down the stairs to see Myra in the arms of one of the gentlemen who brought her to the schoolroom. Lady V.

would not have her in the drawing-room. A Doctor was instantly
fetched by another gentleman. He held out v. little hope. My
little Myra had received a spinal injury and lingered, I believe, for
the inside of one year.

'I never once heard your Mother discuss the Tragedy with
her sisters, save in a general way. It seemed as tho' Anne were
dumb, yet she was always ready with a laugh and a joke in Myra's
room where I had to *command* myself not to give way many a
time. All I can say of the weeks which elapsed after the Accident
is that at least Myra was largely beyond the reach of her mother's harshness, for Lady V. soon relinquished her to my care and
the Doctor's visits. To the relief of us all she seldom visited the
schoolroom floor, and was entertaining much at this time and
often out at receptions. If she ever came to the patient's room,
Myra would weep at the sound of her step.

'It made one's heart ache to see how few comforts and dis-
tractions Myra had. I did what I could. And after a while, the
bad *service* reasserted itself with trays of unappetizing food quite
unsuitable to an invalid. It was over this that I attacked Lady Vallant; I lost control of myself and spoke to her as no woman should
to her Mistress, and to my amazement was not instantly dismissed.
I believe that she *did* once actually inspect the schoolroom food
provided, but this led to a great deal of Unpleasantness and even
impertinence towards myself from the Cook and maids. You can
have no idea of the atmosphere of violence and anger which
seemed to envelop that most unhappy home. At last I could endure it no more, it was affecting the nerves and health. Lady V., in
paying me my salary, remarked that from the first I had stirred up
strife and that I was far too indulgent in the schoolroom.

'My h'writing is becoming terribly shaky and bad. I sh'd not
speak of this to your dear Mother. It can do no good to open
old wounds. It occurs to me that Lady Vallant is, as you put it,
"harrying" your Mother *on your account*, trying to discover if you
three children have ever been told the Truth about her. This may
be *conscience* or a desire not to alienate her own Grandchildren.
Anne has probably made her no promise of silence. Anne never
breaks her word. Indeed, there was plenty to tell you all, apart
from Myra.

'In case we never meet again, God bless you all. If I have pained you, as I know I must have, forgive me. "Doubt is a greater mischief than Despair" and the truth sets free. I have told you what I know.

'Yours very sincerely
'Alma Chilcot.'

Somebody, I began to remember, had told me to ring for them; I am fairly certain I made no attempt to do so, yet the Sister was suddenly in the room with me. Incredible woman! she was all kindness and humanity.

'My dear girl! you mustn't give way so! I assure you your friend didn't suffer at the end.' She was speaking, then, over her shoulder to some underling, 'Hysterical. Bit overstrained, evidently', and a vile-tasting sedative was given to me. I had got to that stage when one literally has no control over one's features and precious little over one's conduct, the stage in which one's normal self sits watching the amateur dramatic exhibition and wondering what is going to happen next. One's manners, it seems, are the last thing to go by the board. I managed apologies and disclaimers of illness, and luckily the whole affair was attributed to Miss Chilcot's death. They mopped me up and dosed me and spoke me fair, and I began to deal with Miss Chilcot's 'things'.

There was a writing-case, very worn, which I would keep as a souvenir, a pair of real lace cuffs and a collar – these I would sell for her sisters, a copy of the Hampshire photograph which I already possessed and the usual trickle of little possessions, the deckings of many an alien mantelpiece and chest of drawers, efforts after the home atmosphere which all governesses make, and there was a packet marked *Anne made these for Myra*. Inside was a family of paper dolls coloured in chalk.

I thought I was over my temporary loss of control. Holding the dolls to my cheek I found I was wrong.

III

Anger works in various ways. I reckoned up my chances with it, guessed that when I had come through collapse I should settle down to the fury which is not fire but ice. Forgiveness and softening were out of the question. Some hates are holy things;

the Vallants are good haters, and I hoped I was as good as the best of them.

CHAPTER XIX

I

IF JAMES HAD NOT come home on leave at this period I hardly know how I could have carried on. And quite apart from the presence of him and its relief, there was the rock-bottom duty of helping him to knock up a good time. He relied on me for this, I on him to keep his hand on Vallantry. We didn't fail each other. It had its funny side. By now our Vallant items had grown to formidable size, and much of his leave was an overlapping of indignation and outings, rage and revues, dinners and denunciation – at times we hardly knew what to snatch at first. At some musical comedy, James, ostensibly drinking in the plugged waltz refrain, said quite loudly 'But the old woman's a sadist!', and once or twice we left the theatre in the middle of the show to walk the streets discussing our grandmother.

At other times, James would study my face quickly and say 'We can only knock out Vallant by shock tactics', and he took me to tea at the Ritz or the Carlton (I forget which) carrying a string bag bulging with a tin of golden syrup and a bunch of watercress 'just to see if one could do that kind of thing', and we ate it zoo-ishly under the incredulous eyes of the head waiter and our own man. We were literally a sensation, as James had expected, and the feeling was horrible. But he was right; it had dislodged Lady Vallant for an appreciable time, and is a method I can vouch for, if I cannot recommend it to the squeamish. I once knew a man who cured himself of melancholia by putting £200 out of a Bank balance of £350 on the Derby. His action so shocked him that it drove away his bogeys, and a girl we all know, on being presented at Court, was so ill with nerves that she nearly fainted; she was on the verge of losing consciousness and just managed to lean forward to some dowager sitting by her daughter and to stammer, quite untruly, 'I think your dress is fussy and unbecoming'. In the whispered melee that followed the faintness was forgotten for the whole evening.

11

When I showed James the Chilcot letter he had much ado not to break down, for which (like Kipling's subaltern with his Colonel) I respected him. I was thankful to see that in regard to affairs of peace the war hadn't calloused his mind, although he did his best (as I had done) to be robust about the whole thing.

He said, 'All this happened over forty years ago. It's no worse because we know of it for the first time. It was an accomplished fact when we were at our happiest.'

All true – and all no good as consolation, and he knew it. There is no time in grief. Once more we were back, but reinforced a hundredfold, at our dreadful habit of spying upon mother: trying to read her face in the light of our greater knowledge, knowing the action for the futility it was, and quite unable to stop.

And there was the curse of imagination; vivid, morbid, probably inaccurate, it nagged one with small swift scenes, taking one from room to room of Vallant House, putting the wrong emphasis upon this fact, attaching insufficient importance to that, and egged on eternally by stray sentences from the Chilcot letter. It was the country seat business over again, only more acute: the fact that one didn't know and that the house did.

Sometimes it seemed to me that one's efforts of imagination must inevitably be worse than the actual fact; at other times, lines from the Chilcot letter – infinitely less sensational – surpassed anything one's mind could contrive. It was 'heads I win, tails you lose' with a vengeance.

The Vallants had 'a kink', that was the easy colloquialism current in our clan. It was entirely typical, no less of the dominion of the distaff side than of family injustice, that we all termed anything which offended against our codes 'Vallantry' and 'Vallantish', casually loading the sins of the mothers on to the inadequate shoulders of our grandfather, Sir Frederick. Susan Stonor had married him and become a Vallant. It was enough! The Stonors, so far as we could discover, had never been or achieved anything spectacular, or fallen into any historic disfavours or under those eminent and readable displeasures which penetrate the history book; they were just the county family which is the Imperialistic backbone of the nation, monotonously produces children and is called 'of' their native earth. The Vallants of Hampshire, the Stonors of Lancashire.

Information was difficult to wrest. The elder Seagraves, Stonors, Vallants and Verdunes were uninterested, rooted in the social security of generations and incurably averse to the personal touch, shying from anything which might develop into a tie.

James, fresh from the clean straightforward violence of war, had less tolerance than ever for the family temperament; he had his moments of seeing them all entirely objectively, which was male and wholesome but quite useless to me as it only saw results instead of exploring for causes. And yet, hasn't all evil (like all talent) from crime to idiosyncrasy, to have its beginnings which need not necessarily be remote? In years to come, as yet unborn members of the family would have their Susan Vallant (she was a Miss Stonor, my dear) upon whom to load all blame, all excuse for personal lack and frustration. We who were living in her actual period had no such landmark.

And I know now that lack of love isn't a matter of an unsatisfactory ending to a novelette, but that it has results which are beyond computation. I know that the withholding of tenderness in families, even where there is no actual physical neglect, can warp character, enfeeble initiative and spoil careers. It was, I feel sure, something of this truth that Alma Chilcot had meant to convey when she said that I might be looking for something sensational which was not there, guessing that the young demand a target, large and clearly marked, at which to aim its shots.

'The Stonors make bad mothers.' It was Great-aunt Jane Stonor who had said that, a woman whom we had never seen, who mattered to nobody, who had probably hit the nail squarely on the head and who was to exist for future generations through one short sentence.

III

We went to Alma Chilcot's grave bringing a big bunch of flowers. James tipped the sexton to keep it neat 'for as long as the money lasts out. I mean – it mayn't be able to be a regular payment'.

The man looked at the khaki uniform and gently concurred, as he made out the receipt upon which was the cemetery number. I couldn't afford anything, there seemed to have been a lot of unforeseen expenses, lately.

The problem of Myra's grave was less easy of approach. We tracked it – incredibly – through uncle Maxwell, whose unconsidered existence was thrown in as makeweight upon James's duty-round of family visits. Aunt Sophia's conventional sprightliness had its tricksy uses. 'You men will like to have a good talk,' quite ignoring the fact that their very respective positions upon the family tree had to be tentatively re-established and stabilized. But Uncle Maxwell was an in-law – once removed from clannish considerations, eternally free by blood.

'Old Max has quite the makings of a person,' James put it to me, but we both guessed that this uncharacteristic smoking-room session would do no real spade-work for intimacy, and that when the doors of the Emperor's Gate house-closed upon James, our uncle would fade once more into always-a-nose-in-the-paper, an alarmed retirement from feminine gaiety and into the eternal Mr. Jorkins whose caprices aunt Sophia worked whenever plans or pleasures not of her own contrivance were mooted. But his value for us was that he was an outsider, who, if not seeing most of the game, at least was willing to explain it without bias. Myra Vallant to him was sheerly an unknown and defunct sister-in-law, casual query about whom would be as casually dealt with and forgotten – another point in our favour.

James admitted to me that on going upstairs to the drawing-room to say good-bye to aunt Sophia (who, it seems, was at her desk, which made him grin), the fact of being in that large parqueted space in the morning almost robbed him of his bearings and gave him 'a feeling of nudity and prying', plus a genuine interest for the first time in his life as to what 'these people' were really like. Quite soon a gong would sound in the hall, and they would assemble and eat food. Just a family – and for ever obscured because they were relations, about whom we should never see clearly for anecdote and joke, disparagement and facetious rumour.

But for all that, it was a Seagrave who made quite plain to us where Myra was buried.

It was a very small grave, this marble-rimmed oblong of turf in Brompton Cemetery, and we exchanged surprised relief that it was not spoiled by abominable sentiment of stout angel pointing heavenward – though there might have been reasons for that omission. ...

'– and probably were,' said James, although I had not said a word.

On the way, we had argued the question of flowers or no flowers. James thought that as she had never lived, for us, this years-late tribute would be as dead as an undelivered letter; I took the line that if all time is one and the present co-existent with the past, our offering could not be belated. We grew so interested over the argument that with no more than a glance at Myra's grave, we strode past it altogether, by headstones and memorials to eminents – a Lascelles and some Victorian actor whose name I have forgotten. Also, when shepherded back, we had forgotten the flowers themselves, and when we approached the grave, there were flowers, a sheaf of lilies of the valley.

We looked at each other. 'Somehow, I swear those weren't there just now,' he murmured. I didn't believe they were, either, and said so. We tracked an official at the lodge. The Myra Vallant grave? He consulted the cemetery plan.

'Oh yes, the lady brings flowers regular, very regular, though not always at the same time, like. She's brought flowers for years. I've bin here sixteen years ... She's just come and gone.'

'Excuse me, but who is she?'

'Buchan, the name is. Mrs. Austen Buchan.'

We moved on.

'That was a close shave,' muttered James. He had turned rather white, and my hands were beginning to shake.

IV

During James's leave, Dolly Verdune married her 'Arthur', whose non-committal surname turned out to be Hillman.

Once more there was a tendency for the younger generation to ring up its contemporaries and for the elders to proceed in semi-secret to shake heads in each other's drawing-rooms. Or perhaps I am judging by the telephone calls to our little house, and the visits directed to our door. There seemed, as in the old days, a universal wish to converge upon mother, who gave us the cream of the debates at meal-times and said, with her pleasant sub-acidity, that she felt 'catastrophically honoured'.

Aunt Emmeline was sunk in pessimism; there was a rumour that aunt Sophia had ordered a new hat and had been heard to say that the wedding was 'such a solution', which we all dispassionately and instantly interpreted as a backhanded allusion to aunt Emmeline's upbringing of the Verdunes. The views of uncle Bertram were, if formulated, drowned in the voices of his females in Palace Green and Dolly herself tackled me upon the bridesmaid question.

'Mother, of *course*, is against my having *any* … she's being too *chrewnic!*' and then with the Verdune candour, 'I wanted you for one, m' dear, but I suppose we'd have had to ask Lalage, as she's the elder.'

It was mother herself who settled that question, putting on her hat and flitting on foot to Palace Green, telling us all at night, 'I told Emmeline she *must* let the poor child have her bridesmaids'. Sophia, plumed and Daimler'd, had failed to gain the point, although, always good-natured, she had made the attempt, and nobody else, including Lady Vallant, had tried at all. And after all it was I who played bridesmaid; Lalage shrank from the publicity, which concerned without surprising either James or myself. Dissatisfied, he argued the point.

'But … is it usual for girls to balk at that kind of tamasha? After all, it means a new frock and a present and flowers, and so on.'

I shrugged. 'It's all of a piece, Jamesey. You know what mother was about parties, and look at the uncles! Lalage is one of the family.'

He was impatient. 'Not a fair analogy. There was a reason for that, with Vallant snubbing them all round and throwing her weight about.'

I said, suddenly and to myself unexpectedly, 'Lalage will never be herself until she's out of our family.'

He stared through me. 'You mean, married to Hugh?'

'Hugh being Hugh, yes, though I think the same result might be achieved in other ways.'

'You mean – to cut loose from all of us? ... Somehow, I can't see her on her own, or as one of a gang of female hearties in khaki calling each other by surnames ...' He propped an elbow on the mantelpiece. The appearance of Lalage, I knew, had shocked him, seeing her anew after all those months in France, although he had said nothing, even to me.

'Vere, this about never being herself,' he began again. That was the price one paid for James, for the instant understanding he gave; it also meant that he had noted all one's vague gropings, letting nothing pass as unimportant because it was incoherently expressed. Like a barrister, he allowed witness no margin for ill-considered remarks.

'I sometimes wonder who she is to *be*,' I brought out unwillingly.

'You feel that, too? That she's a mould into which any personality could be poured?'

And then mother came in, to tell us with a schoolgirlgiggle that uncle Julian had sent Dolly a bronze stag paperweight. 'Out of stock,' said mother. 'Lor! don't I remember it! It used to stand on the Pater's writing-table in his study.'

'Then its vibrations are low and I shall tell her to pop it,' said James. It was an unwritten law that one could 'out' with that type of thing, where Lady Vallant was even indirectly in question. Mother accepted it that we were anti-Vallant on her own account. And upon principles more or less carefully general.

Dolly Verdune drew James into her immediate affairs with that direct courage which was part-innate, part-careless. She quite simply wanted her Arthur vetted. Her family, it seemed, were no use. 'It's uncle Bertram's job,' James told her at once. She agreed, and stood her ground. 'You never knew, with father.' Besides, Arthur mightn't get a fair opinion owing to the possible influence of aunt Emmeline. Dolly's sisters were sympathetic, with reservations, to the Hillman cause, but, Dolly insisted, negligible as social referees. In short, no member of the family –

('But, I am one of the family', put in James.)

'No, you aren't. You know what I mean! So be a saint. ...'

James was a saint for a week, dining, golfing, theatreing and bear-leading the Verdune-elect ... he gave Dolly his findings, retailing them to mother, Lalage and me no less frankly.

'Quite a harmless chap. Will pass along, though not off the top shelf. Pleasant, bawdy sense of humour which will suit her a treat. Snags: that he can't wear all kinds of hat and get away with it, and plus-fours search him out. Rather a half-sir run. Isn't it odd that men who aren't quite grade A can't move properly? I notice it so much in France. We've got some perfectly A.I temporary gentlemen in my outfit, good discipline, game as you make 'em, good company – everything, but oh God! when they walk or sprint! ...'

v

From my subsidiary place in the procession, partnered by a Seagrave and preceded by Barbara and Evelyn Verdune, I had an excellent view of church events. It was impossible not to be physically proud of my kinsfolk, as I scanned their fine-drawn, hawk profiles and damned them all for this reason or that! The Seagrave cluster provided the relief of stuff to all that steel. Aunt Sophia was 'in' her new hat, inevitably bought at the oldest-established and most traditionally ladylike of the Knightsbridge shops. I knew the model of old; to Mrs. Seagrave all hats (like the three persons of the Trinity) were one hat, and that meant an almost exact reproduction of the headgear carved upon the periwig of William of Orange in Kensington Gardens.

It delighted James who, officiating in the aisle, tiptoe'd to me in the porch, wreathed in grins, or full of query. He took it for granted that anyone he indicated in the pews must be a relation and therefore a potential humour.

'That,' I would mutter, 'is uncle Stuart.'

'Hah ... what's *his* dossier?'

'Refused whisky to two Hampshire neighbours,' I rapidly hissed, 'and says the War will be over by Christmas,' and James, suffocating, returned to his post.

Or:

'Who's the Godfearing geyser in mauve bits and pieces?'

'Lower, brother, i' God's name! A Stonor cousin, I *think*, but am not sure. Judge by the nose when next you pass, and keep the thoughts clean.'

As we advanced up the aisle James said to me, 'The complete Vicar's daughter', as he looked at my frock.

'I know shut up', I answered all in one sentence. We had long mastered the trick of ventriloquial conversation − it consists in keeping the lips stiff and using only your tongue, and it is absolutely possible to let off any insult behind the barrage of a fixed and brilliant smile. My dress was a failure and I knew it. It had been conceived to suit alien and majority-taste. It contrived to look too ingenuous for me while appearing far too *rusé* on Helen Seagrave; also, it clashed with my hair, in which Bertram Verdune was taking a non-avuncular interest, to judge by the things he was doing with his eyebrows whenever he caught my glance, plus a tendency to hum at me under his breath when he was near.

Aunt Emmeline drew into my view as we neared the chancel; aquiline, in steel-grey, she was looking stonily ahead. Dolly, pale, competent, striking and determined, was summing up her groom's best man and finding him a give-away, as we all did. He would probably commit facetiousness later and I would warn James to stage-manage him, for Dolly's sake. Mother, with quiet, masochistic pluck, had selected a place next aunt Emmeline, and Lalage, noted, I saw, by many eyes, the obvious subject of confabulation, was at her side.

In the vestry I was kissed − thoroughly − by my uncle Verdune, and said 'Don't be a chump, Bertram', counting on many factors to get away with the remark. It was a kiss I recognized at once; also, I was disgusted at the petty bad taste of the business.

The Stonor-Vallant uncles and great-uncles were round mother, speechless as usual, and we drifted to the porch and began to await cars. James was surrounded by three of the Seagrave girls, and I wondered once again how it was that they always contrived to suggest a mob, just as they would, probably, look frizzed and Edwardian for life, follow they the current and future fashions never so madly. I edged James into a car with the best man, from whose painstakingly convivial expression I judged he had begun already, found a nameless Stonor for Lalage and managed to include a woman as well, against accidents, and let mother chance her luck – she was a match for anybody.

On the steps aunt Emmeline was saying, 'We don't know how it'll turn out. Let's hope it won't be the most *ghastly* mistake … oh, we're *sick* about it! …'

Lady Vallant had sent an empty brougham. The devil entered me and I got into it, and the coachman, nonplussed, flicked his horse. Somebody would catch it, later. …

From a passing car I received an incredulous grin from Barbara Verdune, aunt Sophia's voice rang out from another. 'That naughty puss! Alone, mah'ee dear!' I leant out of the window.

'Manners, good people! I am the Protestant whore,' I called, and turned to the coachman. 'Beech, we will take a turn in the park before returning.'

Bouquet'd and furbelow'd, I leant back and closed my eyes.

VI

There was much to think of, more which insisted on getting itself thought.

The War was being some ordeal of the spirit to Lalage that I could not even guess at; mother, overstrained herself, had this burden to bear, plus anything that Lady Vallant might be up to. There was my own job to hold down. A bunch of lilies of the valley in Brompton Cemetery, and the years of Myra-flowers brought by sister to sister, and the way that fact sapped one.

Miss Chilcot …

Mother and Lalage, I was certain, ought to be taken right out of London for months. Money question. And anyway, where could they go?

There was Vallant, in Hampshire. I would tackle the uncles at once about that, at the Verdune reception I must return to. It must be done openly, lightly, publicly – I mistrusted Stonor-Vallant capacity for nuances and finesse, must make the invitation seem the obvious, unremarkable thing it should be; after all, the place actually belonged to our grandmother until her death, a large, rambling house with plenty of room. The scheme seemed fool-proof. And yet the uncles, as we all agreed, had surpassed themselves over the honeymoon ideas of Dolly Verdune – even the Seagraves had jumped to the humour of it.

Dolly, a month before her wedding, had written to her uncle Stuart to sound him as to finding her a suitable cottage on the estate, the Hillmans to occupy it for a month with option of acquiring it permanently. Stuart Vallant wrote back (the letter was now a Verdune exhibit) that he 'and your uncle Julian' feared there was no cottage available, and a fortnight later bought up the two empty dwellings to make assurances doubly sure. It was a Stonor great-cousin 'up for the day' and lunching in Palace Green who had blamelessly given the show away. The Verdunes had preserved poker-faces (at least we have the tumbril spirit) and aunt Emmeline's silence had acted as another reminder to Dolly that the marriage was 'a pity'. It was to us Buchans that the Verdunes streamed hysterically, and mother who, half-laughter half grief, soothed poor Dolly down. 'My dear, we're *like* that. You've just got to accept it. I do apologize for my family!'

But, would mother leave me? One was cramped for the relief of open discussion about almost everything. But in any case we were a close-tongued lot to whom silence was second nature. James was my safety-valve, more so than ever since the Chilcot-Vallant-Myra affairs had come into our lives. And James's leave would soon be up.

Uncle Bertram …

Enjoying kissing me because I was not his niece by blood, getting away with it because he was my official uncle.

Hugh Lyne and Lalage …

I prayed over my limp bouquet, there in that stuffy, odious little equipage of my grandmother's, that Hugh would consider himself free to marry her soon. I saw, as it were, for the first time quite clearly what I had meant when I told James that Lalage would never be 'herself' until then. It was a continuance of that earlier discussion we had once held, when I suggested to him that our sister had lost her continuity, and I began to see Lalage's marriage as literally a new life for her, a direct though possibly dangerous challenge to whatever her psychic malady might be.

One rejoiced, apart from that, in the prospect of Hugh. It was disturbing how few reliable men there were in our family; their swamping by the female element perhaps had something to do with it? Or did their women override them because their men were ineffectuals? But in case some girl one day took James from me, and because Hugh must be free of the lot of us to love and guard Lalage, it was essential that I should not obtrude any difficulties of my own upon him. I would be a good in-law, so that future members of the family in their dens and schoolrooms should have no additional story or inherited grievance against my name...

That palmist ...

How they all loved promising one mysterious men; God alone knew which of my crew of raggle-taggles if any she must have been alluding to or when he had supervened and passed! She had very nearly taken me in, too, with her positive manner and hints about paternal care. But that father-manner was an old trick; it paved the way, was always vilely done and never lasted beyond one evening. It offended me more than any other form of approach, being a travesty of what could and should be one of the beautiful relationships of humanity, and being – to me, at least – ideal element which might well enter into associations more intimate. And that curious insistence of all our shoddy seers that two children marked our hand.

And it was over-time to return to Palace Green. I pulled the rug over my knees. Organdie fal-lals went ill with London in November. Men were sweeping leaves in the park and covert-coated children being led home to warm nurseries. One would like to be a child again. Swaddled in perfect ignorance.

CHAPTER XX

I

AND AFTER ALL, my suggestion to the uncles about mother and Lalage was received in a way that upset the lot of my carefully bright approaches, and left me uncertain of my victory. The thought of having their sister under their roof – a guest – to stay – filled both Stuart and Julian Vallant with an astonishment they were too naive to conceal. Uncle Stuart positively chuckled at the notion, with a wrinkled, sardonic smile which instantly recalled our grandmother.

'I don't think Anne would care for that very much,' he muttered, and brusquely turned right away.

Uncle Julian, always more easily identified by his thick-lensed glasses, was at once more human and articulate. It is possible that he remembered having once ventured into our Campden Hill home. He was vague obstructionism incarnate, misleadingly ready to consider the idea, and blocking all avenues with disparagements.

'Well, you see … the maids mightn't like it.'

'Oh, damn *them* –'

'The old place is really shockingly uncomfortable. No modern conveniences …'

'Mother wouldn't mind –'

'The Mater would never have electricity put in …'

(*Me*: Charm of lamps, interesting shadows cast by incandescent burners.) I was brazen. There was nothing to lose by it, here or hereafter, and I think I won.

'Well … Anne and whatshername'd have to amuse themselves…'

(Why, why, why? you inhospitable old devil! Why the hell don't you and your blasted old brother pull yourselves together and put in light and behave like Christians?)

'… she'd have to take a cab from the station. The road's very bad and Masters wouldn't like the trap used … oh … come if she's set on it. …'

And, having introduced the subject to mother, I left the pair talking to each other, mother faintly flushed as she worked at the old man. Wonderfully soon she had got him (like a crab) out of the major portion of his shell and I left them, with a mental picture of uncle Julian bashfully chuckling over remote, mutually-shared and remembered catchwords and jokes. I realized then that the maddening, time-wasting depreciation by him of all that was his was not sheer cussedness, and certainly not oriental etiquette, but plain, downright inferiority complex. And you battered it with brazen persistence, it seems.

I crushed my way across the room to find James. Outside the door aunt Sophia plucked me absently by the arm and shouted,

'Sly puss! In granny's carriage. *How* I laughed! We must find you a nice little husband, next.'

I ran James to earth in the library, a room which had, so to speak, long lost its character and never recovered it, as the perusal in it of books was entirely subordinated to aunt Emmeline's capricious preference for 'doing' the flowers there. For years and years she had arranged blooms and filled vases all over uncle Bertram until he had been driven elsewhere – the house was large, and could stand it.

James, Helen Seagrave, Barbara Verdune and Dolly were sitting at ease, the girls in their spreading skirts, their Victorian-bonneted heads engulfing whiskies and sodas. I added my bonnet and flounces to theirs and stacked my bouquet with the others upon a side table.

'Really, Dolly! *You* ought to be upstairs in tears, assuring aunt Emmeline that although she has lost a daughter she has gained a son – whoa, Jamesey! Don't drown the sperrit.'

Dolly grinned. 'One doesn't want to rub it in. And mother mayn't have lost me entirely, after all.'

'I see. No. There's always that. Well … bless you, m'dear, whatever.'

'Hear, hear,' assented James. We clinked glasses and I told them what I'd done about the uncles. Helen, sipping cup, looked at me brightly in that way an audience waits upon the traditionally humorous utterances of the low comedian, and it was Barbara whose gaze became fixed, taking in the true inwardness of the event, and Dolly who ejaculated *'Lor!'* We were all making rather a noise. Discussion of the family seems to invite it, among the younger branches. And then aunt Sophia passed, looked in and droned 'Cranford! All those naughty bonnets!' and to Helen, '… all the men looking for you!' and vanished. Her place was immediately taken by Aunt Emmeline, tall and lamenting. Her eye took us all in.

'You *must* go upstairs at *once* and *change*, Dolly.' Then, tragically, 'How much longer will they all stay? I mean, the servants are getting rather restive … *such* a bore. Better take the bouquets off the table, they'll mark the polish.'

We rose at once. The party was over.

11

That evening James and Lalage and I went out with a young brother officer whom I had liked on sight, quite apart from James's private testimonial ('He's quite one of us'). He had first met me with the remark, 'I have to tell you that my Christian name is Claude. You will want to go away and practise it quietly.'

He was, we all thought, a most dear person and the most unselfconscious; his inconsequence of thought, about which mother once tackled him, was astonishing. Like myself, he was unable to take anything for granted, and, looking like the more preposterous of west-end revue 'dudes', he would eagerly fall upon any triviality and put it under the microscope, or discuss the most solid social questions with a sense and fairness of outlook for which, owing to his appearance, he got no credit at all. With regard to the charge of inconsequence he said quite simply, 'I know what you mean, and I think it's France that does it. I like arguments and ideas, and when you never know from one minute to the next whether you'll be alive or not you have to get everything said as it occurs to you. I wonder why the words "Holy Ghost" are so funny? I once woke up laughing my head off at it.'

He was often with us at home, and called our outings 'trying to get the point of view'. The trenches had left his critical sense completely untouched; he could never accept as infallible the current scale of values on humour, morals, the cost of pleasure and its bearing on value received or the frightfulness of Germany. He even failed to lose his head over the daylight raids which began, that November, and when a baby was killed in its pram in Folkestone and the newspapers had hysterics, said that the bomber wasn't aiming at a baby but at an English town.

We came by our good times in ways many and strange. Claude was fond of us all and from the first I had had to exert no vigilance over his expenditures. He would come to fetch me, announcing, 'I've got thirty shillings for the day, if we go beyond it we're sunk. That'll mean decent booze at a dive, or a refined meal and undrinkable catlap. There's a waiter in Soho who told me he'd reckoned the distance he'd covered in twenty-four years of service. He makes it just under five hundred miles, in a room twenty-four by sixteen.'

One Sunday night we had suddenly followed a Salvation Army band, and Claude was so worked up over it that by the time our third pitch was reached he was singing with the best of them and calling out Praise the Lord! Another pitch and he would have testified. James headed him off in the nick of time and Claude was as sincerely relieved as any of us. 'They're such fine dramatic stuff, but I dare say one couldn't stand the pace. And personally I've only got two sins to confess, and one of them's pretty old-fashioned for these days – I mean, they'd get to know them too well at street corners.' He smote his thigh. *'That's* why you have to be such a sinner! It's for the repertoire! Where do we eat? I say, I wonder what the first woman who accidentally made scrambled eggs thought? I've often imagined how alarmed she must have been, because even when you know what to expect, the eggs are rather an uncouth spectacle.'

I discovered very soon that everything interested Claude, and I think he cultivated people in every rank of life and of most occupations through an unconscious necessity to feed his avidity. Once or twice I nearly gave way to the temptation to talk to him about Lady Vallant, but one mustn't take advantage ... Claude must be allowed by James and me to be himself, untouched, for the leave that remained to him. Also, I'd given a badly misplaced confidence, before. Men didn't want one's troubles ... I wasn't prepared to give the old woman another opportunity to break a friendship.

Claude had a quality of social moral courage which was my perpetual admiration. If he didn't catch a name on introduction he would say so and ask for it to be repeated; I have heard him ask a head waiter 'I say, does one tip the wine-wallah as well as one's own?' and he had none of that queasy fear of ridicule which causes so large a proportion of the world to shy from approaching policemen as to the locality of famous buildings or exclusive clubs. I was told he said to a bishop visiting G.H.Q. in France, 'I'm frightfully sorry, sir, but I don't know how to address you. Is it "Bishop" or "Doctor" something?'

III

I took him to a cocktail party; I too wanted to 'get the point of view'. Such affairs don't come my way very plentifully; also, for some time, I had had no social fish to fry, with Hugh safely hovering over Lalage and James in France.

The party, in some mews, smelt of petrol and lipstick, and was full of an atmosphere which we both agreed we couldn't do very much for. Always the victim of my surroundings, I was willy-nilly forced into the rôle of Gummidge. We arrived at our conclusions by divers routes, I, through the instantly-sensed fact that these girls and boys and intermediates of both sexes and of none had left their personalities elsewhere. They said things as variously, reliably and slickly as the well-kept gramophone, and like the gramophone seemed compelled to keep within the limits of the record album. I relapsed into helplessness at once where Claude investigated.

A stayless skeleton in henna and cretonne looped up to him and said affectionately, 'My trouble is that I *cannot* give up fornication'. He regarded her civilly. 'Fornication … I always mix it up with adultery and incest. Oh, yes, I get you. Well, of course, I daresay you'll find that if you put your shoulder to the wheel you may shake it off in time, what? But how did you get like that in the beginning?' The woman, who was not prepared with reasons, but only with long-respected sexual identity discs, looked haggard and glided away.

By the window, the names of Proust, Havelock Ellis and Freud were in circulation.

'*Too* final. The only writer, don't you think so?'

'I've never read him, I'm ashamed to say,' answered Claude.

'*What!* My dear lad …!'

'Awful, isn't it? Is Ellis an essayist or a scientist or a philosopher?'

No definite answer, except that Ellis was extremely frank and rather 'difficult to get'.

'What nationality is Proust?'

Nobody knew. That, somehow, wasn't the point about Messrs. Proust, Ellis and Freud. The discussion flickered and went out.

In another corner screeches of laughter and cries of exceed-
ing great joy went up as the names of Ethel M. Dell, Berta Ruck
and Elinor Glyn were tossed into the air.

Claude took another drink. 'Well, I liked *The Bars of Iron*,' he
said. 'She *can* tell a story, you know.'

For a second the listeners wavered, uncertain.

'*So* did I!' plunged a six-foot wraith in blue.

They joined her. The ayes had it. Confession and laughter
resounded. They revelled in their apostasy, searching their very
souls for praise and reasons.

Going home, Claude was plucking at his chin.

'Go on. Say it, we shall probably agree,' I remarked. We
pounded on.

'It isn't the lies I bar, Vere, or even the attempts to be daring;
after all, that shock complex is the earliest instinct of kids who
chalk up dirty words on fences: it's that that lot isn't being itself,
or any self. These people mayn't have many guns, and probably
what they've got are the wrong pattern, but they must positively learn to stand by them. Isn't it a mercy that there's nobody
recording our conversation for the future? "At a Cocktail Tea:
Double-sided ten-inch record. Red label," my God!'

'Some people believe that conversation *is* recorded, Claude,'
and then, to make my point, I had to tell him about Hampton
Court and Henry. He fell on it voraciously.

IV

It was on the evening of the Verdune wedding that we were
still hard at the topic of the resuscitation of lost scenes and voices. Claude, waving a fork upon which a small sausage was im-
paled, said that it could be done through the wireless. James said it
would always remain uncontrollable and capricious, 'because the
ether is already so overloaded with material.' He leant forward,
arms on the table. 'It would only become more possible, less liable
to overlapping with previous scenes, by localization … allotting
each conversation to its known venue. I mean that supposing we
wanted to re-hear the trial of Catherine of Aragon, we should
obviously have to shift to Blackfriars Hall … and that's long been
demolished (that's another snag).'

'Not a bit,' I chipped in, 'it's the *site* that probably counts. The point is that even if Blackfriars Hall is pulled down and covered with warehouses and shops, the four walls of the hall weren't the chief factor, but the air-space, and it's that space which must still be saturated with the voices of the Cardinals.'

'But ... the four enclosing walls must have been a conserving medium. ...'

'Not necessarily. When a "haunted" house is pulled down, in quite five cases out of a dozen the hauntings continue, because the trouble is deeper than just bricks and mortar. *You can't destroy the air in which it happened.*'

James agreed. 'An additional proof of that is that there are plenty of houses in England whose hauntings are only to be seen and heard on the anniversary of the tragedy; in other words, the air is subject to the time-limit; it lies fallow for three hundred and sixty-four days, then functions ... receives some stimulus ... the condensation of remembered evil, and history repeats itself.'

'Then, Jimmy, you mean that when you saw the Tudors at Hampton Court, say on the third of January, it was on *a* third of January that Henry made that remark about tennis and his bad leg to Edward?'

'What I think doesn't count, granted that the laws governing this sort of thing aren't understood. But on the available evidence, I'm inclined to suspect that the time-factor only applies where there has been violence or tragedy, and that these – shall we say – humdrum, domestic flashes-back may turn up at any time. Look at Versailles and the Petit Trianon. Marie Antoinette was so much in evidence all the time making her butter and what not that trippers got cold feet, and the window has been boarded up.'

'But, about the wireless. How would you work that?' I asked.

'Wait till all stations are closed down for the night, then tune in,' answered Claude, promptly.

We never tried, in those War days; first, because then the privately owned wireless was by no means as common as it has since become, and second, because life was too full and leave too short for patient theoretical experiments – incidentally, the military authorities were too suspicious of strangers hanging about in the small hours with heavy square boxes.

But since that day, James and I have pursued our intermittent investigations. Thanks to friendship or influence, we have sat overtime in a huge deserted cinema built upon the site of a famous Victorian music-hall, and there in the darkness, our portable in the gangway, we have re-heard the voice of Dan Leno, the fainter one of Jenny Hill singing 'The Coffee-Shop Girl'; at Hampton Court tuned in to a feast eaten four hundred years ago, and hum the minstrels' music to this hour (and didn't think much of it, it was thin and monotonous and a little repetitious, and gave the effect of being slightly off the key), and once we heard a quarrel in the Banqueting Hall in Whitehall, which (infuriatingly) we were unable to 'place'. Scraps ... one burned for more.

'Sire, it is impossible!'

'Heh? No one says "impossible" to me.'

Then crackling from the machine, and

'She must learn.'

A dispute which probably never penetrated the textbooks: just some royal huff, so infinitely more revelatory if one could return night after night to hear it all!

I believe that this, one day, will be possible and free to all, and that if we do not precisely win through to the touch of a vanished hand, at least we shall repossess for our life the sound of a voice that has been hitherto, and quite avoidably, 'still'. Meanwhile, we must muddle along with such rare extra senses as we have developed, or which have elected, arbitrarily, to lodge themselves in us.

It was inevitable that as we sat in the little eating-house and argued, the sick memory of Myra should wash over me and leave me raging; inevitable that our elementary gropings into the possibility of tuning-in to the past should immediately have, for me, but one value and purpose, and though James and I were never to approach the miserable business in exactly that way, the insertion of the Hampton Court episode into our discussion suggested another line of enquiry. And I suppose it was then that I guessed what I must do.

I looked at Lalage, and against all logic and reason, blamed myself for encouraging the subject.

She had turned very white and her eyes were clouded and apprehensive.

'What do you think, Lalage?' It was Claude asking that, so my kick upon James's instep went for nothing.

'I – hope – it – will – never – be,' she stammered, and began clutching the table cloth.

'But … my dear! Think what we're missing!'

'And – think – what – we – might – hear,' the thick, toneless voice went on.

'Yes! And we might learn, in time, to see.'

I think that, at this point, Claude began to sense trouble, and at a loss, started to make hasty, general remarks.

'D'you mean to tell me that Tower Hill isn't still *clamouring* with the voices of the beheaded … and Tyburn … or that the steps of Canterbury Cathedral don't still possess the cry of à Becket where he fell?'

I don't know if there are many people who would have grasped Lalage's dis-ease through that sentence and her reception of it; I know that I failed to, at the time, though the indication was, possibly, clear enough. For Lalage gave a tiny, thin cry like a wild creature's and slid sideways against James's tunic. His arms were round her in a flash.

CHAPTER XXI

I

WE TOOK HER home in a taxi, and mother, paper-white herself at sight of Lalage, was told by Claude that the heat of the restaurant – Lalage seemed not quite herself all the evening – rather silent – and was silently disbelieved, and presently he went.

James and I had been able to prepare no story, thanks to the presence of a third party, and I don't know of how much knowledge or curiosity mother suspected us. We three stood there unable to start any sentence at all, and it was I who rescued us temporarily by the bluff-and-hearty method. They were both badly run-down – must go to Vallant at once. And I really think that if mother had hesitated or deprecated her own popularity with the uncles, or been obstructionist in her own Vallant manner, I should have screamed. My own nerves evidently needed watching. …

Two things prevented that: one, that the statement of her health and Lalage's was self-evident, the other that next morning a daylight raid took place, and when the anti-aircraft gun began roaring on Campden Hill, Lalage became worse and fell into fits of trembling which nothing seemed to stop. And I was grateful even for this as happening to be a fairly commonplace contemporary symptom.

James would accompany them to Hampshire and send the telegram to the uncles; I wrote to Hugh Lyne telling him where Lalage had gone and praying that a non-fatal wound might bring him back to England, and then began the business of overcoming mother's reluctance of leaving me alone. The fact that we had two servants in the house made no difference to her, she seemed to believe that her 'desertion' of myself would immediately loose the entire German army into our road; she even stated that 'the uncles would love to have you', which reduced me to just looking her in the eye. I had an answer, actual as well as merely plausible, to everything. My work, James and Claude who must be seen off at Victoria, three Buchans too much for Vallant hospitality. ...

'But, what will you *do* with yourself in the evenings, darling?'

I tried not to look grim. 'Oh, *I'm* going to Vallant House.' It occurred to me, a split second too late, that I had made my announcement with a shade too much of cheerfulness and decision. Even in my own ears the words rang with a preconcerted effect, also, the state visits to our grandmother were not hallowed by any precedent of lightheartedness. Luckily, again, I had long ago told her of Lady Vallant's wish that I should be at hand if the air-raids became worse. The antick notion gave one scope for facetiousness.

'One can't live with her but one can die together.' And James, later, had said, 'Always die from a good address if you can'.

'I only pray you'll get enough to eat,' said mother, a little unguardedly, forgetting these perverse feasts with which the old lady plied us. She meant that, once sure of me, Lady Vallant might revert to type and return to the old regime. But as, officially, I knew nothing about that, I was reduced to replying that I hoped so, too ... I went on, determinedly: 'It's quite my turn, anyway, to take over. I'm afraid the old creature's been rather a flail to you all this time.'

'She – can be awful.'

'She's been more than that,' I snarled, then, keeping my face as empty as is ever possible between two members of a family who know all each other's range of expression far too thoroughly, 'She seems to have been rather *extra*, of late'.

Mother began drifting about the room, a signal of uncertainty. I tried to brace myself against what she might say, and prayed that it mightn't be something about the old woman's mental brutality to herself which would haunt one. I felt *crowded*, couldn't admit any more material for hate and fury and futile compassion. ...

Mother was in her own difficulties, obviously selecting and grading, just as, no doubt, I should have to do in my answering comment. She had swung round, one hand (it irritated me) flapping the blind tassel up and down.

'Look here, old darling, I didn't mean to say anything about it, but granny's really been worrying me sick, for ages now. She's got it into her head that I've been letting her down to you three. I haven't, have I?'

Mother's voice was wistful as a child's; it was the measure of the strain Lady Vallant had been putting upon her, on and off, for years now, that she should look to me for assurance and comfort.

'You wouldn't need to,' I said, 'we dislike her quite on our own. Besides, everybody gossips about Vallant, you should hear Dolly and Barbara Verdune!' That was misleading, but technically true enough, and mother took it the way I meant her to, as being that ancestor-dissection, ribald and joyfully inaccurate, which goes on in schoolrooms. I had said the right thing, so far, but mother, frail and obstinate, hadn't finished, was goading herself to keep the subject alive.

'Yes. I'm afraid she's not very loved. It's very lamentable.'

'And anyway,' I cut in, 'why does she mind *us* being put off her? She doesn't care a toot for any of us.'

'I wouldn't say that. I think, in her way, she's got a sneaking admiration for all of you, and I really believe she's genuinely devoted to James.'

'God,' I said cheerfully. Mother smiled apologetically.

'Anyway, she's stood him treats her own sons never got ... poor wretches ... but what I wanted to say was: as you'll be seeing rather a lot of grannyma soon, better keep off' – she floundered – 'I mean, if I were you, I wouldn't mention the old days in the Square.'

What mother expected me to make of that I don't know. I was commonplace and brisk.

'No. All right. I see.'

'She – she's got it into her head that – my dear, did I ever mention Miss Chilcot to you? She was one of the govs, you know.'

Now we were getting somewhere.

'No, you didn't, but Hutchins did, once.'

'But, how did she crop *up*?'

'I think we were talking about family photographs. I rather liked the sound of La Chilcot.' I went on being casual. 'There *were* a crew of govs, weren't there? No wonder they upped and left.'

'And,' mother was being elaborate and casual, too, 'what did Hutchins say about her?'

'That he liked her.'

'Oh yes, we all did. She was a rattling good sort.'

Interesting, but I had no time for side-issues if we were to get out of this in safety.

'And that she fell rather foul of Vallant ... Hutchins was vague about the reason ... I suppose he was too used to that sort of thing!'

'There weren't any more changes after we got Miss Chilcot's successor. She was a *beastly* woman.'

I caught my breath. But one mustn't head towards that. Somehow, in all one's scourging inventions, groupings and imaginings, one had overlooked that situation – the governess, upon whose harsh, bleak methods Lady Vallant could count ... Faugh!

I went on, 'And then James spoke of Miss Chilcot in the drawing-room and Vallant was "not amused".'

That was over, and the chronologic juggling was undetectable. Mother's face had cleared. 'I wish I'd known before.'

'Well, I'm awfully sorry, darling, but one treads on Vallant's corns so often that once more didn't seem to be worth telling about.' Half-liar though I had been, I felt half shriven.

One more thing occurred to me.

'Don't let her know that Hutchins mentioned the gov. to us.'

'What d'you take me for?' responded mother.

It was evident that the old woman had concentrated her ire solely upon James's mention of Miss Chilcot's name, and that she had dismissed as a piece of vulgar practical joking the possibility of her nephew having seen the governess in her own drawing-room.

II

It is apparently impossible not to extract laughter from our family, and we all succumbed as we helped or watched mother pack for Hampshire. Here, it was a question of leaving out for all the social events which would not take place. 'What is the correct wear for the days that Masters doesn't want the trap used?' 'Semi-evening for bridge? No, but a High Street coatee for a good rousing evening of solitaire.' 'Pass the moth-balls, if I'm not robbing *you*.'

It was James who bought mother and me each a service flask and filled it with whisky. For rather different reasons, we were both to empty them before we had done with our relations. Lalage – her disappointment at what she believed to be the clashing of gifts was keen – gave me a thermos flask.

'Keep it filled at night, Vere, and Hutchins'll smuggle you up some biscuits.'

On thinking it over, I'm bound to admit that Lalage had been present when mother made the remark about hoping I should get enough to eat – and yet there was a quiet, special quality of urgency about Lalage's apparent fears for my material welfare in subtle contrast to mother's semi-humorous tone. It was as though, to Lalage, I owned no longer that self-reliance she, at least, knew so well: as if, suddenly, my age and experience were non-existent, and I was beginning life once more with all the vulnerability of youth.

If this was an elder-sisterly attitude, it was one that I had never thought of expecting from her, or she of extending.

III

And so I saw everyone off and divided my days between work, Lowndes Square and Campden Hill, and knew what loneliness could be. Difficult though families can be, I can imagine no much greater woe than that absolute freedom which enables one to live for oneself alone. For, somehow, even friends are not the same, their praise or sympathy, however genuine, is eternally once-removed, their knowledge of one too intermittent and gappy to make of their encouragement anything very much deeper than the compliment.

At all times prolonged absence from James gave me a sensation of instability and lack that was distinct from the pang of a mere parting.

Hard work in the daytime and the impact on one's nerves of settlement into a strange house, though wearing, helped me over the first few days; that, and letters from Hampshire.

'… last night, with the soup, sherry was handed round *in a medicine bottle*. We tilted in each a drop, like perfect ladies. There was whisky on the sideboard and nary a hollow toothful offered. My tongue was hanging out, and at almost the end of dinner, uncle Stuart said "What do you care to drink?" so of course I made stockish noises, like Kipps, and it ended with some quite decent burgundy, but I foresee the day when I shall fly to me trunk and quaff James's whisky, bless him!

'We had a leg of mutton and not a solitary dem of mint sauce, though the kitchen garden is still *rocking* with it.

'We are still on lamps and candles here, and I take mine at ten o'clock and with a Lud Love You, Gentlemen, disappear to my *enormous* bedroom. I do trust it isn't boged! It never used to be, but if an elemental of the Elliott O'Donnell type appears with its "eyes of hellish malignance" I shall pack me box! Lalage's room is smaller but really charming, and overlooks the park, and there's a bookshelf with *Ministering Children*, and *Jessica's First Prayer* and *Mrs. Edgeworth* – our old tomes. I read two off at one blow, last night, and they are one long unmitigated scream. Find some more of ours at Lowndes Square. (Top back room.)

'Lalage is much better already, and I think we shall make out, though to-morrow I must tabor into the village and buy a spirit lamp and kettle. The hot-water bottles here are tepid, and *no* early tea. Lor!

'Wrap up warmly, pet, and if you feel low, let me know *at once* and I'll come home *ventre absolument à terre.*

'Bless you,
'Mother.'

In the first of my answering letters it occurred to me that it might well be distinctly necessary for mother and Lalage to send me 'Vallant despatches', separate from the real letter, as James and I had done to each other, and mother's reply, 'it won't be the least necessary, Grannyma is never tiresome about letters', surprised me, until I reflected that this accommodating normality about her daughter's correspondence was all a part of the Vallant indifference to its children.

IV

Hutchins had welcomed me warmly; even Lady Vallant had seemed grateful for my arrival.

I was put into the spare room on the third floor, and found it to be an awkward, L-shaped affair with a brass bed far too large and the dark, flocculent wallpaper hung with an assortment of Empire mirrors, all valuable and all spotted, and which had apparently drifted there from somewhere else. The toilet set was rotund and cumberous and one spent one's time sidling when not actually in bed.

I wondered what mother's version of the room would be, and wrote off to find out. Here, at least, one should be on safe ground. … Her reply was, 'Yes, it is rather a beast. We never went into it, though I suppose it was kept aired. I believe one of the uncles was turned in there, in the holidays'.

And so the room had nothing for me, for good or ill, or I for it. We were mutually pointless. It was at the end of a thickly carpeted passage running parallel with the stairs, and was a flight above Lady Vallant's bedroom. By means of lifting the weighty jug and basin on to the floor, I was able to type at the marble washstand, secure that I was disturbing nobody. The only table in the room was a small bedside one of mahogany, with a drawer and twisted legs. At the moment, I was engaged upon the parts of a play about Gladstone; I had asked my chief at the office as a favour that I might be allotted as much work as possible which could be done at home in view of my grandmother's apprehensions. I would give Lady Vallant her money's worth, and if my presence 'comforted' her she should have it. I could wait. ...

Once, already, when the maroons went off, I had joined the antick procession down all those stairs and installed the old lady in the subterranean wine-cellars, labyrinthine and coldly fusty, kindly refraining from pointing out that if the house was struck, we all stood a sporting chance of getting the dining-room table on our heads plus the bomb. When the skyward droning was over, my grandmother led us upstairs and prayed with us in the dining-room. She then proceeded to the drawing-room and was herself again.

For one thing I admired her: the fear of domestic mockery did not seem to exist for her. Eccentric, she yet contrived consistence and dignity. I saw very soon that the staff all detested her, but their manner was invariably immaculate. An impertinence shrivelled in her presence, and suspected deficiencies were laid bare and trounced then and there with dismaying publicity. And even here was fineness, of that kind which lays all its cards on the table.

When I told mother about the cellars, she wrote that she never knew there were any, and asked for a full description.

V

Sometimes, in the afternoons, Lady Vallant and I entered the little brougham and were driven stuffily to the park. It did not occur to my companion that an airing with closed windows was an outing of which horse and coachman alone received the benefit. I once let down one of the windows, and the grey pleasantness of the winter day seemed to surprise her. I did not ask permission, I simply let down the window. If there was a scrap, all right; if not, it would be as I had discovered with other members of our family; that any argument was futile and direct action the only means of getting anything done.

Sometimes, we clopped our way to the elder of the Sloane Street and Knightsbridge shops where – whether it was a relic of more spacious days or tribute to personality I don't know – assistants trickled out to the carriage and the pavement became a bazaar of flicked lace and *gros point* squares for Lady Vallant's fancywork. And once I was taken to pay calls. The call, I found, persists in the big London squares, and butlers still loom in Adams doorways to receive The Card, and on the railings of one of our destinations was the link-boy's extinguisher.

I tried not to let myself become enchanted overmuch, though that episode in my life has given me a taste for space and beauty which I have never lost; and even now James and I will walk the squares of south and west at all times of the year to catch up on the life within them. We have loitered in high summer to savour a party in Grosvenor Square and followed the putting up of the awning and the putting down of the red carpet; have marked the delivery of palms and gilt chairs earlier in the day, thanks to announcement in the social columns of *The Times* and *Post* (read by us at breakfast). In autumn we have sauntered to Belgrave Square to follow up the reported arrival 'from Scotland' of the earl and countess of so-and-so (James looking up the trains), and seen the quiet, unremarkable couple unremarkably arrive and safely installed. In winter, Berkeley Square has given us the secrets of neighbourhood amenity, and we have watched at all hours the emergence from pillar'd doorway of The Companion airing the dog, and — oh pleasure undiluted! — the departure of footmen bearing 'floral offerings' and 'seasonable greetings' of fruit for the Christmas sideboard to numbers farther up and down the square; and vans arrive from Fortnum and Mason, as is meet and right, and deliver (so we have arranged) that green satin and sequined casket filled with 'bonbons', gift from old flame to old flame (who married very prudently, thanks to mamma, but of course the wrong man). And it is in these quiet backwaters that, quite perfectly, one finds the forgotten Italian and his monkey and the family of love-birds who peck one up a fortune from a drawer of cards. And once we held our breath at a revolving ring of puppets who danced their legs jiggishly to the lost music of the harlequinade (and followed the show for an hour). And so home, bursting with it all, and talking about it for the rest of the evening.

My bedroom at Vallant House overlooked Lowndes Square. Too high to see the activities below, not high enough for view of roofs and chimney pots, it gave me little pleasure. There were no longer those jinglings of hansoms of night, midnight and early day of which mother had sometimes told us 'I liked to listen to them, they were company'.

CHAPTER XXII

I

IT WAS, after all, quite easy for me to explore the schoolroom floor. Why I had expected the clever advance-move of locked doors, conflict and veto I don't know. One flight above my own room and I was there, where my mother had lived, and Myra, for somehow the presence of my aunts Emmeline and Sophia had no mental meaning at all.

The stairs leading to that storey were covered with scuffed linoleum, a delicate reminder to me, who didn't need it, that anything did for the children.

I had postponed the visit for days, partly in fear of the distress I knew was waiting for me in some form, partly in order to get the atmosphere of life in the lower part of the great house settled, one way or the other. The children's floor, I knew, one must approach with mind unconfused.

And there I was at last, after all these years, receiving fact against guesswork.

There were four bedrooms and the schoolroom itself, the number of rooms accounted for by their smallness. Mentally I began a provisional allotment of the accommodation; this, possibly, Miss Chilcot's bedroom, the second Emmeline and Sophia, third, mother and Myra, fourth; two uncles (and the third uncle, apparently, put into the room below). No den for the boys at all.

Here, from most of the windows, was the view which, to me, is London incarnate; of backs of houses, faintly tinted as in a colour print, with their occasional box balconies, the Georgian bow-windows of smoky brick, the glass dome of some dining-room on the leads below, a grimy bubble; a livery stable where grooms made ready the little equipages of the old dames round about (including that of my grandmother), and serrated black against the sky, chimneys, angular, contorted, cowls slowly turning – the outlook that thousands of nursemaids of the Jubilee, arriving in growlers to their Victorian situation, had looked out at.

> Sally go round the stars,
> Sally go round the moon,
> Sally go round the chimneypots
> On Sunday afternoon.
> (Whoop!)

lines which I had first heard sung (to the tune of 'Guy, Guy, Guy, stick him in the eye!') by a chaperoned school treat, chanting it in a walking circle.

Sally … somehow one pictures her as persistently rakish, wearing check silk taffeta and a bustle; she is to me a capable, rortily chuckling daughter of joy, and was in her heyday in the early days of the Alhambra, when gloves and scent were sold at the back of the dress circle. She had, I fancy, a 'combined' room off Drury Lane and her favourite 'perfumes' were Jockey Club, Opoponax and White Rose. Not long ago, I actually found a bottle of patchouli behind the pills, cough cures and horse drenches of a country chemist, and instantly bought it for the sake of the old days I never knew in fact, but know so utterly in every other way!

And I stood in that back bedroom and gazed, and murmured the anthem of London Sally.

11

Emboldened, I made many visits to the top floor as the days passed, examining on my knees the poky little cup-boards, touching the rusty fireguard round which those children had clustered, and the mean and grudging grate – I even found the coal scuttle in one of the bedrooms. In the schoolroom, a broken-down wicker settee; from a chest of drawers more suitable to the servants' quarters, I drew the red tablecloth, and know every inkstain by heart. I shook it out, folded, and replaced it. On a wall I found pencil marks:

> E. 5ft. 3ins.
> S. 5ft. 1ins.

A. 5ft.

M. 4ft. 8ins.

Myra. And another set of measurements of an obviously later date.

E. 5 ft. 5½ ins.

S. 5ft. 3ins.

A. 5 ft. 2 ins.

M. 4ft. 8ins.

Myra, who remained at four foot eight inches. And mother hadn't made the progress of the aunts, either ... I clenched my teeth.

Lady Vallant met me once on the landing. She saw where I had been, and I braced myself automatically. I really believe that if she had stood there, a fury, or eyed me inimically, or forbidden me the upper storey outright, I should have been happier.

She only glanced at me, said absently, 'Ah, dear', and flitted into her bedroom.

Subtly I felt robbed and a little defenceless. I wasn't uneasy – she was no actress – therefore no plan was behind the greeting. It was the cool assurance of it – nothing to hide – my house is yours ... mother had evidently soothed and convinced the old woman about us, either that, or the direct fear of air-raid had thrown Lady Vallant out of gear, or she liked me, after all, when tested as an inmate? That would be quite typical of Vallantry; letting one go to seed for the best years of one's life, and suddenly, by hazard, taking to one, too late.

III

The schoolroom suite was neglected. It was left to me to air it, and gradually, whenever I had a spare moment, I got into the habit of cleaning and polishing it – I even put a little pot of flowers on my chimneypots window-ledge.

The rooms could make nothing of my presence there; their atmosphere reminded me of the person whom life has injured and rendered hopeless, it was as one feels when taking fruit and flowers to the doomed case in hospital; one received a languid gratitude and then apathy again. There was the hint that one had come too late … absurdly one was stung by the injustice.

Once, wrapped in my thickest coat, I spent an afternoon up there. I chose the least of the bedrooms and took a nap on the bed, but was thankful for waking. There was nothing definite about the dreams I had had, simply a sensation of misery. I awoke crying, as one sometimes does, with the difference that for quite five minutes after full consciousness, the tears continued to roll down my face. I was robust with myself about the business; dreams were beyond all reason, and so on. James and I once dreamed for two nights in succession of the same woman. She was quite unknown to us, but over the breakfast table we compared notes and our description tallied to the last detail, and I have dreamed of one or two people never seen by myself, and have subsequently met them in the street, or in buses, although we were never destined to know each other. I have often wondered, therefore, if the dream created the person, or the person the dream, and if the latter, what was our initial point of contact?

I made a point of 'resting' in that upper room, once more, and the same thing – the distress and crying – happened as before. And then I knew it had been Myra's room.

IV

I left it with coward's haste, prepared though I had been for something of the sort. And far downstairs the telephone was shrilling. Hutchins was at my side with annoying promptness. 'A gentleman wishes to speak to you, Miss.' I don't know what the old man thought of my manner to himself, what he made of the way in which I turned my head from him – there were reasons – when I saw him, or indeed of my voice when I thanked him. At the best of times I am at sixes and sevens when torn from sleep, and such a sleep as I had fled from had left me tenfold more inadequate than usual. It was the cursed crying. This afternoon, for some reason, it wouldn't stop, and my eyes enragingly filled and filled again as I lifted the receiver in my grandfather's study off the hall.

'This is Mr. Cosmo Furnival speaking. Would that be Miss Buchan?'

In spite of everything I was slightly thrilled. This was one of those preposterous moments which life occasionally holds; it was almost like a piece of one's childhood being handed back to one, as though Hayden Coffin had sent one a postcard, or Alexander suddenly came to tea announcing that he 'often dined with Sir Frederick and Lady Vallant in the old days in the Square'.

My silence while savouring all this must have lasted overlong.

'*Is* that Miss Buchan? I'm Cosmo Furnival, perhaps you know my name?'

'I was brought up on it,' I answered, 'and I'm Miss Buchan.' The laugh in my ear pleased me instantly. Just so, I feel certain, must Irving have reflectively chuckled when, as Iago, he sat upon that Lyceum table plotting, and eating raisins and spitting out the seeds.

'Well, of course, it's about this Gladstone business. Now, Miss Buchan, in confidence, I've acquired that play, the original option has lapsed – you have the script I believe?'

'I'm working on it now.'

'Thank you, yes. Well, I want to get ahead with production, and – do forgive my mentioning it – but I must ask for absolute secrecy, you understand? They tell me at the office that you are kindly undertaking the typewriting.'

'We don't give away clients' business, Mr. Furnival.'

'No, no, no. But you know, things leak out in the most disconcerting way. I assure you that if it was known that a Gladstone play was on the stocks we should have three rival versions in as many weeks, because unfortunately with the public it isn't a matter of who's written the best play on any subject, but of who gets in first with the idea … now, there's a point or two I want altered. D'you remember the Sandringham bit?'

'Yes.'

'Well, I wonder if you'll bring the script to the telephone? To begin with there's quite a page got to come right out. The Censor. It appears that one mayn't have the Queen on the stage. I think it's ridiculous, but there you are.'

'I remember. I don't have to bring the script. You mean about the grants for the Prince of Wales's children. *"At such a time as this, Ma'am …"*'

'That's it! *"… the feeling of Parliament, of which I, an unworthy representative …"*

'*"Mr. Gladstone, we would prefer your meaning quite unwrapped. Frankly, we do not recognize in you this diffident approach."'* I replied.

'*"Ma'am, I have not deserved this …"'.*

At this moment, the footman, hearing voices, passed through the hall and peered in at the door while we were Gladstoning and Ma'am-ing each other quite oblivious. I gave it up and emitted an hysteric scream of laughter. The man vanished like smoke. I bent again to the receiver. 'It – it was my grandmother's footman. He – he *heard* us.'

Again that soft snarl of amusement. 'I hope he isn't preparing a version belowstairs.'

'He would call it "The Grand Old Man", and it would inevitably be a success.'

'And we, with just "Gladstone", are going to antagonize all the expensive seats. I wonder if you could, perhaps, come to the theatre and go over the whole script with me?'

When the conversation was over an idea occurred to me, and I went round my grandfather's bookshelves for the first time in my life. There was one biography of Gladstone; it looked dullish, but you never knew. I abstracted it without a with or by your leave. Lady Vallant was no bookworm. When one came to think of it, one had not an idea what her interests were, if any, beyond, of course, dress and chicanery. She thought she was fond of music, but her occasional performances at the still draped and littered piano made me wince, she played everything with the loud pedal, and never let wrong notes stand in her light. Crash, bang, out they came with an equal arrogance. It was all very typical of the woman.

v

The theatre was in Shaftesbury Avenue, a locality in which, for some reason, I have never been able to be happy; it always strikes me as being remorseless to young things, and if it were a woman, it would possess hard, drugged-looking eyes, and a cruel underbred snigger. Should any ill befall the daughter of the rectory, up for lunch, a little shopping and a matinee with Aunt

Bertha, I think that Shaftesbury Avenue would take the pitiless line that she had only herself to blame. Leicester Square, perhaps first cousin to Shaftesbury Avenue in, as it were, social standing and visitor's list, should affect one in a similar manner, but about the square there is a warm, stale geniality like that of a slightly tipsy serio of the 'nineties – no harm in her at all. Perhaps it is owing to the sense of space, and above all to the garden where children from the Soho courts play, and one receives an optical illusion of innocence.

Walking down Shaftesbury Avenue that morning and receiving the usual impression, I was remembering a game that in the first years of our settling in London James and I used to play, and have played, on and off, ever since. And it came into being through my dislike of certain local atmospheres, of which Shaftesbury Avenue was typical, and of the fact that from my later teens I had had to pursue my affairs very largely unescorted, and therefore extra vulnerable. James, when he knew that I was due in any street at a given date, would make a point of going up it himself in advance, and of leaving me a token. He would say casually, 'Haymarket? I've thrown a halfpenny down the first grating past the Carlton', or 'Shaftesbury Avenue? You'll find a pencil behind the pit placard outside the Lyric', and, looking for the halfpenny or pencil, one forgot to be intimidated, and when one found it the entire street became, for a minute, changed and friendly. And he once twisted his theatre programme into a little cocked hat and poked it behind a restaurant mirror. I found it six weeks later when dining with somebody else, and the somebody else was, as usual, the wrong person, and the little hat saved the evening for me, and made me able to cope with everything. And now there was nothing. And I had had difficulty in getting away from Lady Vallant. She was extra nervous that morning, and as pessimistic as aunt Emmeline at her worst about the safety of 'London'. She was feeding and housing me, but I must earn, and told her so point-blank. It silenced her. The obvious solution of giving me an allowance (which I should not have accepted) never appeared to occur to her, but, as always happens, one felt put in the wrong. Also, she would turn me out whenever it suited her. One had at times, when considering her objectively as a frail and close relation, lonely and a woman, to keep a grip on other

aspects of her which were eternal, as against merely immediate
and dramatic.

There was no place in my life for cheap appeals to the emotions.

VI

At the theatre, I made the usual novice's error of enquiring
for the manager in the foyer, and was sent into a back alley.

I was left after the sergeant had passed me in to find my own
way, and my reward for posting along corridors was ultimately
to discover that the room I was destined for overlooked the Avenue; its floor must, I calculated, be the very ceiling of the foyer from which I had been indulgently displaced. Then why not
run a staircase to it direct? I found Furnival's name on the door,
knocked and waited, and knocked again. As I received no sum-
mons I did as I always do: assumed it to be the Enquiry office to
the inner room, opened the door and found I was badly wrong.

Cosmo Furnival had fallen lightly asleep on a sofa.

I recognized him at once in spite of the fact that he was not
in everyday clothes and yet not made up at all – a baffling combination of effects. Gradually I smiled as I looked. One ringed
hand, the knuckles veiled in a ruffle of lace, hung down almost
to the carpet, the other was snuggled into the flowered waistcoat,
while a triangle of stiffened silk coat jutted beneath his elbow. On
a near-by table were a rapier, a snuff-box and a handkerchief; on
a wooden stand like a bedpost his queued peruke.

I stood there and frankly gloated at the spectacle, and admired
his legs in oyster-grey silk which had that right and satisfying
length from knee to ankle which is so uncommon, with the an-
kle-bones clear and sharp. He was subtly older than I had quite
expected in spite of the calendar and of my flatulent words to
poor little Gladys, whom I had forgotten until this moment. She
had left the office quite inevitably to make munitions, which
quite directly and simply to her meant extravagantly better pay
and the dual opportunity for wearing trousers and collecting
scalps from among the fitters. She had outgrown Furnival, if indeed she had ever 'ingrown' him. But so, it seemed, had everyone
else. I thought of the mantelpiece in Palace Green, of my very

father and mother going 'up to town' to see him. People didn't run Furnival any more; his epoch and its emotions were as dead as Lewis Waller's. It positively dated a woman. One could appreciate that, just in the way that the world no longer sang 'The Lily of Laguna' or 'You are queen of my heart to-night', in spite of the fact that their charm and melodiousness remain the same as ever. ...

Meanwhile a point of etiquette confronted one. I hesitated to sit there and wait for Furnival to wake, it seemed a sort of spying on him. I was even more unwilling to wake him myself. People asleep are in a no-man's-land, between death and life, and I have always felt that to drag them back by a sudden noise, movement, or touch is, possibly, to endanger them, that such sharp translation must harm them in ways of which we know nothing. He must return in his own good time. I closed the door noiselessly and took a comfortable winged chair near him, I even took off my hat to fit more snugly into its depths and wedged the Gladstone biography down its side. One must chance startling him when he did awaken. There was plenty of time, it was still an hour and a half until luncheon which I must take with Lady Vallant as a peace offering. Warmed and relaxed I went on looking at Furnival. He certainly didn't resemble Gladstone, with his fine Wellingtonian nose, also, Furnival's mouth was too thin and humorous, his length too long and slender, the planes of his face too fine.

I am told I 'ought to have seen him thirty-five years ago, he was a beautiful young man'. I *have* seen him, and on post-cards, and silently disagree. Age had brought out the character in his face and the delicate bony structure, and the knife-line along the jaw and the hint of kindly crows' feet. Still, there were ways and wigs, and even I saw that the point about this play was that it was an innovation – it preceded by many years that flood of biographic dramas which, pioneer'd by *Abraham Lincoln*, in 1919, was to be a feature of the 1930's. One would like to see Furnival complete in the peruke which was on the stand; at present his head, a study in black and white with one white streak that ran across from forehead to crown, was far too modern for ruffles and quizzing-glass. And yet, why not? All the beaux and fops of Bath tossed their wigs aside in off-moments, and Charles II himself had admitted to being 'a very grizzled old gentleman' without the shelter of his own tumbling curls.

And so I sat and watched my grizzled old gentleman.

VII

I woke to find him at my side. He smiled down at me, his eyes crinkling.

'Now, try and forgive me. Dear! what tired people we are! Why does one go on?'

'Mr. Furnival, I can't expect you to believe me, but this is the first time I've ever gone to sleep on my job.'

'Then I'm really flattered.'

But I was neither soothed nor amused. What I had done struck me as being neither whimsical nor charming; I was disgusted with myself, and a little apprehensive. If this was going to happen in the future it meant one was sub-standard. ...

'It was cheap and slack,' I rapped.

He held out to me an acorn-shaped glass. 'Brown sherry, from the Cock Tavern. Isn't the colour rather wonderful?'

One didn't go on hammering a subject and I took the glass and sipped at the syrupy sunshine. Also, I was immeasurably grateful. He seemed to divine all that. He hitched himself on to the sofa end and the band of brilliants winked on his long leg. 'I was glad to see you sleeping. You looked as though you needed it badly.'

I couldn't meet that and just answered, 'I'm really quite efficient you know'.

He shook his head over me. 'Too much conscience. You must find yourself very difficult to live with ... now, we'd both like another glass and we both mustn't have one. This may feel very innocuous, but believe me it gets there.'

'You are playing this afternoon?' I flicked my head at the peruke.

'Another special matinee, for the Red Cross. A scene from *The Bath Comedy*.'

'Do you ever forget your words, Mr. Furnival?'

'Oh, we all have our lapses, you know. My private trouble is that when I dry up I cannot wait for the prompter like a sensible man but go on improvising. It's a kind of vanity, I believe. Old Tree once enchanted me by exclaiming "Odds Fishikins!" in a costume show at His Majesty's when he couldn't lay his tongue to the period oath.'

'And you?'

'Oh, my nicest effort was once in a modern piece. I can always remember the sense of a speech, and its rhythm, but it's agony when the words go. The line was "You cannot clean a pig-sty with rosewater", and I said "You cannot clean a pie-dish with newspaper".'

I tried to put the glass down to laugh and he took it from me and pressed me back into the chair.

'And did the audience notice?'

'No, bless them, except those who thought it was a biting epigram and were able to feel cynical and disillusioned.'

The ridge of the biography caught my side and I sprang up guiltily.

'I brought you this.'

His glance was for me, not at the book in his hand. 'Can't you *rest*?'

'No. Now you mention it, I don't believe I can, any more.'

He cocked an eyebrow. 'Any more? ... this book, I'm entirely grateful to you. Candidly, how much it may assist matters I don't know, but not everybody would have thought of bringing it.'

His eyes on the opened book, he murmured, 'And so you're living with your grandmother'. It seemed so much a part of the text, and the firelight and the temporary general security that I did not at once realize it as a personality.

'Oh yes ... for a little. Lady Vallant.'

'Vallant ... one knows the name.'

VIII

I ground my palms together. Inwardly I was crying, 'Not here! If she gets in here as well then I *am* done'. And I think that if his expression had become grave, or his manner wary, above all if he had changed the subject with obvious tact, I should have despaired, but even allowing for the fact that his profession included the control of feature, I believed that there was nothing to disturb me in his look.

'She was rather a beauty in her day, wasn't she?'

So that was all … I relaxed. 'Oh yes.' I could have enlarged upon that side of things, on her fear of air-raid and facial damage, on her bursting wardrobe, but I would fight clean, and regard my silence as fair payment for my own relief. Furnival was only a man, and a stranger.

'*I think* we will reverse our decision and have some more sherry. But only half a glass each. So …' Evidently my face had been doing things on its own, giving me away at mention of the old woman.

'I wonder why total abstainers are so often alarming, unlovable and humourless?' He sat down close to me and gave me – it reminded me sharply of James – his entire attention. 'Now tell me: don't you find it very difficult to combine being a gentlewoman with business?'

I thought, 'No, you don't! If this is an approach, I'm not having any. I don't happen to have had to cope with any actor's-charm business before, but I can quite imagine that it would be ten times more clever and concentrated than the ordinary man's.' At the same time, one might as well plumb disillusion from the start. …

I said, 'Oh, I suppose so', and he sighed and looked at his shoe buckles. I felt squarely put in the wrong, for once, and made as instant an amend as possible. 'You mean that the two qualities clash?'

'Of course. And the eternal tragedy of gentlewomen is that they give a hundred per cent value for ten per cent return. Full measure, pressed down, and nobody thanks 'em.'

'My God! that's true.'

'Ahh …'

He'd got that from me, but somehow it wasn't just pumping. Yet I meant to be under no misapprehensions; would judge him by the most exacting standards, and impute to him the lowest motives. One got on best, that way, in the long run … and I would never more be lulled by trusting into any complication. I would, for the present, begin by envisaging the possibility that this social atmosphere of sherry and small talk was tribute to Lady Vallant and Lowndes Square. She should serve me that way, by putting vulgar suspicion before me. And I would face up to his

172 | RACHEL FERGUSON

attraction, first as last: that makeweight which, in dealing with men as fellow humans, so unfairly confuses the issues if you let it. And before the task of describing charm one throws up one's hands. How can one expect to convey that a laugh, a walk – even a personal way of clearing the throat between sentences, can possess actual beauty? I only know that sometimes I have caught my breath at the sight of Cosmo's walk across a room, have often set myself, since, to discover it elsewhere that there should be no mistake at all, and found it never, except – faintly emphasized and conscious – in other men of the stage. But of course there is no getting over the fact that men like Cosmo Furnival who have spent a lifetime on the stage at a time when it was a profession and not a hobby acquire a mellow grace and flavour the young 'uns will never catch up on. Fumed oak against chippendale. And more's the pity for the modern theatre, with its catchpenny popularities and get-rich-quick methods. Since meeting Furnival, I know that a man must love his art, and sweat for it, and be by it brought low – even unto fish and chips in Bradford and a combined room in Highbury New Park (or perchance Kennington Road), and so cleansed, and that his religion must be 'What can I put into the theatre?' not 'What can I get out of it?'

I wanted to go on talking to him, to listen to his voice, which, quite apart from anything he said, was what Claude would term 'well worth the price of admission', and so I announced, instead, 'I'm keeping you. Oughtn't we –?' and I put the script of the play upon the dressing-table.

'You're being very efficient, this morning, but no doubt you are perfectly right.' He put a chair for me, supplied us with pencils and we got to work.

I was to find out that Cosmo Furnival's mental processes were as sharp and clear – as his ankle bones! In his quiet, suave way, he knew exactly what he wanted and saw that he got it. It often reminded me of the clash between Irving and Ellen Terry over her desire to wear black as Ophelia, except that, having got his way, Cosmo would go off and chuckle silently to himself. If one tried to catch him at it he would swerve upon one and look attentive and civil, and bend above one, deliberately exploiting his height, and make one feel a fool. As they say, one couldn't get past him over anything. I have seen him at his desk deep in correspondence at the fluttering in of some actress armed with her beastly little yap-dog, and although I swear that Cosmo hadn't glanced up, he murmured 'You are looking most delightful and charming Mary, but … the dog, you know. The barking … and … ah … other possible manifestations. I must sincerely apologize to you for the obscurity of the notice in the entry prohibiting the presence of pets at rehearsals. It shall be placed more prominently. Most thoughtless of me.'

He was saying, 'I see Queen Victoria having to come right out'.

'But – couldn't Gladstone speak to her through the door?'

His smile at me was the exact equivalent of a pat on the head.

'Miss Buchan, have you ever heard an audience laugh in the wrong place?'

'Yes. It's awful.'

'It is worse than awful, it is a tragedy to actor and author, and may spell finis to a play.' He screwed his monocle into his eye. 'A certain margin of stupidity one must allow to every audience, but one must positively not play into their hands by inviting ridicule. I see you don't quite get me. Now may I show you what it would sound like if we pursued your plan? You see, I'd so like you to be interested in your work with me.' He went to the door and set it ajar, then retreating, poddled towards it and conducted a dialogue largely extempore in which the State squabble was reduced to a loud protest from Gladstone and remote, offended gobblings from the Queen. I couldn't even laugh. I saw what he meant, and said so. He smote his hands and tossed them into the air. 'The audience isn't going to care tuppence what the Censor allows or doesn't allow; all it will imagine is that our late dear queen is in one of several intimate inabilities to receive. The real damage is that the Imperialistic atmosphere is killed dead – yes, Murton?'

'What will you take for lunch, sir?'

'Sole, a bottle of sauterne and some Brie – ripe. For two.' He turned to me. 'You'll lunch with me?'

'Thank you, but I must get back.'

'Then half a bottle, Murton, and phone through to the garage, I want the car round now.'

'Very good sir.' The man vanished.

'I wish you'd stay. Must you be quite so conscience-struck, all the time?'

'No, it isn't that exactly, but–' I hadn't quite meant to say it – 'when one's meditating a mean thing ...'

'Mean? You? I don't believe it.'

It came spontaneously, even I sensed that. It would warm one later, privately.

'I think it's true; justified a thousand times or I hope I shouldn't be doing it. Perhaps "a betrayal of hospitality" would be a better expression.'

He looked down on me. 'I give it up! Then ... tomorrow at eleven, here, if that will suit you? My car's waiting for you, and forgive my mentioning it, but don't tip the chauffeur. I pay him thumping good wages and he quite understands I don't intend to have my friends victimized, shelling out in the end more than they would for a taxi.'

'Oh but I can't *not*!'

'Oh yes you can. Now, please. Do believe me. Promise?'

'Very well.'

As I stood in the hall of Vallant House, it seemed to me that the children's storey would like to know about Cosmo Furnival. It was, to me, as if those top rooms would be reassured as to my goodwill if I told them – a sort of testimony as to character! But go into Myra's bedroom again so soon I could not. And yet it was that room, somehow, that would be most relieved of all. ...

CHAPTER XXIII

I

AT LUNCHEON, my grandmother was what aunt Sophia calls difficult and aunt Emmeline going to pieces; she was offended and impertinent by turns, and intolerable to the footman, on whose behalf I soon began to have sympathetic nerves. She told me with what sounded like bitter sarcasm that I was 'looking very handsome' and enquired as a corollary in whose motor I had returned. On being informed, she merely said 'Waste of time: you can't marry him', before the butler, at which it occurred to me that possibly I had given her too much rope over trifles all this time, and I deliberately caught Hutchins' eye and smiled at him. The old man met it quite admirably with a slight, shocked shake of the head which conveyed perfectly both the terms on which we mutually stood and an assurance that he had, in his time, weathered the table through many similar crises.

Lady Vallant said measuredly, 'When you have quite done ogling my manservant we will have the sweet'. And by a hairsbreadth I let even that pass, for I suddenly realized that she could not tolerate any hint of sympathies going on elsewhere, above all, any *sub rosa* alliances. It could be engrained autocracy or fear. ...

And one couldn't even campaign against her as one having committed flagrant vulgarity; it was all too assured and superb and outrageous for that. The pearlie queen on her donkey-barrow can never be vulgar. It is only when you get into the queasy timidities of those suburbs which would draw their very skirts from the buttoned, feathered, chy-iking donah that you achieve vulgarity.

I suppose everybody in that house was always glad when luncheons and dinners were over, and when one thought of the years in which that sort of thing had been going on!

After luncheon Lady Vallant adjourned to the drawing-room, there to sit until tea, unless the carriage was ordered round and she paid calls. Satin skirts pinched up, she was already ascending the stairs.

In the hall I found the young footman with crumb-brush and tray who wellnigh leapt into the air on seeing me. I suppose he assumed I had vanished upstairs with the old lady. He was more or less openly blubbering. The shock of encounter was mutual. I stopped.

'Henry, is it her ladyship that you're upsetting yourself about?' The boy gulped and muttered. 'Because, don't. It isn't worth it. She – I mean, it wasn't you she was scolding, it's just her way.'

The fat being in the fire he faced me. 'Beg your pardon, miss, but I 'ate that old lady.'

'Yes. Well, what about going?'

'I couldn't face the row, miss.'

'Oh, nonsense. Why, it'd be over in ten minutes.' Why is it one can always see straight for others, never for oneself? 'Besides, you haven't done anything; you know, I think you're an excellent footman, if I may say so.' I did. My varied experience in dining and lunching had taught me that. Trained by Hutchins he was deft, quiet and anticipatory, never kept you waiting or tweaked your plate away before you had finished, or fidgeted you at chair back or sideboard, and he could pitch his eye in the right place during courses. 'If you want to leave, go up now and tell her ladyship you wish to make a change.'

'It don't give a man a chance, picking on 'im, and before company too.'

'I quite understand that. You go down and tuck in a good lunch and then put it to Lady Vallant.' A thought struck me. I counted upon my position in the household for it to pass muster. 'Henry, are your meals satisfactory?'

'Mr. Hutchins sees to that, miss. *And* cook.'

The old gang, operating again … this time, united. But then servants, unlike growing children, could fight for their own hand. …

'Her ladyship thinks she keeps an eye on everything, but she don't know half what goes on.' The boy had, by now, quite lost touch with diplomacy, had completely forgotten my own relationship to his employer. Involuntarily I smiled. 'You'd better not tell me too much, Henry.'

And after all, he put it off for weeks; it was almost as if he had caught the germ of our family inertia. Like us, when he acted it would be suddenly and clumsily, with amazement that the affair was simple after all, and plenty of self-scourging that he hadn't done it before. The house itself discouraged action, and it was time that one coped with that, for by now, as missionaries say, I 'knew the field' as much as one was ever likely to.

Going upstairs, I was thinking, as I had thought before, that as a Vallant granddaughter, I was once-removed from the house's slaveries, vulnerable at least through my own choice, by having ranged myself on the side of my mother and Myra.

I went up to my bedroom and from my locked trunk took out and re-read the Chilcot letter.

It was past twelve o'clock that night before the coast was clear. Those thick Victorian carpets have their uses and I achieved passage and the staircase outside my grandmother's bedroom in absolute silence. I took candlestick and matches with me and thought how thoroughly and generously the house would burn if an accident occurred. But it mustn't burn. I had something to discover, and was extra careful in my disposition of the light. Besides, burning down wasn't always any good at all for a certain type of trouble.

I sat in the middle of the staircase which led from drawing-room to hall and remembered our discussion in the little Soho eating house. It was the site of events which counted. And here I was, on the site. Fragments from the Chilcot letter came back to me. My sealed orders.

Myra was lame from birth … did you know? … then came a cracking sound and a cry, two cries, I think … Lady Vallant would not have her in the drawing-room … Oh God! one ought to be hardened to it all, by now, but I buried my head in my hands and tried to remember I was here on business. On Myra's business.

Mean? You? I don't believe it. I'd forgotten that. It was a beautiful voice saying a beautiful thing to one, no longer ago than that morning. Mentally I clung to it. But one mustn't go that road about Cosmo Furnival; waste of time and life and feeling, also incredible that he meant it. One would see him to-morrow. The hall was so still. Large houses, it seems, have the gift of silence. Nothing to hear but the *muffled* toot of taxis. I was — oh curse it — beginning to be afraid. I exercised my mind with the first thing to hand. *Mr. Gladstone, we would prefer your meaning quite unwrapped.* Bless Mr. Gladstone and his unwrapped meaning! The front door with its oval panels was just such a door as he might have come in at, dashing down inverness and top hat which, I felt sure, was a size too large for him, as was our vicar's in the village in the old days. One's hands were shaking. *Those stairs are beastly cold.* James off to his prep school, telling me that in our Campden Hill home. Suddenly I was glad of the chill and the trembling. I thought it meant that things were beginning to move, guessed that They were coming. I didn't pray because, quite plainly, all set forms of prayer eluded me; I just said over, instinctively, the names of those on earth whose various associations brought me comfort by day. 'James … mother … Claude … Cosmo.' I left out Lalage, I remembered later, and wondered why. But I was to find out.

Already the air was beginning to vibrate – a sort of buzzing and undulating – in which one knew that one must keep control of one's very thought, and then I was aware, without seeing, that people were passing me. I ducked ridiculously, and this I swear: that as they went by, their mood no less than their bodies went through me, and it was Vere Buchan who experienced two closely-following emotions. The words did not so much present themselves as the sense, which poured through me. So, I thought, 'I am pretty to-night, more girlish than she is', and 'We shall get no partners. Just like her to send round the carriage too late. I will dance and I will be a success'.

Remorseless, nervy and ill-humoured.

The faint crack – it seemed to come from the banister rail above me – went through my immediate consciousness and suddenly (Oh, I admit I muffed it all, that first time), there was a humming of voices, more like a change of vibration in the air; the stair on which I sat gave sharply and all the nerves in my body twanged. In the flame of my candle I saw for a matter of seconds, imperfectly and incompletely, as at Hampton Court, a strip of white nightdress and a small foot. It was on the stairs below me. In those seconds I was to be momentarily a third person, and I instantly knew (and shall never forget) what it was to be without love and without hope. I thought 'My life is over, and I know hate'.

III

And, tangibly, in my own self, I almost knew despair. I sat on those stairs and told myself that I had failed; I had at most confirmed suspicion, not from the little I had seen so much as from my sensations at the passing and their temporary possession of my brain, of those three figures. But I had proved nothing that wasn't in the Chilcot letter already.

I was never sure. And neither was I.

It then occurred to me that there was, perhaps, a little more to be gleaned, and I made myself go down to the hall and re-ascend that flight.

The picture evidently had not entirely faded, for just as one passes through a fog belt to clear weather, I too passed through sensations on my way. A faint twist of physical pain on the fourth step from the bottom one; two steps farther and it was gone. It was on the topmost step of all that suddenly, sometimes separately, sometimes merging, two intensities of feeling rushed into me and battled for my possession till I staggered.

At that moment I would have enjoyed depriving Lalage of Hugh, seeing and savouring her tears. I spared a hope that James would be killed, and while sick with compassion and that hate which is a holy thing I was praying, deliver us from evil.

And then I was filled with an emotion which revolted me more than the first, and I was just a coward, surprised, wrapped in mean anxiety for its future.

I suppose I leant too heavily upon the banister, that is a sound, official explanation of the ascending light which illumined the wall below, and, turning, flickeringly picked out that dado of china parrots at my back. The sight of the candle held up by Hutchins somehow shook me more acutely than what I had just been through. Perhaps it was the too-sudden impact of physical upon psychic … or the look on his face. He should have been a ridiculous figure enough, dishevelled, alarmed and blinking, portly in dressing-gown and pyjamas, except that when you saw the type of alarm in his eyes even the last ditch of hysteria was denied you. But I had, it seemed, a few remnants of consideration left.

'Miss Vere!'

'It's all right, Hutchins, I couldn't sleep and I badly wanted a drink. If you'd like to save my life get me some whisky.' It was just luck that I didn't happen to say brandy, the implications of a need for brandy morbidly excite all servants, as telegrams do.

Blessed are the burglars. Hutchins, if questioned by myself, could riposte with that. He led the way into the dining-room and mixed me a drink, and indeed I was glad of it. His hands were shaking and like a fool I let common humanity get the upper hand and asked him to have some whisky too. It tore down his respectable defence, showed him at once that I had seen that in his expression which wasn't accountable on the score of thieves. He took a drink, excusing himself, as I might have foreseen.

'It was seeing you on those stairs, Miss Vere.'

I just nodded and finished my whisky. He watched me going upstairs, lighting me with his candle, not stirring until I had disappeared.

I wrote to James all the rest of the night and was careful to turn off the light a few minutes before the maid was due with my hot water. I knew I was almost at the end of my tether.

I re-read bits of my letter. '... and it looks as if, tonight, I had been aunt Sophia and Emmeline ... and Myra, too. I suppose the last two people I became were Vallant and Miss Chilcot? Or would the good one have been mother, or Hutchins, do you think? I didn't see properly, oh! it's infuriating! You've got to remember I was only a *feeling*. I guessed Sophia and Emmeline because, with them, it was all dress and looks ... Hutchins discovered me, and hated it for me though he said nothing you could take hold of. ...'

And on the breakfast table was a letter from Lalage. Hugh had been slightly gassed and was coming home at once.

I was too drained to know what I felt about that; like a glass which has been breathed upon – and had I not been? – I felt blurred all over. But I must have made the small, involuntary sound of surprise for Lady Vallant asked me what was the matter. I told her, and she said, penetratingly for her, 'That should make the marriage easy', then she added, 'Your sister shall be married from here'.

There is a type of thought which screams. Hitherto I had met it only over trivialities: over the unwanted visitor, the bore or the guest who, having risen, will not make a clean exit, but wanders stickily about the room fastening on to any pretext of opened novel or new cushion for creation of further delay. This time, my thought was a scream of denial. 'Never, if I can prevent it. Never, never, never.'

And even that one couldn't take to mother. If she too balked at the sheer idea of Lalage's wedding from Vallant House it would be on her own grounds, by reason of private memory, or – for public use – by a pot-pourri of semi-humorous, sub-acid distaste.

It was a Vallantish touch which worked out so that our grand-mother offered an unprecedented and costly favour and I was to be the one to deny it to Lalage without explanation.

CHAPTER XXIV

I

I WORKED IN Furnival's rooms for nearly three weeks after that, going to the theatre every morning, to the enormous satisfaction of the good Miss Royal. Sometimes Furnival was there and sometimes not. On the latter occasions the key was handed to me by the sergeant.

It was impossible not to be interested in the work, although my life, then, was in such a confusion that I couldn't give my all to it, or when I did, felt that my hand was removed for just so long from Vallant House politics and that something, as a result, might get the better of us... In one of the intervals where the scales dipped to Furnival, I even wrote in some lines which I considered would improve the play. I really never believed that anyone would notice – the author certainly didn't and said 'Look here, where I've made Gladstone say –' and quoted my speech. Furnival, leaning on the window, accepted it charmingly, and when the other had left, screwed his monocle into his eye and murmured 'The G.O.M. was in a very *talkative* mood that morning, wasn't he?' and began to walk up and down the room and I knew he had found me out. I said 'I'm sorry', and took up the blue pencil. He took it from my fingers. 'Oh, but you wrong me. I liked the lines, and our friend's face when he read them', – here the crowsfeet rayed round his eyes – 'was what is too often quite erroneously termed "as good as a play". Now tell me: honestly, do you think I should come better sitting down or standing up in this bit here?' and he dabbed at a speech quite four inches long.

I laughed a little. 'I think you'd look right whatever you did'. I enjoyed saying that. It isn't often that one can combine raps over knuckles with absolute truth. And then I shot a glance at him and saw I'd hurt him. It was something about his lips that gave the show away so that, for the moment, he looked the age with which the person, unenglamoured by memory and seeing him for the first time, would debit him. Well, it wouldn't do him any harm. I, of all people, wasn't there to establish too great a personal relation, and if it alienated him that was all to the good and would make our ultimate dissolution of partnership in the work more smooth. All my experience went to show that this was the line to take; tactics which conflict with one's impulses commonly are. But Furnival had hired my fingers and intelligence, not my impulses.

It wasn't as easy as it sounds. So often, sitting there, cutting out slabs of bombast, typing in fresh lines, I thought 'if he takes no notice of me I shall die of disappointment and if he flirts with me I shall despise him at once'.

Of course one loved him. Frankly I don't see how anyone could help it. These rare, irresistible old wretches are usually absolute fakes, *au fond*, but I had to admit that, so far, I hadn't succeeded in tripping him, for all my suspicion and alert disparagements. The knowledge that I loved Cosmo neither surprised nor troubled me. I have never been able to credit those women who, whether in plays or books, fall in love quite suddenly, and the women who, after prolonged, sparring association with a man, realize with a shock of incredulity that their heart has been insidiously won are, to me, damned liars. I am certain that every woman knows whether she loves or is in love, and nearly every woman could tell you exactly when it all began, and more, whether at first glance she is capable of doing it at all. In my case Cosmo had rather put my eye out by bringing with him a tradition of attraction and success with women against which one had to campaign. One watched out for him to be fatuous and quite quietly he put one in the wrong by failing to oblige; indeed I'm bound to admit that as far as appearances went he wasn't getting much encouragement from anybody but myself! From all the actresses, major and minor, who peeped and fluttered or strode in upon us, never once could I succeed in tracing a love-look or even a flirt-look. They took him — crass, extraordinary females — so absolutely for granted that the whole business was a cross between an At Home and a college lecture. The young ones were the worst offenders: said their little say and hardly glanced at him though they seemed, as I once found out when crossing the stage itself with a packet of amended parts, to have plenty of eyes and conversation for the juvenile lead, a shining young sprig who had found himself an actor through the nursely care of the university, and who would continue to believe he was an actor until something better came along.

Fools!

As for me, I knew I was born susceptible, and that had to be dealt with as well. Whatever was going to happen about this, I wanted the best for Cosmo; also not one man in a hundred seems capable of realizing that you can love, even quite intensely, without necessarily wishing to fly to extremes, and I didn't propose to be misunderstood in that way by him. With his training he would inevitably regard even a smile as a desire to live with him.

All of which was, as we say at home, not too good for the complexion, and the glances I took at myself in the theatre mirrors with their surround of electric lights of appallingly high candle-power, so kind to make-up, so gruelling to nature, assured me that I resembled nothing so much as a family banshee – all white face (too thin) and copper hair which had turned an entire shade darker, as hair so unaccountably does when one is thoroughly run down. And that, too, was well. Once again, only more intensely, I was glad that Cosmo should see me at my worst. By the time he had also seen me in a temper, or sulky or moody, we might perhaps begin to build up a friendship – by which time my work would be over and I should be gone.

I I

Lalage's definitely announced marriage brought a certain amount of emotion to the boil. Aunt Emmeline, I gathered, let it be understood that it was a hole-in-the-corner affair and was inclined to query our cumulative eccentricity in 'having no bridesmaids'. 'You'd almost think there was something *in it*. And it *looks* so odd.' This more or less expurgated version was given to me by Barbara, whose humour it was to pay a formal call at Vallant House while I was installed there, and who, with cheerfully sarcastic Verdune grin, took in everything and exploded intermittently into laughter while we sat *tête-à-tête* in the drawing-room. Our grandmother was fortunately out, to Barbara's disappointment, for she preserved a delusion that she 'could manage old Vallybags', and if imperviousness to personality and atmosphere is anything to go by I suppose she was right.

'You know it kind of makes me *die* to see you *poor* little thing on your own here, coping with Vally.'

Mother, who was extremely fond of her Verdune nieces, once said that in the way of gossip they were excellent germ-carriers, and it was this side of them which I utilized that afternoon.

Aunt Sophia – and here one had to separate, so to speak, the chaff from the grain, was finding some difficulty with her face over Lalage's marriage, 'because of Flora, you know'. Flora, instead of producing Seagraves, was grooming horses in the stables of a friend, and aunt Sophia was driven back on to the line that it was such a thousand pities that she wouldn't look at all the men who, by implication, wanted to look at her 'in the days when all the young things were getting settled'.

'You see, that story's been blown sky-high by Lalage,' and here Barbara and I exchanged the same look of instant appreciation. 'But lor! I'm sorry for poor old Flora, because honestly I don't believe she's particularly keen on getting hitched, and she told me once she's never had even the ghost of a love affair ... I suppose I oughtn't to say that, but I know you're safe. One's sorry for poor old Sophia too, because they're both telling a different story that dishes the other's. Main an' okkard it du be. And of course Sophia obviously can't imagine any gurl not wanting to be married. I'm not sure that I'm particularly keen on it myself, but I mean to do the civil thing.' And I believed her as she sat there, rather perilously dangling Lady Vallant's tea-cup by one finger. If Barbara Verdune didn't precisely marry the man she wanted or needed, at least she would, as the comedians say, marry 'when and how', and where and why, into the bargain.

'And you know, Vere, when I do, I've made up my mind not to start a family. I should make a thundering bad mother; I don't know anything about kids because they've never come my way and I don't even like them much. They've got to make good with me just as friends have to before I fall for 'em, but I can't adore babies *qua* babies.'

Neither could I, but I did say 'You'll have to warn the man, it's not playing the game not to.'

'Naturally I shall, but you know, Vere, when I look round on our lot it's not exactly encouraging, is it? *You're* all right, of course, with aunt Anne … but *will* you think of all the rest of us!'

I did, and I had, and could find nothing to say.

'And when I think of grannyma! I mean, could one condemn anybody to grow up Vallantish?'

It is curious how some people, without suffering or experience, can fluke to conclusions it has taken others half a lifetime to arrive at. Yet this, I saw, was a backhanded slap aimed actually at aunt Emmeline's career in maternity, rather than a knowledgeable indictment of our grandmother. The Verdunes, I had always suspected, would eternally miss the real point about Lady Vallant. All the same, I was sorry Barbara felt like that. The older generation at least had filled their schoolrooms, given us Buchans, Verdunes and Seagraves, a tilt at friendship, kept a flag of a sort flying, where we, from very liberty and reaction, were tending towards emptiness and eventual disintegration. Which brought me back to the everlasting thought of the importance of love, given punctually in its time and place. And I wondered what Cosmo was doing. At the Garrick, probably.

Dolly, Barbara was saying, was 'shaking down'. Already the formal meal in Palace Green was open to Arthur. The War had, in Verdune argot, tended to pass him along with my Uncle Bertram and aunt Emmeline and Dolly herself was 'as happy as could be expected, might even produce when the War's over'. But would she? In my experience children are only born through an impulse utterly removed from child-love in the parties concerned, or – more rarely – through the considered, practical wish for family, a desire high-minded, eugenic and untypical. In either case, genuine mother-love may or may not develop, capriciously, afterwards. In our own case it had, but there was no getting over poor mother's dismay at the prospect of James and myself. And Dolly was extra-burdened by public opinion of her husband, which might well have the effect of chilling the impulse or slaying the considered wish. And then in the Verdune manner, which is inadmissible, disarming, likeable and blatant, Barbara cocked a bright inquisitive eye.

'We've often wondered why you haven't married, Vere.'

I wasn't having any, and dealt with that fairly cleverly, for me, as I am seldom clever for myself.

'Of course you have, bless you!'

'Because, you have got *about* a bit, haven't you?'

'Perhaps that's why. More tea?'

Now over the bridesmaid business, Barbara, alert for my laughter, was as usual cynically willing in the Verdune manner to share what humour could be extracted from the family. And I did laugh a little, but only as tribute to ancient alliance; for the no-bridesmaid decision, arrived at by our various private ways, was one which certainly in my case and James's, and I suspected in mother's as well, was emphatically not a presentable one. We elected, originally, to base it upon the score of expense and of the venue, but such a risk in these motoring days, and with the possible but improbable advance cheque from some uncle or aunt Sophia, we eventually decided not to take. We just told the relatives that we wanted a very quiet wedding and no fuss. I suppose we all hoped that that whipping-boy, the War, would account for this. The real reason was a desire to keep Lalage and Hugh's wedding free of the entire clan, to send them forth together at mental peace, above all to hear their blessing pronounced in a church void of Lady Vallant herself. It was at this consideration that our silences and evasions with each other set in, so that we fell back on the bluffer, more obvious humours and aspects of the old woman.

III

Hugh was acquiescent in all our tortuous schemes. Back in England, he came to see me at once from a flying visit to Hampshire, and he met me in our Campden Hill house, at my request. It is probable that we found each other's appearance mutually distressing. I could see that although he had escaped the worst results of being gassed he was far from absolute normal. He seemed to concentrate with a slight but definite effort, and my heart sank, quite selfishly, with the fear that after all the marriage would be postponed. But his illness had done this much, in wiping out his old scrupulousness; it was, I imagine, one of the many intimately personal castings-off which heaven alone knew how many other men on active service were practising.

And thinking it over, above all watching and listening, I thought that even this could be turned to Lalage's advantage. I had had my moments – what guardian or intimate relative hasn't –? when I feared that the tremendous change of habit and the shock of mutual concession and adjustment might have upon my sister's peculiarly delicate balance some disastrous effect. But, half brutally practical, half painfully compassionate, I saw in Hugh's transitory state just such a general dimming of personality as might weather her safely through the first weeks of strangeness and alienation from mother, James and myself. Now Hugh had his moments of suggesting the eternal child in its half-world, as Lalage did so often. It would pass, and it must pass. Even for Lalage's sake I wouldn't keep him so, but while it endured he and she would be as two children, confiding, trustful and a little helpless, going through their days with all their actual adult knowledge blurred and softened. The afterwards of return to normal I could leave safely in his hands. Of Hugh one had never had any doubts at all. Also, as I discovered later, his state of health had blinded him to Lalage's own flaggings and to that apparently psychic sub-normality which James and I had sensed so long, and possibly mother too, when she said to us as children 'She's not a bit like either of you'. Apart from that, anyone could see that Hugh was steeped in the very thought of Lalage. He said to me, stammering a little, 'She was so extraordinarily glad to see me'. I could well understand that, obvious reasons apart. Wasn't it possible that she recognized some salvation that should come from Hugh? And, in point of fact, had I been so wide of the mark when I blurted to James that until she could cut loose from all of us she would never be 'herself'?

IV

James's delayed letter in answer to my account of that night on the staircase at Vallant House arrived at last, grimy of envelope, worried-between-the-lines in ways that I could so well interpret, anxious for me, hastily written – the letter of an overwrought

man torn between conflicting urgencies and knowing he is doing full justice to none.

I blamed myself for having written as I read his letter again –
rapidly, for Cosmo Furnival had bought my time and attention,
yet I knew James would have blamed me more if I hadn't. We had
always been in this together and through force of circumstance I
had acted alone and gained nothing.

Sometimes, when the memory, hot and sickening, of that
small foot on the stairs swept over me (had I sat on a lower step
would it have lain across my lap?) I steadied myself with unper-
ceived glances at Cosmo. It was a point of honour that he must
never catch me at it and I allowed it to myself for the help it gave
me. And I knew that the Vallant business must be gone through
all over again until, somehow, I got the rights of it.

Cosmo Furnival was loping about and murmuring to himself
of waistcoats and shirtfrills, occasionally referring to some steel
engravings on his dressing-table. I caught 'I like that one best …
but it's ten years too early… tah! …' And what would one feel
when Lalage had gone from us? That was an aspect of future life
I hadn't bargained for in my direct anxiety for her welfare. And
with James back in France … and Lady Vallant eternal. …

'These betwixt-and-between dress periods are the very deuce.
Ugly, too. …'

And any day now I should lose Cosmo. There was one thing:
I saw no real compulsion to stand life with my grandmother any
longer. I would go back to Campden Hill and set up house with
the two servants until Lalage's wedding, and until it seemed that
mother had sucked all the benefit possible from the Hampshire
visit. Furnival was still murmuring to his engravings. I received
and rejected the impression that he wanted me to come and help
him complain of his Gladstonian waistcoats too. Well, I was ready
even for that, and sat there underlining in red ink and looking
respectable and cuffed.

CHAPTER XXV

I

Life has quite a little sense of humour of its own.

Ever since that morning when I crossed the stage during a lull in rehearsal, the juvenile lead had elected to bestow his attentions upon *me*. Reasons: my own unawareness of his brilliantined charms and undeniable profile plus a ray of amber limelight which the electrician accidentally played upon me like a hose. Mr. Furnival had invited me to watch any rehearsals I cared to come down to, said it would teach me a lot and might interest me. It did both and I wasn't going to be done out of watching him, seeing him walk, hearing his voice which no superimposed characterization, to my delight, could quite conceal, by young Bavin Wraxe. But I dodged, sat in the stalls – and was sleuthed there. And yet, for all my slightly entertained irritation, I couldn't deal too harshly with the creature. James had been that age, once, and Peter, and given the conditions might have behaved in just this way to a youngish woman flattered by a deceptive light. I chaffed Wraxe, and was aunty, and I'm bound to admit it wasn't much good. That amber beam had – as some equivalent always does with youth – fixed me in his mind in spite of the contradictions which daylight fairly shouted; that is, that until the boy fell in love, I should always be to him as he had seen me at a fixed moment in time.

The ridiculous business did not endear me to the sprinkling of girls in the company. I found that this world magnified every trifle, realized the amount of mischief I could have made had it suited me. Enmity, poker-faced or open, I can cope with at a pinch, but the Wraxe affair had rather fatally focused me with some of the cast and, on the principle of snatching victory out of defeat, at times they made me a species of dump for 'workings' of 'old Furny', for favours, for privately conveyed complaints. Enormously interested in spite of myself (a mistake) in any clash of humanity, I listened as tactfully as might be. Once again I was Chiffinch to a Charles. I 'had his ear', but on looking back I don't think I abused my place. I sorted, selected and presented the petitions to Cosmo with dispassion if they were in my judgment legitimate. Of course I made mistakes and on at least one occasion gave way to personality and suppressed a perfectly reasonable grievance because I saw that Cosmo Furnival was overstimulated, overtired and depressed; and because I am to this day dissatisfied at my conduct I remember the *casus belli* – a question of precedence and the allocation of dressing-room, which was not my province at all. I can only imagine that the company, knowing that far better than I did, easily believed that Cosmo was in love with me, and used the situation for what it was worth, and if that was the general notion, all right! I too took what advantage I could in the way of nursing Cosmo's interests when he wasn't looking. There were plenty of things to do and I did them, cautiously at first; matters of minor research for details in the British Museum, inspecting his lunches if he was not taking them at one of his clubs, keeping bores off his bones – and paying myself by being brisk with him when he went dramatic on me about the play and his part. And when he got no particular change out of me over that (I even said to him 'Shall we both have a good cry together? I'm ready if you are', at which he burst out laughing), he seemed to be playing his own game as well. There began to be a tendency to bring out old photographs from albums and drawers and to sigh, 'You ought to have seen me then', ... 'I really was rather good in that'. Impossible not to be interested in the photographs for themselves. There under my eyes was spread a handsome portion of Victorian-Edwardian stage history, the later plays in which he had figured bringing me back my own youth.

But it wasn't the historic side that he wanted me to notice.

Of course he was handsome in those days – just that and nothing else if the courts and cabinets spoke the truth, possibly even rather unusually good-looking, but lord bless my soul! aren't presentable faces twenty a penny? He had picked the wrong audience this time, and inevitably, in that I was astounded at his taste between then and now and the false self-comparisons he drew, I said the wrong things, commented upon the plays themselves, questioned him, even remarked 'They are charming, aren't they?' (politely, in the wrong voice), 'You must have been really devastating in so-and-so', naming a cloak and dagger drama. And he slowly swept up the lot and said sadly 'They said I was. But you never know, of course ... I wish you could have seen me in that show', and sat down at his dressing-table and began to sort grease paints. I'd failed him, but at least sincerely. Young beauty-men I have no use for at all. And there was nothing permissible to say.

There was silence in the room except for the passing carts going in the direction of Shepherd Market. Cosmo was absorbed in a trial make-up and had forgotten my existence.

He turned in his chair. 'Tell me: is Wraxe making a nuisance of himself?'

'Oh no, not at all, thank you.'

He sighed. 'I've been keeping an eye on him.'

Off my guard I looked my astonishment. He rewarded it with a suave smile. 'You thought old Furnival doesn't notice anything', he remarked with acidulated sweetness.

'Well, hardly that, perhaps.'

'Then I am to take it that his — shall we say? — attentions are not displeasing to you — wait! … because if they are, he goes, quite unobtrusively, but he goes, he goes …' And go the youth undoubtedly would. This was Cosmo Furnival, the business man of the world I was seeing, and upon my word I believe he could have turned a dismissal to such favour and prettiness that the victim would bundle off positively flattered! I smiled at the thought.

'Then, he shall stay, my dear — ah — young lady.'

This needed dealing with. I was exasperated, would see justice done but didn't propose to flatter Wraxe to the extent of getting him his notice on my account.

'Mr. Furnival, you've seen a bit. I only wish you'd listened in on the whole!'

'Ah?' He was waiting, gazing down at a stick of carmine.

'My dear — oh gosh! the boy's a *flesh-pot*!' I faced him. 'In any case I'm almost old enough to be his mother. D'you know I'm nearly thirty? But if I were thirteen or twenty-three, could I ever take that sort of little object seriously?'

'Don't like the youngsters, eh?'

'Oh, *like* them, yes, to look after and stage-manage and get out of fixes and dry their little eyes and blow their little noses. But that *you* … oh well, I do thank you for being ready to fend him off me.'

'Nearly thirty … indeed. That doesn't seem much to me, you know. I'm getting on for seventy.'

I looked at him. 'I know you are.'

'It's pretty obvious, eh?'

'I know what you mean, but you're wrong. Sixty-eight as a
sign-post to age has ceased to exist; people are themselves, not
their birth-certificates. One can be a pretty old thirty, you know.'

'That's a comforting theory.'

'It's just convention. Forty years ago I should have relapsed
into a cap and the shelf and good works.'

He smiled at me – so kindly. 'Yes. It's quite true. I never
thought of that ... how nice you're being to me.' He swung
round, arms over his chair. 'One does need it so, at times.' I nearly
cracked at that, but I was taking no chances; if any restraint of
mine, of tiresome eyes and tongue, or a reckoning with the too-
apt time and place, or the general glibness of our opportunity
could save either of us from cheapness I would save us, and we
both set to work again, and intermittently he began to hum fragments of musical plays. It is very catching. If he had hummed or
sung these melodious clichés nearer me, or when idle, or looking at me I could have got on with my job in silence. But set a
congenial companion working and absently buzzing with tunes
your own cradle rocked to, airs and choruses you emitted with
the school satchel thumping on your shoulders, that as débutante
however *manquée* and penniless you waltzed to with your hot,
kid-gloved fingers in a hand whose owner is probably now a
grandfather and more dead to you than Queen Anne can ever
be, and not to join in is very nearly the impossible thing. I found
it so. Between us, we covered much ground, and thank God the
door was shut.

COSMO (sotto voce)
> Li *ta* ta-ta-ta *tar* dee-dee *dee* dee
> You are queen of my heart to-night.
>
> Swing high, swing low,
> Swing to, swing fro.
>
> . . . .
>
> Mary, oh they call me pretty Mary
> I don't believe them
> For they always tell me fibs. ...

BOTH   (La-la *lar* la *lar*)

Why do they call me 'pretty Mary'
When my name's Miss Gibbs?

(Pause)

COSMO   Don't be a man, San Toy, oh,
Ev-er remain a boy, oh. ...

ME *(firmly)*   There's many a slip between the tip
And the horse that wins the cup.

COSMO *(not to be outdone)*
Back your fancy, back your fancy
Come and join the gamble. ...

. . . . .

Arcadians are we. ...

ME *(con brio, to suggest the re-entry of the chorus in Act I)*
We're soldiers of the Netherlands
Of the Netherlands
Of the Netherlands. ...

COSMO *(catching the idea and actually singing)*
We guard Brabant and north Friesland
And all that lies between
(Pom-pom-pom POM POM)

And then, in a slight, sweet tenor, delicately worn, like his face:

Under the De-o-dar
Lit by the evening star. ...

One could watch him, at leisure, from one's own place.

Pearl of the wond'rous Eastern sea. ...

'"Star of the"' I corrected mechanically.
'Pearl.'
'Star.'

My own voice speaking brought me up with a jerk, but Cosmo hadn't noticed my vocal share – I hardly had, myself. We were both living in the past, in our differing set of memories which the songs had brought back, and I wondered what his pictures had been. A part of him one could have no share in. It was of a piece with the general stinginess of life. It could have been so simple to have got born a bit earlier, even if it did involve bell

skirts and feather boas and flyaway chiffon hats and goggling under fringes – one would have had that much longer of Cosmo
– who, I suddenly saw, could watch me quite comfortably too, in
his mirror, and I told myself 'This is my fault.' I've muffed it after
all, at the last minute', for without coming over to me or touching me – only his hands had stopped their rapid movements over
his face, he said, 'My dear, you love me.'

It was half statement, half query.

11

I got up and began putting my things together and spoke to
his reflection. 'Yes. But I shan't be a nuisance to you.'

'Nuisance? Why … you little duffer …' He came over to me
and his hands were on my shoulders. 'I thought for some time I
must have got it all wrong. It's so incredible.' He seemed almost
excited and I swear he suddenly looked fifteen years younger. I
said so – I must have, for I do remember adding 'but don't get
too young on me. I should hate that, you know. You see, I prefer
you as you are.'

'Now listen: this matters a lot to me. I'm going to sound extremely fatuous and deliver myself,' here he smiled down at me,
'bound into your dismayingly efficient hands. Are you what is
described as in love with me, or do you just love me?'

I attempted a shrug with my weighted shoulders. 'I don't
know. I don't think I do know the difference. In the last resort
it seems to amount to the same thing, except that I rather fancy
my kind wears better. I suppose the popular test is that I don't
feel that my life would be over if I didn't get a week in Paris with
you. You see, I know that life goes on and on – oh, *how* it goes
on! and that it would be just a lie to say that when I don't see you
any more it will stop. I may wish it would, but it won't. I can do
without you.'

It was true. I've gone without so much and weathered it, and
knew for all time the terrible strength of engrained self-control
and inherited reserve, aspects of my destined make-up which had
never oppressed me before. Yet even in those minutes I couldn't
honestly regret any of my second-rate experiences. If they got
home on me it was purely emotionally as the meaningless make-

shifts that they were. 'And yet,' I meditated, 'on the other hand
– now I'm playing into yours – there's no blinking the fact that
I've had to give up going to concerts. ...'

'... because?'

'Because you get in my way,' I answered baldly, 'particularly
with my favourite composers. Dammit! I can only *hear* Chopin
with relation to ... look here, don't you think we'd better pack
up and go to our respective homes?'

'So, you can't hear music ... and that's about the most beautiful thing anyone has ever said to me. And I do nothing for you
at all, except give you my love ...' He took my face in his hands
and kissed it. 'You dear!' and kissed it again. 'You're about the
only woman I've ever met who didn't want things from me.' He
was striding about the room, his hand in mine. 'You know, ever
since I saw you asleep in my chair I thought, that child is – there's
no other word for it – hagridden. Now, what can I do about it?
How am I going to look after you?'

It warmed one's heart so that answering was difficult. He was
helping me, and I said so, by just being there. 'And I may as well
tell you that you're about the only man who has ever thought of
that particular thing.'

'Is that really so? Well, we're a worthless crew, my dear, and' –
here I caught a twinkle in his eye – 'I don't say that twenty years
ago it might have been an aspect of you which I too might have
ignored.'

'Then how right we were only to meet now.'

'Um ... that rather brings us to the Paris week-end, doesn't
it? You'd hate it, of course?'

'Not at all, Mr. Furnival,' I answered, between chaff and ear-
nest, and we laughed together. 'And now I must bundle off to
Vallant House.'

'And now you are coming home with me.'

'Me? Why?'

'To meet Enid, of course.'

'Who's she?'

'My wife.'

I took my hand from his. 'I wish you hadn't said that. Don't
you see it's impossible, now?'

'And why now?'

'I mean, since we have failed to keep –'

'Our heads?'

'No. They were never in any danger. I was going to say something on the ponderous and prim side, about having failed to keep the situation at the suitable level.'

'And a very good line *too*. It never misses … only the word is "proper". "The proper level".'

'Mr. Furnival, I'm not coming to your house.' I was rude and bitter because Cosmo had hurt me badly. 'I've had some. Wives! They litter the ground like paper bags!'

'I don't *think* Enid's a paper bag,' he considered, twirling the ribbon of his monocle, 'and so you think that because I gave myself the pleasure of kissing you –'

'Oh, I was in it too. That makes it worse.'

'Yes. You were unmistakably "in it" too; one of the nicest things, for me … but to revert to my wife: don't you *want* to meet her?'

'Oh, *want* to, yes. In a way …'

'You know, child, you distress me a lot. This darting defensiveness … and sudden flights out of one's reach … it's as though you'd never been fairly dealt with. And you should be having such happiness … Enid … yes.' He moved towards the telephone.

'No!'

'Will you try trusting me, just for an experiment? Don't be arrogant with me, Vere. If there's any arrogance called for, I'll supply it myself.' He took up the receiver, then replaced it. 'By the way, what is your idea of my wife?'

'No you don't, Cosmo!'

'Oh, but please. I'm immensely interested. Now try and think you're prophesying to a third party … no reflection on my taste, and so on.'

Unwillingly I smiled; it was as if he had climbed into my very brain. 'I – I really couldn't. It *would* sound rude, whatever you say.'

'But it's not I who am saying it. Now!'

I'd heard that 'now!' at rehearsals. It usually produced results.

'Well,' I began dubiously, 'she has henna'd hair that's blue at the parting, and is what used to be called a fine figure of a woman, and she dislikes girls and is clever at eliminating them, and she

calls one darling with an eye like a stiletto and makes scenes …
semi–public ones, you know.'

'Thank you so much,' responded Cosmo blandly, and lifted
the receiver again. 'I do admire you for that. I really mean it. It
– Lenox 0717 … Mrs. Furnival … Oh, Niddy, I've got someone
here for us. I think she loves me and I could knock a house down
… no no no! company be damned! Don't be an actress, Enid! …
what? … getting on for thirty, she says. Yes, of course it's the one
… How like a woman you are, sometimes! … No she doesn't
think age matters, even if you do … oh yes, I've told her and it
made no difference at all. Yes, and I've rather unsuccessfully been
trying to come the heavy father over her … Certainly. Twice.
And I want to bring her along. Let's have some champagne for
dinner. Of *course* it'll kill me but you like it, like all the chorus …
and you're another! But seriously this needs celebrating … right,
bless you.'

He made to replace the receiver and put it to his ear again.

'Oh, Niddy, just sing me one of the old crusteds, will you
dear? Never mind why. Just do it.' In the little pause he twitched
me with eyebrow and finger to the telephone. 'Listen', he murmured, and put the receiver into my hand.

From heaven knows where came a voice, silver–true as a bird's
but as a bird which has served an uncommonly knowing appren-
ticeship; only a light soprano, certainly, but full of that appeal
which we seem to have lost in these overcrowded days: a voice
which conveyed person and manner and which, to me, accounted so thoroughly for the forgotten days of hero–worship and pit-
full notices and gallery boys and girls and autograph albums and
picture postcards. No voice at all, academically speaking, but with
intonations that told you beyond doubt when the singer was
smiling and when immobile. And with it and through it came the
tinkle of the Furnival piano in some unknown drawing-room.

> 'A goldfish swam in a little glass bowl
> As dear little goldfish do …
>
> . . . . .
>
> And she said "It is bit–bit–bitter". …

and a little laugh at the end. She was singing for Cosmo; to me
quite obviously flirting with her own husband.

III

Involuntarily I said, 'Oh, thank you!'

Cosmo had gone back to his dressing-table and was removing his partly-begun make-up. The things he didn't say were positively noisy, but he caught my eye and looked arch and prim as he so often does when he'd scored off anybody. Whether he had this time remained to be seen. A man's recommendation is seldom the right – or any – passport for another woman's invasion of his home. Well, he ought to know, and on their own heads be it. At least he'd put me straight with Mrs. Furnival from the start, conventionally speaking, if she should decide to turn nasty later on. Yet one was hurt by it in deeper ways which didn't bear investigation ... and if one was going to be lured into becoming attached to Cosmo's wife, the old unsolved query presented itself of whether it is, then, a worse disloyalty to love her husband. And then Cosmo disarmed me utterly, if temporarily, by catching up my hand as I passed his chair, looking at it and dropping a kiss on it before dealing with a smear of cold cream on his nose.

'Isn't it wonderful the way all novelists say he "washed the make-up off his face"?' he chuckled. 'I should prefer to try and clean the enamel off a yacht with a bottle of rosewater, personally. If ever ... you do any amateur shows ... never ... use cocoa butter. It's guaranteed to grow hair on a plank. There! Now we'll get your Vallant House rung up.' He pressed a bell. 'Murton, ring up Lady Vallant, Lowndes Square, and say that Miss Buchan is dining with us and we're sending her home in the car. And to-morrow get on to Clarkson and tell him the wig's still too young. Too much hair on the temples, and he must stand by to make me another one, too. Five years elapse between Acts Two and Three and it'll have to be whiter and thinner. Well, we're going now.'

'Very good, sir.'

I was thinking how strange Lady Vallant's name sounded, spoken by Cosmo, and that he had, after all, deprived me of the gesture of mentioning it first.

IV

Furnival tossed on a wideawake and pulled the rug over us. We drove to his house in absolute silence. My thoughts were upside down and I didn't attempt to cope with any of them. I knew the address – had seen it on many a brown bundle of script packed for the post at our office. It was in one of those suburbs which pay back in gardens and space and carriage drive and house-room what they borrow in off-colour address and a tendency to redundant steps in black and white tiling.

'In here. Enid!' I heard a rushing step and Cosmo's wife appeared.

Nell Gwyn, thirty years later. Naturally curly hair, pale-gold in kindly light, silver by day, which giggled all round her head and matched her sudden laughter. Even her clothes suggested Lely, lacy and beribboned, and hinting at masked adventure at St. Bartholomew's Fair. She came but little above Cosmo's elbow and her blue eyes took me in as she gave me a small hand.

In that moment it was I who felt the elder: worn and unsure and staled before this little thing from whom assurance – the security of mid-Victorianism, untroubled by wars and unpestered by our plague of introspection, fairly radiated.

'This is so nice of you ... my dear, your *hair*! It'd look quite heavenly from the front – and from the back, too,' and she gave a tiny giggle. And Cosmo was watching both of us.

'This, Enid, is the one girl in the world who loves me, and now I'll leave you both ... oh, by the way ... she says *you've* got hair that's blue at the roots.'

'It *isn't*, Val! I've let it grow grey *absolutely* naturally. Oh, you're being funny.'

'I'm not in the least funny. And you have an eye like a stiletto.'

'But – didn't you show her some of my photographs?'

'No,' I paid back Cosmo, 'he showed me some of his.'

'*Wouldn't* he!' and the blue eyes crinkled.

Well – perhaps he was right. If that was the note he meant to strike ... yet for all one's tranquil conviction that one's intentions were honest one was already indignant at the idea of ever so delicate a circumvention of Mrs. Furnival. ...

It is ironic that that storm-centre, the other woman, is by reason of her sex usually the penetrative and pitiful party, the perceiver of baseness however trivial and, more times than is admitted, its demonstrator to the man in the case. The other woman is the unscrupulous villainess of the piece, and the woman who is an ex-blonde and who giggles is brainless and a fool-cat. I had found one who was neither of these things, and she had found – but her case is a better one than mine, when all's said.

v

She walked by my side down that Edwardian drawing-room, whose gilt and watercolours and chintzes reminded me of ours in our first suburban home except for the electric light and the gleaming grand piano, and pulled me down to a sofa by the fire and gave her head a little shake and smiled at me and complained 'There's such a lot to *say*, isn't there?'

I said, 'Thank you for *The Goldfish*.'

'Oh … aha! So that was his doing, was it?'

'I thought, from the way you sang it, that you'd once played O Mimosa San.'

'Oh, you are a nice person! My dear, think again! When *The Geisha* was going strong I was over forty! And though I don't say it's too old for the part if you've already got a name, the thing was that I hadn't. In those days the unknowns and the on-ly-slightly-knowns like me had to be as pretty as pinks or they got scrapped at *once*. Looks mattered far more than voices. Oh, I could have been rather good, you know, but the conditions then were very difficult, though we did far better work than is be-ing turned out now. The musical composers, people like Sydney Jones and Adrian Ross, Caryll, Paul Reubens and Lehar seemed to write for the love of it … you can *hear* it. Nowadays the new lot write to make money or to fit some actress with type-songs, all hit-or-miss stuff, written with no unmistakable personal urge by men who have nothing particular to say and aren't even very keen on saying it. Am I boring you? I'm afraid we old dears are very trying when we get started … and what's the result? We *have* no musical comedy actresses now. Evelyn Laye, perhaps, though she seems to have deserted to the films, Vera Pearce, yes, but she's more a character lead; Maisie Gay same thing, and there may be one or two more. Oh they all think they can do it! Have a pop at anything, you know, and the result is that musical comedy has fallen into bad odour and has simply faded out. But look at the names *we* had! Florence Smithson, Ada Reeve, Marie Studholme, Adrienne and Amy Augarde, Gabrielle Ray (no voice but a darling figure and face and a good dancer), and Ruth Vincent (did you see *Amasis*? *Very* poor book but she could sing), and Olive Moore and Evie Green and Jean Alwyn, Edna May and Ellaline Terriss. ...

'Oh, if you want to find old Enid on the programmes, you must go back further than *that*! As a matter of fact it was in one of 'em that I met Val. He was filling in – not his line a bit and he wasn't much good; the new conditions and conventions bothered him and he made some quite killing mistakes but always saved his bacon somehow. And then, thank goodness, we fell in love with each other ... he could have had *anybody*, if he'd waited a bit, you know. And so I more or less left the stage after a few more years of it. Oh they were good days. Such *fun*! Of course Val is fearfully well known now, but it isn't the same, to him anyway. He misses the fussing and admiration, though he's a *far* better actor to-day than he used to be. Luckily the public still likes us and I come in on the reflected glory.'

She smiled and thought and went on, 'There are two ways to keep real to the public; one is by having sensational rows that get into the papers, and the other is by never having any – like us! We're the kind of couple who parents trust and ask advice on careers of. It make us feel awfully old, but it's rather nice as well ... dear me! what a good listener you are.'

'You'll never be old, Mrs. Furnival. You're one of those people who wring the best out of every age. You make me not mind my own.'

'I must tell Val that. And you mean it, too. No wonder he grabbed you.'

'Well, I meant to mention that,' I thought, as quickly as might be.

'But, must you? The great point is that you're here.'

And that remark accounted to me for the entirely dignified youth of Enid Furnival; sincere, typical, directly happy-go-lucky, it was a point of view which the prolix, tortuous and nerve-wracked younger generation could never conceivably have either held or expressed, yet it piqued one to be so lightly dismissed ... even if one's common sense and decency told one that it was the best possible line to take. Whether it was a considered line or the fluke of natural kindheartedness did not, after all, matter; my work for Cosmo was nearly over and then I should withdraw into my family and the next job. And meanwhile I would allow myself the happiness of the moment; I would watch Cosmo quite openly, walking about his own drawing-room. It would pass as the look of a woman who to the Furnivals seemed to be still a girl, belatedly stage-struck: the fact of her puerile enthusiasm being quite a quarter of a century out of date probably wouldn't occur to them, either ... and yet Enid seemed to know. 'He misses the fuss and the admiration.' Meaning women and girls falling for him wholesale at long distance, and stacks of albums and post-cards to sign 'Yours v. truly, Cosmo Furnival.'

And how one would have ignored him at the right and suit-able age! The romantic actor, the bulk of whose admirers would inevitably put the accent on the first syllable – the adorers who, in his beautiful elderliness, had happily deserted him *en bloc*.

'He misses the fussing ... no wonder he grabbed you.' H'm! So I was to be the peg on which Cosmo was hoping to hang the shreds of his personal vanity ... oh, one could edge in a lot of fun with Cosmo! Delicately pull his nice long leg, like the urchin who tweaks the front-door bell and scampers away ... and one was so sleepy that one could have dropped off then and there, over-stimulated by Enid Furnival, keyed up for Cosmo to come into the room.

And then he did come in, in dinner jacket, the ribbon of his monocle making a loop of shadow on his soft shirt, and he gave us each an arm and we dined – quite perfectly by candlelight, the best light of all. I said so, and Cosmo said for Regency effects, yes, but for appearance give him gas light every time as it threw such wonderful shadows, and that the artificiality of the bulk of mod-ern plays was directly traceable to their electric lighting which left one no illusions to stand up in.

And that brought us all back – they included me without apology, almost, so to speak, snatched me from each other's jaws – to the Lyceum, the Adelphi and the Haymarket, and 'the floats', candles set as footlights on little rafts of wood in saucers of water. 'And,' declaimed Cosmo, 'I defy any company however experi-enced to play melodrama wholeheartedly as it *should* be played in a light you can control by switch and depend upon. And surely everything that is tended by hands has a greater meaning because, willy-nilly, more thought has gone to it, and thought breeds affection, if it's only for a lamp you must keep trimmed? But to-day our effects are so slick and labour-saving there's no love left.' He leant back in his chair and looked mockingly at me, 'But then, I over rate the importance of love, no doubt'.

'I don't think you do,' I answered, '*I* ought to know … machines *v.* personal service is all the difference between tinned peas and the kind from a Georgian kitchen garden, or between a Hepplewhite chair and something on the instalment plan from Tottenham Court Road, or between a service flat and, say, your home here.'

His eyes lit, but he said nothing to that. It was his wife who exclaimed 'But you oughtn't to understand that at your age! You ought to be all for modernity'.

'Only, for some reason, I'm not – except in one respect: the treatment of children by their parents' … I broke off and tried to change the subject and couldn't. Cosmo saw, and gave me some more champagne and Mrs Furnival smiled at us both, suggesting to me a happy woman glad to share with her guest the protectiveness of her husband. And in spite of everything it was the happiest evening of my life, therefore it couldn't endure.

From some other room the telephone shrilled. The maid came in and murmured with a side-glance at me that it was for the young lady ('that rules *me* out', sighed Cosmo's wife, with a wink).

It was Hutchins, apologetically thinking that I had better come home.

CHAPTER XXVI

I

THAT MEANT that Lady Vallant was raising Cain among the staff and that Hutchins wanted to break my fall for me, guessing I should say nothing to her. As ever there was tacit conspiracy between the old man and myself.

I returned to the drawing-room. I had not meant to say anything at all about the message, also I was desperately unwilling to carry over the Vallant atmosphere into the Furnival's home; it had even disturbed me that Cosmo had been put into the position of ever having had so much as to mention her name, and I hastily told Mrs. Furnival that I must go, thanked her – and Cosmo, as though I had not spoken, walked over to me and said, 'Who *is* this person who troubles you?'

'It sounds pretty comic, but it's Lady Vallant, my grandmother.'

'Cannot you tell her to go to – bed?' insinuated Cosmo, his elbow on the mantelpiece.

'I'm going to do more than that. I'm going to leave her.'

'Where are you going to?' It was for all the world like a suspicious father, indignant about latchkeys, and delighted me.

'To our house on Campden Hill.'

'Alone?'

'A servant is there.' The second girl had walked out on me, days before, as I discovered on calling at the house. She had, I suppose, left to make her pile 'at munitions' and it was no doubt only a matter of days before the other followed suit, a fact I had deliberately kept from mother as I knew it would bring her posting back to town and undo, in worry and indignation, all the good of Hampshire.

'… who'll come in at all hours and waste the food and steal the wine and feed the postman and lose her head in any emergency,' remarked Mrs. Furnival.

'And what if you were taken ill? It won't do, Vere. I don't like it,' decided Cosmo.

'But of course she must come to us, Val!'

I suppose I knew, then, how much I had subconsciously longed for her to suggest just that; the fact that as a wish it had never become active was due to its essential improbability.

And this, my temporary parting, was enlivened by Enid Furnival's plea, head on one side: 'You don't still think my hair's blue at the roots?'

Cosmo put me into his car and his arms over the door.

'I don't like you harassed … quite unnecessary, you know. We will go into this business later. Enid will write to your mother to-night, of course … now, one more thing: would you like me to come with you?'

I shook my head. 'Bless you for that, but I can manage Vallant.'

'– and it's telling on you, my child. Why not try being man-aged, for a change?' He looked at me, tapped me lightly on the cheek and the car drove off.

11

Night at Vallant House seems peculiarly suited to anger and scenes, even if I had not felt it myself there was the Chilcot letter to remind me. ...

Hutchins was waiting up when I returned and we seemed to gravitate instinctively to the dining-room.

'Am I in disgrace, Hutchins?'

He permitted himself the nearest approach to a shrug that I had ever seen in him. 'Nothing that I should take notice of, Miss Vere, but I thought I would let you know. It isn't right –' he hesitated, found himself committed, and went on – 'that young ladies should have to come back from a pleasant evening to this sort of thing.'

I thought, 'to him I'm a Sophia or an Emmeline, even perhaps an Anne. He's *remembering*'. 'The young ladies.' And now, a gen-eration later, here was another young lady to steer through the current storm.

'I hope you have had a very pleasant evening, Miss.'

'I have, a singularly pleasant one.' His gratified look fair-ly showered rice and confetti upon me as proxy for decorous tongue. 'Please sit down a minute – no, please, I really mean it.' He took a chair quietly, facing me across the immense mahogany table, hands folded upon the red cloth. 'Look here, I'm leaving, Hutchins, but I'm coming back without letting – I mean, would it be possible to get in quietly at night, say?' It was on the face of it a preposterous question to pose to the house's official warden, and I hoped that he would regard it as test of friendship.

Whatever his sensations were, it was a test I had passed.

'I would see to that, Miss.'

'I give you my word that it is nothing you oughtn't to allow. It's some – family business I can't do during the daytime.'

He thought a moment. 'If you would tell me the date I will let you have my own key.'

'You're always my standby, Hutchins. I promise to turn off all the lights when I go, and don't wait up for me. I mean it. It would – you know – fidget me to have to think of that kind of thing.'

'Very good, Miss Vere.'

'Well, good-night, and thank you for all your kindness.'

III

Lady Vallant was in the drawing-room – but Victorian walls are thick, its doors well-fitting and its floors solid; no murmur – hadn't I tested it? – of conversation could be heard from the dining-room below; the double curtain were drawn and the Furnival car a silent affair.

'You are very late,' the plangent voice was possessive, authoritative, but from her it gave one no pleasure. My grandmother was merely trying to make out a case against me in which I had 'kept her from her rest', which was ridiculous, as she went upstairs whenever it suited her, but logic was ever jettisoned when Vallants were annoyed. 'I have been alone all the evening'.

'I'm sorry. It was a final pressure of work,' I lied civilly. Her disbelief was partly automatic and was, no doubt of it, her method with her own daughters. One felt quite sorry for her for what she must have gone through all these years in enforced suppression of her nature through sheer lack of victims ... except for Anne ... Anne the vulnerable and the most available.

'You are making yourself conspicuous with this man. Are you supposed to be in love with him?'

'Certainly. Why not?' I answered, deliberately baiting her, for I thought I saw what the matter was. Quite plainly, Lady Vallant had convicted me of a private happiness, and happiness was suspect ... meant underground contrivings against herself ... was almost insubordination as in the old days any snatch at it must have been ... something to be exposed like a nerve and with jeers before people where the maximum of hurt shame could be exhibited. She had made a joke of Myra's lameness before the servants. Who was I to mind this enfeebled version of old tyranny, I with my whole body and background of sane home and laughter? Yet she could still inspire fear, encourage awkwardness and confusion of speech, and touch up any tendency to innate self deprecation ...

it was her damned assurance, and as with the uncles, her sons, one met it with obstinacy, drive and bogus frivolity.

'You were always troublesome,' she said levelly, and for the moment made me believe it, 'you are making yourself undignified. That is no doubt why you have never found any man to marry you. Look at you now! Grinning all over your face.' This was her version of my facial attempts to get upsides with her, or was the atmosphere of Cosmo and Enid Furnival still so thick about me?

'You would rather I cried?' I suggested. It was quite a nasty one, and a line, as Cosmo would call it, that the audience could take in two ways: one, as superficial impertinence, the other as a hint at past things. Her look of open suspicion satisfied me entirely. But one wouldn't go too far. Time for that, later.

'Don't be insolent. Go to your room.'

With an effort absurdly great I stayed where I was; I believed that all my backers, James, Cosmo, Enid and Miss Chilcot, would approve.

'I'm not a servant, you know.'

'While you are in my house you will do what I tell you, or go.'

'Only in reason, and I came to tell you that I must go. The arrangement isn't answering, is it?'

'If I had had the bringing of you up, I'd have made you sing a different tune.'

It was that which drove me to the door, with shaking knees, not on my own account, but for her poise in retrospective power over two children some forty years ago.

My manner obviously strengthened her; if one could say of that sardonic face that it was charmed. ...

'Come here.'

I could hear the wrong quality in the voice with which I answered her: thin, without body, produced from the head – what Cosmo at rehearsal once called 'that silly *white* tone'.

'I'm going to bed, Lady Vallant.'

'Don't call me that. Say, "I'm going to bed, granny", or "grandmother".'

'If you prefer it so – grandmother.'

'You are going to this actor, I presume?'

'And his wife, yes.'

'Reduced to that already!' The wrinkles rayed on her face at the taunt. 'You will never come here again, except for your sister's wedding reception. I shall have to admit you for that, I suppose.'

I left her in mid-scene. It was no matter of bravado, simply that I was in tatters. I can only suppose that in this action I was a pioneer, that in all her years of cowing a peace-at-any-price husband, trembling children and fainthearted governesses, not one had attempted that solution. The effect was possibly more enraging than I had quite realized or intended, for – and somehow it was, to me, the most unnerving item in a wracked evening – the old woman followed me, skimming up the stairs on tiny feet with incredible lightness and speed. It should have been a profoundly humorous sight. I can only say that it was beastly, for I knew in my heart that this furious pursuit wasn't the first; that once there were those who ran before her as I was running, and one who could not run so fast ... what she had done then I don't ever wish to know, and try not to think of. What she did now – and the futility of it must have been a torment to her – was to hammer on my door with her stick. I had no time to lock my door, I merely pressed her out with my weight. Physical strength can at no period have been her weapon, and my defensive action was tribute to her sheer atmosphere.

The house was roused in that gradual, decorous way of the large mansion; the maid evidently came out of Lady Vallant's bedroom and stood there. I heard, 'Since you are there, open that door', and nothing happened at all, by which I judged that Palmer was suddenly robbed of all initiative or (more likely) had no intention of becoming embroiled with another, and stronger, of the Vallant clan. The heavier step ascending the stairs I thought I recognized, and my grandmother said – and it was part of the revulsion which she inspired that she never raised her voice: plangent and sibilant, she seared her world in tones almost conversational:

'Get that woman out of there,' and at the crack she dealt my door the wood of her stick splintered.

Lady Vallant, in short, wished to continue the conversation.

'Go to bed, your ladyship, the young lady needs her rest.'

I wasn't going to be outdone by Hutchins and opened the door. He stood his ground. Together we waited for the mistress of the house to move.

I wrote letters to James and mother and packed for the rest of the night and am not ashamed to admit that I locked the door. Later, I was to feel a twisted pity for the old woman, for the night she must have spent and for her knowledge of waning powers of dominating her scenes that, to-day, had no climax and fizzled out into ineffectiveness. The loss of her first beauty must have rendered half of life meaningless to her, the loss of power to inflict damage to bodies and susceptibilities, the other. Unlike Cosmo, she had no second appeal of age, no lovely autumn-life, so far more full of meaning than its spring and summer. Her good times were long gone and for ever. She had failed even to flatter the youth of James, had never been clever enough, as the ex-beauty is seldom clever enough, to put by for the future in the way of attracting and securing members of her own sex, those traditional enemies. In all my life, I think, I never heard her laughter.

I wondered what sort of exit would be mine in the morning, even dallied with the notion of bread and water on a tray, and – such was my debility – welcomed the thought as being a communion bread associating me with the children. But nothing happened. Lady Vallant did not appear at all, and Hutchins looked after my wants as usual. I was fretted by the streak in me that actually felt regrets at leaving my uncomfortable bedroom, but there it was; live in any room if only for a few weeks, and you begin to throw out shoots which bind it to you. There among that plethora of Empire mirrors and ponderous furniture I had typed *Gladstone*, there read my mother's nursery books (*The Robey Family* and *Anna Ross* were still on the table by my bed; heaven knew when or if a spasm of orderliness would ever seize the under-housemaid and relegate them to the schoolroom once more from their first outing for well over a quarter of a century!')

'Hutchins, you won't forget to water my plants? They're on the schoolroom windowsill?'

'I'll see that is done, Miss Vere.'

I thanked him, then (it was bound to get said sooner or later), 'Why do you stay on here?'

He spoke more freely now, thanks to the night before. 'Well, you know what it is, one gets set in one's ways, and I shouldn't like, after all these years, to lose touch with the family.'

'But you needn't. There's Miss Lalage, going to be married, she'd adore to have you. I only wish *we* could.'

'Thank you, Miss Vere, but the fact is I'm used to the large house. I could never shake down in a small one, or a flat. Here, I've got my staff and things as I like them … in spite of all.' I admired that: there was no pseudo-sentiment about Hutchins, no tearful family retainer stuff, swearing *à la* Belvawney to live and die in the service of everybody: he would stand by you to a finish while keeping a placid eye on his and your own creature comforts – a reassuring combination. 'But I can't say how I shall miss you, it makes one almost wish you'd never come here, Miss Vere. The house has been a different place –'

I was so touched I could say nothing in thanks. I told him where I was going and he looked slightly bewildered and said 'Not *the* Cosmo Furnival? the actor? … well there now! I re-member him, it must have been in 1882, as quite a young man. I saw him many a time since. A very fine artist, we want more like him.'

'I'll tell him you said so, Hutchins, he'll love it. You two must meet. I like to share my friends when I know they'll make a hit with each other … well, it's about time I left.'

'If I might suggest … I should like to tell Miss Palmer and Henry, Miss. They wish to say good-bye to you.'

'Don't let's disturb them. Might I come down to them?'

He led me down to the rooms I had never seen. I asked to see the kitchen and was shown it. The warren of sitting-rooms and pantrys was small and freakishly ventilated; some of them, including the larders, had no windows at all and gas light burnt there all the year round, they told me. Furniture obviously taken from the upper floors made the staff comfortable enough and I saw that the dining table of the upper servants, still covered with breakfast things, sported an imposing array of our family silver. The cook was drinking a jorum of tea out of a cup that looked uncommonly like Crown Derby. And said nothing: neither did Hutchins, for which I respected him. If you appropriate, do it in the grand manner. And that underworld of men and women, the majority of whom had so far only materialized to me as a row of decorous behinds at dining-room prayers, emerged as human beings, and I think we pleased each other reason ably well. Their laws of precedence, I knew, were tricksy, but I managed to make only two mistakes: confused the upper with the under housemaid and 'spoke' to the kitchenmaid who is, socially, dumb.

CHAPTER XXVII

I

ENID TOLD ME months later that my appearance positively shocked her. She was 'doing the books' when I arrived, told me she was a perfect devil at them and had got the habit ever since her days of theatrical landladies and their extras, and indeed her domestic accounts seemed to be models of efficient balance which mother could never rise to, as I told her. Lalage, now, used to be arithmetically sound, but James and myself –

'James? Is he a brother?'

'We're twins.'

'No! What great fun! Is he anything like you?'

'Exactly like me!'

'Then I shall fall into his arms at *once*. A male version of you, my dear, must be too much!'

'You won't have the slightest difficulty! He's yours already.'

Cosmo was at the theatre, he had veto'd my joining him there in a note I found on my dressing-table. 'Be happy here, and take it easy. C.' By my bed was a photograph of him – as he used to be. Enid's doing, from wifely pride? Or his from vanity? A mistake, either way. I wanted no popular young pain-killers in my bedroom. I moved it to the mantelpiece and saw, hours later, that Enid Furnival had noticed.

The new house was taking its usual toll of me, even though it was his, and his atmosphere and his wife's after Vallant House was, that day, as psychically upsetting as is the physical change to Alpine height from stifling valley. And his arrival at night exhausted me, also I was fretting to know that all was well at the theatre. He said yes, gave me a rather searching look and began to choose at a built-in bookshelf.

'Do you like poetry?'

'Sorry. For some reason it eludes me. Embarrassing ... you know. So out of the picture ... isn't it?' I managed a sardonic smile.

'Ah ...' He selected a volume, took an armchair and cocked an eye at me.

> 'Sing God of Love and tell me in what dearth
> Thrice-gifted Snevellicci came to earth ...'

read Cosmo Furnival, and made beauty of it (which was hitting below the belt). It happened to be a portion I particularly liked, leading as it did to the Phenomenon, the sandals, the Benefit and the parasol down the grating, and a voice said, 'She's off' and Cosmo picked me up and the next morning I was in bed, and outside spread his large garden, under frost and be-robin'd, like the type of Christmas card the bores tell me I ought to feel contempt, for, and plenty of it, and that I so love. Enid Furnival told me that they often had rehearsals there in the summer.

We had breakfast in the morning-room which took in another view of the garden: a stone bird-bath and a mass of michaelmas daisies, pink and mauve, fell to my share. 'But you were to have had breakfast in *bed* in another hour!' lamented Mrs. Furnival, more Gwynish than ever in a tightly fitting lace cap that tied under her chin.

'Was I? I'm so sorry,' and I thought instantly and guiltily of the upset I had probably caused, of de-laid tray and re-laid place at table.

Cosmo was waiting to pull my chair out for me. 'Always punctual – and conscientious,' he murmured reflectively, and moved to his place opposite mine. 'Excuse me, but what do you weigh?'

'Seven stone something.'

He shook his head. 'Too little. I thought so, last night.'

'Oh Lord!' I gave it up. 'I meant to have apologized about that. I seem to spend my time going to sleep at him, Mrs. Furnival.'

He turned to her also. 'Isn't it curious the way she's always apologizing about something?' then to me, 'Sheer worry, in my opinion'. I had nothing to say, and he changed the subject. I enjoyed seeing him chipping an egg 'just like a person', as we used to say. He looked after both of us and when his wife wanted anything walked all round the table to give it to her. It was part of my cultivated defensive system that I was for some time unable to credit that this old-world mannerliness could be genuine. It was more helpful to assume it to be a set of charming actor's tricks with one eye on the gallery; breakfast in some Sweet Lavenderish romance with everybody called Lydia and Vernon ... or the brittle tea-cuppery of a Robertson comedy.

At this point a dry rustling caught my ear and a stout hedgehog handed itself into the room from the garden. 'Come on Trotty. He wants his bread and milk,' said Mrs. Furnival, 'take him, Val, till I've made it. He will stick his spills – quills –'

('Spines.')

'– into my lace.' The creature laboriously crawled up Cosmo who looked austere and resigned and it sat on his shoulder with two minute and perfect pink hands clutching his collar. 'Val dotes on him, but always pretends to hate him. Aren't men oddments? He came in in a bad thunderstorm, once, and has boarded here ever since. He likes his Actor's Orphanage, bless him! I must remember to tell cook to make him a custard ... Val, I don't think this child ought to do any work to-day.'

'She's not going to.'

'Oh, but I must! I mean, what use am I unless –'

'Oh dear, oh dear! Is it never permitted to any of us to be ornamental?'

I smiled at him. 'Exceedingly so, sometimes', and he cast down his eyes and said to the hedgehog, 'Ah, she doesn't mean it'. It was the merest whisper, but Cosmo's whispers had the knack of being as penetrating as other people's shouts. And – so soon – he was off to the theatre. His wife called out, 'Don't forget the footwarmer in the car', and I said, 'Or that Clarkson's man is coming at eleven, not half-past', and he shook his head at me and told me to go and rest.

'Good-bye my dears, be good.'

'Why, sire, we are always that', I retorted, quoting my favourite Stuart biography.

'Oddsfish! Would you disgrace the family traditions?' he finished it, flooring me completely, and flipped me under the chin and swept off.

11

A week later came letters from mother and James. He was in the usual torn state of rage and worry over Lady Vallant and myself. 'She's like a curse. Is this sort of thing going on for ever? I often think I'd be doing a better job of work at home fending her off all of us than out here trying to do in Germans I don't even hate.' But the chief point was that he had got leave for Lalage's wedding. 'I mean to give her away, and tell mother to take a firm line with the uncles. I wish to God we didn't have to have them there at all, but it's their stamping-ground, after all, and the alternative of Vallant's rooms makes one spit blood, I agree — and *quite* wrong for Lalage. I say, don't you pity Hugh marrying into *our* lot? ... I'm distinctly thrilled *re* Furnival. Have you ever told him about us and the queue and the pennies? My love to Enid! ...'

But mother's letter was another story. The Vallant part was a battleground of conflicting loyalties in which belief in myself and my action warred with her inability to justify me entirely by being explicit about her own mother. For the sheer look of the thing (that 'thing' we had spent our lives in preserving) she had to appear to think, with reference to my grandmother, that I had 'rubbed her up the wrong way', 'got her back up', and similar synonyms for the tactlessness of relative youth. Such a line had to be, as things were, for I, too, had taken my full share in the non-explicit game, and the cumulative tension of being able to speak of it all to nobody except James, who like myself was saturated to rotting point in the whole thing, gave me its moments of almost physical nausea.

Lady Vallant had written to mother at once, that was evident, and worried her in the old way, with promise of more to come, if I knew my grandmother; and the further business of keeping her away from the wedding wasn't going to make for harmony. 'Of course grannyma is most *frightfully* difficult and tiresome ...'

It could not have been an easy letter to write; too honest to express amazement at the Lowndes Square scenes or to pretend that my grandmother's behaviour was in any way unprecedented, poor mother had, at the same time, to withhold the 'comfort' she longed to give me in assurance that what I had endured from the old woman was not a circumstance to what she had herself. She fell – one sensed the almost wild relief – upon the topic of the Furnivals, doing the only possible thing of making Cosmo the scapegoat for Lady Vallant's outbreak. For several lines mother thoroughly enjoyed the drawing of a picture in which a conventionally old-fashioned relative was outraged at the typical, loud-spoken candour of a modern grandchild, complete with cigarette and lipstick ... but for the rest of the letter she was herself again. 'I've had a perfectly charming letter from your Mrs. Furnival; she must be a great lamb and I love her nice actressy handwriting all rather large and loopy. She seems to be really fond you, and as for Cosmo – lead me to him! I shall go down like a ninepin before him. Gosh! how I lurved him in the old days, and father *was* so shocked (yours, of course Fool!). Lor! It's like going back to Noah. Well, he ought to be safe by now! By the way, you'd better watch you step a bit in that direction; I'm certain his wife's a dear but you don't really know her, do you? and you don't want that sort of scrapping-match. She's probably got tongue warranted to blast the barnacles off a battleship and you'd be nowhere. I screeched over you, and her hair being blue at the roots, and think she took it amazingly well, but *how* naughty of Cosmo to tell her!

'The uncles are being really quite decent, and I'm liking them. I was horribly afraid they'd be Vallantish about the wedding but they're taking it wonderfully well and Julian has actually forked out £50!!! The church is a little pippit –*so* small and fairly rocking with old brasses and a marvellous Saxon door, and we're hedging and ditching to make it pretty for Christmas and Lalage. The uncles have asked you to spend Christmas here. Come if you feel you can, darling. I really think you'd like it and we needn't see too much of them, and I've wheeled the staff into line in heaps of ways. ...'

I I I

That night at dinner I said, 'My brother writes, "Give my love to Enid,"' and she cried, 'Oh, lovely!' and clasped her misleadingly inefficient-looking little hands.

'Doesn't anybody send me their love?' enquired Cosmo.

'Well, mother said she adored you.'

'Charming of her. When was that?'

'When I was about six or seven.'

'Ah!' He lost all interest.

One of the few ways in which I could repay the Furnivals was to make myself as scarce as possible on all occasions; I was determined not to be the guest who had to be amused and kept in talk as her writing-table is in notepaper. Enid and Cosmo must live their lives as nearly as though I were not in the house. The good secretary learns the plausible exit, and I left them now, after coffee, and went into the library. Enid would be in the drawing-room and Cosmo in his study. I had done it before, and from the way neither attempted to deter me I guessed how right I was. Meanwhile in those seven days I learnt much about the Keans, Wilson Barrett, Toole (by whom I was probably quite unjustly bored), and Fechter (whose legs looked wrong for Hamlet), and dipped into books on period costume and production and wondered if I agreed with Gordon Craig and Reinhardt, and came to the conclusion that theories, however noble, were cold things for repellent audiences and that a theatre must ever remain a theatre and look like one unmistakably, even unto gilding and plush, and not resemble a Cornish cave or Valhalla during a spring cleaning. And could William Terriss ever have aged into anything as good as Cosmo, had they let him live? Had Barrett really been as handsome as his legend? To me he suggested overmuch the young Roman Emperor. Could one have loved Irving? Too aloof for me. ...

'And now we've let you rip for an entire week,' said Cosmo at my elbow, 'and suppose we talk about this Vallant business.'

I shook my head. 'I want to forget her, here.' It was typical of life as I knew it that the one person to whom talking with was always a joy should divert me from that particular relief by pull of his own attraction. 'And it's a long story, and I think it possible that it might occasionally "recur" with you and prey on your mind when we've got to keep you in fighting form for "Gladstone".'

'And you only come up to my shoulder! Or just a little higher than my heart –'

'–and that distance removed from it. What's the new wig like, Cosmo?'

'– and therefore it seems to point to the fact that what you can stand I can.'

'It isn't fair. You're a *happy* person.'

'And you aren't, and so you want to keep me like a débutante. Good Gad! that ought to be amusing, but it isn't.' He turned on me, 'Or have I got this all wrong as well', he asked suavely, 'and am I the silver-hair'd veteran – but beloved by all in his saintly feebleness whose faculties must be nursed over the first night lest he drop down dead in his dressing-room, still blessing all concerned?'

He was almost glaring at me and my burst of laughter had a slightly hysteric edge. 'No, I honestly never thought of that. Cosmo, you're really rather awful when you rend one.'

'Good. *When* I rend you, my child, you'll know what trouble really is. And now for your affairs. *I'm going to do a mean thing …* remember?'

I had said it to him at our first meeting, when (even then!) Lady Vallant's name had crawled into our farewells. 'You've not forgotten that?' I marvelled.

'It's my business not to forget important lines. May I smoke?… Have you ever noticed that if anyone has a ingrowing toenail, say, he sends for the doctor to deal with it, and quite a nasty little business it can be, involving a minor operation. But if anyone has an ingrowing anxiety, he indulges it or ignores it or does anything under heaven with it except cure it … and there was, apropos some little remark of mine about overrating the importance of love, *I don't think you do. I ought to know.* Now,' he dropped his eyes to the signet on his finger, 'who hasn't been loving you enough?'

'Cosmo, what about Enid?'

'She rather agrees with me that this is probably not a three-cornered discussion. Fond of her?'

'Love her.'

'Good. *"They litter the ground like paper bags".*'

'Devil!'

'Now can't you get started? Just think of me as an old friend (in years, of course), or as – all right! all right! I very likely mightn't have said it, anyway. Shall we make it a father?'

'Yes. Let's make it that.'

And to that aspect of him I told the story of Myra and Anne and Vallant House, and later went upstairs and slept as I had not slept for weeks.

I V

I had told it badly; one does, with harkings-back and wrong sequences and feelings for the right word, but Cosmo hadn't spent half his life listening to incoherent playwrights stammering their scenarios to him for nothing, and he sorted out essentials and pinned down apparent contradictions and generally speaking 'produced' my account.

'And, you see, I must go back; the job's only half done. That foot on the stairs … Cosmo,' I was imploring him now, 'what do you think it sounds like?'

He hesitated, but only for a second. 'I'm afraid I agree with you. These things and people *are*. *I* could explain the Victorian point of view to you. I've had some, you know, though my own experience, admitted, wasn't as acute as yours. But I've at least shed what didn't suit me All my people were black Dissenters and they very nearly succeeded in making me dislike God very much indeed. But I was determined they shouldn't do me out of Him entirely, together with the other things they scamped me of in my boyhood, so I saved my soul alive by running away. I never went back, either, though I very nearly had to, once or twice. I wrote to my own mother for ten bob to pay my landlady, once, and she refused to send it – with a long homily about my sin, and my soul; it never occurred to her that she was making my land-lady suffer for it. And then – this'll show you – when I became a success, they were willing to overlook the past … no logic and reason aren't in that generation.'

'It does sound a bit Vallantish … did you ever consent to see them?'

'No. It had bitten too deep. But I always feel I've been de-frauded of something irreplaceable, even now, even in the posi-tion I am to throw my weight about.'

'She's spoilt my life, all right; hitting at me through other peo-ple … she wrote pious things as well …hymns.'

'It often goes with cruelty. It can be a form of suppressed sex, you know. Old Lady Vallant is an ex-beauty.'

'Oh … and you, too, think she minds?'

He looked at me swiftly, but answered the mantelpiece. 'It is very understandable to grieve over one's looks going, if they're what one has lived by.'

'*If* they are.' It was the only hint I dared give him that I had understood he wasn't thinking of the case of Lady Vallant.

He sheered off that. 'Of course when you go to Vallant House, I come, too.'

'Never, Cosmo! You'd bring some of its atmosphere back to Enid and we can't risk that … do you know, there's never been anyone as kind as you in the world.'

He looked at his shoes. 'That's bad hearing.' I could see his hand as it lay along the chair-arm. I prided myself then that I sat very still; I pride myself on it now, in spite of everything. I was thinking disgustedly, 'I've the instincts of the worst type of kitchen-enmaid', for Enid was upstairs, and I loved her too, and she had risked this interview with no second-rate qualms in a way that I could never have risen to, and I thought then that the successful marriage was the one in which its Enids took their Veres cleverly, philosophically, and could have wept then and there.

He was standing now, looking down on me. 'And so, you've got "the sight" … it must be a mixed blessing. And your brother?'

'He, too, and as far as I know, more focused than my own.'

'Twins … you being one eye and he the other, perhaps? In that case I stand aside.'

I was overwhelmed at his penetration. Confusedly I had always schemed to go back with James to Lowndes Square, once, or as often more, as might be necessary, but rather to bolster up my personal courage with his presence than deliberately to exploit our joint psychic resources. The result would have been the same, but the lift to me was that Cosmo had seen it first, that I had found a confidante at last, above all that he believed me with his own brand of calm and had meant to be with me in that house. One is a woman, when all's said.

'And when you have got what you went for, what next?'

I had never quite faced up to that in words, only in emotions, and I answered slowly, 'To be quite brutal, I want my pound of flesh and so does James. I want to make her suffer. One isn't half a Vallant for nothing I suppose.' My voice cracked. 'Do you blame me? ... when you think of Myra and the trays ... "she wouldn't have her in the drawing-room ..."'

It was then that he came over to me – and almost casually twisted my arm until I winced.

'You'll have to try and forgive me for that, later. But hysteria, you know ... never any help. I slapped my leading woman in the face, once, on a first night, and she thanked me. Blame you? No, Vere. As a piece of fatherly advice I might have recommended that you stay your hand if the affair had stopped at the damage to Myra's body. As it is –'

'– as it is?'

'– it's the damage to your mind which I find so unforgivable.'

v

And after that one had to be more careful than even about Cosmo. As the Americans say, I had got him where I wanted him, and there our relations must stick. Sometimes he seemed to me to be unfairly trying to bring all the batteries of his charm to bear upon me; began to arrange, his profile at me and even wore the ties that in a careless moment I had said I liked, and generally speaking made me feel like a demented flapper at the stage door. I quelled him with chaff, looked pointedly at the ties and said nothing at all and remarked to the profile, 'It's all right, Cosmo, I saw it the first time!' I thought 'after all, he's like all the rest of 'em', yet every moment with him one wanted to spend in bracing him about *Gladstone*, and one's concern must be everlastingly edited lest it be construed as philandering.

We got on best together when he openly bossed me, told me what was the matter with my dress and why, sent me upstairs to remove 'just one layer' of excess lipstick and altogether treated me as a cross between a daughter and a super, to my great and concealed delight. I once called upstairs to Enid: 'It's an awful bore, but I've got to go over to our house this morning for letters.' Cosmo was reading the *Telegraph* in the hall, threw it aside and remarked, 'Isn't it marvellous! And what, my dear, my sweet and my own, is "a nawful baw?" Enid!'

'Coming!'

'Enid, we are to lose Vere.'

'No! If that's going to be a joke, Val, I'm too *busy*, dear.'

'Fact, I assure you. Vere has discovered a nawful baw and has gotter go over to our house for lettahs. Now!' He stood and barred my exit.

'Cosmo, you beast!'

'Now: "It's an – awful bore – O-R-E, but I've got (mind your t's) to go" – and so on.' And he made me repeat it three times.

I leaned on the banisters and laughed at him. 'Honestly, I've a most correct aunt who lives in Palace Green and says "baw". Lots of our family do too.'

'Then I suggest that they all need lessons in diction, *and* throwing the voice. There's never any need to shout to make yourself heard – no no no! It doesn't disturb me, there's a great deal about your voice that I like, but don't forget that.'

'Oh Val, do leave off bullying her!'

'Don't mind me, Enid. Darling Cosmo (I repaid him for that sarcastic endearment) is just giving us a cameo study of the celebrity at home; "nor will Cosmo Furnival permit slipshod speech in his own home, and will take the greatest pains to secure that tonal harmony …"'

But he had gone, and I went too.

He sometimes took me out in the evenings when Enid wanted to stay at home or to go to her own friends, and usually veto'd every suggestion I made as to our after dinner destination.

I remember one particular night. We were in the car alone; I was, I suppose, trying to match up to him, throwing all the London lore I had ever scratched together into his lap. He said after a long pause, 'Is that the kind of place you like?'

'No, not particularly.'

'Then, why?'

'Oh, just because I've been there, you know.'

'With whom? Tell me.'

'Oh, this and that.'

Another silence. 'Vere, I do trust you're not one of those girls who don't know a gentleman when she sees one. I'm right out of this … my dear child, we're none of us gentlemen!' At that I laughed aloud and (I really couldn't help it) buried my face in his coat. He was apparently too fretted to notice. 'This night club, d'you mean to say you were taken there?'

'Yes, and got ditched into the bargain for a lady of colour.'

'But of course, of course. Didn't your man know it's got a rather nasty reputation?'

'It'd adore you for that, Cosmo! I saw nothing but bad fizz, black jazz, tired waiters and bored people.'

'What I'm trying to convey is that it isn't what goes on inside as much as the wrong set it gets you into. You don't want people going round saying, "Oh yes, I saw Vere Buchan at the so-and-so, she's always there", or "she's often there". It places you at once. Not that any woman is ever safe anywhere, in the last resort,' he added whimsically, 'nature sees to that, and don't you forget it. But one *can* help the set one heads towards, and remember, I don't like it, and while you are in my care I won't have it.'

'Cosmo, I do like you.'

'Thank you, my dear, but you don't love me any more.'

I answered, and the politeness of it pleased my conscience, 'You're perfectly wrong, I do very much'.

'It's a test, of course, living together in a house and colliding in the bathroom – '

'But I *like* colliding in bathrooms! And I like your dressing-gown.'

'Which one? I've got seven.'

'You would! It's the coffee-coloured silk.'

'King Edward gave me that.'

'My dear, what a nice ending! I must start a bedjacket knitted for me by Queen Alexandra.'

'Now look here, Vere; can you promise me that if ever you contemplate – ah – falling in love, you'll give me the opportunity of sizing up the fellow first? I'm not a bad judge, you know.'

'Yes. I can promise you that, Cosmo.'

Incidentally, I had girded myself for the battle over the question of paying for my own outings, and Cosmo just stared through me and settled the bills. He seemed unable to understand the point of view (and indeed as applied to him by myself it was ironic enough), or deliberately turned into a Chesterfieldian museum piece and made me feel cheap and nasty.

And once he played me a low trick, and I found myself with him in a box at the Albert Hall, and there was Chopin on the programme. And I could say nothing at all, and he knew it.

CHAPTER XXVIII

I

JAMES WAS IN London again, was to pick me up, meet the Furnivals and go with me to Hampshire. He stayed at his club; I mistrusted the Campden Hill *ménage* and the solitary servant who might take advantage of the situation – I quite saw that he was an opportunity not to be missed. Enid had suggested that he should come to her home, but James and I agreed, and kept to our decision, that there were limits beyond which hospitality should not be taxed.

His meeting with Cosmo's wife gave me another pang. He stood in the doorway and beamed all over his face at her, and she at him.

'Hullo, James!'

'*Hullo*, Enid!'

It was all to be so happy for them, and they fell from the beginning into one of those easy relationships which are eternally possible between the elderly woman and the young man of the right sort. He would kiss her quite openly before Cosmo; they sang duets and solos by the hour – what Cosmo called the good old crusteds, and indeed James's repertoire was almost as long as hers, if slightly and inevitably more modern, and where there was laughter in the house there were Enid and James gathered together. And Cosmo and I looked on like indulgent grandparents.

It accounted to me for my own failures in the past when my self-imposed maternal cossetings of my young men had broken down. In the last resort I had been a girl, and they knew it, something to which you could switch over at any moment. But Enid Furnival was the real thing, secure in her charming late middle-age, and when James invested her with a youth non-existent in all but spirit it was a pretty joke between them, holding no complication.

He told her about the pit queue and the pennies and she poised on the edge of laughter, blue eyes widening. 'But James! you poor midgets! Why didn't you come up and see us – oh, but you didn't know us then, how silly! I wasn't in that show and you'd have probably found me darning stockings in Val's dressing-room. Val! do you hear that? Vere! come and sing the *ex-act* song with James. I want–'

But I had gone, and so apparently had Cosmo. We met in the hall.

'Our young people too noisy for you?' he suggested sweetly.

'No, I'm just sulky.'

'So am I. Can't we go and get over it together somewhere?'

'I'm busy, Cosmo dear.'

I was. I had to finish packing and fussing with my Christmas presents.

'You're coming back to weather me over *Gladstone*.'

'May I?' I thought a moment. 'There are lots of things I could do, you know. Pasting in press cuttings, and so on.'

And next day Enid was on the top of a step ladder, decorating hall and drawing-room with holly and mistletoe.

I had filled stockings for them both; in Enid's, a mass of tiny sparkling silliments including a celluloid goldfish in a talc ball and a doll's tin grand piano; in Cosmo's, a property monocle of window glass to which I had attached six yards of watered silk ribbon, and a tiny booklet I had made and written, containing a tragedy in verse called *Seneca*, which consisted largely of the di-rection, *Another and more expensive part of the Forum: Enter Cosmo Furnival as Seneca*, and whose concluding lines ran:

> Bleed, wrist! and free my spirit from its chains,
> Rome take my blood that gushes from these veins.

(His later comment on it was 'A promising subject, from what I could read of it with my ribboned monocle; action perhaps a shade too swift; very costly production and *not* a box-office draw, as entire piece plays two minutes and one quarter. I think the public would want to see even me for longer than that.')

And I went up into his bedroom and tied it to a chair: 'From Vere and Trotty.'

On my last morning Enid picked her way off her current ladder and hugged me good-bye and was plucked from me by James, and Cosmo resignedly waved his hand at the mistletoe and we kissed each other, the traditionally facetious caress permitted annually.

II

Those ten days at Vallant were a disturbing Christmas to me, at least. Faced with the immediate loss of Lalage, meeting Hugh in lanes where London friends are apt to look so crude and strange, breaking in an unfamiliar house, seeing my own mother for the first time since my association with Cosmo, and weathering the uncles as my hosts. Here at least I found that mother had worked improvements; already they spoke to her at table with a passable imitation of that freedom which prevails among acquaintances and the unrelated, but that their worm died not entirely was evidenced by the set-back of my own arrival, and for nearly the whole of my stay my mother's brothers addressed the bulk of their conversation with me through her, and answered my remarks with averted head. Away from the table, one received the impression that they meant well, but that a substratum of confusion lingered still in their mind as to my precise identity. With Stuart and Julian Vallant, Hugh and James made the most headway by virtue of representing the law and the war, and James, blazing with secret grins, would form plans of campaign with salt-cellars, spoons, forks and napkin-rings upon the table cloth, while mother looked pink and apprehensive. He even developed an atrocious knack of inventing French villages for his maps, of which 'Passyle-Poivre' and 'La Soularde' stick in my memory, and which the uncles, fated wretches! took *au grand serieux*. And once again my ears and James's heard references to 'the Mater'. It was typical of the family that not one of them paused to speculate about the Christmas Day Lady Vallant was spending. Only James and I gave her a thought, who hated her more actively than anybody.

But when, from my window, I saw mother walking in the splendid neglected old garden with Uncle Julian (she even took his arm and laughed at some joke), I looked upon my work and saw that it was good.

That at least I can lay to my credit.

We Buchans tacitly accepted the fact that a Vallant Christmas would be a joyless affair, but the presence of James, as representing the less resigned and adaptable sex, redeemed it in some measure. It began by the uncles not giving anybody anything but embarrassed breakfast greetings, heavily facetious lest sentiment be suspected, followed by a bad ten minutes which convicted us of tactlessness while they unhappily unfastened our own conventional and stultified offerings and hurried them behind toast-racks and silver entrée dishes on the principle of least said soonest mended (uncle Stuart, we realized later, had quite cleverly contrived to say nothing at all. It was in mother's room that we did our heavy giving, a James called it, and could laugh as much as we wanted to, and be silly. After all, as mother said, the uncles were feeding and roofing us, 'and I've seen to it that there an enough crackers. If I'd left it to the housekeeper there'd have been one each, or none.'

At dinner, which was excellent, I said to nobody is particular, 'Isn't it rum that if it hadn't been for Susan Vallant, none of us would be here, except Hugh?' and James, rising as though for a toast, raised his glass and announced genially, 'And has it been worth her trouble? No!' and tossed off his burgundy at one blow, and even the uncles cackled.

That morning James had come to my bedroom with two boxes. 'The Furnivals gave me these for you,' and he left me alone with them. Enid's box held a dozen pairs of sheer silk stockings. Cosmo's a coffee-coloured silk dressing-gown 'with love from Queen Alexandra and that much more uninteresting person, Cosmo Furnival'.

Oh my dear Cosmo! It must have cost you quite three guineas (a fortune!) – and I would so much have preferred one of your old wraps!

I had headed him off giving me things, even trifles, always; it was partly my engrained outlook on life, but more that I wanted nothing of him at all. He could give me nothing that I could ever take, and he didn't even want to: I had already given him what he mustn't accept. I had hurt and plagued him a dozen times by my bright grateful refusals, but in the last resort he stayed his hand and I had deprived him of a small pleasure, rightly, wrongly, how do I know? One can only act hurriedly according to one's lights, and life is short.

Wrapped in his dressing-gown I sat down to write to them. My first letters.

'Cosmo dear. ....'

And, 'Darling Enid'.

That at least was no understatement. She was dear to me then and is to this day, after all the years.

III

In the lanes whose hedges creaked with frost James and I discussed the Vallant business ahead of us. We would get it over during this leave of his, but if possible not before the Furnival première. I didn't know how Cosmo reacted to nerves: he had asked me to be there with him on the day and that was enough for me; he was evidently of the type which needs companionship in crisis, where James and I gravitate instinctively towards the lone furrow, and if we were together over the Vallant matter it was that we were so very nearly one person. And then I told James about our talk in the library.

'One *does* like him, doesn't one?' stated James.

'Yes.'

He looked at me, a direct question.

'Yes, Jamesey.'

'Oh Vere, my dear! Well, well … and yet I'm not surprised, you know.' But there seemed to be something on his mind, extra to anything I had disclosed. I had too much to say and let it go and we trudged another quarter-mile. 'You must write to Hutchins for the key', he said dully, and I wondered why his pace was beginning to flag.

And on New Year's Day Lalage was married to Hugh at the church 'rocking with old brasses', and what there is of good in me was glad to see her go, for even then she moved down the tiny aisle beside Hugh like one half-awakened from a very bad dream indeed as they passed out through a line of kindly, curious villagers into a white world.

IV

James and I travelled up to London together, he to the club and I to the Furnivals. All the long journey home, I was thinking that I was one of those semi-courageous people so much more unsatisfactory than the open coward too fine by a hair's breadth to swerve from the line I had laid down myself in Enid's home, not fine enough to keep away from it altogether.

On the hall table was a letter for me in a hand I knew and I was childishly warmed by the postal identification of myself with that home. It could wait. Claude was one of those intensely amusing people who seem unable to give full measure on paper; endless reminders of how amusing they were are dotted all over their rare epistle and their letters are invariably far too short. With the envelope in my hand I went in search of Enid. She was writing letters and murmured 'Ah, that's nice', and gave me a hand to hold as she bit her pen and asked about the wedding and 'her' James, and quite soon told me I looked tired and sent me to get warm and called to me – she was great at last-minute messages – 'I don't know where Val is but do go and find out.'

I went, and found him in the garden, in the bright chill. He had huddled a cloak round him and cocked an astrakhan cap on his head – anyhow, and crooked, and perfectly right, as usual.

'Aha Tovarish!' I called, and he turned and came to me and I surveyed him from head to heel and kept my greeting at chaff-level.

'Cosmo, I've yet to meet the hat that didn't suit you. I believe you'd get away with even a bowler. Tell me about that cap.'

'Little fool, I'm very glad to see you.'

'And I to see you. Please go on.'

'What? Oh, this? Lord, now … I had it in a preposterous Russian drama in – what? – 1908.'

'And there was a vamp called Sonia.'

'No, a beautiful Vera.'

'With green eyes and a tigerskin you raped her on.'

'Now! I don't like that. Keep it for your cocktail teas.'

'My –? Well, I like that! And me the dullest of the pure.'

'And I learnt four Russian words during the run: two I frankly never knew the meaning of, the third was inevitably samovar and the fourth I should call you now if I dared.'

We walked on. From a shrubbery, Trotty scraped and rustled to meet us and put up his little face at Cosmo for notice. I said, 'Aren't Trotty's hands *exactly* like Enid's?' and Cosmo stooped to the hedgehog and put Trotty's little hand on his finger and said he saw what I meant, and straightened and turned on me.

'I may be going to be rather a trial during the next week or so. Production isn't all interviews and applause, you know. This isn't only a question, as it used to be even twenty years ago, of first-night nerves, because one could pick oneself up then after a fall and go ahead; it's a case of theatric innovation, to begin with, and new wine in an old bottle to crown all.'

'If Enid can stand it –' I smiled.

'Enid and I have practically grown up together. She knows me.' So true. And I deserved it, even if I hadn't meant to sound arrogant.

'I'm ready.'

'I wonder … You've seen, shall I say? the more presentable side of me all this time (and even that's apparently gone bad on you).'

'You asked me to stay, Cosmo, and weather you over it.'

'That was a piece of self-indulgence. I've been thinking …'

He hitched at his cloak. 'There's a side of you that doesn't seem to me to grow up at all, and a side of me that's curiously reluctant to disillusion it. Now's your chance to emerge with false impressions intact,' and the lines round his eyes were sardonic.

'But, I don't want to emerge … Cosmo, do you really think I'm just a stage-struck flapper?'

'Can you honestly tell me that glamour isn't half the battle?'

'It has its place, no doubt,' I agreed reasonably, 'or there'd be no more theatre, but it doesn't happen to apply here.'

'I think, then, you'd better stay … and finish up for good.'

I was so dismayed that I refuged in laughter – it sounded like a hyena. 'If this is a scene, Cosmo, I don't know my cues or my lines.'

He stopped in the middle of the path. I have often read of a voice of ice and dismissed it as an effective but unreal flourish. It is no joke when you run into it, and it is combined with height and the strength of eyes.

'Can you never take me seriously? I'm getting rather tired of this, you know.'

Well … if this was a sample of Cosmo as he really was I would learn it. Yet it wasn't his fault that one was so shattered, shattered but eternally interested. The words as words were nothing at all; I thought 'If he can do this to me on an ineffective sentence, what cannot he do to an audience on a good one?' and would console myself with that later. And I stood waiting for him to stride away or do something showy and obvious, and he turned quite quietly with me and walked me back to the house, and later (as we were both to do in time) we ended at Enid, heading to her for comfort.

And if this was part of knowing him, then it must have its place, hurt and all.

I went up to my room and found I was sitting at the writing-table with an opened letter in my hand. Gradually isolated sentences sprang at me from the pages, and it was Claude asking me to marry him. I struck my hand on the desk top. 'Well, God damn it all …'

Oh, my dear Claude, whom I so like! with whom I have laughed so long and fooled so happily always! And it was all so cursedly suitable on the face of it; Claude, who would be mine entirely without bar, and the pleasant, healthy father of our children. And for ever impossible, even had one hankered for matrimony and offspring, because of a pacing, looming old wretch downstairs with crowsfeet and acidulated eyes, my pacing, looming old wretch who gave me what sheer youth could never rise to in brief, intolerable glimpses of understanding and affection.

Claude would give me love and plenty of it, and laughter and nothing else at all. And it wasn't enough. I was no young girl to bask in admiration and deference to my whims and opinions; I needed a reasonable amount of opposition backed by experience, and above all was it essential that it should come from one who not only maturely appreciated me, but who had a good, considered opinion of himself as well and no self-deprecations at all.

Claude in between his work would want the things that young men call good times, in which the newest cabaret is a lark, and getting raided by the police and your name on the society black–list at Vine Street, an adventure and a joke and a titbit you dined out on; I wanted to be steered away from the wrong places and people which never had amused me.

Claude and I would live and learn together, and make our mistakes, and that was no good to me at all, who wanted one who had learnt and could point to where my own feet should tread, and who had long made his representative selection of mistakes and got the worst of them over. Also, I discovered I enjoyed ups and down and unforeseen fiascos and success that the slow, certain advances of army life could never offer. If I married Claude we should end up at Tidworth or Farnborough and I should become a 'mother' to the junior officers or 'that cat' to the tea-parties, and in time (oh glory!) should be heavily flirted with by majors with stomachs.

And if the still–young marry each other, they have to watch the creeping on of age with all its small physical humiliations. Cosmo had not been young when first I met him, nor should I have looked at him twice when he was. I could wane in his sight and was doing it, heaven knew! but he never in my own.

And finally, James must have known of Claude's letter, that day in the Hampshire lane … the way his step had slowed. …

One couldn't even pack a suit-case and escape from the Furnival's house. One doesn't. It is a social impossibility, involving explanations even more impossible to one's hostess. To Enid, in short.

There were just two ways to answer Claude: one by telling him I didn't care for him, which wasn't true, and the other by telling him openly that there was someone else. Slang has its uses. I used plenty of it. And I let him go with a considerable pang and no doubts whatever, and dressed for dinner and went down to meet whatever might be waiting for me.

Enid, I remember, was looking particularly charming that night. Whenever I think of her the word 'adorable' springs to my mind, and after dinner we had coffee in the drawing-room and I said 'Play to me'. She dawdled to the piano in her mist-coloured chiffon, cigarette in hand, and turned to us where we sat side by side on the sofa, and tilted a silvery-gold head. 'Are we sentimental to-night, or lively, or just plain cussed?' and her lip curled back over her little teeth.

'Just plain cussed.' Cosmo and I said it together.

'Ah well ...' and she sat at the piano and turned off a light and thought, and twiddled a screw in the piano stool – and sang a song of Marie Lloyd's.

Oh Enid! It was so exactly like you, when one had been keyed for Schumann, Beethoven, or even 'Star of my soul!'

'I'm one of the ruins Cromwell knocked about a bit ...'

It is a splendid ditty, fruity and lilting and with minor modulations that Wagner himself would have relished! Coming from Enid and not the dear rorty originator it was funnier still, but she followed it with German 'The way that he looked at me', 'Dream o' Day Jill', and was well into 'All for a green ribbon' when Cosmo put down his cup and leant over to me.

'Can't we forget it?'

'Yes, but it was my first evening at home.'

'At home ... you have the devil's knack of saying the beautiful thing – and not meaning it at all.'

And I was happy again, as happy as I expected to be, or probably deserve.

CHAPTER XXIX

I

GLADSTONE WAS A *succès d'estime* for statesman and actor which is to say that James Agate whipped and scorpioned the public not to miss it and some of them obliged, backed by an intelligent minority whose opinion, socially, did not count, and further supported by what remained of the Old Guard of Cosmo Furnival's following. The paying public to whom the theatre was a place of entertainment treated the play in the manner in which the confirmed convivial eyes the bottle of limejuice on the sideboard, and murmuring praise at the interesting and instructive nature of the experiment went off to a Charlot revue. But it ran, with nursing, for three and a half months and the important thing about it was that it replaced Cosmo on the map, lined him up with contemporary stage evolution, put him among the moderns who are paid the compliment of controversy, rather than affectionately accepting him in his own line for the sake of old times with an indulgent pat on the peruke.

In his home, I watched it all, vicariously stimulated, flustered, despondent and nervy, while Enid Furnival sat in the drawing-room and plunged into a large and nameless piece of knitting. I looked upon her work and saw that it was good, so to speak, and even started a piece of *gros point* myself, and the strange, sticky puckered object lay about and was cast down anywhere at the call of the crisis of the moment. I don't know, after his caution, what I had expected from Cosmo himself, and for days I didn't see that the fact that I got nothing at all was part of the business. He would look right through me if he met me about the house, or was terse and abstracted, and once when I was in his way he lifted me by the elbows and put me somewhere else as if I were a chair.

Gradually I grew to expect it, saw that this concentration was right, knew I wouldn't have it otherwise, guessed that this was one of the ways by which creators get results. And just as I was settling down to that, another phase set in and put me at sixes and sevens; Cosmo on the semi-suppressed rampage, with the back of the work broken and the trifles crowding on him. And Enid knitted through it all.

'What? Val? Oh *he's* all right. It's always like this. Darling, pick up that ball like an angel. No, it's under the table.'

'Enid! Where in heaven's that registered letter?'

'Niddy! If Clara's moved that book I shall go out of my mind.'

'The eggs are hard-boiled, you *know* I hate them like that.'

Oddly enough it was over the hard-boiled egg side of it all that I wavered. There were moments when, losing all sense of context, one saw Cosmo objectively as any husband being tiresome over trifles, and try as one would the knowledge that this was only offshoot of overstrain and miles away from Cosmo as he could be and nearly always was didn't immediately reassert itself, and one thought 'This is him as he is'. I know now that it was of just that petty side of him that he warned me in the garden, and why. Oh, but he knew! He was clever. Retrospectively I revel still in his mind. For during those moments it was impossible to re-capture him, almost incredible that this was the man whose eyes and mouth had ever said the lovely thing to one, in whom one had found the exactly right listener, to whom one had entrusted the story of Myra. My sole excuse is that myself was pitched in a pretty high key at that time worked up for two, upset over Claude's letter, and watching the days drawing me nearer to Vallant House that would upset me more.

Sometimes James dropped in in the evenings. He was always careful to telephone first for permission as I could never count from day to day upon Cosmo's mood, and wouldn't have him overtired, even for James, as I told Enid. And the result of that was that on James's next visit Cosmo blandly scooped him off to the library and left us both lamenting!

I took myself right off. When or if Cosmo wanted me I was there. Meanwhile I gave as good as I got, when we did speak!

And next day, Enid, needles flashing in the firelight, laid down her wool and said, 'Vere ducky, I do *wish* you'd be nicer to Val.'

II

It was the unexpectedness of it that drove me to just stammering.

'My *dear* Enid …!'

'Keep him petted. Make a fuss of him. He's dying for notice. He wants heaps of affection, you know, and more these days than ever. Don't I know him! And I thought you loved him.'

'I do. That's the whole difficulty. D'you mind going on knitting?'

'Well then, go and tell him so. He'd adore it. He thinks more of you than I've ever seen him do of any girl. He used to come back full of you – called you "my girl" and "my dear little friend" and "my nice child". He says you're the only one who wants nothing for herself from him, and that's true – even I wanted to marry him! And (if I'm being impertinent, stop me), there was a young man at the theatre –'

'Wraxe,' I said mechanically.

'My dear, Val was jealous of him! *I* saw that fast enough. I've been it too often myself to mistake the symptoms! Oh, I'm so thankful that's all over! You know, I'm sorry for all you young things. It seems to me that the men you get a chance at now aren't a patch on *our* lot … and their *manners*! There's James, of course, but I don't believe he's typical, any more than you are ... so do be nice to Val. There he is, putting on his most becoming ties for you and you crush the poor thing off the earth!'

'Well, is he fair to me, Enid? Is it necessary?'

She did put her work aside at that. 'Well! I did think you had brains, oh, but heaps more than me! But my dearie child, he thinks you're bored with *him* – off him – disappointed. – '

'He *doesn't*?'

'He *does*! I've watched you muffing him three or four times when a ha'porth of sense would have kept him happy.'

'That's all very fine, Enid, but these things are apt to get a bit above and beyond, you know.'

'Oh, I see. You mean you're afraid he'll touch you and flirt with you and give you the glad eye?'

'Now we are down to brass tacks, I've had my moments in which I've been much more afraid that he wouldn't!'

She giggled delightedly. 'One *is*, isn't one? Oh, I've been all through that! It was touch and go once or twice, I can tell you, in the old days, and I only had my face to carry me along.'

'No, it could never have been only that, Enid, he's not that sort of a fool. You're the one right person for him.'

She leant to me, hands round knees like a schoolgirl. 'No! Do you really think so?'

'Yes. What a haven of refuge you must be to him – after me!'

We both laughed at that. 'Oh, we have our uses,' assented Enid Furnival, 'my present one is to keep him quiet by keeping quiet myself.'

I thought. 'Enid ...'

'M'm?'

'I've meditated once or twice walking out on you, and if I'm not doing it, it's because there's nothing to walk out *for*, or ever will be ... on the other hand, being human (and the heart desperately wicked and so on), I can't promise for always and all the time not to break down here and there, though I'm pretty steady on my feet, I will say that for myself.'

'More than anyone I've ever seen. You scrupulous honourable people do have the *nastiest* time! I couldn't have done it, I tell you flat ... so go and play with Val, my dear. You've got to remember that every time anybody fails him they're undermining him, at his age ... he was so lovely! And you've hidden away the very photograph in your bedroom – '

'– because I prefer him as he is.'

'Tell him that. You must!'

'I have.'

'When?'

'At the theatre.'

'Oh ... that accounts for it. He probably had inches of grease-paint on his face and thought it was that you were admiring. You know, it's terrible for them when everything they've lived by and for begins to go.'

It surprised me, the stress she laid upon physical beauty it seemed, with her generation, altogether to overshadow the subtler matter of charm, where we with our more tortuous and so-phisticated minds can at least appreciate that and rate it at its true value. I answered, 'Of course, if that's all he sees, or thinks other people do ... *he who lives by the sword must perish by the sword.*'

'Is that the Bible?'

'Probably. It usually is when it isn't Shakespeare.'

And it ended by Cosmo's wife virtually comforting *me*. '*I did* so want you two to be happy! It seems such hard luck ... well, go and make friends with Val, and save something for me, too!'

I went to her and put my arms round her. 'Enid, there are times when upon my soul I don't know which I love the most, you or Cosmo!'

She smiled up at me. '*I* do.'

'Isn't it curious that nobody ever admits that it's possible to love the wife in the case? At the cocktail teas which your good husband assures me I frequent there is a notion – pay attention, Enid, this is serious, and contemporary thought and bulky things like that – that if you hate a woman and say so you are a cat, and if you care for her and show it you're a pervert. Don't we have great fun among the Bright Young People?' and I went down to Cosmo with Enid's kiss on my mouth.

Even then I doubted a little if she understood. As for myself, it seemed to me at that moment that I had no real place in her home in spite of everything. Enid in her youth had risked what Cosmo might be going to turn into, even unto the obese professional failure, whereas I had skipped his early, problematic future

and come in on what, to me, was the crest of the wave. It made
one feel extraordinarily humble, unworthy and brittle. It made
me plague myself with questions as to my ability to have grown
up with him as she had dared to do … those other women …
or his own demands upon one … the conventional and rather
meaningless demands of young manhood. As things stood, he
at his age and I at mine, we were temperamentally nearer than
we should be at and other period, for if I was at concert pitch,
his tempo was slowing down, and granting the relative force of
emotions between man and woman we had, in point of time,
drawn about level.

He was writing in his study.

'Please don't get up. I just came to see if there was anything I
could do for you.'

He began to sketch noughts and crosses on the blotting paper.

'So you don't cast me off entirely?'

'I never did; that was your idea.'

He threw down his pen. 'That's good. But I'll make you say
more than that, one day.'

And so he did, so he did – when it was very nearly too late.
And there was peace between us, or quite enough to satisfy Enid,
and always after that Cosmo kissed me good night as naturally as
he did her, and if I have imagined that he sometimes shaved this
side of the fatherly we let it go at that. Even for the other aspect
I could not have lost the safer one happily.

I I I

And then the Press descended on us, and Enid put away her
knitting and turned on another side of herself and became the
hostess, seeing that the young men had whiskies and sandwiches
and cigarettes, and directing the servants where to move furniture
when the camera man wanted to photograph Cosmo in various
rooms or called for screens and sheets as photographers nearly
always and unaccountably do, she told me, 'like plumbers only
with them it's ladders and candles', and she smiled at them all
and sympathized when anything collapsed and insisted on Trotty
being 'done' with her husband and told the immediate young
man how hedgehogs should be fed, and laughed at me for being

so interested in it all and protested against being corralled and photographed too. They even included me in one shot and for the first time I became that sub-human 'and friend'. ('She's Vere Buchan and no friend of mine' murmured Cosmo for my ears, and with a face completely impassive for the camera he poked me in the ribs and I hacked him on the heel and we managed between us to get off a delicate assortment of stingers behind our teeth – I hadn't forgotten my ventriloquial tricks.

'They said, "Who *is* that handsome man?"'

'"It's Mr. Toad,"' I purred.

'Your princess slip's coming down. Half an inch below your skirt. I detest ramshackle women.'

'What *d' you* know about slips?'

'I could tell you every stitch you've got on, *and* in its proper order.' All this with fixed and pleasant smiles.

After that, the scene of battle shifted to the theatre where I didn't follow it, for photographs from the stage of sets and the principals, and of Cosmo in his Gladstone make-up, and Enid went back to her household affairs and I to the library to paste in the advance notices and answer letters and the suddenly almost incessant telephone; over that job Enid frankly said she hadn't got the touch and 'had never been much use that way to Val. I get too interested in the poor souls who want things from him, whether they're firms asking for testimonials for shaving-creams or actors out of a shop, and that does confuse life so.' I didn't let it, and for all that week I became a hard-boiled office executive and if I did occasionally permit the use of his name to the boosting of some toilet preparation at least I scuttled up to the bathroom or his dressing-room first to find out if he used it or called down to his wife, in the last resort. '*Enid!* What toothpaste does Cosmo use?' and a faint scream of 'Kolynos' came from the unknown.

'That settles it, then he mustn't give his name to the one on the telephone.' And then the first night was upon us and Cosmo passed into his final phase and became himself again – he seemed to realize that all that could be done and foreseen had been, and just waited on results; he even played a round of golf with us in the morning with walking sticks and tennis balls, and broke the kitchen window and said what a wonderful shape the pane has splintered into and tried to do it again while Enid faintly shrieked that he would 'hurt cook', and Cosmo, addressing the ball, said that that would be unfortunate as she was the only one they'd ever had who understood quenelle (Fore!) and sent the second missile after the first.

Days before, Enid had offered me a seat in her box, and I refused it; it was her night and Cosmo's, and I told her so. 'James and I are going to sit in the pit and pay Cosmo half a crown and suck oranges.'

She thought it over and let it pass. Actually, of course James and I had booked our seats weeks ago, in the upper circle. I had no time for standing in queues. Also, as I had been careful to tell the Press when the Furnival weren't listening, I was Mr. Furnival's secretary. I had taken far too much from them, always, and had had a set-to with Cosmo already into which we had imported Enid as referee over the question of his paying me a salary. It was ridiculous and I told him so; my work at his house had been intermittent and only really concentrated in the pre-Gladstonian fortnight … I was taking a vulgar line over it … also I hurt him … I mightn't think it but I was worth it to him, and anyway he was using my time … now as a favour to him … don't hit below the belt Cosmo … well then, would Enid let you go? Couldn't you consider her for just five minutes? … did Vere seriously consider that two miserable pounds a week was adequate payment for her companionship?

And Enid ruled in my favour, but told me plainly that she thought I ought to get a clear two pounds because of the commission to my office. And I stayed, and took Cosmo's two pounds four shillings a week.

A minor reason for my refusal to appear in the Furnival box was the clothes question; on such nights he must have his womenfolk do him credit and a bit over. It wouldn't do him any good to be mixed up with *démodés* who are so much more fatal than the noticeably shabby, who might be duchesses (and very often are). At his six o'clock dinner I sat with him in my ordinary house frock and if he thought I was going upstairs to change into splendours, let him. Enid and I were dining together later; at present we kept him company over his omelette and sauterne and put our elbows on the table and were all rather silent and

I suppressed the yawn-after-yawn of nerves. Enid said, 'I hope you'll like my dress, Val', and I held my breath. Dress, at a moment like this! ... but probably she knew ...

'So long as it doesn't put my eye out, dear. What colour is it?'

'There's a new powder-blue and a silver lace.'

He considered, peeling a peach. 'The powder-blue. The silver ... those highlights glancing off that material do distract one so.'

I had sent him my telegram to the theatre and was careful to omit my surname lest in the dog-days of the run members of his company, remembering me, came to his room and read it. Mother had sent him a wire as well, and later on I enjoyed thanking her in the third person on Mr. Furnival's behalf.

And then we three were in the hall; I could see the outline of the waiting car and its headlights through the window, and Enid said, 'Well, God bless you, my dear old boy', and put her arms round his neck, and he hugged us both and I wished him all the good in the world and told him I was jealous of every last woman in the company which seemed to please him immensely.

And then it was lights, and a huge arch of red curtain and a theatre filling and the orchestra (which I had forgotten to allow for, in the scale of mental strains), and wondered what personal belongings were thrown on to that armchair in Cosmo's dressing-room that I had slept in, and quite soon there was a glint of silvery-gold hair and James said, 'There's Enid'; a mist of blue tulle, and I saw what Cosmo meant; it blended into the shadows of the box. She was sitting well back so that the stage lighting shouldn't pick out her head and 'put his eye out'.

The house-lights dimmed down leaving a glow on the curtains, and I sent up a hasty prayer, and found that James's hand was in mine, gripping it.

A built-in set – the study in Gladstone's house – maid moving about and Wraxe appearing and saying four lines, and a door opening casually and Cosmo's casual entrance, walk to his desk and absorption in correspondence and a cup of tea.

I saw then how dangerous what is called 'natural acting' can be to an actor who must capture audiences against time and a house which unknowingly expects a star to throw his weight about from the word go. How dangerous, lay in the fact that for several seconds it timed him wrong with them, and their recognizing burst of applause cut in on his opening lines. Du Maurier was wrestling faithfully with the public; since then, George Arliss has taught them something of theatric values, his beautiful restraint enormously aided by his accessibility to the wider public of the screen, whose audience is mercifully dumb, but in the early weeks of 1916 naturalism was still a risky game. Also, one sensed the danger to the actor of a too-faithful make-up. Cosmo had scrapped everything in him which took the eye, every mannerism I knew had gone by the board since the earlier rehearsals, and in the last resort average playgoers want to see Gladstone as Cosmo Furnival, rather than the other way about, lest they be forced to concentrate upon history and the statesman, which will probably bore them. If Cosmo had pandered to them just the little more, been a little less self-denying; if he had given them as makeweight the Furnival laugh or eyebrow, the 'ah?' and the caught breath, that play might have had a longer run.

'Interesting but stuffy,' a voice in the foyer was saying in the interval.

'I give it a month.'

'But – what's he *done* to himself? I didn't know who it *was* until some woman called him William.'

'Mother says he was simply *adorable* about ninety years ago, and *made* me come. Aren't one's parents grim?'

One's fingers were clenching at one's side; this wasn't one girl speaking, but several million.

And the final curtain at last, to rousing cheers!

And home to the Furnivals, and finding yet another facet of Enid; no italics and adulations here, but a woman very much on the spot, so keenly interested she had no need to show it.

'Tell Wraxe he mustn't come on so soon on his cue, Val. It looks like a fire, from the front, or as if he'd been listening outside the door.

'And I don't like that scene of yours with Mrs. G. played with you standing at the back of her chair. That speech is a bit on the dull side already and more movement wouldn't do it any harm. Besides, she masks you.

'Oh, and those trousers of yours … I'm afraid we'll have to get a smaller pattern after all. Yes, my dear, I know they're correct and shepherd's plaid and so on, but you want an *effect*, not a photo.

You've got some terribly important lines in that scene and they're going to be very nearly dished on that pattern. I wonder what it is about even a suspicion of plaid that's funny? ... low comedians I suppose ... Vere darling, be an angel and ring up Sackville Street and tell them – and *much* more neutral and *quick*!'

They taught me so much! Cosmo told me once that it was first-rate material; heaven knows I had the best teacher. I suppose it was the business of my inner ear over again which, baulking at the drudgery of crotchets and shying away from all the grammar of music, yet had its instinct for the ultimate rights and wrongs of harmony that operated over Cosmo's profession, and made me immediate, if inarticulate, to sense a theatric danger or false note, and instant in knowledge of the rare and perfect thing.

IV

The 'and friend' photograph which appeared in sepia and one of the shilling weeklies had the unforeseen effect of bringing up my relations once more, those – I realized it with a shock – dim and half-remembered people who were my uncles, aunts and cousins. The magazine had evidently gone the rounds.

Aunt Emmeline, via Evelyn Verdune, seemed to be cynically accepting some unspecified downfall on my part which, if vague, was strong through my grandmother over this – they all took the line that if Lady Vallant had anything to contribute the matter must be worth attention – Dolly herself actually wrote to me. It seemed (but of course Vallybags has got it all wrong) that I had been practically turned out of Vallant House: 'Grannyma says she couldn't keep you. I *ask* you! *Naturally* I don't believe a word she says, but *do* tell me.'

The loyalty of contemporaries tinged with incurable Verdune curiosity; colloquial lenience in the air because Dolly herself had made what uncle Bertram called a mess of things. And I was the current family mess. Meanwhile, they asked me for free passes for *Gladstone*. Aunt Sophia, always sublime, thought that I was living with a Mr. Furnace, and it was bound to happen – such a quaint mite – with poor little Anne away. And, in short, if I hadn't exactly taken the wrong turning I had sidestepped into an uncommonly fishy one.

The unmarried Seagraves more or less frankly gaped and when I met them again would stare at me with that mixture of suppressed virginal repulsion for the soiled plus the spinster's fascinated curiosity, and Flora, still watering horses, expected in a note that my Mr. Cosmo Furnival could be worked to recite at a drawing-room concert in Emperor's Gate 'lent by the parents' for the benefit of the Blue Cross, impressing me matter-of-factly into the business of giving an actor the chance to serve a Seagrave and a Buchan. The poor farouche lamp-post probably hadn't meant it that way, but it was my mood, and at times anything which will feed one's fury is a gift from above. I enjoyed answering that. I read, and said at breakfast, 'Cosmo, I seem to be living in sin with a Mr. Furnace. It's all rather baffling.'

'It would be. But are there, as it were, no marks, or signs of a struggle?'

'I don't know … wait a minute … no … I seem to have gone quietly.'

'Let's have Mr. Furnace to dinner,' said Enid.

'It's no good. He's here,' and I resignedly tilted my head at her husband.

'Oh no, oh no! Oh how lovely!'

'Mr. Furnace …' Cosmo took a piece of toast. 'He would, I think, have sideburns and be a stickler for the conventions, and probably a solicitor who never handles divorce … yes … the Dickensian unattached extra who fills in at Christmas parties. Well! I'm sorry to hear he's gone wrong, too, but we all do it.'

But beneath all our laughter I was frayed. I showed the letters to James who said, 'Blast them! It's the damned cheek of it … doing nothing on Gawd's earth for one and then reserving the right to criticize.' Heads together, we pointed each other out the plums.

'Taking one's character away quite cheerfully on no evidence and then trying to make a bit on it …'

'"Drinking champagne that she sends us, but we never can forgive –"'

'Oh, distinctly Vallantish.'

Dolly's letter had at least one effect, of bracing my spirit to cope with Vallant House. Cosmo was now settled into his run: he had weathered the Press notices with a calm and common sense that surprised me, James's leave was drawing to an end and there was no longer a shred of excuse for delay. Tell Cosmo? But it might worry him. Actors seem to have so many apple-carts whose delicate adjustment a tap will upset. At the same time he had a right to know; James and I argued it back and forth. Finally, I was against telling him, and we arranged that we would go back to Campden Hill to sleep.

But the Furnivals would expect to know why.

Tell Enid, then, that we were going to a dance.

But she'd see me leaving the house, not in evening dress.

'Then tell her we've gone out on the tiles and you'll be late back, and I'll slope off to the club.' And we made it so.

James was prowling up and down my bedroom, occasionally looking at me out of the corner of his eye.

'Go on, Jamesey, say it, say it!'

'Does Enid know about this business?'

'I don't think so. Cosmo and I rather agreed that it wasn't an Enidish thing −'

'Furnival was definitely worried about you and Vallant?'

I looked out of the window. 'He was ... concerned,' I assented.

Then it came. 'Vere, is he in love with you?'

I could have taken it from no one else on earth.

'I hope not. I don't think so.'

We managed fairly smoothly. James took the thermos that Lalage had given me and had it filled with coffee at his club − I shied at stealing Enid's! − and from the same source awaited me in Lowndes Square with a packet of sandwiches. And I sat with the Furnivals at Cosmo's early dinner, and do what I would it was hard to be natural, and the contemptible instinct to cling to them both had to be dealt with as well. I even followed Cosmo into the hall and said good-bye, and patted his arm, which seemed to take him aback.

And Enid: 'Au 'voir, ducky, have a good time.'

CHAPTER XXX

I

WE ARRIVED AT Vallant House at a few minutes past eleven. James went upstairs to sleuth out bars of light under doors, and found none – it was evidently one of our grandmother's early nights.

In the hall I found a note from Hutchins, confirming this, and I called up softly, 'Now for it, Jamesey'.

'Yes. This is the dam' drawing-room.'

'Got the thermos?'

'Here.'

'I wonder how long we shall have to wait for them to-night.' He rejoined me, padding soundlessly.

'Vere … who's a red-hair'd child on the top landing?'

'Oh God, Jamesey, I don't *know*!'

'In a nightdress … I think. I only got the meres glimpse. She was looking down. …'

We went into the dining-room, and after all, Hutchins had put out food and drink for us.

'Good chap,' James stammered.

'One of the best.' I was pleased with the way that remark had come out. A memory returned to me. 'By the way, Jamesey, if I should disgrace myself would you mind twisting my arm – *here*, like this?'

He nodded brusquely. We fell to eating sandwiches, and presently James said, 'What are we doing this for? I don't want 'em … and we've cleared the dish.' He looked ridiculously astonished.

The pillar'd clock on the mantelpiece ticked on comfortably, as one who had marked off the seconds that led to the approach of a thousand many-coursed Victorian meals. The belly-god of the house. We went into the hall and James said, 'Where does it happen most?'

'All down the stairs, but there's a lot on the landing –' I stopped for a phrase to convey the impression I had received, '– people hating each other worse …'

'We'll camp here, outside the dining-room door.'

'Chairs?'

'Better not. We might have to move in a hurry.'

Later, from the dial of his luminous watch, we found that we had sat there, crouched on the floor, for two hours. And nothing happened at all. It seemed as if, with the glimpse of that red-hair'd child, the house had exhausted itself for the night.

James said, 'Look here … about this time factor: we might be a year before the staircase affair came round again.'

'I don't think so. I've seen bits of it already and it would be too much of a coincidence if my short stay here had included the night it happened. It's our affair, as Vallants, and that being so I suppose we have some extra link with it through our physical link with the people concerned. You see, I *know* those two who came down first were Emmeline and Sophia.'

In the taxi he shifted and said, 'That child … what's your theory?'

I answered, apologetically because for some reason the idea to me was the only incredible one of the whole business, and a dawning probability which had only reached me in the manner of a light ray much later during the wait in the hall, 'Personally, I believe that it was mother'.

Sleeplessness invariably leaves its mark on me. At breakfast, Cosmo murmured to his plate, '"A very considerable bend, gentlemen",' and I decided against time to take him up on that.

'Yes. Late nights are apt to fly to the old face – no more bacon, I implore you, Enid.' And later on I had to tell her that I should be in late again that night. I was fretting that she wouldn't have been human if she hadn't been hurt at what must appear to be the heartless action on our part in failing even to suggest that she come with us too, with me and 'her' James. But you can't touch Vallant business without hurting somebody.

11

That night, we arrived in Lowndes Square a little earlier and had hardly taken up our places on the hall floor when the air became charged as it had once before when I was alone in that experience; it is the only word by which the sudden vibration, like the effect of an electric bell on the ear, can be described, and it was then that I saw that our positions were strategically wrong. By the time the hall had been reached, the picture was – must have been — already fading: the Chilcot letter supported this, and my own imperfect test.

I said 'Up the stairs, quick', and we made for them blindly. How correct my theory was I found by the fact that, even so, we very nearly missed the thing in its entirety as I knew it; we were, for instance, too late for Sophia and only caught up on Emmeline whose entirely material, peevish apprehensions again passed through us as she went down the flight — this time far more strongly, as far as I was concerned. Whether the accident of sex operates in the matter of intensity of vicarious thought I don't know; all I can say is that James has told me since that his own irritation which passed through him with Emmeline's rapid descent of those stairs didn't appear to have been equal in intensity to my own. But about the rest of it there was nothing unequal at all. Every sound was louder, including the blur of voices from the landing; we heard isolated words, even sentences.

'*You* here! What are *you* doing here?' and a pause in which we had apparently missed something. But we missed nothing of what followed, and the splitting crack and thud were to my ears life-size and set my heart beating lest the house be awakened, and for the first time I saw completely, and James as well. I whispered, 'Down, two stairs down, quick'.

We got there in time. The sweat was dropping off his face as he peered, flashing his torch.

'Vere … it's *Lalage.*'

'No. Don't you see? It's Myra. They're — they're the same person.'

And it was time for the next thing; you can't skip that kind of sequence, and through the despair we both knew and for which I at least was prepared, James stammered to me — so naturally I was appalled until I remembered it was a voice dead for forty years and more — 'There is no love. My life is over.'

But his life wasn't, and I gripped his arm. 'The landing. They'll be there, next.'

It was as we trod upon the stairs where Myra lay that we both stopped, our faces twisted with pain.

'What's matter?' James mumbled.

'My back. Oh Jamesey …' and then I saw that he was grasping the banisters.

'Same … here. Sort of red-hot knife.'

'Come up, come up! It'll stop then. It's only on those two steps … after it happened, to Myra, you see.'

And on the landing we were plunged at once into that humming war of emotions that I knew so well. This time, the sense that they were battling for my possession was less acute: perhaps the presence of James was diverting their attention, or weakening their force? But one thing I had forgotten, and that was to allow for the passage through oneself of their violence, and I was horrified no less at the hates which poured into me than of the murderous look that James threw me.

And here, too, was vision, patchy as at Hampton Court in our childhood, with this difference, that incomplete as it was on that night, at least our sight tallied on detail. We saw a face set and white with anger, the black, close-set eyes looking with that fixity which accompanies power and behind it, seen almost down to the waist where it faded abruptly against the passage wallpaper and dado, the red-hair'd child, her small face pinched and mature in its contempt and puny valliance. And we heard – this was new to me –

'*Oh God forgive you, what have you done now?*' and the tiny scream of a child so frightened it can hardly find even that relief.

'*Myra!*'

'*Go back to bed, you!*' and hurrying steps.

'*Lady Vallant! What on earth has happened? Seymour, come here … I don't know … carefully … he should be here in a few minutes.*'

'*Take her upstairs.*'

And just as any material object will rock to a standstill so that scene ended, and the silence of the house settled about one with a lurch.

The aftermath of shock takes unromantic forms, and for quite fifteen minutes James and I were occupied in futile efforts to control our jaw muscles, fending off nausea and yawning and yawning. …

It was followed by a craving for sleep that a remnant of caution warned us must be dealt with and which dragged us just in time to our feet and kept us walking up and down the hall, then, because there was much to say, into the dining-room.

'We shall have to run it through again.'

I just nodded. I knew we must come back and re-see in more detail but I was beyond facing up to that at the moment.

'"Seymour" would be one of the two men Vallant was entertaining … that Chilcot spoke of.' This was talking for talking's sake and I didn't even nod. 'Vere, it's awful, that landing, you know. I swear I could have done you some dirty trick, for a few seconds. I didn't even want not to. …'

'One doesn't. I've been all through that already, only with me it was Lalage and Hugh as well. But – I hoped you'd be killed in France.'

He was propped against the sideboard now, staring at his feet. He looked up suddenly. 'Exactly what d'you mean about Lalage and Myra being the same person?'

'I believe that mother's state over Myra and her life and death –'

'Now then, stop that!'

'Sorry … well then, isn't it possible, isn't it probable, in view of what we've always seen and known of Lalage, that mother's mental condition over Myra affected her first child?'

'Reincarnation?'

I shrugged. 'I wouldn't go as far as that. Take it or leave it. But intensive brooding and thought leave their marks. Lalage is in the birth-mark category, only with her it's a psychic one. Why, I tell you she even remembers part of life as it was here. *I know hate. I remember hate.* She doesn't, on detail, but she carried something over when she was born. And she's like Myra too, even aunt Emmeline told the Verdunes so. That photographed well.'

'And mother hating dances …'

'Lord, James, I'd forgotten that … that coming of age ball in the village, and mother going white … you see? The dance Emmeline and Sophia were going to that night was a coming-out dance … and now, Lalage collapses because the War has brought a version of violence to her door with air-raids, and she associates conflict with the house.'

James stood up. 'That seems to cover the ground. We must slope. Come on.'

Back at the Furnivals, I was badly tempted for the first time
to behave like a guest and to leave a note for Enid, asking that my
breakfast might be brought up to my room. I mistrusted what my
face might be doing in the morning. It was her concern against
Cosmo's observation, but in the end I elected to bluff it out. Even
to my own eyes the rouge and lipstick I applied looked all wrong
and amply justified the very slight lift of eyebrow with which
Cosmo favoured me, and the fact that he said nothing consoled
me not at all. I was beginning to know him too well for that.
Later in the day there was Enid to be got over once more.

'But my dear, again? You're looking most *terribly* tired; can't
you take a night right off and go to bed early?'

I decided hastily to throw James to the lions. 'Oh, I wish I
could! but James's leave, you know; they want to pack all they
can into the time –'

It silenced her at once.

That third night gave us what we wanted: it was almost as if
the first two efforts at vision were the picture rehearsing itself and
that now, at last, it was ready for us, or we for it?

For the first time we saw the ball gowns of Emmeline and
Sophia, mauve tarletan with sash waists of old rose, the wearers
abundantly recognizable as the women we knew even allowing
for the softening and rounding of the rolled back years. Then
came two childish chuckles and a coppery head over the banisters, by its side another, smaller dark one – Lalage over again at
the same age.

'Hope she moves soon, I want to see,' I murmured. She did,
and even at that distance her uneven walk with its sideways jerk
was plain enough.

'We can't watch everyone at once,' James's voice was strained
with anxiety.

'Never mind Sophia and Emmeline. They've gone.'

'What happens next?'

'Listen, I'm not sure.'

'Wasn't Emmy lovely!' The opening of a door and a broad bar
of light showing us everything: the still-young woman, brilliant
in her elaborately draped yellow dress cut in a wide oval off her

shoulders, the small figure curving at breast and hip in the fashion of the day with tiny waist two hands could have spanned, the short train rustling.

Susan Vallant had been smiling, she bore the traces of it to the stair head. And then she saw the children.

Never could I have believed that features could have so regrouped themselves; in that moment she looked years older, a sardonic mask of fury, and yet a trace of pleasure in the close-set eyes at an opportunity …

'You here! What are you doing here?'

'It was my fault Mamma, I brought Myra downstairs.'

'Who's speaking to you? I'll deal with you later. Isn't it enough that I have to keep you at all that you must show yourself downstairs?'

I whispered, for it seemed impossible to believe that I was not interrupting them, 'Look out, keep your eye on her. See what she does with her hands.'

There was no mistaking that. Violent temper often self-confessedly goes too far, and whether Lady Vallant intention was a definite one or the mechanics of sheer passion our eyes couldn't tell us, they only showed ringed fingers wrenching at a child's fragile shoulder, and the missed footing.

'Myra!'

'Go back to your bed, you!' and the men's voices, and figures hurrying from the drawing-room, and the set face of compassion of the one who knelt on the stair – I could have touched him: I should recognize him to-day if I met him in the street. And from a flight above ran yet another person, a thin and distraught young woman in a high necked gown.

'Carefully … I don't know … better get the doctor. He should be here in a few minutes.'

'Take her upstairs, not in the drawing-room.'

'Oh God forgive you, what have you done now?' Even had the face baffled me I should still have recognized the voice of Alma Chilcot, and she and Lady Vallant stood there, eyes battling in scorn and loathing, temper and fear.

'What is it, your ladyship?' Another voice I knew, from the hall this time, and a young man in livery looking up white and scared. And the staircase rocked and blazed and the picture went out like a blown candle.

When I could trust my voice I said, 'You see? Mother knows. She saw it all. Hutchins got there too late. He never saw. And Miss Chilcot was never sure ... and the aunts missed everything.'

CHAPTER XXXI

I

I WAS IN the Furnivals' hall, stumbling into the dining-room; brandy and whisky, I seemed to remember, were always on the sideboard as nobody ever knew who would drop in. I poured myself a two-finger peg and drank it neat, and began pouring another.

'Ah ... I was rather expecting something of this kind,' said Cosmo from the doorway.

I looked up and saved the glass by some miracle. He was in his dressing-gown, hands sunk in the pockets. I surveyed him blearily, I felt nothing at all, even at seeing him.

'You can have half that second go and no more.'

'I – I – I –'

'Three o'clock. H'm.'

'That – sounds – awfully – fatherly.'

'Fathers have their uses. Well ... had a good time?'

And it was only then that I began to cry, if one can so describe the uncontrollable torrent which poured down my cheeks without check or punctuation, glazing them. Both his arms were round me, I didn't know or care from what impulse.

'You do have awful fun with me, don't you, Cosmo? The perfect secretary ... when she isn't sleeping at you or swiping your brandy she's in floods of grief... never a dull moment.'

'When are you ever going to stop hurting me?'

It, if anything could, shocked me back to normal, and that wasn't saying much, at the moment.

'Hurting you ... Cosmo?'

His face was very close to mine. 'Doesn't it occur to you that I've almost a right by now to have been told you were out on this cursed business?'

'Gladstone –'

His face softened. 'Oh God help the child. *Toujours la poli-tesse*. But another time when you want to hoodwink me, don't plaster an obviously white face with rouge. Come along.' He got me upstairs to my room where I proceeded to do that which in our family we call 'circling' – taking off a bangle and putting it on again, throwing down a coat and looking for it, and hanging it up and moving it somewhere else, beginning a dozen things and finishing none.

'Come along,' and he rapidly unfastened my frock.

'Cosmo, you oughtn't to be doing this, ought you?'

'Now we're not going to be conceited and insulting, my child.'

'*What?*'

'Certainly. You're practically telling me that you believe your charms are such that I shall be unable to withstand them. But I daresay we shall find that you're singularly like everybody else, with nothing on,' and he eventually removed every rag I stood up in, before putting me into my pyjamas and throwing me occasional remarks. 'What a boon these zip fasteners are,' and 'Why do you wear combinations? Enid doesn't. She uses silk vests'.

I suppose there ought to have been embarrassment, and plenty of it. I can only say there was not, either at the time in retrospect or at that tremendous test of overnight indiscretion, the breakfast table. And all through it, while I was answering his comments and even laughing at them a little, and long after I was in bed, the tears continued. We tried everything we knew to stop it and at last had to give up and just accept the manifestation. Cosmo said, 'Would it help things if you told me all about it, or shall we have a chat about something else?' and I smiled at that too.

'You must go to bed, my dear. It's twenty minutes to four and matinée day to-morrow.'

'Can't you ever think of anything but my work?'

'I think of you.'

He sat down on the end of the bed. 'I agree that the arrival of the early tea and can of hot water must be timed.'

'Oh Cosmo! Nobody but you would think of that.'

'Maids and cans of hot water represent what might be described as the eternal dilemma in cases to which our own bears a superficial resemblance (very superficial). Now then!'

I lay and looked at him; nobody could say he hadn't seen me at my worst, and he seemed to be weathering it. His presence was having its usual effect in pulling me together, and even that must only be just enough to help me through the Vallant story: invalids – and I was at the moment in that class – are traditionally to be humoured, but one mustn't help oneself to overmuch incidental attention. ...

I have said he was a good listener: he was more, a singularly expressive one, so that it was helpful to watch his face, shadowed though it was, with sunken eyes and harsh lines, and you found that it was collaborating with your words and oddly spurring you on.

'... it's a thing one's never going to forget. Suspecting, even knowing, isn't the same as seeing. Cosmo, what she said to that lame child will be in my ears for life, and there's such a lot of life ahead, perhaps. And she's gone beyond one's reach, to comfort and pet. Like a murder. Final. And what happened afterwards, all those months that Miss Chilcot wrote of... "Myra would weep at the sound of her step" ... aren't phrases terrible? the way they can haunt ... and yet it's old-fashioned wording. Hit or miss ... oh damn this crying! And even going to see Lady Vallant won't kill memory.'

'No.'

'It isn't so much what she did, even if it were deliberate. It's the state of mind that made it possible. ...'

'It was a fairly large family?'

'Seven.'

'M'm. Well of course even in those days there may have been married rebels ... especially in the case of a woman who valued her appearance and the social life a marked degree. Resentment at another baby and all that. Bearing grudges isn't only a figure of speech. Unfortunately.'

'Mother made Myra a family of paper dolls, I've got them still –'

'And you're going to give Lady Vallant the pleasure of spoiling another life as well as your mother's and Myra's.'

'One is as one is.'

He shifted his position and I said, 'You look dreadfully uncomfortable'.

'I am, and I'm not used to it. Mind if I put my feet up …
That's better.' I threw him a spare pillow and he settled it under
his shoulders. 'I wonder if I'm going to risk your friendship by
telling you how it would help us best to get over this affair? My
angle isn't yours, of course, it's the professional one, and that's
where I'm going to risk you, but it's an idea as well. Now, first of
all, you've got to hold on to the fact that you're grieving over an
event which happened before you were born.'

'I've tried that and it's no good.'

'No? Then you've got to hunt for something else, and my
something else would be to encourage myself deliberately to get
the whole story in detail, and that means scene, motives, character, psychology – even speeches and dress.'

'What d'you mean?'

'I mean, think of it as a play you have got to put on. Don't
evade anything. All this time you've been dramatizing it just
enough to make yourself miserably unhappy; you have brooded
over Lady Vallant until she's acquired a power over you that you'll
have to fight against. She's a rather bad woman, I don't doubt,
but not the goblin damned you've made her, all-powerful and
all-malignant. All she is is a hard, selfish and repellent Victorian
type with a bad temper, and the fact that your parents have given
you nothing but affection has made you mentally extra-vulnera-
ble. I've told you about my boyhood and its lack of softness and
charity, and the result is that your grandmother doesn't dismay
me to anything like the extent she does yourself. And so I suggest
that you use what is past instead of letting it use you. We come by
our reliefs in strange ways. Try this one. And don't be pestered by
the idea that you're being callous or doing a thing in execrable
taste. In any case that would be my fault, but I won't plead guilty
because I'm convinced that Myra's death was her best solution.
As an ending one shrinks from it, but have you considered what
the alternative was bound to have been? Not yet sixteen, which
means two years more of life in that house as she knew it, even if
she made an early marriage. But would she have? With her disa-
bility? We men are pretty brutal, you know, and can afford to pick
the sound and perfect thing and damned few of us look further
than the physical, and would this poor child have ever been given
a reasonable chance of marriage? On what we know already isn't

it more likely she would have been kept in the shade, kept short of pretty clothes that might have turned the trick, relegated to her own suite except perhaps for meals, at which Lady Vallant would have plenty of opportunities for rallying her about her husbandless fate and its reason … why Myra might be there now – and you're looking as stricken as if it were all happening, which only goes to prove my contention that your sense of proportion is all over the place and your imagination undisciplined. Now, have you been able to go with me so far?'

'Oh God yes, Cosmo.'

'Be quite sure. You mean you believe with me that Myra's better out of it all?'

'Yes.' And I did, for the first time. Until that moment I had not been able to look beyond the short life and its termination, far less explore all round it.

'Bravo. If you concede that you've nothing much else to fear; all that's left is the shrinking from the incident which led to her release, and that's where I want you to ride over everything, to see it all as actors, walking. First of all, cast it, humanize it to yourself by associating this player and that with your people in your mind's eye, never forgetting that Lady Vallant is your principal interest; she's, theatrically speaking, an illegitimate one but in the right hands she'd be tremendous. You'll find the fascination of it will grow on you, and there'll come a time when your play and cast will be so much more telling that they've gone one ahead on the sheer facts. I could find you at least one actress who'd play your real Lady Vallant right off the stage and out of your mind and almost send you off to Lowndes Square for comfort. And why? Because she has the technique of unease and evil at her fingers' ends, and your old woman's a bungling amateur. It's all in the sight. You've just admitted so much yourself.'

He broke off, glanced at me and continued. 'And on with your play. We should have to begin earlier than your trouble. I should show Lady Vallant –'

'Susan Stonor –'

'No no no! We must show her as a young married woman, carrying over with her into the Lowndes Square house every fault she had as a girl: vanity, love of finery, of power, and her awakening delight in acquiring more and more people to exercize it on, beginning with servants, admirers and her husband to whom she is faithful because she is conventional, not big or warm hearted enough to throw her cap over any windmill. There are no children in Act I. It's what the French call the *scène obligatoire*, a necessary building of character, a preparation for the future. And this, plus just one small incident of callousness, to give a hint … and one flash of temper, only one, and slight, as another hint, but less than half-strength because we shall need all her thunder later.

Then we come to the children, and here the technical difficulties begin. In the first place, real children ruin any adult play by side-tracking the audience, hanging everything up while the surplus matinee woman goes maternal over them; therefore we must show them all at the age where you saw them, and that means a lot of poignance lost. One can't indicate neglect extending over a period of years except by retrospective dialogue. I'm not pretending to have got it all cut and dried, I'm just trying to suggest the lines along which I want you to think in future. We'll assume that apparently insuperable difficulties have been overcome – the problem of playing out your principal scene on a staircase isn't the least of them, and of an excess of sets that must include the schoolroom. Very well. From then on you get the unequal and foredoomed conflict between Anne, Myra and their mother … you hear through that schoolroom doorway the sound of music and of guests arriving and talking and laughing, while in the room itself Lady Vallant, brilliantly dressed, is rating two miserable girls in shabby nightdresses. And Myra pretends to fetch something from a table and move away — d'you see the value of that?'

'Go on.'

'The way that move will be made will tell your audience all she has, and has had, to fear from her mother. Nothing marked or melodramatic. Just an instinctive recoil glossed over by petty deception. To suggest present emotion is fairly easy: but to convey *arrears* of feeling is no small thing. Laurence Irving did it in *Typhoon* … and as she moves, she shows that she is lame. Why was Myra lame, by the way?'

I was sitting up now, staring. 'I don't know. I never thought of that. I just accepted it, as the final touch that *would* be reserved for her –'

'Exactly. That's what I complain of. You accepted it but it won't do for an audience. It means that earlier in the scene we must put our cards on the table, and make some character tell another what caused it. Sophia and Emmeline won't do, it's too sophisticated a scene for them and they'd have been too young at the time of Myra's birth to speak with authority. I suggest Lady Vallant's personal maid to the nurserymaid who brings up the trays and this gives us scope for another development of Lady Vallant's nature. This is, of course a scene that cannot be shown. I doubt if any audience is up to it; they'd see nothing of the macabre in it, only cause for laughter – confound them, but those lines *are* macabre, all the more so because they are spoken matter-of-factly ... or jocosely, that's worse ... by an undramatic woman. It's of course the vanity point operating. Now, which shall we have: Lady Vallant riding and dancing, or drugging — your "Seymour" might be a doctor, you know, an infatuated, unprincipled admirer — to prevent that child getting born, and that would be an effective touch where he picked Myra up from the stairs fifteen years later. ...

'Or shall we make it, *"Well, what can you expect? She tightlaced right up to the last moment although the doctor warned her"*. Something like that? ...'

I hardly heard his concluding words. I was seeing again that tiny figure in waspish yellow with its waspish waist, and the regrouping of feature as the ex-smiling face caught sight of the children on the landing.

'... and the rest is up to you. And if you are ever in danger of making a fetish of your memories come to me and I'll find a set of situations for you far more harrowing than anything *you* ever thought of! And when you go and see Lady Vallant next and find yourself trending towards the old slavery to her manner or expression or words, say to yourself "Furnival knows an elderly actress who'd do this sort of thing far better". Artificializing ... the veil of illusion ... it's a very healing thing. If it comes to that, the only real difference between the theatre and life is that our everyday speeches are extempore. You've got a part to play at Vallant House. Play it well. And tell me – this time – when you are going there, and for what it's worth I shall be backing you up, and envying you the opportunity!'

He rose and came over to me. 'And it may surprise you to know that the crying stopped' (he glanced at the clock) 'one hour and ten minutes ago.'

I took his hand and put my cheek against it. The circumstances, as the Verdunes would say, would surely pass it along?

Through the curtains another day was beginning and in the trees the tentative, long-spaced 'chip' of birds.

CHAPTER XXXII

I

I ALLOWED MYSELF all the following day, fixed up two appointments for Cosmo with a photographer and for a stray interview, and the rest of the time was spent in strolling round the garden, sleeping the entire afternoon and playing silly games with Enid – I remember that over Snakes and Ladders we both, for some reason, became almost hysterical when three times running she was sent bundling down the longest ladder pointing the sternest moral of all when within one throw from home. And the next day I went to Lowndes Square. James and I chose our own time, immediately after luncheon, as I told Cosmo. The excuse was to be the termination of James's leave, and that a pretext was necessary the face of Hutchins as he opened the door was ample proof.

'I am afraid her ladyship won't see you, Miss Vere. I don't advise –'

'All right, Hutchins, she's in the drawing-room, I suppose? I'll be sure to let her know this is my fault. Don't announce us.' And we went upstairs, both careful to walk heedlessly over certain of the treads. ...

She was sitting in front of the fire doing nothing at all, an old-fashioned handscreen of peacock's feathers and gold thread shielding her face. She looked round casually at our steps and the opening door – it was as though a start of surprise was reserved for the less assured, that she knew no domestic situation could presume to challenge her into discomfiture.

'Ah, dear boy ... what is your sister here for?'

'To see you. We made Hutchins let us in,' and James uninvited drew a chair for me and one for himself and sat down without shaking hands. 'There's a fug in this room. You ought to have more fresh air.'

And she was utterly unaware, encased in traditional security.

'I told Hutchins I would not receive your sister. Ring the bell.'

I said, 'Don't be silly, Lady Vallant, and don't talk at me.'

That penetrated, but she was still half-credulous. 'Hold your tongue. You' (to James) 'ring the bell.'

'No.'

'You are very insolent. I don't wish to talk. Go away.' He shook his head. 'Then what is it? Do you want money?'

His answering look was one of such sick disgust that she almost wavered.

I took over for him. 'You've tried that once before, haven't you, Lady Vallant? The nice-looking grandson being taken up by you, overpaid even as a child of thirteen to be on your side because you were afraid of what he might have heard about you. Or have I got it wrong and was it through a shortage of admirers – like Seymour, for instance?'

She seemed, with a certain fineness, to accept by this time that she was in for something, and the plangent voice was very much as usual when she turned to me. 'Seymour?'

'One of the two men who lifted Myra off the stairs that night. Do you want any more names? Alma Chilcot, for instance? *"Oh God help you, what have you done now?"* Remember?'

'Miss Chilcot is gone.' I had never until now seen signs of her age as evidenced by mental confusion in Lady Vallant.

'She died last year in a workhouse, of starvation, my dear grandmother, but she has never left this house. She is here now, and so is Myra.'

'Are you mad?'

'You don't like that idea, do you?' James said. 'It upsets your comfortable luncheon and deprives you of your nap to think that Myra – that comical encumbrance – should have the presumption to come back and lie where you pushed her, down the staircase.'

' *"Not in the drawing-room",* ' I cut in, 'that would never have done. How right you were. There might have been something that would have stained one of your rugs. As it was, there was nothing, nothing at all except an injury to her spine.'

'Your mother shall hear of this.'

'No.' James looked at her squarely. 'You've bullied her enough. She's never given you away – God knows why, but it wasn't out of love or respect, make no mistake about that. Love! Does anyone love you? Even at best you're a wry-mouthed joke to the entire family except ourselves, and that's because we know about Myra. The rest of 'em have been fobbed off with the usual story about declines and weak backs. You're a lucky woman, but the luck's out.'

On looking back, I don't know now which of us, dispassionately considered, came out of that interview worse; James who within a couple of hours outraged every known law of chivalry to age and sex, using as incidental weapon all he had ever learned about bullying at school with that dazing rain of repetitive questions, or myself, who took full advantage of the different method open to the worst type of woman, in betrayal and detraction of a fellow woman before a man, plus that terrible memory for detail always more thorough than his. Also, it was two to one.

James was saying, 'You must understand that if we find out that you've been worrying and nagging and rendering Anne's life a burden as only you know how to do because of some notion that she has told us, we shall know at once by her face. There's a look which comes on your daughters' faces that is unmistakable, after any interview with you; we've both seen it on Myra's as well. And that will be our time to tell the family, who at present merely see you as an over-dressed, narrow-minded bad-mannered old woman–'

'– who can't even drop to pieces decently,' I added. 'She has enough cosmetics on her dressing-table to set up a leading lady, James. Rouge on half-dead skin isn't pretty … and those dresses in the wardrobe; more than Myra and Anne ever had, evidently, when it comes to the governess – the paid dependant, I'm sorry – having to renovate your cast-offs for them because their appearance made her "ashamed", and to bring them invalid food when they were ill. Food, you devil …'

'You've forgotten, she doesn't know that,' said James quietly.

'She knows now.'

'Leave me. You are making me ill.'

'Aren't we justified?'

'Aren't we justified?'

'Aren't we justified?'

'Nothing would justify this scene.'

'Making you ill … it might be a stroke, you know, and strokes have a tiresome habit of distorting the mouth in an unattractive way that will give your maid a lot of trouble … they're apt to fly to the speech, too, and make it difficult for people, like Anne, for instance, to hear you when you're struggling to say something hurtful.'

'Stop this ranting. I can see your mother's hand in all this, deny it as you may.'

'You're wrong.'

'She was always troublesome, always daring with me. I had great work to subdue her.' I sickened as James was retorting 'She hated you, no doubt, and for the best of reasons. What sort of a keeper were you? Of a home? Or of a menagerie for wild beasts? And as for telling us about Myra, we saw what really happened, I tell you, just as I saw Miss Chilcot at your elbow that afternoon.'

'Did your mother tell you to say this?'

And I might as well say first as last that up to that point there was no shaking her conviction, biased and materialistic, nor at any stage could we wrest the slightest admission from her. She had fineness, of a kind. They say that finely tempered steel cannot break, though it may bend and bend and ache for the relief of snapping which its very quality denies. Her entirely human certainty of human tattling was her safeguard. James, again:

'You think it was Anne who told us what you did? You have been remarkably anxious all these years to keep *something* dark.'

She faced him, looking him up and down. 'Your aunt Myra, led on by your mother, was grossly disobedient, and in defying me, met with a severe punishment, poor child, which I sometimes feel to have been excessive on the part of God.'

'Faugh!' We were both so utterly shocked that for a second there was an absolute silence. And then, explain it how you may, something stirred in my brain, independent of all my private thoughts and feelings, something which began to work through me, using me, so that as with the practised pianist and his hands

I was able, as it were, to sit back and listen to what I myself was getting accomplished. For an instant I couldn't accept such possession, even fought it with my own words. I was about to say, 'Would that, supposing it were true, cover what came afterwards ...', only the sentence was swamped by sudden, absolute conviction which, translated into words, would have said *Get down to it. Cut out that line. Close with her now. And stand up. This is what you must say.* And I succumbed and stood and spoke.

'There was one year between Myra and Anne. Would you believe us if I told you what happened before Myra was born, at a date, therefore, when Anne could have known nothing? Do you remember a woman who loved herself to such an extent that she clung to admiration from any source right up to danger-point? It didn't kill her. That was a pity. It only maimed a child. And she stood with her maid, very pleasantly, perhaps, and jokes about over-large families passing between them ... or perhaps the maid protested, and she turned on her, gave her a taste of the Vallant temper. *Tighter, you idiot. The gown still looks awkward ...*' I found that my fist, shaking in her face, had unclenched, throwing my hand up in a gesture so foreign to me that I looked at it stupidly.

It was hit-or-miss, but apparently I knew what I was about. ...

It had told. Upright always, consistent to herself, she did not buckle now, but her eyes were very dreadful, for in them even the light of malice had gone out. James had made a restraining gesture towards me but I hadn't finished, for mingled with that possession of my speech was my own individuality of desperate fury.

'And so you had a cripple, someone at whom you could laugh before the servants.' I dropped my voice and the rest of what I had to say was pitched in a key that to any entering visitor was purely conversational. 'I wonder who will be with you when you die. A handful of those servants? The doctor? Or will you set them to sending for the family? They'll come. They always do the correct thing. And perhaps the hymns you composed will be a comfort to you then, especially the one you wrote after the Myra affair. But there won't be a man or woman there who minds, or is pitiful to help you through. Even Myra had Anne ...'

'Oh, for God's sake, Vere ...'

I turned on him. 'She's crying at last,' I shot at him thickly and avidly, 'come and have a good look.'

And I pointed like a guttersnipe.

And even now I am not sure that those tears were of remorse and not, rather, of rage, fear and the sham of helplessness.

We went out on to the landing and I rang the upstairs bell for Palmer. In the hall the menservants were bringing the tea-things and I thought quite grotesquely, 'That's a bad touch. Anti-climax. That incident ought to be cut right out'.

II

I went in search of Enid and found her in the drawing-room.

'*At* last! Aren't you dying for your tea, my dear? I've had mine but there are muffins in the fender. Oh why do they go out so soon? It's so hidebound. It isn't as if it were game that has to have close-times.'

'Yes, I could do with some tea,' I agreed, then, and very casually, 'by the way, where's Cosmo been all the afternoon?'

'In the study. He had something he wanted to think out and didn't want to be disturbed.'

So, Cosmo? …

CHAPTER XXXIII

I

AND THAT WAS nearly twenty years ago.

The War is over, and Lady Vallant is over.

But Cosmo is dead. Even to-day the temptation to indulge in cheap embittered cynicism is sometimes overwhelming.

I never particularly hankered to be young with him: I wanted to grow old with him. All the Vallants have a kink. Perhaps he was mine. I hope so.

Lady Vallant died nearly two years after our visit to Lowndes Square. She never changed much outwardly, at least she kept her shattered, lonely spirit hidden from us all, for which I applaud her. She had her points, and reserve and the high hand were two of them. There were several of the relatives with her at the end, aunt Sophia and aunt Emmeline within immediate call, the uncles standing by to clear up the business aftermaths of death. Mother came from Hampshire and stayed at Vallant House, the first to come to her, the last to leave her, and although I am pretty sure there was no deathbed repentance, no very perceptible softening during her last weeks, there was *something*, that a remark of mother's put me on to: 'I think she felt she hadn't been quite what she might have to us all.' I never learned or asked the exact phrasing, but it indicated at least one sentence which, for Lady Vallant, amounted to a stupendous admission.

In our conventional mourning we all counted visually equal, and the uniform at least concealed the graded poignance of our individual thought. We went, of course, through no antics of bogus emotion, we just stood about, and foregathered, and knit up each other's ravelled life as scattered families will.

Later on we were to realize that power, even wrongly directed, can hold a clan together whether in the unity of a common rage or humour. Personality will out, and in a sense when Lady Vallant fell our family wavered, disintegrated into non-significant units. Tribally speaking dictators have their uses.

And that is my tribute to Susan Vallant.

Her grave in Brompton Cemetery is nowhere near that of Myra. I never ventured the enquiry as to whether this was due to accident or design and my suspicions I keep to myself.

The house in Lowndes Square is not closed. Some of its rooms are occasionally occupied by those of the family who live in the country and Hutchins remained there for years as caretaker with a skeleton staff. The original idea that he should end his days and service at the Hampshire house the dear old man, incurably *pavé*, would not listen to. For him the lamp-posts of London, and in default of jingling hansom, the horn of taxi, the chimneypots and the autumnal muffin-bell. He was the best friend I ever had. Except one.

Mother has made her home with Julian Vallant in the Hampshire house; he is now so nearly blind that the official explanation 'he must have somebody with him' has long been issued to the relations. I happen to believe that there is another, better reason. ...

As for uncle Stuart, cranky, grudging and farouche, he too has left his gap: eccentricity seems to be a wonderful stimulant to regret and very nearly a substitute for merit! and the individual who is all-good, all-worthy is apt to be forgotten sooner, which is a very shocking state of affairs, pointing to no moral that I can think of.

Aunt Sophia, we Buchans agree, will indubitably live for ever and I hope she does. Complete good nature and low brain-power are powerful preservatives. She never had a vice to her back and I pity her. Emmeline Verdune on the other hand will always find fuel for her fire among the lot of us. *Why* did James and Vere give up the Campden Hill house and take that one in Phillimore Terrace? It's *just* as small, even if Leigh Hunt and Baroness Orczy *had* lived there before them … wouldn't it be *better* if James lived at the club or in Lowndes Square and Vere settled in Hampshire with Anne as she doesn't seem to be going to marry? …

Poor Emmeline! She reminds one so inevitably of that Bensonian character in *Account Rendered* who shut a window if she found it opened and opened it if she found it shut in the single-minded determination to impress her will upon existing conditions.

I I

When uncle Julian dies, both Vallant and the house in Lowndes Square will pass to James. The town house is virtually his already as nobody seems to want it, but in spite of the fact that Lady Vallant's death has made a tremendous difference financially to us all, and that James is doing well in his business, he is not, we both agree, doing as well as all that!

Besides, there are other reasons. …

We have had an offer for it from Hugh, and the prospect of Lalage and Hugh as tenants forced James and myself after much thought more or less to put our cards on the table with him.

For by that time there was a child.

The first child of Lalage and Hugh was a girl; that, I suppose, was the contribution of our side of the family which runs to daughters. In looks she is a Lyne, and I hope in deeper ways as well, and it was my business and James's to steer her through her early years, so that we blocked all attempts of Anita's parents to so much as let her see Vallant House from the inside. They wanted to call her Vere and I was against that too. Any link, even the most apparently irrelevant, that can be snapped must be. When she was older, tougher, grounded in love and secure in ways she understands she shall go over Vallant House at will, and be happy there.

That was the line we took and kept to from the first.

As for Lalage, her marriage with Hugh has done that for her which we had hoped. It has not of course achieved everything; to her life's end she will have her moments of abstraction, of involuntary brooding, withdrawal from the immediate scene, but the Myra-shadow is fading, very slowly if never entirely, and with her grandchildren it will become fainter until it has passed for ever.

And I suppose I might as well admit that with Lady Vallant dead and Lalage married and a mother and the house at our disposal, I had seen a future in which Lalage and Hugh would live as our tenants in Lowndes Square and that with the first fearless laughter of their first child the light would come in to remain, and the darkness be driven out.

Very pretty – and entirely mistaken. Things don't happen like that. I know it. That house is *stained* with memories of unhappy things, and those of us who own blood kinship with the movers in that story may be peculiarly susceptible to what it still may do. That is why it is futile to destroy the staircase. Until that picture has worked itself out with time or the superimposition of a set of events serene and normal, and until the atmosphere has so been reconditioned, that picture will remain, ever re-enactable, eternally to be guarded against.

Mother is immeasurably relieved by our attitude. She is happy and in her eyes there is a look of reprieve. She has said nothing at all to James or me; inarticulate and evasive as ever with each other where Lady Vallant is concerned, we have put our action over the Hugh and Lalage affair upon the flippant grounds of our humorous exasperation with our grandmother, and all that was hers.

III

I divide my time between our Kensington home, mother in Hampshire and work. Better off financially than I have ever been, I still have no talent for graceful idling, and began by buying a partnership in my office where, when the spirit moves me, I look in and see that the girls aren't being overdriven and drink the

horrible tea the good souls will offer me and even run off man-
uscripts occasionally on the machines myself. For some months,
I believe, the staff speculated upon the curious refusal of Miss
Buchan even to glance at dramatic scripts.

I try not to live in the past and in the future. There is still my
little, dear Enid to whom so much of my time is devoted entirely.
It is incredible that she is over seventy and even as I write the
words I sit back in amazement.

Enid seventy-two. *Enid!* No, it can't be done! For there is a
type of woman to-day who, whatever her birthday certificate
may have to say, remains persistently in the attractive young-mid-
dle-aged class which can still be made love to, and she is one of
them, if her curly hair is undisguisedly silver.

She gave me the sole use of Cosmo's study. I often spend an
hour or so there and Enid leaves me quite alone and goes whistling revue numbers about the house like the wise woman she is.

On the desk is still a half-emptied bottle of ink, and a mem-
orandum pad.

Tell Murton change lights in d. room. New one over my
l. glass *before* matinée.
Rem: subs: to Garrick due. Write cheque.

Between the leaves of blotting-paper is an unfinished letter.

Dear Sir, I find after all that I shall not be available on the 29th
and much regret –

and I wonder who the sir could have been and what it was
that Cosmo 'regretted', and sometimes the helplessness of this
type of not knowing that can assail one at the smallest trifle and
that death renders so inevitable sweeps over me and I have to go,
or find Enid, or plunge into work – anything.

He died at seventy-four. I had just six years of him. I was
not always troublesome to him; there was an occasion when I
was able to see him through one of *his* bad moments, a thing
which I had first glimpsed in the foyer of his theatre through
the criticism of a young, unknown girl. It was some time after
the *Gladstone* premiere which, in the hazardous way that plays do,
had established him once more as an actor to be reckoned with.

He revived a costume piece, that very one the photographs of which he had shown me in his dressing-room. It was, I saw (I also read the script in advance) an excellent play of its kind, romantic, pictorial, full of action, humour and excitement plus that quality of suavity – that bland and polished over-reaching of the lesser characters – that was Cosmo Furnival's hallmark. But, he was sixty nine, and the break from what to the younger generation of playgoers was a suitable synchronization of years with actor and rôle as previously offered them in the Victorian play was too sudden. They had no memory to carry forward to his current account. The older audience came again and again. The Press was affectionate, save for two newspapers who possessed critics with vision – I myself could not have said more! But inevitably there was the fool of the party who indulged in regrets at a wonted fire which would not realize its ashes. Just one paper, and what it did to Cosmo is probably beyond computation. He dramatized it of course out of all proportion to its real significance, saw in it the writing on the wall. Up to that time his career was still fluid, a potential adventure with the notion of the braving of which he yet might dally, and although he acted in a dozen plays after that, his motive power I think was gone, and for him the great game over.

Why I was always able to range myself with the older generation I don't understand; perhaps I should be happier if I had had the eyesight of my contemporaries which saw him merely as an elderly man in a young part. Be that as it may, I can only state that whenever I saw him in this rôle I saw him subjectively, with the intention of the past and the finished execution of the present in a perceptive appreciation which was undatable. It was a case of 'simultaneous time' over again, and indeed as regards the theatre absolute art can't be confined to calendar, whether the type and quality of its medium is high or low. Enid herself told me that he was giving a far better performance now than ever he had done in his forties. And it was to be neutralized by an older, leaner face.

She rang me up a week before the opening, told me she was worried about Cosmo and asked me to come to them.

'Worried?'

'My dear, he's not being like himself – *you* know, not all over the place and going off the deep end. He's silent and quiet and I don't know what to do.'

I stayed with them until his Press notices had come in.

The day before production he came to me and said almost shyly (Cosmo *shy*, with *me*!) 'You've got "the sight". I'd like to know if the show's going to go or not', and he put his hands in his pockets and looked at his shoes.

'I can't see the future, only the past, and that capriciously.'

'Ah ... thanks, dear.'

And it was my turn to go away and pray for him and his affairs.

And then that newspaper came in ... unimportant, second-rate, written by a critic who didn't count for a public who preferred football scores and wouldn't read it. And Cosmo shut himself up the whole morning in study and for the first time I saw Enid inadequate, and tears in her eyes.

I went to my room, found a letter, knocked at the study door and went in. But he managed a smile for me. It was a heart-twisting affair. 'Well, I've got my *congé*. Nice of you to come. There's nobody else I could stand. Enid knows me too well ... thinks too much on the same lines, bless her dear heart.'

'For one newspaper, Cosmo?'

'These things are apt to show which way the wind's blowing. One can't live on minorities. Well ... I should have no complaint against the present verdict of the young. They've done me well enough in the past.'

'Cosmo, you're talking like a film-fan of nineteen. God, how I'd like to smack your head. Do you propose – an artist like you – to tell me that you'd rather be a matinée idol catering for the immature taste, appealing only to the adolescent emotions of girls who'll forget you the moment they've got a young man of their own and a semi-detached villa at Pinner? I tell you, I've seen it happen.'

'There's a lot in that. But the point is that once there were relays, so to speak, and when your young women had retired to – ah – Pinner, they instantly replaced themselves. Oh of course they were a confounded nuisance at times, and sometimes worse than a nuisance.' He got up and began to pace the room. 'But it was – life. I don't suppose I can convey to you what fun it was. ...'

'I think I know what you're getting at, but go on.'

'It's very good for one, all this. Searching test, and so on. But even now, Vere, I can't believe it's only vanity. It was a *sustaining* thing … creating that love-atmosphere … I don't think I abused it unreasonably … and the kick one got out of making the quixotic gesture. …

'Once or twice I was sent for by girls who were dying, or by their parents. It wasn't always hysteria … many of those young women who didn't know me, who'd never even met me, loved me, I swear. There was a quietness about them, a look in their eyes – oh kick me, I'm sorry!'

'Go on, dear.'

'– a look, incredulous and yet as though the dear friend of their life had come in unannounced, a fulfilled look, and peaceful. And how much more could I bring them now, with all I know … and they died happily. Can you understand that?'

'Why not? A woman's imagination can be a holy thing. It's so often all she has to live by.'

'I stayed with them always, until the doctor turned me away. It wasn't only self. …'

'Oh, Cosmo –'

'I caught an echo of all that with you, quite apart from the fact that I love you in other ways as well. And then I found that I needed more than that from you, my child. I wanted your love, certainly, always, but I wanted to annex the discriminating side of it as well; it was a combination I don't remember to have met before. In my experience, young women are either glamoured children, like your Pinner girls, or definitely women and all that involves, of *blasé* demands on one, material and emotional. And when you came here – well, I admit the racket was difficult to stand, but you did turn rather efficient on me, didn't you?'

I tossed him over the letter. 'Oh very, Cosmo, very, and shall again. Just run your eye over that.'

He did more; he read it twice, from end to end.

'You oughtn't to have shown me this, ought you?'

'No.'

'And seeing the gist of it, I shouldn't have read it.'

'Probably not. We're both cads together, a comfortable couple.'

'Are you fond of this "Claude"?'

'Enormously.'

'Love him?'

'I could almost go so far. Yes.'

'How old is he?'

'Two or three years older than me.'

'Gentleman?'

'Yes.'

'Private means?'

'Yes. Entirely suitable all round, so I'll take that out of your mouth; also intensely amusing and completely reliable.'

'You've refused him?'

'Yes.'

'Why?'

'I give you one guess.'

'When?'

I smiled at him. 'After you and I had had a set-to in the garden.'

'What about?'

'Nothing much, as usual. You'd asked me if I could never take you seriously, or words to that effect.'

'Oh, that … you're going to marry Claude, Vere.'

'Not a hope, my dear. Think it over. You see, I'm not the only pebble on the beach, from your point of view. Given my opportunities there would be hundreds of Veres refusing hundreds of Claudes, only you don't happen to meet 'em.'

'Well, I'm damned.'

But he wasn't. Cad though I'd been, I had brought him the mental security he needed. If he was wrong to take comfort in it I neither know nor care, and I'd do it again to get the same result.

IV

But there was still laughter. There was a sequel to the Claude letter over which I chuckle to this day.

The Furnivals gave a party and until a quarter of the evening was over I didn't see Cosmo's game. It must have been a week or so after the revival of the costume play was withdrawn and Enid sent out the invitations when he was only rehearsing for the next, or he could not have appeared until midnight. She took me to her own dressmaker, a well-known theatrical one, and insisted on giving me my frock. I didn't like that much, but certainly could never have afforded it myself. 'Cosmo will want you to look your prettiest.'

Well, of course if he was treating one as so much dressing of the stage, all right; left to my own devices and finances I supposed I ran the risk of 'putting his eye out'. Mystified a little and not quite happy over the bill, I let them rave. Cosmo himself came to the last trying-on and walked all round us both and was so taken for granted by Angele and her fitters and pin-bearers that I supposed they'd been all through that before over productions. My dress was a wispish affair in waterlily green-white and Cosmo said it was exactly right for me and for my hair and made me have a square neck when I wanted a round one. He was satisfied, but I thought there was a substratum of depression in his face and manner when I came downstairs in it....

'You're going to have some devastatingly pretty girls to contend with,' Enid said, 'but I don't think you need worry.'

'Only I shan't contend, Enid. I'm like America, too proud to fight. *And* too old.'

'Old? My *dear*! You look about twenty-one, doesn't she, Val?' and Cosmo assented, and didn't, I fancied, seem to enjoy the admission. She was looking down at us both from the first landing in a flutter of that cyclamen pink which has a tinge of blue in it. 'And thank God poor Enid's got some flames coming. To-night, Val my love, we will test the damage wrought by matrimony. I feel ready for the lot of 'em!' and she burst into a schoolgirl's giggle.

'So long as you don't go too far,' said Cosmo, 'they're a respectable crew.'

'I'm only afraid they mayn't want me to. I adore going almost too far. One foot over the edge. So much more thrilling than both. Heavenly! Come on!' In the hall glass she surveyed herself from head to foot. 'Yes, we still light up well, and I'm always so thankful I haven't got a Land of Hope and Glory bust, like contraltos.'

'"Wider still and wider shall thy bounds be set",' I suggested.

'Cat,' and we three took each other's arms and went into the drawing-room.

It didn't take me long to discover that here was a party which would send aunt Sophia into the seventh heaven, although she would not have been so happy over the women, who seemed to be all well under thirty and all beauties into the bargain, for the men outnumbered the women by quite two to one. It took me a little longer to see that they were all middle-aged and attractive. Forty-five to sixty seemed to predominate, and most of the professions and arts had at least one representative. It took me a good while longer to realize that apart from introducing them all, Cosmo was neglecting *me*.

Later, everyone danced, and Cosmo and I had *The Choristers* together; waltzing *is* waltzing with him, I found, and during it he gave me exactly three words. 'You dance well.'

'Am I in disgrace, Cosmo? Oh well, you'll have to sit out with me anyway! And we'll have one again later, won't we?'

The music had stopped and I made for two chairs. He saw me into mine and took the other.

'I'm so very sorry but I'm quite full up,' he said.

It was like a slap in the face, but at least I met it without blinking. 'Of course, you must be.'

He took my programme. 'In any case you're full up too.'

'Ever heard of crossing out names, Cosmo?'

'I don't like it. Besides, that's an exceptionally interesting man you're booked to. Foreign Office. And so's the next ... but you know his name from the posters, besides being the best looking man in the room.'

'Yes, but I've got two others who run him pretty close in the decorative department.'

'Good. Who?'

'Sir Timothy and Mr. – can't remember his name. Man with a mouth.'

'Oh, Standish. Yes. He's got me whacked all to pieces.'

'Yes, I suppose so. His chin isn't so long,' I agreed pleasantly.

'That's it! I'd always wondered what it was,' mused Cosmo. 'Oh well, the Lord giveth and the Lord taketh away,' and he left me as soon as he decently could and I saw him one-stepping with a golden head that had *me* whacked all to pieces.

I wanted, badly, to cut a dance and go away to think all this over; I was in one of my moods in which the craving to leave gaiety, if only for ten minutes, becomes a part of my nature, but I fought it off and plunged into what I hoped was a flirtation with the next man in. He met me more than half-way and in a naïvely flattered manner which disarmed me so completely that I began to be quite fond of him! At least once I thought I saw Cosmo watching me from the door, and on his face there was a look I couldn't read.

He was pleased. And he didn't like it.

I ran into Enid in an interval. She was, I found, one of those hostesses who even in the middle of a party is as avid for personal conversation as she is in off-moments at home. It is an attribute which I find singularly endearing, and oh how rare! I firmly believe that if at that moment I had said to her, 'What are we having for lunch to-morrow?' she would not only tell me, but would develop several reasons why other dishes were impracticable.

'Darling, don't dance too much if you're tired. You're a tiny bit white. Come and have some rouge. You're being a success, you know, but I'll tell you all about that to-morrow … oh what a night! My old flame – the worst one, I mean – is being *so* chaste. It's awful. But I live in hopes. I can see he's dying to kiss me and I'll make him before I've done. *And* it wouldn't be the first time.'

'I put my shirt on you, Enid. If I were a man I'd elope with you.'

'You angel!'

'By the way, the women here are all rather *young*, aren't they?'

'Oh yes.'

'What I mean is, there don't seem to be very many wife-looking people about.'

Enid Furnival looked at me uncertainly, thumbnail between her teeth, her head tilted like an enquiring thrush on a lawn. Well, I – I don't believe there *are*, now you mention it. Wives do cumber the earth rather, don't they? It's more fun for *me* without 'em.'

I just looked at her. This wasn't being Enid, the warm and kind and gay. I said, 'And Cosmo: it's more fun for him, too?'

'Well, these things always are, aren't they? Jealous husbands …'

'Then, these men have left their wives at home?'

'What? No! Most of 'em haven't *got* any. We know lashings of bachelors. You *do* like them?'

'I adore them all. Honestly, Enid, I've never seen such a pleasant assortment.'

And I left her and thought a bit more, and shivered with silent laughter all by myself, and then went back to my man with the mouth.

v

And there was the day that my mother first met the Furnivals. She had come from Hampshire for a day and a night, to shop and investigate the situation at the Campden Hill house; James brought her to the Furnivals, for I was staying with them, and in the middle of her first words with Enid I was suddenly overcome by the 'tongue warranted to blast the barnacles off a battleship', and glanced at mother and saw a reminiscent barnacle look in her eye as well, and gave it up and left them together, and went into the study and sorted up Cosmo's bills and watched them all from the window. Presently Cosmo joined them and that left Enid free for James and they vanished round a corner.

Cosmo strode over to mother and smiled down at her, and loomed over her and gleamed at her through his eyeglass, and she looked up at him with a child's gaze of delighted remembrance and recognition and her face grew pink. How the late-Victorian contrives to go on doing it I can't imagine. Cosmo has never made *me* blush yet.

I ejaculated 'Hah!' and he looked up and saw me. He shouted 'Come out'.

'No, my dear, I should strike too modern a note; you've gone all *Sweet Lavender* and I'm more on the Frederick Lonsdale side this morning. And you *must* settle that tailor's bill. It's twenty-nine pounds six and eight.'

And Cosmo and Anne disappeared round the other corner!

Later, I said to Enid 'This is all very "teaching", my sweet life, but what does one do when jealous of one's own mother? Wouldn't Freud love it? He'd call me something damaging ending in "'phobe".' She screwed her eyes in delighted anticipation of laughter.

'Oh! what *has* he been doing now? Do tell!'

'My dear, vamping my mother. Item: one exit round shrubbery, so far. But – she's very like me, and nearer his age.'

'This *is* one of life's nasty corners, but I dare say things haven't gone too far. Your mother looks so *good*, doesn't she?' soothed Cosmo's wife.

CHAPTER XXXIV

I

I WAS WITH Enid during the whole of the week before Cosmo died. He said himself, 'It's always better to leave the stage before it leaves you, and the wrench of leaving Enid and you I can't realize at all, so let's talk about other things. There are several matters I want settled.' And, on and off, in those six days we talked, he and I.

'First of all, I've left you five hundred. I'm not going to urge you to be careful with it because I know you're incapable of being anything else, and in the second I'd rather think you were having a good time with it. Don't interrupt! It's not left you in my will because, amusing as the idea may sound, there might be talk. Enid will see to that.'

I shook my head. 'No, I'm sorry. I couldn't quite stand that, you know.' And, amazingly, he gave in. Also, I told him that since Lady Vallant's death I was receiving a generous allowance from my mother − naturally my grandmother had not left me a direct penny. Then, there was my work. And he closed his eyes and opened them on the abrupt nod I knew so well, and let it go.

'Then − what?'

'*I think*, unless it's valuable, of course, the quizzing-glass you used in the costume play.' He was pleased, I could see.

'Why d'you want it?'

'Perhaps I shall see your audiences through it, Cosmo. Have you used it *a lot*?'

He smiled at me. 'About six hundred times, not counting the revival.'

'Good. And I'm going to be Ikey, my dear: I want the script of *Gladstone*, and your own separate part with your insets (and lor! how you messed up my good typing!).'

'They're yours, but if anyone should ever want to revive it you'll have to allow my executors to make a copy.'

After a little, he said, 'Those men you met at the party. I want you to keep up as many of them as you can. They're all good sound sorts or I wouldn't have picked 'em. They may be useful to you, you never know. There's a surgeon and a judge and a banker – in fact most of the professions who can deal with life for one. They're all old friends of mine and I've written to all of them about you. Don't lose them. Enid'll give you their addresses if the need should arise, but I rather fancy that at least two them may want, shall we say?, to cultivate a more social side. I won't tell you which, because I know you, and don't want to get their pitch queered in advance! You like them?' He shot it at me.

'Oh, I like them enormously, and they're your friends, too.'

'You'll be safe and happy with either of the two I'm thinking of and safe with any of 'em.'

I managed to say 'That party … it was the only time I've ever really danced, Cosmo, and you gave me one waltz. …'

He looked at me long, and I forgave him the blonde who'd whacked me all to pieces. His hand was in mine as he said 'Now, you're going to do something for me.'

'At last.'

'Look after Enid for me.'

'Always.'

'We both love her. I don't know any other woman I'd trust her to.'

I believe I laughed. 'What's left of me, Cosmo, is hers entirely.' He was thinking, and his eyes never left my face. 'It's curious, and rather interesting, how when one knows for certain that one's days are literally numbered, one gets a feeling of recklessness, and is able to ask questions which, if life were going on, would be almost impossible … a sense of boundless privilege, and rather to be guarded against; but I'm not high-minded enough to rise to that, personally.' His hand tightened in mine. 'I want to know.'

'I'll tell you anything on earth, Cosmo, if I know the answer.'

'If it hadn't been for Enid, would you have married me?'

'Aren't you the damfool?' I marvelled.

'At the age I was when we first met?'

'Yes.'

'With the risk of my career going downhill?'

'Yes.'

'And of my turning semi-invalid on you?'

'Yes, yes, yes.'

'At your age. ...'

'Cosmo, I can't go on saying yes all the afternoon, it makes me feel like the ceremony, except for the bridesmaids and the obey clause. I bar that.'

'You would! ... we *have* kept each other on the boil, haven't we? ...'

11

On another day he said, 'And this Vallant business ... there's no more trouble in your mind there?'

'It's fading, chiefly I imagine because she's dead and I've seen the new look on Anne's face: I feel as if one had got just that much the better of Lady Vallant, a fresh start. And because of that I'm going to be able in time to *feel* that story is in the past, instead of only knowing it is.'

'Ah, that's good. And you can't see the future at all?'

'Never could.' I bit back the inevitable accompanying comment just in time.

'Well, the past's pretty good ... I wonder if we can all re-see it at will?'

'I've always believed that's possible, Cosmo. It probably needs practice, though.'

'As you saw at Vallant House?'

'Of course.'

He was leaning back and his shadowed eyes were gleaming. 'God, that would mean reliving all one's best plays, hearing the *entr' actes* one's forgotten, and proposing to Enid and listening to the words one actually used, and waking up and meeting you asleep in the dressing-room. ... Now tell me: do we go on from that point, saying new things to each other, comparing notes and so on?'

'No, I don't feel that. That sort of thing isn't heaven Cosmo, it's a law we know nothing about, but a law just the same and we must stick to the rules. That means that if we meet again, in episodes that actually *were* in our lives, the action would be as exact as a film you run through twice; down to the last detail and the smallest movement it's the same film.'

'It's good enough for me.'

'And me. Where one really scores is over things one had forgotten, and there the absolute-exactitude business is salvation. You'll be able to propose to Enid again and again (and find out what it was you *did* say!) just as with any luck at all I shall be able to go on and on and on meeting you for the first time. And all the other things … And there's one way in which you score all along the line, Cosmo.'

'Ah?'

'By dying, my dear. You can come back to us but we can't go over to you, however tempted some of us may be to take that short cut to you.'

'Never that, Vere darling.'

'No, never that. It isn't from fear or religious scruples or any truck of that kind, with me. It's just that I'm certain that's not the way. It's cheating. We've got to sit out the show, and *then*! … You mayn't be allowed to come back, or perhaps not at first, but if you want to enough –'

'If I want to! … I wonder if it would frighten Enid? Frightening Enid … what a very preposterous notion.'

'I don't know. You'd better come to me first and I'll find out and tell you. Some people can't stand it, remember. It's nothing to do with how much they've cared for you.'

'And you think one has a freer hand that way?'

'Certainly, it's in a different class to the Vallant House thing which was purely photographic, with no freewill at all.'

'And now tell me this: will you be able to come along with me and see me, at about forty-two say, in my best plays?'

'Ah, ah, ah! you're at the millennium again! I wasn't *there*, you see. Oh, if it could be! … as things are, with you going and leaving me, I don't fancy we can rise to that. If you could have lived, and we could get the place and the right conditions – that means the actual theatre when it's empty, and absolute silence, you might see and hear again and help me to by dint of concentration on the past. But by myself I should be like a mountaineer without his guide. No. Where I come in on your plays is only about seventeen years ago at a show called *The Tulip Tree*, at the

Coronet Theatre. I saw it with a most dear old lady who told me you were 'a very good-living man'.

'Hah!'

'I know!'

'Did she know me?'

'Well, naturally not!' And Enid came in and wanted to be told what we were 'sillifying about'.

III

He died the following night, alone with Enid. But before then, I had him to myself for over an hour. It was she who sent me to him. And just as he had found that the nearness of death gave him a sense of 'boundless privilege', so I too discovered that it could break down the reserve of a lifetime, and with my arms round him I told him all I'd ever thought of him, all I'd ever felt for him and always would.

Enid guesses, and James knows, and Cosmo, and nobody else in the world.

I suppose minds of the Verdune and Seagrave type would look upon him as the 'tragedy' of my life. If I could ever conceivably so regard him it would be simply because his death has brought me a volume of grief to which officially I have no right at all.

What he saw in me heaven only knows.

I've had my time with him, and in that hour he said things to me which have made the rest of life not only endurable but even happy. Half father, quarter friend and quarter lover – and if I have got it in its wrong sequence and proportions I don't know, or very greatly care.

IV

Meanwhile James and I have slowly humanized Vallant House. I think it will be ready very soon now for Lalage and Hugh. Sometimes, returning from one of my Lowndes Square parties, I still see fragments of that story playing itself over as I turn off the lights, but I think, I am almost sure, that the figures grow fainter. There is a mist-like quality about them to-day, and – a great point, the picture is dispersing into episodes in their wrong

sequence, meaningless to the uninitiate. I think that to-day it
would take all of my concentration and James's, and much time,
plus our special faculty of seeing, to recreate the thing in all its
force. And that is well.

Two rooms in the house are mine entirely, the schoolroom
and Myra's bedroom. I'm not quite sure of them even now –
luckily, nobody gives them a thought, up all those stairs, and
so poky … In Myra's bedroom I succumbed to cowardice and
cleared out every stick of furniture. It was cheap enough. The
room is repapered, too, and on the mantelpiece is a statuette of
Cosmo Furnival by a sculptor friend of his.

Already we have let Lalage's daughter see the house. She was
greatly struck with the size of the drawing-room and there was a
gramophone-and-rolled-carpet look in her eye, and she has her
dances there. But she doesn't have it all her own way, and there
are many nights when I am the hostess to my friends and let in
no relatives at all.

House-warming … I'm warming Vallant House in my own
way, and incidentally myself as well. To these gatherings come
the elderly and the old and I let them do what they like, cards,
talk or dance, gossip or glad eye! I loathe gramophones, they are
all wrong for those evenings and we have the piano instead, and
if there is an itinerant harpist in the square, James brings him in
and the difference that golden strings, however weatherbeaten,
make to any dance is unbelievable. We practise the Lancers and
discover that I have forgotten the figures and that there is nobody in the room who can remember quadrilles except one or
two who won't date themselves by admitting it!

Cosmo's friends are often there: all of them sometimes and
two of them very often. They are my friends now and what I
should do without them I don't know. Together we three go
down into that labyrinthine basement and make small-hour
snacks for whoever may be still upstairs. Sometimes I treat myself to one or two old retired actors and actresses; Enid finds
them for me and comes herself in her prettiest clothes, for we
very soon abandoned the tactful 'don't dress' clause finding that
the old people loved the chance to exhume their sequinned finery and put it all on. They have, these veterans of the stage, the
most beautiful manners in the world but their notions of caste,

I was to discover, leave Debrett at the post, and not soon shall I forget the night I introduced an extragedienne of the 'sixties to a low comedian. I didn't (very kindly) hear the last of it for weeks.

Sometimes I comb the highways and by-ways for lonely gentlewomen; one is careful of them, they need, at first, the treatment you give to eggshell china, but if once, by cup of coffee, by joke, by tactful placing and partnering you've won them, they are yours. I've got three Alma Chilcots already and hope for more. They are pitifully easy to find. Standish, who admires one of my Almas and her life and her pluck, kissed her hand once, and I saw, quite accidentally, and I can only say that that faded little woman, pinched of graciousness all her life, was transfigured. Life had, at last, a meaning, a past and a future. ...

One of my old actresses, in the way that some women of the stage unaccountably do, believes that she can 'tell hands' and has fallen more than once upon my own (she is the one who always rejects our sherry and wants cup after cup of strong tea with – oh God! – cherry brandy in it). On the first occasion she seized my fingers I said, 'Now then, Mrs. V—, you're going to tell me that "two children mark my hand", so get it over.'

She looked at me. 'But dearie, they *do*.'

She was as insistent as all the mercenaries have ever been. I've joked her out of that (my age), but sometimes James and I talk it over. We have reduced the possibilities slowly: for years I saw what conclusion he drew, and I suppose, when all's said, his now discarded theory was no more fantastic than my own. For I have come to the unswerving conviction that, somehow and somewhy, those children in my hand are Myra and Anne.

Why not? They are the only children with whom I have had intimate dealing. They have accompanied me nearly all my life long. And I shall be fifty on my next birthday.

And the parties go on. If the action flags, we take everyone downstairs and give them supper and play charades and are silly, or Enid sings to us all.

I have had my failures, of course; three of my theatre veterans have had to be eliminated owing to feats with the bottle, and one of them told the wrong story (which exploded *me* with giggles) to the very, very wrong woman indeed. It was Enid who got us out of that fix, staging a charming little scene of outraged

purity before rushing on to the landing to cry with laughter
on James's shoulder. And poor Miss W—went back to her bed-
sitting-room in Pimlico convinced that the world was not only
a sad place, which she knew already, but a nasty one into the
bargain, and I never saw her again!

And once my host came himself.

V

I wasn't unprepared. Although it was over a year since his
death I was always waiting, consciously or subconsciously.

He was suddenly there, in that room he had never entered
in life. He went straight over to Enid who was laughing with
Standish and she never glanced up. And then he looked about
and found me.

I went next day to Enid's home and told her, careful to be
matter-of-fact and she took it as I had hoped, and if her attitude
was a little doubtful, it was that over this side of me she had
ever been uncertain; it is about the only matter upon which
we aren't in mental accord. It was the child-side of her, I think,
which shrank quite normally from the unknown. She asked me
what he looked like and I told her he was an outline, faint but
unmistakable.

Since then I have seen him constantly. He seems, as far as I
with my limited physical opportunities of tracing his movements
can discover, to prefer his own house and garden. And every
time I see him his outline is more distinct.

On the second occasion he was sauntering down the path
with a natural air of possession that delighted me. I hurried in-
doors to bring out Enid and we went to look for him.

'There!' and I pointed.

She could see nothing at all and said so. My heart stopped
for the way she might be going to take it, but she added, 'I'm
not really sorry or disappointed. I don't think I *like* to think of
him like that'.

'But you're not frightened?' I shot at her.

'No, oh no …'

She wanted her Val in flesh and blood; unlike myself she
could take no comfort in the second best. Some people are un-

able to see at all, and there it is. It is possible that by this time
Cosmo knew all that himself.

And now that weight is lifted from my mind I can give myself up to looking. Incidentally, it is fun, for I never know how
Cosmo will be dressed. I have twice seen him in garden and
study wearing the oyster-grey court suit, and the band of brilliants below his knee which is in my jewel-case upstairs. At our
second meeting I was wearing it on my wrist and the sun im-
partially struck sparks from both our ornaments, which seemed
to amuse him.

Sometimes, but less often, we have succeeded in running
through again pieces of our old life together. Once more I have
seen his house for the first time and with him hummed *Miss
Hook of Holland* in the dressing-room, but apart from the fact
that Enid can share with us those scenes in which she had her
part I have found this form of reunion on the whole a disap-
pointing affair. For while it is happening *there is no memory of
the future* with which to savour and anticipate. Switched back
in time, we are condemned to our set lines and to the exact
progress in intimacy at which we had then arrived (I have, for
instance, in certain episodes to call Enid 'Mrs. Furnival'). The
price one pays for re-living the past means also no possibility
of modifying, no hope of avoiding old mistakes and misunderstandings. Out they all come – like Lady Vallant's discords and
mischords on the piano!

Often in my daily life I have sworn that, next time, Enid and
Cosmo and I must overcome this; that on my waking in his chair
Cosmo should say 'Ah my dear, I thought you were never going
to wake up and talk to me. Now tell me …'

Not a bit of it. I wake in his chair and he is standing by me
with a glass of brown sherry, and his words to me for all time
are, *'Now try and forgive me. Dear! what tired people we are! Why
does one go on?'*

And so it is with everything else. And that is why I prefer that
he should get through to me in the other way, for it is continuity,
always with the element of surprise, as in life.

I talk to him and tell him the news (and am careful to keep
a poker face if we should pass the gardener, or if we happen

to stop outside the kitchen window, because of what Cosmo would call the 'eternal dilemma' presented by the domestics in 'our case').

James has promised me that when Enid dies the Furnival house and garden shall be ours by hook or by crook, if we have to sell all we have – and *not* give to the poor! For Cosmo is so clear to me at last that I have to remember hard that he is not as I am. And once an amusing thing happened.

He came back as he was at that 'forty-two or so' upon which he and Enid used to dwell so fixedly, *and for ten minutes I was two years older than him*! I suspected it must be one of Cosmo's pranks because, to put it baldly, the spectacle of a young man in a very familiar garden, clad in officers' uniform of 1815, at eleven-thirty in the morning is at least unusual. Anyway, I advanced upon it and walked all round it and surveyed it from every angle before I spoke. Yes, there was a look of him, reminders … more in the manner, perhaps. Eyes and height unmistakable but mouth too indeterminate and face too smooth and well-covered. Dark brown hair and more of it and not a white thread, let alone a whole streak, in sight. H'm. …

'Very nice indeed, Cosmo, I should think, for most people. I quite see the point of view. A Waterloo play, I suppose.'

I never told Enid, fearing to distress her at being unable to share in that particular phase with me, but I sorted dozens of photographs until I found the right one and frankly asked her about it.

'Oh, that! it was one of his big hits, a romantic comedy called *The Queen's Own*, at the Avenue.'

Next time we met, I told him what I felt about the personal futility of that form of approach. For Enid, yes, but for me – never.

And, I hardly dare believe it, but I rather think that with time, and as Cosmo becomes ever more tangible to me, we shall arrive at exchanged speech. Such things have been, and why not for us? What makes me think so is that once or twice already when I have spoken to him *the sense of an answer* has streamed into me, rather in the way in which the thoughts of Sophia and Emmeline passed through me on that staircase. As yet it is no more than a yea or nay emotion, a feeling of confirmation or rejection of anything I myself have said to him, but that, too, will take more solid form. Patience. One must be terribly patient. There should be many years yet for me.

Or it may come any day.

THE END

FURROWED MIDDLEBROW

Made in the USA
Monee, IL
07 May 2021

67515198R00167